11 $\frac{95}{g}$

D0813965

Onesimus
Rebel and Saint

Onesimus

Rebel and Saint

by
Lance Webb

Bishop

THE UPPER ROOM
Nashville, Tennessee

Onesimus: Rebel and Saint

Scripture quotations set off from the text are from *The New English Bible,* © The Delegates of the Oxford University Press and the Syndics of the Cambridge University Press 1961 and 1970 and are reprinted by permission.

Scripture quotations identified RSV are from the Revised Standard Version of the Bible, copyrighted 1946, 1952, and © 1971 by the Division of Christian Education, National Council of the Churches of Christ in the United States of America, and are used by permission.

All other scripture quotations are the author's paraphrase.

Portions of "The Letters of Ignatius" reprinted from EARLY CHRISTIAN FATHERS, edited by Cyril C. Richardson (Volume I: The Library of Christian Classics). Reprinted and used by permission of The Westminster Press, Philadelphia, PA.

Book Cover: Bill Myers
First Printing: October 1988 (7)
Library of Congress Catalog Card Number: 88-050242
ISBN: 0-8358-0585-9

Printed in the United States of America

To Professor Albert C. Outler

My long-time friend and mentor whose counsel and constructive criticism have guided me since the publication of my first book thirty-five years ago. In recent times he has encouraged and aided me in combining scant historical fact with my imaginative recreation of the bravery and courage of some of the early Christian church leaders. To him I owe a debt of grateful thanks!

Contents

Part One

The Reconciler

*T*wo weary young travelers on tired horses climbed the steep mountain pass on the main road from Ephesus to Smyrna. The hot afternoon sun was disappearing behind the lofty peak of Mount Kizil to the west, its golden beams still reflecting dimly on the red granite cliffs of Mount Mimas to the east. The evergreens of scrub pine and cedar growing from patches of sand between the rocks remained visible. Bent over and breathing heavily, Onesimus slowly led the way. The younger rider, Glaucon, was guiding a donkey laden with richly colored silks and woolen cloth from the famous dyer and merchant, Philemon of Colossae.

Suddenly from around one of the huge granite boulders forming the escarpment of Mount Mimas, several horsemen charged out with spears raised threateningly.

"Halt your horses! Dismount!" the bandit leader shouted harshly as his men surrounded Onesimus and Glaucon. The chief's voice was strong and resonant with authority. "What's the donkey carrying?"

Onesimus and Glaucon got off their horses. To the utter surprise of the seven robbers, Onesimus addressed them with strange kindness. "Greetings to you, my brothers. We welcome your unexpected coming! Our journey has been long and arduous. Please lower your spears. We don't want to be robbed, but we'll do what you want."

"What kind of trick is this?" the bandit chief roared, cursing. "We're not brothers! When you're stripped of your possessions, you won't welcome our coming! We're not here on a friendly call, you fool! We're here to rob you!"

"Very well said," Onesimus replied. "I know how this works. I, too, once robbed for a living. In fact, I was even a runaway slave. If you take our valuables, we won't try to stop you. We are carrying gifts for friends in Smyrna, Sardis, and Pergamum, but we can't stop you from taking them if that's what you want to do. Go ahead and look at the cloth you are taking—the best colors and texture to be found anywhere!''

As he spoke, Onesimus and Glaucon untied the pack on the donkey's back and displayed the beautiful silks and woolens they had brought from Colossae.

The bandits looked at their captives, the cloth, and each other in amazement. Never in all their deeds in these mountains had they met such agreeable victims.

''That's a new line,'' the chief snorted, ''but we're not as dumb as you think.''

In irritation, the chief roughly grabbed Onesimus, tearing his tunic and revealing ugly scars on Onesimus's back. The bandit lowered his voice and muttered, ''By Zeus, you may be telling the truth after all. How did you get those scars?''

Onesimus breathed easier. His reply was calm. ''They were put there ten years ago by my master, Philemon. He was angry that I was bold enough to hold the hand of his daughter Helen, so he tied me to a tree and gave me forty stripes with his whip. He'd bought me five years earlier in the agora in Ephesus. I became his chief clerk, and I was also used to teach his daughter the best of the Greek philosophers. He caught me unawares one evening during one of our lessons when, for the first time, I expressed my love for his beautiful daughter!''

After a few moments of awkward silence, one of the bandits spoke. ''Captain, we may have something here that's more interesting than these costly fabrics! I'm intrigued by this story, and I'd like to hear more.''

The chief looked around at the other men, who nodded in agreement. He replied with a laugh, ''Ha, this is indeed something else! To be called 'friends' and 'brothers' by our intended victims!''

His fury somewhat cooled, the leader of the bandits turned to his captives. ''We'll take your cloth and all the gold, silver, and jewels you carry, but you possess something else we can't touch. I'll admit, robbing the fat, filthy rich who pass our way has become monotonous. We don't know who you are or if your story is true, but just for a change of pace, we'd like to hear how you became free men. Of course, I'm not sure I'll be ready to believe your tale until I see your papers of manumission. But first,'' he said with a grin, ''we need to finish our business!''

Unhappily, Onesimus and Glaucon pulled off their money belts and jewel cases. From their pouches they each took the papers their former master, Philemon, had given them when they were set free. They watched with concern as the bandit chief examined them.

''These papers appear to be authentic, though your words and appearances tell us even more about you.'' Turning to his band of thieves, he said, ''I think we can trust these two. How about it?''

''Sure, let's hear them,'' Demetrius, the sub-captain of the group, replied. ''We don't have anything to lose since we've already got their money, jewels, and this beautiful cloth.''

By this time all of the bandits had dismounted and stood curiously around their astonishing victims—two men who were neither angry nor afraid! This experience would be a break in their lonely existence.

Again, the captain spoke, ''Since it's nearly time to make camp for the night anyway, why don't you join us for a meal and conversation? Tell us who you are and why you're not afraid of us!''

''We'd be delighted to visit your camp and tell you the story of our past and present,'' Onesimus replied.

''As you probably already suspect, we're all runaway slaves. We've shaken off the diabolical chains of slavery, and we're now free to roam these mountains and breathe the fresh air of liberty. Of course,'' the captain continued with bitterness, ''we're unable to return to our homes, and we may never possess the freedom which you two know. The Roman governor in Smyrna and the commander over the Roman legion stationed there would enjoy nothing more than catching us and nailing us to their crosses. You may be freer than we are in several ways, but we'll hear your story later. The legionnaires who patrol this road may be here any minute. Mount your horses and follow us.''

Before being allowed to follow the bandits, Onesimus and Glaucon were tied up and blindfolded with a burnoose. "You appear to be trustworthy," the chief told them, "but we can't take any chances. We don't want to risk your leading the legionnaires back to our mountain home."

Onesimus and Glaucon sat quietly on their horses for several minutes as they and their donkey were led off the main road over rough terrain. Onesimus knew they had crossed a stream when he heard the rushing, noisy water. When the procession halted, the captain and Demetrius took the burnoose from Onesimus's and Glaucon's eyes. The captain enthusiastically cried, "Welcome to our lovely home!"

As their eyes became reaccustomed to the light, the two travelers looked around in delight. "It is indeed a beautiful place," Onesimus responded. The bandits' hideout lay behind a tall clump of pine and spruce near the side of a steep cliff of red granite. In the cliff was a cavern large enough for several horses with riders walking beside to enter. To one side of the cave was a spring of fresh, cold water. Four more members of the gang were in front of the cavern busily cooking a kettle of savory vegetables and roasting several hares on a spit over an open fire. As their captain and his men approached with their captives, the men at the cave assembled with curiosity.

"We've returned with two of the most interesting people we've ever tried to rob!" the captain announced to the four. He retold the strange account related by the two "agreeable victims."

Addressing Onesimus and Glaucon, the leader introduced himself as Carias and introduced each of his men, telling a little of the history of each one. All were escaped slaves. Over a period of months, they had formed one of the several gangs of bandits preying on travelers in Ionia. Four of the band were from Smyrna, one from Pergamum, one from Thyatira, two from Sardis, and three from Ephesus.

"All of us have endured severe beatings," Carias told the newcomers. "We're bitter enough over the injustices and cruelty of our former masters to risk mutilation or our lives in order to be free."

"I understand just how you feel," Onesimus responded. "As you have seen, I was also beaten by my owner, a master generally kinder than most."

"We've heard enough, Onesimus, to know that the two of you have been victims of the same cruel injustices that we have. But let's not dwell on the past. I'm hungry. Simus, is it time to eat yet?"

"It's ready. Come and get it!" the pudgy, good-natured Phrygian ex-slave from Smyrna announced. With a huge wooden spoon he dished up the vegetables while each in the group took a large piece of roasted hare. Captives and captors alike sat on the rocks in a semicircle. As Onesimus shared his meal with Carias, he saw revealed the confident, vibrant personality that easily made him the leader of the band.

The men ate ravenously with the silence punctuated by grunts of satisfaction. Onesimus marvelled at the abundance of good food and wondered how they had managed to get it. Carias explained that the vegetables and bread came from caravans they robbed, while the meat was generally wild game hunted or snared by the bandits themselves. Onesimus smiled to himself as he realized the bread and some of the fruit they were eating had come from their friend Joanna, who had made careful provision for them before they left Ephesus.

The motley group of robbers and robbed sat around the glowing fire until late that night as Glaucon and Onesimus told their stories. Glaucon recalled his boyhood and early youth in Smyrna, where he was born of a poor family.

"My father was employed by the owner of one of the largest vineyards in the valley of the River Hermus. The wine-maker kept a stable of good horses for work and pleasure. My father taught me much about horsemanship on those horses. One of the untamed horses, though, accidentally kicked my father and killed him. After my father's death, the wine-maker was attracted by the beauty of my mother, so he took her against her will as his concubine. When I was only fifteen, he sold me as a slave on the block in Ephesus."

Clarus, recently escaped from Smyrna, leaped up with excitement. "That sounds like my cruel former master, Anacreon! Was it?"

Startled, Glaucon replied, "Yes, that's the man! I remember well my hatred for that devil." Glaucon paused to consider the implications of this situation. "You must know my mother! Her name is Erica."

"Indeed I do," Clarus replied. "She is one of the kindest, bravest, warmest, most wonderful persons I have ever met!"

"How is she? Is she . . . is she well and . . . and happy?"

"Yes, she is well. As far as being happy, however, no doubt she dislikes being a slave, but her spirit reflects elements of happiness other slaves cannot know. She was one of the strongest influences on me when I was younger. I recall her remarkable kindness to the slave boys. After you were sold, she found time to talk with us about the virtues of patience and courage. She truly became our friend. We knew she suffered terrible humiliation and abusive treatment from Anacreon when he forced her to submit to him. My own inability to help her and my rebellion against this man who, through his wealth, popularity, and power among the leaders of Smyrna, was able to get by with his horrible injustices . . . ," Clarus paused momentarily. "This and my desire to be free were the reasons for my bitter anger and my fortunate escape to these blessed mountains!"

He continued speaking almost reverently of his newfound freedom in his mountain home. Speaking with strong voice to Glaucon, he said, "You can understand why I take pleasure in robbing men like him who cross our mountain pass. If only we could meet and rob and beat this devil himself some day!" As he spoke these words, Clarus raised his fist, and Glaucon could see his face suffused with anger.

"We know how deeply you feel, Clarus," Onesimus broke in. "Perhaps you can tell us a little more about Anacreon. If possible, we plan to find Glaucon's mother. With the help of some of our money," he smiled and looked knowingly at Carias, "we had intended to buy her freedom and take her back with us!"

The men sat quietly with deep interest in this development.

Even Carias said nothing, though Onesimus thankfully noted the sympathetic look on his face.

The silence was short-lived as Glaucon went on to tell the story of his purchase by Philemon. He described the vast difference in his treatment at the hands of a kinder master.

"But wasn't Philemon the same master who beat you with forty stripes, Onesimus?" Carias inquired.

"The same man but with a difference! Let me tell you my story to help you better understand what Glaucon is saying."

Onesimus began with the dreadful morning when he, seventeen years old and the son of Aristarchus, a former treasurer of Ephesus, and his mother, Alcestia, and two sisters were sold on the slave block to Philemon of Colossae. Onesimus's original name had been Gaius, and he had been born of a noble family, yet he was reduced to this. His father had worked closely with Governor Gaius, the youth's namesake, in Ephesus, but a plot by old enemies of the governor led to the removal of both the governor and treasurer from office, after which they were taken to Rome and executed under Emperor Claudius. Consequently, the enemies of his father sold the family on the auction block and took the profits for themselves.

His life under slavery had not been all bad, Onesimus told the bandits, as new hopes aroused in him when Philemon and his family listened to a traveler named Paul tell of a new religion. Shortly after, the master and his family became "Christians."

"I rejected this new religion," Onesimus explained. "One reason was that my Aristotelian philosophy could not accept Paul's story of Jesus' crucifixion and resurrection from the dead without more evidence. Mainly, though, I could not accept that faith because of the hypocrisy of Christians like Philemon. They talked of loving each other as brothers and sisters in the family of God, and they even began to treat the slaves with more kindness, but they continued to keep us as slaves. I still could not touch the lovely Helen . . ." Onesimus's voice trailed off wistfully.

As the former slaves listened with intense interest, Onesimus continued. "You can surely understand how, in my anger and frustration, I decided to run away, no matter the costs."

Snorts of appreciation and sympathy came from several of the bandits.

"I carefully planned my escape, waiting months for the proper opportunity. That opportunity came as I attended the annual market in Ephesus with Philemon's son, Archippus. As we finished marketing our goods in the agora, Archippus and I were enjoying a final celebratory dinner. I drugged Archippus's wine and robbed him of most of the money and jewels derived from our sales. Even though he had become a real friend to me and had promised to intercede for me with his father, I did this anyway. I could no longer be someone else's property. I quickly found a ship for my passage to Rome. In order to escape detection, upon my arrival I buried myself in the Subura quarter, where I was befriended by two escaped Phrygian slaves, Marcia and Nicia, who were making their livings in prostitution. When I refused to join them in their profession, they drugged my wine and stole the money and jewels I had stolen from Archippus. When I awoke, I was so angry that I went to their apartment to confront them. I was stopped by Nicia."

The group laughed heartily as Onesimus told of being kicked down the stairs by Nicia. Marcia, his sister, mockingly intoned the question of Socrates that Onesimus had twisted to excuse his own robbing of Archippus. "Isn't it better to do unjustly to others than to suffer unjustly yourself?"

"Well, Onesimus, that is our reasoning, too!" Carias said pointedly as he recognized the irony of the situation. "I am interested to see that you no longer agree with that reasoning."

"No, I don't," Onesimus responded. "In the dark hours that followed, I found a far better response to injustice. Let me tell you about it."

The bandits became quiet again as Onesimus recounted the dramatic story of the despair that led him to find the apostle Paul. Paul knew Onesimus from his time with Philemon in Colossae and could have turned him in, but instead, the apostle accepted him and let him act as his *amanuensis*, copying out the letters Paul sent to the churches in Asia. Onesimus betrayed his deep feelings as he described the amazing joy and freedom possessed by this little man imprisoned by Nero. He described how he came to faith in the Christ he had previously scorned after he saw moving and convincing evidences of the mighty power of God's love in the handful of persecuted Christians in Rome.

"With the courage of my new faith," he continued, "I returned to Colossae at the risk of my life, with a letter from Paul asking Philemon to forgive me and take me back as a brother rather than a slave. To my amazement, I was received with love and incredible forgiveness by both Archippus and Philemon. I had the privilege in the presence of my dear Helen and my mother to write my own manumission letter."

"What about Helen?" Clarus interrupted eagerly. "Were you able to marry her?"

"Yes, I was promised her hand by Philemon, though we were not married until later. First, with Philemon's blessings, I returned to Rome, where I resumed ministering to Paul in the Mamertine Prison."

Onesimus went on to relate the events following Paul's execution by Nero and the burning of Rome, which Nero quickly blamed on the Christians and used as an excuse to order their persecution. Onesimus told of the coming of Simon Peter, who insisted on ministering to the brave young Christians soon to be thrown to the beasts in the Coliseum as sport for the crowds as part of Nero's persecution. He described his own imprisonment with the apostle Peter and the miraculous gift of freedom through the good offices of his once enemy, Nicia, who had become a Christian! Onesimus told the story of Nicia's brave meeting with his former lover, Rufus Faenus, who had risen to captain of the Praetorian Guard, and of the way the tough soldier was persuaded to let Onesimus go, to the delight of the men sitting around the fire.

"That was a very gutsy thing for Nicia to risk his life in such a way!" Clarus exclaimed.

"Yes, he risked his life out of his love both for Jesus Christ, his new master, and for me, the one whom he had once robbed!"

Onesimus concluded his story by telling of his happy return to Colossae, his marriage to Helen, his partnership with Archippus and Philemon, his journey to Ephesus, and now his being sent by the Christian leaders in Colossae and Ephesus to tell his story in Smyrna, Pergamum, and Sardis. The only interruption from his listeners was an occasional exclamation over the astonishing changes that had taken place in Onesimus's life.

When he had finished his story, Carias spoke. "So that explains your genuine welcome to us who came to rob you and why you and Glaucon are not afraid of us! If you forgave Nicia and Marcia for robbing you, you would forgive us, if we took your valuable gifts! You wouldn't like that, but you could still accept us. Is that right?"

"Yes," Onesimus answered. "We could accept you because we really do care about you. We join in your painful experiences as former slaves."

"You truly possess a remarkable freedom, which we, as former slaves like you, cannot know in our physical freedom alone!" Demetrius exclaimed.

"We have found the only true freedom that no man or group of men, no evil circumstance can take from us: The freedom of the sons and daughters of God, members of the heavenly family," Onesimus responded. "We welcome this opportunity to get to know you, for we earnestly desire for you the same freedom we have found in the love of Christ!"

"Hmm . . . ," Carias mused. "This man Jesus Christ must have been a wonderful person to have had such powerful influence on so many! I would like to know more about him!"

For the next few minutes, Onesimus did his best to describe something of the life and teachings of Jesus. He tried to explain such difficult but hopeful sayings as "He who would be greatest among you must be the servant of all." He told them of the prayer which Jesus taught his disciples, "Forgive us as we forgive those who sin against us." Onesimus shared as simply as he could his conviction that the supreme God of all creation has been made known to us in the life and death and victory of Jesus, God's son, who taught that God's first commandment is to love and forgive, as children of God.

"As Christians," he summed up, "we believe that the loving, victorious spirit seen in the human Jesus is the very spirit of almighty God. God, the creator of us all, we believe, is not a vengeful God, but a God of mercy and love who calls on us to live as brothers and sisters in the heavenly family."

The men listened intently, sometimes shaking their heads in disbelief.

"We have heard your strange 'good news,' as you call it," Carias said for the group, "but it will take some time for us to understand it and to decide whether or not we can accept it for ourselves. The witness provided by the two of you is most convincing. The fact that you, Glaucon, came to accept this faith as you saw what it did for your master Philemon, who set you free not only physically but internally—this adds up to some very strong evidence. I, for one, will pursue it further. But it is late. In the morning we would like to hear more from you." Pointing to a smooth grassy spot, he suggested, "You can put your bed rolls there and have a good sleep. As for me, I will have to do some thinking before I sleep!"

Onesimus lay awake for some time after the others were asleep. Looking up at the stars and the full moon shining over the tops of the trees, he was thankfully aware of the providence that had made this experience with the runaway-slaves-turned-bandits an inspiring opportunity to share his witness of the only true freedom in the love of Christ. Because of the possible danger, he was glad Helen had not made this trip with him. But he missed her greatly, and his mind went back over the blessed times they had shared together after his return from Rome and since Bishop Papias had performed their marriage. He thought of the three months in which he had enjoyed her loving companionship. He remembered his excitement at the revelation of the child she was bearing. Onesimus was thankful for so many blessings such as his new partnership with Philemon and Archippus. By the love of Christ these whom he had once despised had become more a father and a brother to him than he had ever dreamed possible. *There is nothing more powerful, more creative, more joyful than the experience of the love of God through the son Jesus Christ!* he thought.

These were no longer strange words for him. As he looked at the stars and the celestial heavens, Onesimus remembered the apostle Paul's statement from prison to the Christians in Colossae in a letter that Onesimus himself had copied from Paul's dictation:

> It is now my happiness to suffer for you. This is my way of helping to complete, in my poor human flesh, the full tale of Christ's afflictions still to be endured, for the sake of his body which is the church. I became its servant by virtue of the task assigned to me by God for your benefit: to deliver his message in full; to announce the secret hidden for long ages and through many generations, but now disclosed to God's people.... The secret is this: Christ in you, the hope of a glory to come.

Onesimus knew this was the secret of his new life. Christ, who brought the love of God very close to Onesimus, was in him—not somewhere off in the stars, indifferent and uncaring toward the sufferings of individual people. Christ was living in him. He fondly remembered the words of Paul, "The life I now live, I live by faith in the son of God who loved me and gave himself for me." What a secret this was—to know what Paul meant when he said, "It is now my happiness to suffer for you." No wonder the bandits could not understand why he and Glaucon had welcomed the danger of being robbed in order to identify with this group of former slaves! This was something unknown to the world! Onesimus knew this was to be his task for the remainder of his life. He thought ahead to the next day, when the two riders would go to Smyrna where he would tell this "good news" as he had heard it through Paul, Simon Peter, Luke, John, Mark, and his other dear friends in Rome.

Onesimus's thoughts next went back to the two nights he and Glaucon had stayed in the home of Tyrannus and Joanna in Ephesus as they were beginning this journey to several of the churches in Asia. Tyrannus and Joanna had been friends of Paul and now were his dear friends as well. Onesimus remembered what Tyrannus had told him of the gathering storms of persecution in Smyrna and Pergamum. In Smyrna, the travelers were to meet young Bishop Tavius, whose father was the Roman governor. The governor was very bitter now that his son had become a Christian. Tyrannus told Onesimus that the break between father and son had already resulted in an edict, similar to ones in Pergamum and other Roman cities, that every person must sprinkle incense on the altar before the statue of the emperor to prove loyal citizenship. This action was directly aimed at discovering and rooting out the people called Christians, for if they were true to their faith, such an act would betray their Lord.

Tomorrow I'll meet with Bishop Tavius and some of his people. Over the next few days, I hope, I can help reconcile father and son and stop this terrible threat to the Christians in Smyrna. Onesimus understood the same threat to be facing the young bishop of Pergamum, Bishop Antipas. He wondered, *Will I be worthy and able to suffer with Paul and Peter and my other dear friends who have been killed in Rome?*

As he asked himself the question, he realized that this chance meeting with the robbers was turning out beautifully. What happened at Smyrna and Pergamum—and in the other experiences ahead of him—would not likely be so delightful. Instead, the experiences would doubtless test his faith and his inner strength. He went to sleep with a thought of quiet assurance on his mind. *Christ is in me, therefore, I'm able to do anything through the One who gives me the power.*

As dawn came, Onesimus and Glaucon were awakened by the sounds of Simus and his helpers preparing breakfast. The air was fresh and cool, smelling of fir and balsam trees all around. The band arose and went to the stream for a drink of cold water and to wash their faces and hands. Breakfast was plentiful, with eggs, cheese, fruit, and bread toasted over the open fire.

As they ate, several of the men asked questions of the two Christians. One was the same question that had bothered Onesimus: "How could a man who is dead and in a tomb be alive again?"

"There is no visible or tangible proof," Onesimus tried to explain, "but the evidence that convinced me was the experience of Paul and these brave Christians who daily practiced the presence of God. As Paul put it, 'It's not I who lives, but Christ who lives within me, and the life I now live, I live by faith in the son of God who loved me and gave himself for me!' "

Several of the men spoke of their biggest problem with this new "way" of Jesus. As Clarus phrased it, "How could I ever forgive this devil of a master who has done such evil things to me, to Glaucon's mother, and to others?"

"In the same way that Jesus forgave those who crucified him," Glaucon answered. Jesus prayed, 'Father, forgive them. They don't know what they're doing.' When Onesimus and I go to see Anacreon and attempt to purchase the freedom of my mother, if I hate him for all he has done I will have blocked the channels through which the spirit of God is working. We may not succeed, even though we are willing to pay a high price for her freedom. But whether we do or not, I must and will forgive him. Though I hate what he did, I know that God loves him and seeks to make him a new person in Christ. It happened to Philemon. It may not happen to Anacreon! It is a wondrous thing to believe that Christ came into the world to save sinners, and if I am forgiven and made new, then anyone who accepts Christ can be accepted and become a new person!"

After breakfast, Carias walked over to Onesimus and Glaucon. Putting one hand on each of their shoulders, he said with deep feeling, "Your coming with us last night and all you have said and done are the brightest hours of my life. I am sure my men feel the same way. You have given us a gift worth far more than many pieces of beautiful cloth or bags of gold and silver. I am going to follow the example of your life and work. Since I am an ex-slave from Thyatira, a long way from Smyrna, I am going to risk being detected as I seek to find and talk with you in the house of your friends. I want to know more about your Christ—and someday. . . someday, I may be ready to be baptized into him and become a Christian."

With a broad smile, Carias said to his men, "Too bad we can't rob these two. They are the richest men we have ever encountered!"

The men laughed and nodded their heads as they understood what he was saying.

Turning to Onesimus and Glaucon again, Carias announced, "Let it be known that I, Carias, chief of the bandits of Mount Mimas, do hereby release our captives with their silks, their woolens, and all their money. I also acknowledge that you, Onesimus and Glaucon, have become, through your Christ, our friends and brothers." In a quieter voice, he added, "If we ever become slaves again, it will be to your Lord Jesus Christ. You are the freest persons we have ever met. God go with you!"

All eleven of the men shouted their approval and gathered around to bid their newfound friends and brothers good-bye. The two men loaded their donkey, mounted their horses, and followed Carias, who led them without blindfolds from their mountain home back to the highway leading to Smyrna.

2

*T*he morning was bright and clear, the mountain air invigorating as Onesimus and Glaucon rode out of the mountains toward a spectacular view and into Smyrna. Ahead to their left was the Mountain of the Two Brothers, twenty-nine hundred feet high, about a third lower than the mountains through which they had just come. The Mountain of the Two Brothers would easily be visible from Smyrna.

The riders galloped into town and quickly arrived at the splendidly colonnaded agora. Glaucon looked to see the slave block where he and the three thieves he had recently met had been sold to slave-traders. The two rode up near the crowd gathered around the raised platform on which, even now, a slave auction was under way. A young, muscular boy was on display, the subject of the bidding. Heartsick, Onesimus and Glaucon turned away and rode to the part of the agora where silks and woolens were sold.

"Compared to the agora in Ephesus, this is well arranged, but it's only about half the size," Onesimus observed.

From the position of the sun, Onesimus realized that it must be close to noontime, when the *familia* of Antonius Tavius expected them. Glaucon, obviously familiar with the city, led the way to the house with directions provided by Tyrannus.

Onesimus and Glaucon turned their mounts back to the main thoroughfare, known as the Golden Way. As they rode north, Glaucon pointed to the many temples of which the city boasted—temples to Cybele, to Zeus, to Apollo, to Aphrodite, to Nemesis. There was even a copy of the famous temple to Asclepius in Pergamum. All were built of white marble and were detailed with Ionic columns and the delicately sculptured figures for which the city was noted.

"Before we leave, you must see the huge stadium where the famous games are held each year and the Odeum music hall, one of the largest theaters in Ionia," Glaucon told his companion. He went on with his tour of the city.

"That's the public library," the youth said, pointing to a magnificent building on the right. "The house of Antonius Tavius should only be a short distance to the west. Tyrannus described it to me, so we shouldn't have any difficulty finding it. The building has been the ancestral home of the Tavius family for several generations. When Antonius's father was made the Roman governor, he and his family moved to the luxurious Roman palace, leaving his son's family in the old home. That, of course, happened before Antonius became a Christian. Now the little church of Smyrna meets at the house!"

"I'm sure," Onesimus observed, "that this is what most rankles his father. Not only has his son become a Christian, but now, the last straw, his son has openly invited the Christians to meet here for worship!"

As they came upon the home, Glaucon reined his horse at the front gate. They stood before a large, three-story stone mansion that bespoke wealth and aristocracy. The gatekeeper, one of Antonius's Christian freedmen, was expecting them. He greeted them warmly as he opened the gates and led their horses to the stables at the rear of the house.

When they arrived at the house, the travelers were met by young Bishop Antonius Tavius, surrounded by his excited family. "So glad you made it across the mountains!" the bishop exclaimed. "You must be Onesimus, about whom I have heard so much," he said as he shook hands with the older of the two. "My *familia* and our church expect to share such inspiring times with you." Turning to the youth, he continued, "And you must be Glaucon! Tyrannus has written us something of your family tragedy here in Smyrna. I hope we can help you in finding your mother." Bishop Tavius spoke with a rich warm voice; his strong, well-formed face was wreathed in a broad smile. Though he was not as tall as Onesimus, his black hair and eyes and his intelligent bearing revealed him to be a person of charm and strength, a natural leader.

Onesimus responded joyfully for himself and his companion. "We are certainly glad to be here and to share your hospitality. Our brother Tyrannus in Ephesus has told us something of your situation and expressed his and Joanna's loving confidence in you. We both look forward to our times with you."

Antonius led his two visitors into the tastefully appointed atrium opening out to the garden. The table was set near the entrance with white linen, exquisite dishes of painted china, and delicately carved silver. A bowl of red and white autumn flowers was in the center. Antonius introduced the guests to his wife, Octavia, a beautiful dark-haired, dark-eyed, winsome woman. The couple's three children, aged seven, nine, and twelve, stood around wide-eyed to see and hear this tall, handsome man who had been the secretary and friend of Paul and Simon Peter. Antonius had told them stories of the courage and bravery of the apostles in Rome. The young father introduced each child, lingering on the eldest.

"We named our first child Simon before we knew there was a Simon Peter. When Simon was baptized, remembering the stories

Paul told of the big fisherman, we added the name *Peter*, which
has stuck. We now call him our Peter!''

Introductions over, the seven sat down to a dinner of roast
lamb, vegetables, and ripe fruit. As the group ate, Onesimus and
Glaucon told the remarkable story of their encounter with the
bandits and their experiences as they shared with them the story of
the Christ and his freedom to love. The three children sat
fascinated by the story and filled the air with many questions.

After several queries that allowed the story to last for hours, the
father addressed the two guests. ''What an unusual, truly remarkable experience of the grace of God working in the hearts of these
embittered men! This is one of the most dramatic and realistic
illustrations of the transforming power of Christ's forgiving love I
have ever heard. I say this reverently, Onesimus and Glaucon, but
you were little Christs to these hunted and lost men. Indeed, there
is no better illustration of Jesus' teaching that we are blessed when
men persecute us, that we are to love our enemies! We may never
hear of these runaway slaves again, but the fact that you cared
enough for them to share so fearlessly will bear fruit beyond all
expectations. I hope we can follow up your work and get as many
of them as possible related to our church as baptized believers.
Praise to the father of our Lord Jesus Christ and to the Holy Spirit
who is mightily at work in you!''

Onesimus listened to his new friend's impassioned summation
of everything he had been feeling and thinking as they rode into
Smyrna. With deep emotion, he answered, ''Bishop Tavius, you
give me great hope. I'm thankful for your gracious judgment on
our surprising experiences. Until we came, these men were like
hunted animals believing, as the psalmist wrote, that no one cared
for them. This is our first witness on this, our first journey in the
service of our Lord. It gives me hope that we may be used to
bring reconciliation between you and your father. Glaucon and I
have been praying for this since we left Ephesus. We have been
praying not only for the hoped-for removal of the threat to your
life and the lives of the members of Christ's church here in
Smyrna, but, just as blessedly, for what such a reconciliation

would mean to you and your family, deeply hurt by your father's alienation and rejection.''

"We have been wounded by my father," Antonius replied. "He has cut us off from all communication. Young Peter is the only one among us to whom my father will listen. Peter reads all the parchments that come our way, and every week he spends a couple of hours with his grandfather. Much of that time, he tells my father what he thinks of several of Jesus' teachings that seem to contradict everything my father believes!''

"It's wonderful, Peter, that you're able to communicate with your grandfather! Remember what Jesus said, 'A little child shall lead them.' Perhaps you can take me with you when you next visit him. Together we might help open wide the door to his understanding and acceptance of, or at least his willingness to hear, the gospel of Christ!''

"Thanks, Onesimus! Your concerns and prayers for my father and our restored relations are deeply appreciated,'' Bishop Tavius responded.

In this time of great sharing, the bishop next spoke of his willingness to help Glaucon find and set his mother free.

"Do you know this wine-master, Anacreon?" Glaucon asked with excitement.

"Yes, he is much older than I, and I have known him since my youth. We have a common love of horses, and through his association with my father, I have often shared in races in which his horses have won medals. I know Anacreon well, but I must tell you—though I'm sure you're already aware of this—Anacreon is a hard man, unprincipled and greedy. He has many powerful friends in the assembly and among the leaders of the city.'' Antonius paused for a few moments and then exclaimed, "This would be a more fruitful visit for you if my father could be more accepting of our new faith. He could do more than I could with Anacreon, as they have been good friends.''

"This means,'' Onesimus affirmed, "that the Spirit is leading me to seek out your father as soon as possible. If he will only listen, I may be able to persuade him that the Christians in Rome

were not the ones who burned the city! They are not the enemies
of Rome! Let us pray tonight that by the grace of God and through
the workings of the Holy Spirit, Peter and I may have a break-
through into the deepest heart of your father!''

All the adults around the table said, ''Amen.''

Peter, with the trust of a child, declared to Onesimus, ''I know
Grandpa loves us, and I believe that you're such a fine man that
he'll listen to you!''

''Thank you, Peter! Your faith is probably more realistic than
our cautious doubts. All this talking has allowed the hour to
become late, so let's go to sleep tonight, trusting in our prayers
that the spirit of Christ will have already visited your grandfather
with a new openness. Can we go as soon as tomorrow?''

''Yes,'' Peter answered. ''It has been almost a week since I saw
him. I know he'll see me, and I'll bring you with me, as my
friend and as a man who knows more about Jesus than anyone
I've ever met!''

With that understanding, Bishop Tavius called the little group
together for evening prayers. He read a portion of Onesimus's
favorite letter of Paul's, the letter to the Philippians. The bishop
closed with the words, ''I can do anything through Christ, who
gives me power!''

Next he led in a prayer of thanksgiving, asking Onesimus to
close with a prayer of petition for the next day's weighty events.
Onesimus ended his prayer with special intercession for Grandfather Pyrrhus Tavius and for all the people called Christians in
Smyrna.

That night Onesimus went to sleep with a calmer trust and
stronger confidence than he had previously known.

After an early breakfast, Onesimus and Peter walked the short
distance from the Tavius house to the palace of the Roman
governor, further north on the Golden Way. Obviously, the guard
at the door was familiar with the young grandson of Governor
Pyrrhus Tavius, for he smiled and opened the door for Peter and
his companion. Peter went without hesitation up the marble

stairway and entered the living quarters of his grandfather. Here again, the guard welcomed him.

"Glad to see you, master Simon! Your grandfather is just finishing his breakfast. Who is your companion?"

"This is Onesimus from Colossae and Ephesus, a good friend of the family," Peter answered wisely. "I want Grandpa to meet him. He has some interesting news, having recently come from Rome."

Onesimus smiled to himself as he listened to the skillful handling of what could be a rather difficult situation.

Peter and Onesimus entered the elegant atrium of the palace and walked on through to the garden, where Peter's grandfather was seated at a table near the pool. Seeing his favorite grandson, the elder Tavius rose with a smile and walked to meet him. Putting his arm around him, he said warmly, "Good morning, Simon."

Onesimus noticed that the grandfather did not call Peter by his baptismal name.

"My, you are early today," the grandfather continued. "Who is this man you bring with you?"

"This is Onesimus, my wonderful new friend from Colossae and Ephesus, Grandpa. He is a partner in a business dying and selling silks and woolens. He brought some beautiful pieces with him as gifts!"

Pyrrhus Tavius, knowing something of the wiles of his grandson, wondered just what Peter was up to in bringing this man with him. But having confidence in Peter's judgment, the old man turned and took Onesimus by the hand.

"Welcome to my house, Onesimus. Anyone about whom Simon is so enthusiastic must be an interesting person. I am glad to meet you. Come, sit down." He motioned to one of the slaves for drinks.

"Grandpa, I want you to meet and know Onesimus because he has some interesting stories from his recent time in Rome that I think you will want to hear!"

"Sir, I am delighted to meet you," Onesimus broke in. "Simon has told me about the good times you have together." Onesimus carefully used the young man's given name so as not to upset the grandfather. "He told me of your great concern over what's happening in Rome. Simon says that you're always looking for firsthand news to help you understand current conditions so you can act more wisely as the Emperor Nero's governor!"

"Indeed I am," Tavius responded. "But tell me why you were in Rome. What kind of news do you bring that caused Simon to think I would be interested?"

Onesimus breathed a silent prayer. He realized that the next few minutes were crucial in his relations with this man who held such power to be used either in leading the persecutions of the little group of Christians or in preventing them. Onesimus also knew how important the time was in helping reconcile father and son.

The best approach was forthrightness, Onesimus decided. He began, "Honored grandfather of my friend Simon and father of Antonius, in whose home I was guest last night, since you trust the judgment of Simon enough to receive me, I trust you will hear me as I tell the most remarkable story you may ever hear. This is a story in which I have played but an humble part!"

Onesimus told the governor the story of his free birth and his misfortune to be sold into slavery as a young man. When he revealed the details of his situation, he was surprised to be interrupted by Tavius.

"I remember well the events you describe," he told Onesimus. "I knew your father and mother well and was dismayed when I heard of the tragedy of which you speak. But go on."

"You can imagine the shame and humiliation my family and I felt! Finally after several years, I rebelled, not only at being a slave, but at what I considered the hypocrisy of my master as a member of this new religion called Christian!"

At the mention of the name *Christian*, Onesimus could see Tavius's face harden, but the old man said nothing. Onesimus continued to tell briefly the story of his escape to Rome and the desperation that led him to find the apostle Paul in his house prison guarded by Nero's Praetorian Guards. He described how, with his training in philosophy, he had completely rejected Paul's "good news" of the life, death, and resurrection of Jesus.

The governor nodded sympathetically as Onesimus told how such a story offended his Aristotelian mind. Governor Tavius's interest intensified as Onesimus described his remarkable experiences with Paul and the little group of Christians, including such well-known Romans as Burrhus, chief of the Praetorian Guard, and Lady Pompania.

"I knew Senator Pompania before his death as well as Captain Burrhus," Tavius remarked. "I have often wondered why the emperor had such a faithful and able man executed. Go on and tell your story. I'm interested in this because everything I've heard has come secondhand."

Encouraged, Onesimus told of his adventures in Rome as completely as he could in the brief time that was his to tell them. He told of his confusion when the freest, most joyful man he had ever met was in chains, while he, having escaped physical chains, was bound by fear and guilt. Onesimus described his writing of Paul's dictation of the letters to Christians in Philippi and Colossae, and how, through the evidences he saw in the loving joy and freedom of persons such as Lady Pompania, Burrhus, and Paul, he had come to his own faith in Christ.

"I realized," Onesimus continued, "that if the faith and freedom of these people were the result of a vain superstition, then there can be nothing in life that makes sense. If, however, a life such as Paul's and love such as revealed in Christ can be the result, then Christ's life, death, and victory over death do make sense."

The governor listened to Onesimus with a quizzical look on his face.

"Honored sir," Onesimus explained, "I found myself coming to believe that the Word contained in Jesus Christ is the highest, most intelligent Word ever spoken—the Word of the mighty creator God. As a result of this new belief, I was willing to return to my master in Colossae with a letter from Paul, even at the risk of my life."

At these words, the governor stood up in disgust. "Well," he spat at Onesimus, "so you, another brilliant mind trained in philosophy, like my foolish son, Antonius, have been captured by the strange power of this Jewish rabbi named Jesus and what you call 'the love of Christ'! It has as strange a hold on you as it has on him! This is an incredible, unexplainable folly! It's already caused a painful break with my son, Antonius.''

In resignation to his situation, the governor shrugged his shoulders and sat down.

''Go on with your story. I want to hear what you have to say concerning these Christians that Nero and his supporters are charging with the burning of Rome and other reprehensible practices. Their stories have reached Smyrna and have inflamed many of our people. We in Smyrna have long prided ourselves on our loyalty to Rome. We've erected the Templum de Roma, the first of its kind in any Roman city. Indeed, I have recently issued an edict requiring every citizen to declare allegiance to Rome by sprinkling a bit of incense on the altar before the image of Nero Caesar. I understand that Christians are foolish enough to die rather than to show this simple obeisance, and this disturbs me.

''From your own experience, Onesimus, please tell me, did the Christians begin the fires that burned so much of Rome? Are they disloyal to the emperor and dangerous to the stability of the empire? Our leaders are levelling these charges against them. For obvious reasons, this is not only a political and governmental question for me but a very personal one.''

The old man fondly put his hand on Peter's head as he pursued his questions. ''Tell me why you Christians are so stubborn. Why do you make such a big thing of a simple gesture of obedience to our emperor?''

''I'll answer your questions as fully as possible,'' Onesimus responded, breathing a silent prayer. ''First, what you call stubbornness is really a courage coming from our faith that Jesus is both Lord of all the cosmos and our Lord. We believe that the spirit of the mighty God who created all things is the same spirit revealed in Jesus. Jesus is the Christ, the one sent to reveal the greatness of the love of God, the creator of all. To Christ, therefore, we give our worship, for he is the source of all that is worthy.''

''I'm disgusted by all this folly!'' the governor exploded with bitterness and irritation. "The whole idea of the man Jesus becoming God, the creator and ruler of everything, is repugnant! How could a fanatical Jewish rabbi, crucified, dead, and buried—how could he be the king and ruler of all creation? My grandson tells me that, in some mysterious way, this rabbi was raised from the dead, but that's totally irrational! How can anyone of sound mind believe it?" His face was red with anger.

The room was silent for some time after the governor's outburst. Finally, in a calmer tone, he continued, "I admit that I'm intrigued by some of the stories and teachings of Jesus that Simon has told me . . ."

The silence returned but was quickly broken again when the governor snapped, "Enough of this foolishness. Neither Simon nor you can explain this 'mystery of Christ.' I want to know why followers of this Jesus are unwilling to put a little pinch of incense in the altar fire before the image of our great Caesar?

"We have many gods in our great empire. Everyone is free to worship any or none of them. Go ahead and worship this Christ. But, as the emperor's representative, I cannot permit any person or group, even my own son and his family, to be disloyal to Caesar! Do you understand?"

"Yes, your honor, I do understand how you feel. I know that you love your family. I also see that you are in a difficult position, what with Nero Caesar's attacks on the Christians. This rebellion of your son and the little group of Christians meeting in your ancestral house has hurt you deeply."

Onesimus could tell that he was beginning to get through to the man. "I respect the loyalty the people of Smyrna feel toward Rome for the prosperity and peace of the Pax Romana. I understand the reason for your edict. But there must be a better way of having the Christians show their loyalty to Rome and Caesar."

"Perhaps so, but all I have is your word that these Christians are not disloyal to the emperor. Where is there any evidence?" Onesimus noted Tavius's hands clenched and knuckles white in frustration.

"Dear Governor," Onesimus responded with deep feeling, "there is a simple answer to your question. There is another way in which the Christians can demonstrate their loyalty and you may uphold the necessary respect and obedience to Caesar. You can . . . you can . . . ,'' he hesitated as he sought just the right word for this crucial moment.

"Go on, I'm interested in what you've got to say."

"Let me put my answer in the words of Paul, to whom I owe my life and my new freedom. In his letter to Christians in Rome, he declared what I believe is the attitude of Christians in Smyrna. It is certainly mine. Paul wrote, 'Everyone should obey the government of the state, because all governing authority comes from God and is appointed by God. To oppose the authority of the state, therefore, is to oppose God, and anyone who does that will rightly be punished. The officer of the state is for your good.'

"This describes the attitude of all true Christians toward the government of Rome. We're proud to be Roman citizens. We'll support the government of Caesar, and we'll continue to pray for him as we have in every worship service I have attended. Of course, I know that Nero Caesar ordered the execution of Paul and Simon Peter. I know that hundreds of Christians in Rome, many of whom were dearly beloved to me, have been thrown to the lions in the Coliseum. But even during that terrible time, prayers of Christians were still offered for Nero—prayers of forgiveness and of intercession for him and his officers."

"Praying for them! By all the gods!" the governor burst out in disbelief. "How in the name of Zeus could anyone do that?"

"We can do that because we follow the example of Jesus. He prayed as he was being crucified on the cross: 'Father, forgive them—they don't know what they're doing!' We prayed for Nero because we believed he also didn't know what he was doing when he accused us of disloyalty and setting fire to Rome. We believe Jesus loves and forgives Nero as he did the leaders of the Jews and the soldiers under Pilate who crucified him!"

"I can't understand such love and forgiveness," Tavius responded dubiously. "It's so unreasonable, so unlikely, so contrary to everything I've been taught! We should hate and seek to destroy our enemies. How could your Christians possibly love and pray for Nero?"

"We don't love his cruel acts, or the selfish lust and greed that drive him to do them. But we love the man he could be. We appreciate all the good things the Roman government stands for. You can count on all true Christians to be loyal citizens of Rome."

"Incredible! What you are saying about forgiving love is unbelievable—almost ridiculous!"

"So I said before I met Paul and Peter and these other brave Christians. But it's true. The Christians had nothing at all to do with causing the fires in Rome. I know, because I was with the Christian leaders and others who escaped the fire by fleeing to the caverns outside Rome. The homes of almost all of the plebeian Christians were burned and their earthly possessions destroyed. I know the suffering that they and thousands of others trapped by the fire endured. No matter the reason Nero Caesar assigned the blame to the Christians, they were the very last people who could have been guilty of such a dastardly deed."

Tavius watched as Peter nodded his head in agreement with Onesimus. He began to speak slowly with deep emotion.

"For some strange reason, Onesimus, I'm inclined to believe you. As foolhardy and unreasonable as it seems, I can see how their deep religious convictions will not allow them to show any sign of worship before the emperor's image. But this only adds to my anguish. I'm not a murderer, and I certainly don't want to see my own family, as mistaken as they may be, suffer the terrible fate they must if my edict is obeyed to the letter. You can see my horrible dilemma! Do you have any solution or suggestion?"

Onesimus caught his breath. This was the opening he had been praying and hoping for. He considered his response carefully and answered thoughtfully.

"Yes, Governor Tavius, I do, if you change the edict that demands every citizen of Smyrna to present a pinch of incense before the image of Caesar. In its stead, make a clear statement of the well-known Roman policy of freedom for all to worship the God they choose, and change the edict to call for every citizen to give a pledge of loyalty and support to the government of Caesar. In this way, you guarantee the loyalty of Christians to Rome in all things pertaining to the rule of the state, but you do not require them to worship Caesar!''

The governor strained forward in his chair to ask doubtfully, ''How could this be done so that my own loyalty to Caesar would not be questioned?''

Remembering a story told of Jesus, Onesimus pulled a denarius, a Roman coin, from his pocket. He asked Tavius, ''Whose picture and inscription is on this coin?''

Tavius relaxed. He began to see a way out.

''Nero Caesar, of course!'' he smiled as he answered.

''Then I suggest that, according to your new edict, all loyal citizens still declare their allegiance to the emperor. They may choose to do it in one of two ways. Those who desire to come to the Templum de Roma will present a pinch of incense on the altar fires before the image of Caesar. Their names will be registered by one of your officers. Others will have the choice to bring a coin of any size bearing the image and the inscription of Nero Caesar to the Assembly Hall, where they will leave it in a royal urn beneath the bust of the emperor. They can also be registered as loyal citizens of Rome. I'm sure, sir, that in that way, every good Christian will be giving a pledge of allegiance to the emperor and his government!''

The governor was elated when he realized that such a plan could work. Smiling, he stood up and put his hand on Peter's shoulder. Tentatively, he gave his approval.

''Onesimus, you've given me hope that this impasse may be removed.''

The young man looked at the governor and realized with joy that the little church in Tavius's ancestral house had been saved for the time being from the vicious persecution he had witnessed in Rome.

In a note of finality, the governor got up and, with one arm around Peter, extended his hand to Onesimus.

''How can I ever thank you for coming to me so openly and helpfully? I still regard the faith you and my son have placed in Christ to be unreasonable folly. But Simon, or rather, Peter, has told me of some interesting teachings of your Christ, and your sharing with me your incredible story of forgiving love makes me wish it could be true! What a difference in this cruel old world if it were! But I need to do a lot more thinking about that. In the meantime, I want to see my son Antonius and my other grandchildren, Toni and Mary.''

Little Peter interrupted his grandfather with a shout of joy. ''Oh, Grandpa!'' he cried, throwing his arms around the old man's waist. ''Grandpa, this is the best gift you could ever give me! I can't wait to tell Dad and Mom. Can you come to dinner with us soon?''

Tavius was deeply touched by Peter's torrent of gladness.

''Not so fast, Peter! Your father hasn't invited me yet!''

''Oh, but I am sure he will. And Mom . . . and Mary . . . and Toni!''

''All right, Peter, if the mystery of loving forgiveness could work for Paul and your new namesake, Simon Peter, perhaps it can work in the household of Tavius!''

Turning to Onesimus, the elder man said warmly, ''With my thanks for helping liberate me from my false and hurtful misunderstandings, I offer to be of any help that I can while you are a guest of our city.''

''I, too, am thankful beyond words, Governor Tavius! This is a great day of rejoicing for all of us! When we have a chance, I'll be happy to share with you a concern having to do with my friend Glaucon, but we have taken enough of your time now. It also may be you'll want to hear more of my adventures in Rome and the new freedom within that I've found!''

''Perhaps so,'' Tavius responded. He walked with his visitors to the door of his apartment. Speaking to the guard, he ordered, ''Anytime this new friend from Colossae asks to see me, give him ready entrance. If I am not too busy, I will give him audience anytime.''

Onesimus and Peter descended the steps of the royal palace with elation.

''A miracle of reconciling love is taking place, dear Peter,'' Onesimus said thankfully as they walked down the street.

* * *

The new edict of Governor Tavius was read in the Assembly
Hall and in the Templum de Roma. There was some grumbling
among a few of the more fanatical Jewish leaders who had been
looking forward to the time when the hated Christians would be
discovered and punished, but most of the Jewish community and
other Smyrnean citizens had been unaware of the risks to the
Christians involved in the first edict.

The good news soon spread to all in the Christian *communitas*,
and celebrations of thanksgiving were held in each Christian
household. Bishop Antonius Tavius, Octavia, and their three
children rejoiced with a special dinner for the grandfather who,
for the first time in nearly two years, shared a meal with them.
The invitation to dinner had been carried by Peter himself. The
note accompanying the invitation had been carefully worded by
Antonius:

Dear Father,

Your care and affection since my boyhood have been priceless
gifts and have made our alienation in recent months all the more
costly. Now that you have received Onesimus and his story of the
loyalty of Christians to Rome, I write to reaffirm what he said. We
are indeed loyal subjects of Caesar and obedient citizens of the great
empire of Rome. We will joyfully bring a coin stamped with
Caesar's image to place in the urn before his statue as a symbol of
our loyalty to earthly matters.

Most important of all, to me and to our family, I ask forgiveness
for the hurt I have caused you in these recent difficult months. I
understand how painful your acceptance of us in our newfound faith
has been. I do not ask that you embrace my faith in Jesus Christ,
though I would be happy if you could. I am thankful for your open
mind enabling you now to accept me and our family, even though
you still may think our faith foolish.

It is with great joy that I invite you to share dinner in our home
tomorrow at the sixth hour in the evening. I promise we will not try
again to persuade you of the rightness of our beliefs, though we will
begin the meal with a brief prayer of thanksgiving by our new friend
Onesimus. Knowing him, I am sure you will not find this objectionable.

We love you in all sincerity, and we are thankful for your love shown throughout our lives and now evidenced in this reconciliation. We look forward to your coming tomorrow evening.

Your thankful son,

Antonius

--*3*

*T*he celebratory meal at the Tavius house became a time of great pleasure for all involved. Onesimus thrilled everyone at the table with exciting stories of his life with Paul and Peter in Rome.

Shortly before dessert was served, the elder Tavius remembered a comment Onesimus had made after his first visit to the palace. Having been introduced to Glaucon, he asked, "What is your problem, and how can I be of help?"

Glaucon related the facts of his situation to the governor and his hopes of being able to buy his mother's freedom.

The governor shook his head sadly. "How well I know Anacreon," he began. "I've no doubt that he's capable of doing this great injustice to you and your mother. He's a powerful man with many friends who protect him. I did not know of this situation, as your mother's case was never brought before our court. But I do know Anacreon personally, and if you come by my office in the morning, I'll be happy to send a personal message asking him to relinquish possession of your mother at a reasonable price."

The entire group around the table was happy for Glaucon.

"Oh, sir, this is more than I had hoped for," the young man exclaimed. "Your help will open the way for us to approach this hardened man who's caused such hurt for Mother and me!"

"I'm glad to help," Governor Tavius smiled. He looked at Peter and imagined how he would feel if Peter had been trapped in such a situation. "Tell me, Glaucon, are you able, as Onesimus claims Christians should be, to forgive this man? What kind of revenge do you plan?''

"I don't want revenge, sir. I've read Paul's words to the Roman Christians. He said, 'Don't repay evil with evil and don't look for revenge. Justice and revenge are the Lord's, and the Lord will repay.' I've already forgiven him, though I hate what he did to my family!''

"Well, Antonius, it seems this strange habit of forgiving enemies is common to all Christians. It's foolish, but I do find it rather intriguing.''

"Father, I promised not to try again to persuade you,'' the younger Tavius answered with a smile, "but I'm glad you're impressed by the spirit of these Christians! Now have some of this delicious dessert.''

When all courses of the dinner had been served, Grandfather Tavius took his leave to return to the palace. A new air of freedom and release from the tensions and fears that had alienated the family was apparent. The strong, loving ties of many years that had been broken were now restored. Evening prayers that night in the Tavius house were precious expressions of renewed faith in the victory of Christ and the divine love that never fails!

As evening slowly became night and after the others had retired to their rooms, Onesimus and Antonius remained in the atrium.

"We have so much in common, you and I,'' Onesimus affirmed. "I'm thankful for all I've seen in you of the love for your family and of your unwavering faith, even as you sought to be reconciled with your father. Where did you receive such a powerful understanding of the Christian gospel?''

"My dear friend,'' Antonius began, "since you've been so open with your story of faith, I'm more than happy to share mine with you.''

For the next hour, Antonius described his spiritual journey, which was similar in some respects to that of Onesimus.

"I, like you, attended the gymnasium in Pergamum. I was fascinated by that gruff old philosopher, Heraclitus. I went to Ephesus to read and study his writings and to spend time in the school with younger philosophers. This was at the very time that

Paul was attracting so much attention with his preaching there. I heard about an inspiring little man who spoke of the death and resurrection of a remarkable teacher-healer, Jesus of Nazareth. When I did hear it, I thought of Heraclitus's teachings that everything carries with it its opposite, and therefore death is always present in life and life in death.

"I was curious to hear what this man was teaching. About the same time, I met Tyrannus and Joanna. You can probably imagine the rest. The three of us took the opportunity to talk with Paul. To sum it up, before I returned to Smyrna, I'd spent the required time as a catechumen under his teaching, and I was baptized as a Christian. I think this must have been just after your own family tragedy when you became Philemon's slave."

"Your story surely shows the working of God's gracious and loving providence!" Onesimus exclaimed. "Both of us owe our new life in Christ to the apostle Paul!"

"That's true. And I'm thankful that our association with Paul goes on even after his death. Since then, I've been able to read his letter to the Romans, his two to the church at Corinth, and the one to the Galatians. Your coming has proven to be very timely. We're all greatly blessed by your presence."

After breakfast the next morning, Glaucon, Onesimus, Antonius, and young Peter saddled their horses to ride on their mission of liberation. It was a beautiful October morning as the four rode abreast up the street to the palace of the governor. When they arrived at the gates, Peter greeted the guard who welcomed him and helped him dismount.

"We'll just wait here," his father said to the guard. "Peter has to get a brief message from the governor for us to take with us."

The guard nodded as he closed the gates and Peter ran up the steps to the palace. In a few minutes, the lad returned, his face aglow from the warm reception given him by his grandfather. In his hand he held the message to Anacreon written on a small scroll of parchment.

"Dad, Grandpa says you should present this to Anacreon with his best regards. He said, 'If this letter doesn't open up the heart of Glaucon's old master, I'll have something else to say.' But he said we shouldn't have any problem with him. He wants us to tell him what happens, and he said that he's eager to meet Glaucon's mother.''

The four remounted their horses and left the palace behind.

As they rode toward the bridge over the River Hermus, they noticed lush vines on each side loaded with ripening purple and green grapes awaiting the harvest.

From the beginning of their ride, Peter was excited and curious. He plied Glaucon with questions about his boyhood and youth, and he asked about the circumstances that led to his being sold as a slave some ten years before. Glaucon, understandably, was even more excited and responded readily as he unfolded the story. He told again of the nobility of his mother in meeting her deep sorrow over the loss of her husband, and of her courage as the brutal wine-master took her to his rooms and as the slave buyer arrived and put Glaucon in the cart with others to be taken to Ephesus for auction as a slave.

''Your mother must be a beautiful person!'' Peter exclaimed. ''What a horrible experience that was for both of you!''

''Yes, Mother was a beautiful woman, and I'm sure she still is. She and my father were sometimes tough in punishing me, but I loved them both deeply.''

''What did you do when Anacreon came to take her? Did you know what he was going to do?'' Peter pursued his questioning.

''Yes, I was there. I heard it all. He told her what he expected of her as his mistress and slave. He also told her how beautiful she was and how much he desired her. You can imagine how I boiled inside as he talked. When she told him she loved my father and would not give herself to the wine-master, he just laughed. He said she'd learn to care for him, but whether she did or not, she belonged to him and would stay in his house, willingly or not.

''He saw me standing there, and he turned and said, 'Don't worry, your mother will be cared for and so will you. If you have any sense, you will cooperate and make someone a good and serviceable slave!'

"In my anger, I tried to hit him with my fists. I only got one good blow in before he fastened my arms behind me. He was hurting me, but he laughed and called me a stubborn little donkey. When the slave buyer came, I remember, I fought with him like a tiger and said every curse word I knew. As he took me off in the cart with the other slaves-to-be, I shouted my hatred and defiance at Anacreon, who stood watching me and laughing. I can still hear him now!"

As Glaucon described his terrifying experience, his companions noticed his face flushed with anger. Onesimus and Antonius were silent, allowing the young man to relive the experience before they arrived at the scene.

Peter, however, did not keep his silence. "I'd do everything I could to pay him back for such treatment," he exclaimed with indignation. Then, looking at his father and remembering Onesimus's story of Christians who forgave their persecutors for throwing them to the wild beasts in the Coliseum, Peter asked quietly, "Did you forgive Anacreon?"

"Yes, Peter." Glaucon managed a weak smile. "At first, my whole being was filled with bitterness and hate. But I remember the last words my mother said to me, even as Anacreon laughed and the cart wobbled down the road. She waved good-bye and smiled through her tears. 'Son,' she said, 'remember, only the weak keep hate in their hearts. The strong take what comes and make the most of it.'

"I knew she would accept her situation. One of the runaway slaves we met the other evening on Mount Mimas who had also been a slave of Anacreon said that she gave herself to befriend and teach the young slave children in Anacreon's *familia*. She was always one to make the best of things, no matter what the situation."

As the horsemen rode up to the gates of Anacreon's estate, a young slave met them.

"Is your master Anacreon here?" Antonius asked.

The slave responded with a nod.

"Please go and bring him here," Antonius continued. "Tell him that Antonius Tavius and three companions are here bringing a message from the Roman governor."

The riders dismounted and handed their horses to another slave who led them toward the stables. A third slave invited them into the house to wait for his master. He called to a young slave girl, telling her to show their guests into the atrium and serve them fresh grape juice.

As the four sat down in the spacious atrium filled with flowers and plants of many kinds, Onesimus breathed a prayer for wisdom and courage to say and do the best thing for this mother and her son.

Antonius and Onesimus had planned their plea to Anacreon for the woman's release. Before the slave girl left the atrium, Antonius whispered his request that she bring Erica, Glaucon's mother, to the *culina*, empty at this time of the morning, after breakfast had already been prepared and eaten. The girl realized something of great importance was going to happen. Erica had been like her own mother since she was a child, and the girl hoped whatever happened would not be unpleasant. She ran to the women's quarters to find Erica.

Antonius told Glaucon, "It's better for you to stay here when Onesimus and I go out and talk with Anacreon so he won't see you. While we're in the garden talking with Anacreon, step into the *culina*. You should be able to meet your mother there. Spend a few minutes with her to see how she feels about our coming. We don't know what her feelings for Anacreon might be. As you've described her strength of character, I wouldn't be surprised if some kind of affinity has developed between them. We need to know what she wants before we go any further. After Onesimus and I have talked with Anacreon, you and your mother join the conversation. We'll have to trust the Lord to guide us in these delicate negotiations."

Glaucon was overjoyed as he immediately rose to go to the *culina*.

Turning to Peter, his father said kindly, "Son, I know you're as curious and concerned as we are about how things will come out.

But I think that it's best for you to stay right here until we return.''

Peter nodded, ''I'll stay here and pray for you all.''

Antonius smiled and patted Peter on the head. ''You're very sensitive and helpful! Your prayers will make a difference.''

Antonius and Onesimus left the atrium and went into the garden. They sat down on a stone bench in the shade beside the pool. They had decided that Antonius would begin the conversation and present Anacreon with the note from the governor, who had been a good friend for many years. At the proper time, Onesimus would say whatever he was led to say.

After a wait of only a few minutes, Anacreon entered the garden. He was a huge man with muscles visible on the left arm and shoulder uncovered by the brown toga he wore gracefully over the remainder of his body. His masculine, tanned face, curly black hair, coal black eyes, and firm jaw revealed a determined, masterful character.

''Well, if it isn't my young friend, Antonius!'' Anacreon said warmly as he and the bishop embraced. ''What brings you here so early in the morning? I hear that you and your father have made up, and that's good to hear. I know your father has suffered. I'm glad for you both!''

''It's good to see you too, Celsus,'' Antonius greeted Anacreon by his first name. ''You and Father have always enjoyed each other, especially when talking about your horses or watching a good race! Yes, I'm thankful that Father and I have again accepted each other.'' Antonius broke into a broad smile. ''You'll be glad to know that we've reconciled on the basis that we won't talk about my new faith! And you can rest assured that I didn't come here to convert you!''

''That's fine with me. I remember our last meeting ending late at night with both of us as far apart as when we started. Your Jesus as man-God, with his impractical teachings, is too much for me!''

Antonius let the subject drop and introduced Onesimus and Anacreon. The two shook hands as Onesimus said, ''I've thoroughly enjoyed our ride through your vineyards and the fragrance of your beautiful garden. I'm looking forward to some of your wine, though your servant is bringing us some fresh grape juice.''

"I'll send a skin of my best wine back with you! What brings you here today?''

"We've come today with my son Peter and a former slave of yours,'' Antonius responded. "You sold him to a trader some ten years ago. In turn, he was sold in the agora at Ephesus to a fabric-maker in Colossae. The former slave's name is Glaucon. Now he's a freeman accompanying Onesimus.''

Antonius pulled the parchment note from his tunic. "I've got a message from my father, Celsus, that will make the purpose of our visit clear. But I can get to the point before you read the letter. You own Glaucon's mother, Erica. When her husband, a poor freeman in your employ for the care of your horses, was killed by a horse's kick, you forced Erica to become your slave-concubine, and you sold Glaucon, then only fifteen, to a slave buyer.''

When Anacreon heard Erica's name, his face became a study in anxiety and anger. As Antonius continued to speak, it was clear Anacreon was ready to explode.

"Now, my friend,'' Antonius continued, "I know how serious these accusations are, but before you say too much, read this message from my father.''

"This is a . . . a . . . a surprise,'' Anacreon stuttered, struggling for self-control. "You're right, though, I'll not respond until I've read what your father has to say.'' He took the parchment and held it gingerly in his hands.

Dear friend Celsus:
   This letter and situation will no doubt come as a surprise to you, as it did to me. Whether or not Glaucon's account of Erica's becoming your slave and his own sale on the slave market is true, the facts, I think, are clear. Erica is doubtlessly valuable to you, perhaps in ways I have no cause to know. But she is also the mother of Glaucon, whom I have come to know as an intelligent young man who has since been granted his freedom and is now employed in the care of his former master's stables.
   Here is my request. It is not a demand I make as governor. But as your friend, I am asking you to consider the offer of Glaucon and his

traveling partner Onesimus to buy Erica, in order that she may be free to live the life she chooses and to be nearer her son. Glaucon's employer, together with his partner Onesimus, offer to pay a reasonable price for her freedom. I ask that you be as generous as possible in restoring to this woman and her son the freedom they possessed before her husband was killed. What she does with that freedom is her own decision.

My friend Celsus, you have supported me in so many ways for which I am grateful. Now I wish to support you in making the decision that will be best for you and for this woman and her son.

Sincerely,

Pyrrhus Tavius,
Governor of Smyrna under Nero Caesar and your friend

It was clear to both the visitors that a struggle was occurring within the mind of this man who had done such a wrong to Erica and Glaucon. The struggle was a mixture of guilt and fear of being forced to account for this act of so many years ago. The Roman governor, though a friend, was also the potential judge and jury over such an unjust act. If the case were pressed, Roman justice would never countenance such a deed.

Knowing the stubborn strength of Anacreon's character, Antonius was surprised at what the wine-master had to say after a few moments of silent thought.

"Antonius and Onesimus, this is truly a difficult moment for me. Yes, I must and do admit that what I did to Erica and Glaucon was indeed, as Roman law phrases it, *Culpa Dignus*. I deserve any blame given me for such an unworthy act. I justified it at the time because of my attachment to Erica. I knew that she would never willingly become my concubine. At that time, my wife was very ill but still alive. I believed, and I've been right for ten years, that with my power and influence, no one could challenge me.

"There are two things I want to say, and you may report them both to your father. First, I have come to have more than a physical passion for this remarkable woman. I've come to love her. Indeed, under the difficult situation in which I placed her,

she's acted with a dignity and kindness to me that is completely
undeserved. Know that I've asked her forgiveness many times,
but I've never done anything to right the situation. Because I love
her, I'll give her the choice of staying with me or going with her
son, whose absence she has never stopped mourning.

"The second thing I have to say is that I will not sell her to you
or anyone else. Here and now, I declare her to be a free woman. If
she desires to remain with me, I will marry her as my wife. If she
desires to go with Glaucon, she will go freely with generous gifts
of clothing as only a small token of my appreciation for her years
of faithful service to one who took advantage of a tragedy in her
life and has no way to repay the debt."

When he concluded, Antonius rose from the bench, and the two
met with a mutual embrace. As Onesimus watched, his eyes filled
with tears.

"Only the grace of God could produce such a miracle!"
Onesimus said as he in turn embraced Celsus. The eyes of all
three were now wet with tears of joy.

"Celsus," Antonius said happily, "ever since I was little, I've
known you as a strong and stubborn man, but rarely have I been
witness to a more noble and Christlike act. You'll be glad to
know that while we've been talking, Glaucon has been meeting
with his mother. Let's go and meet Glaucon and Erica. And let's
pick up little Peter—no one will be any happier than he."

The three walked through the garden into the atrium, where
Peter was waiting alone. Celsus put his hands on the boy's
shoulders and smiled. "Peter," he said to the lad, "your father
and Onesimus have done me a great service today."

Next, Celsus called for Erica and her son to be brought to the
atrium. The three men and Peter waited anxiously as Glaucon and
his mother entered, arm in arm.

Onesimus never forgot the scene that followed. Celsus repeated
much of what he had already said and then walked over to the
mother and son. Placing his hands on a shoulder of each, Celsus
said earnestly, "There's no way I can pay you back for all the hurt
and suffering I've caused, but, after hearing what you've said of
this Jesus of Nazareth, whom Antonius has placed into my

unwilling mind, let me say, forgive and you will be forgiven! I humbly ask both of you to forgive me. This is a forgiveness I cannot deserve, but I long for it with all my heart, and I want to make whatever amends I can.''

Celsus took both hands of the beautiful Erica in his, looked into her eyes, and spoke words that she had never expected to hear. ''In the presence of your son, Glaucon, and these our friends, I hereby give you your freedom. You've had a freedom within ever since I first knew you. I took advantage of your tragedy because I wanted to possess you, and for this I am heartily sorry. But now you're free from all external bonds.''

The big man cleared his throat and continued. ''I've come to love you deeply, and in the presence of all, I humbly and lovingly ask you to be my wife. Since you are free, you have the choice of leaving me and my house to go with Glaucon, or of living whatever manner of life you desire! What is your answer?''

Without a moment's hesitation, Erica responded. ''Celsus, once you were my master, and a very cruel one at that. I hated you for your brutal selfishness. You seized me and forced yourself on me in the very hour of my greatest sorrow. You even sold my son as a slave!''

The wine-merchant accepted the harsh words, but Erica's faith quickly softened her expression.

''But that was ten years ago. Since I had no other choice, I accepted you as my master and determined that hating you would hurt me more than you. Since then, I've learned something of the love of God revealed in God's son, Jesus Christ. I've prayed for you and I've come to love the true Celsus that Christians say God loves. After all these years, I believe my prayers are being answered. I've continued to do what Christ and the highest teaching of the Stoics recommend. I've made the most of my difficult situation, and I've tried to be as helpful as I could to you and to all of the slaves. During these years, I've seen you change. Your brutal and selfish approach to me has given way to a surprising new tenderness and respect. You've even permitted me to tell others what little I know of the Christians' faith in Jesus Christ as Lord. You've joined with me in learning more of the

Christian good news, and now with this offer I'm more surprised
and thankful than ever!''

A smile wreathing her beautiful face, Erica reached up and
impulsively kissed her former master, adding in mock formality,
''Know all you who are present, I accept the offer of Celsus
Anacreon to be married and to live as his faithful and loving wife
all the days of my life!''

With that, she overcame all abandon and flung her arms around
him. In return, he lifted her in his huge arms in an embrace that
caused everyone, including Glaucon, to clap with joy!

When the applause ended, Anacreon put his wife-to-be down.
She turned to Glaucon with a questioning look and asked, ''My
son, what do you think?''

''Oh, Mother, I'm happier than I've ever been. This is a
solution to our loneliness and loss of each other that I never
dreamed could take place—or I'd want to take place. From what
you told me in the *culina* and from all that I've heard from
Anacreon, this is not only the best possible answer to our
alienation and pain, but actually God's gift to us all! As one who
believes in the providence of the loving God, I'm sure this is
God's way of righting wrongs.''

Glaucon reached out for Anacreon's hands and found himself
embraced in such a way as to portray Celsus's desire to be like a
father to him from then on.

''Glaucon, my new son, you're welcome in my home at any
time. I'll do my best to see you proud of your new father!''

A servant brought in glasses of fresh grape juice. Everyone
lifted their glasses to drink to the coming marriage and the
happiness of all!

The noonday meal at the bountiful table of Anacreon was
presided over by Erica, who sat between Celsus and Glaucon.
After an appropriate prayer of thanksgiving offered by Bishop
Tavius, plans were made for the marriage.

''Though I've not been baptized as a Christian yet,'' Anacreon
said as they began their meal, ''I'm sure we want to have a
Christian marriage. I've seen and heard enough of the Christian

good news through what has happened today and through the witness of Erica and other of my friends who are Christians over the past several months to know that I am indeed claimed by your Christ. Though I still have strong doubts, I want to become a Christian!''

Antonius, Onesimus, Glaucon, and young Peter responded with a spontaneous series of joyful *amen*s and *thanks be to Christ our Lord*s.

"It will be one of my highest privileges as your bishop," Antonius responded, "to teach and guide you as a member of our new class of catechumens. Your baptism can take place within the month! In the meantime, with your profession of faith in Jesus Christ, there is no reason why your marriage to Erica should not be celebrated soon."

"It would make me very happy if the wedding could take place before Onesimus and Glaucon depart for Pergamum," Erica said fervently. She put her hands on the hands of her husband-to-be and her son.

"I agree completely," Celsus replied. "Onesimus, you brought Glaucon back to us, and you've brought reconciliation to Antonius and his father Pyrrhus. Will you join with Antonius in the sacred ritual of our marriage?"

"Gladly," Onesimus answered. "I can't think of any higher privilege."

Before the group rose from the table, the date for the wedding was set for the next day, Sunday, at five o'clock in the afternoon. It would be held in the garden of Anacreon and Erica's home.

As Onesimus and his friends rode back into the city, they were exuberant. Young Peter was especially talkative as he described how Anacreon had changed since the times he had met him before and how lovely Glaucon's mother was. "I've never seen a more beautiful woman!"

All the riders were in agreement as they talked of the forthcoming marriage and the new Christians who would come out of Anacreon's transformed life and character.

"We're seeing Paul's 'new creation in Christ Jesus'!" Onesimus declared.

"It's like a good dream taking the place of a bad one," Glaucon remarked.

When the four returned to the Tavius home, Antonius's mood became much more serious. He asked to spend some time to talk with Onesimus, who suggested they walk around the grounds of the home. For the remainder of the afternoon, Antonius talked of his situation as bishop for the Christian community in Smyrna.

"We'll celebrate the Eucharist with unusual rejoicing in our Sunday morning worship tomorrow," he said enthusiastically. "Our Christian family will be relieved that the threats of persecution and suffering have for the time being been lifted by your help, Onesimus, in reconciling my father and me and in the new edict which he is announcing today to all the inhabitants of Smyrna. Praise to the Lord who sent you and Glaucon to Smyrna!"

With sober thoughtfulness, Antonius described some of the problems the Christians were facing.

"Most of us could find our own solution if we had the knowledge of our Lord that you can bring to us, Onesimus. I'd like for you to preach for us in the morning. As you share your interpretation of our Lord's words, maybe you could also share your experiences with Simon Peter and Paul and the other Christians in Rome. Of course, the whole group of believers, including the catechumens, will be there. Before you leave for Pergamum next week, I'd like to arrange for you to meet with the elders and deacons in the church. Here you can go into more detail as you answer their questions about our living in a pagan city, perhaps even as members of pagan families who worship in the main temples all over the city. For instance, what about eating meat offered to idols and sharing in festivities of special feasts and orgies in honor of Artemis, Asclepius, the god of healing, or even the dark god Nemesis? How do we handle the fears and hedonistic sexual abandon that accompany such worship? And how do we live 'in the world but not of it'?"

"I understand these problems," Onesimus responded. "I've heard them discussed by the hour by Paul and Linus, Luke and John Mark. I've made several parchment copies of Luke's and

Mark's Gospels and some letters of Paul and Peter that I'd planned to leave with you."

Antonius was thankful. "Your thoughtful provision of these parchments and your presence to interpret them make the finest gifts you could have brought, Onesimus. How can we ever repay you?"

"Don't worry. That's how I felt about my times with Peter, Paul, and the others," Onesimus responded. "I can never pay back even a small part of what I owe to them, much less to the grace of God, so I just try to do what I can."

The pair approached the house. Before entering, they embraced each other with thankfulness. Nothing more was said as they went to their rooms for rest and preparation. The next day was the first day of the week, and they needed to be ready for the worship.

arly on an October morning, after having substantial visits with the Christians of Smyrna, Onesimus and Glaucon mounted their horses. Leading donkeys laden with the silk and woolen cloth and the gifts from Bishop Tavius, they turned onto the main road to Pergamum. Their hearts were light with the remarkable experiences of the past two weeks.

"What an auspicious beginning to our journey!" Onesimus exclaimed after crossing the bridge at the River Hermus and passing through the vineyards of Anacreon's estate lying on both sides of the road.

As the journey progressed, the horses began to feel the steep climb as the road to Pergamum began its ascent to the summit of Mount Sipylos.

"Let's stop here and let the horses rest a few minutes," Onesimus said. "We're almost to the end of the fir trees."

The two guided their horses off the road to the welcome shade trees. They were delighted to find a small mountain brook from which to satisfy their thirsts with the cold water. Refreshed, the travelers sat on a boulder of reddish brown rock. For a few minutes they talked about the problems they would soon encounter when they met Bishop Antipas and his people.

"I don't know a lot about what we'll be facing in Pergamum," Onesimus began. "I understand that a loyalty test similar to the one in Smyrna is scheduled. I hope this problem can be solved as well, but we'll have to see what the details are."

"You'll be of great encouragement to them," Glaucon affirmed. "Judging from what you've said in your sermons and of your experiences in Rome, your presence will be timely. What do you know about Bishop Antipas and his faith as a Christian leader?"

"Tyrannus and Joanna talk of his stature as a wise, courageous man and a vital Christian. He's the son of a prominent physician and a colleague of Ventulus and several other of the best-known physicians in Pergamum. In fact, he's part of the long line of physicians that have made the city well known as the city of healing.

"As a youth under the guidance of his father and his colleagues, Bishop Antipas began his own studies in medicine and the art of healing. He apparently expected to follow in his father's steps by becoming a physician. His father, Theodotus Antipas, named him Theophrastus, after Aristotle's successor as head of his school of philosophy, because of the father's appreciation of Theophrastus.

"The philosopher Theophrastus followed the examples of Aristotle and Hippocrates, the famous Greek physician of Cos, who did so much to move medicine away from mere superstition. The elder Antipas, though a firm believer and worshiper of Asclepius, tries to balance science and the supernatural. He's worked hard to remove fear and terror from the minds of the sick he serves in relation to the temple of Asclepius, which is devoted to the care and healing of people from all over the world. Antipas is an honest, concerned physician who believes in a combination of the science of medicine with the religious devotion to Asclepius."

"I've heard of the remarkable healings in the temple of Asclepius since I was a kid,'' Glaucon observed. "It'll be interesting to talk with the bishop and his father tomorrow."

As the travelers were riding into the afternoon sun sinking behind the tall peak of Mount Sipylos to the west, they rode along the beautiful Lake Kyz south of the watershed at the pass. They could barely see a glimpse of the deep Lake Kara, just north of the pass where Tyrannus had suggested they might spend the night. Lake Kara was still some distance away, and the young men had grown hungry. They left the road and, after drinking from the cool, clear waters of the lake, spread their dinner on a rock and enjoyed the thoughtful provision made by Octavia and her helpers from Bishop Tavius's pantry.

"With such a background, how did young Antipas ever become a Christian?" Glaucon wondered aloud.

Onesimus related the story he had been told by Tyrannus, who had known the elder Antipas as a physician. A kinder, more concerned healer Tyrannus and Joanna had never known. Antipas had helped them when their young son fell ill with a fever and, despite all their measures, later died. The family had found no comfort in the god Asclepius in whom they then believed fervently, but they had found a friend in Antipas the physician. They continued to make yearly trips to Pergamum for the physician to check on their health.

On one such visit, Tyrannus and Joanna found that Antipas's dearly loved ten-year-old daughter was critically ill. In spite of all the priests of Asclepius could do, she died. Her brother, Theophrastus, became very rebellious as a result of the tragedy. The comfort that his religion could give was not enough, and the boy went to pieces. He rebelled at his father's ideas of the universe as a living organism with an order and purpose that humanity may not be able to understand, but to which it has humbly to submit. He simply could not accept 'fate' as the ruler of human life.

When confronted with such teaching, the youth shouted in anger, "There's no order or meaning in taking the fairest of the fair, in taking the life of my beautiful little sister and leaving her with the decay and destruction of death!"

Theophrastus was equally violent in his rejection of the head priest of Asclepius, who sought to comfort him with the promise that his sister had entered the Elysian Fields filled with flowers and music.

"I'm sick and tired," he announced, "of all this magic, mummery, and superstition!" The young boy planned to go away. His father pleaded with him to stay, but Theophrastus was determined.

Wanting him to have a safe refuge, Tyrannus and Joanna invited the young man to return to Ephesus as their guest. Plenty of ships sailed frequently from the port in case he wanted to go even farther. The couple shared with him their own experience of losing their son, when they had known the same rebellion and disgust over the empty talk of the priests and philosophers.

Theophrastus did go to Ephesus only a few days before the apostle Paul arrived in town. Out of curiosity, Tyrannus, Joanna, and their young visitor went to the agora to hear the apostle proclaim the story of Jesus Christ. The three of them were just as skeptical about Paul's story as they had been toward Asclepius, but they visited with Paul in their home and spent many hours listening to his stories of the life and teachings of Jesus. After learning of Christ's forgiving love on the cross, Tyrannus, Joanna, and Theophrastus each came to faith and were baptized.

"Tyrannus said that he had never seen a more joyful new creation in Christ than Theophrastus Antipas," Onesimus told his young friend. "Theophrastus remained in Ephesus for several weeks, learning all he could from Paul's teaching of our Lord, his new master, before returning to Pergamum to tell the good news to his father and friends."

"That's a fascinating story!" Glaucon exclaimed with enthusiasm. He then added soberly, "During the days to come, I'm afraid we'll see that faith put to its severest test. I don't know how well I could stand the test."

"Only by the grace of God and the sense of the living Christ can any of us stand it," Onesimus reflected. "It seems to me that this is the great evidence of the reality of God in Christ. Over and over I've witnessed it. When I visited the prisons with Peter, I heard about the young Christians thrown to lions or nailed to crosses with hot oil poured over them and set afire for Nero's garden party. These Christians met it all with courage, forgiveness, and even joy." Onesimus was almost overcome with emotion as he thought back on these times. After some time of reverent quiet, he jumped up as if awakening from a dream.

"Come now, we'd better get going while it's still light. We've got several miles before we reach Lake Kara. My story of young Antipas's coming to faith in Christ made us forget time and place!"

As their horses completed the climb to the top of the pass and started down the other side, the two young travelers pondered in silence the remarkable ways by which their own new faith had led them. They wondered what the next few days would bring.

After reaching the lake, staking their horses and donkeys, and preparing their bed rolls for the night, Glaucon built a roaring fire. They sat and watched the flames as Onesimus completed the account of young Antipas's reception by his father.

"Theodotus Antipas must be an unusually open and sensitive person, for although he was disappointed at his son's conversion to this new faith, he accepted him without the break young Tavius experienced with his father. I gather that the elder Antipas was open to his son's witness to the good news of Jesus but could not be convinced of the truth of Jesus' death and resurrection."

"It must have been a blow to him," Glaucon observed, "when his son decided to devote his life to serving as bishop of the little group of Christians rather than continue his studies in medicine."

"Yes, he was profoundly disappointed. Tyrannus has visited Pergamum several times since he and Joanna became Christians, and he says that Theophrastus is an unusually gifted and eloquent preacher of the *kerygma*, the Christ event. Within a few months, he shared the story with a group of young physicians in training and a number of the common people and merchants of the city. Interestingly, his father welcomed the small group who came to hear his son share his experience from the first. As the group grew larger, the physician very generously provided a place for them to meet in his own house. It's only natural that, with the inspired

leadership of young Antipas, he became their pastor-shepherd or
bishop by common acclaim.''

That night Onesimus again felt keenly the absence of his young
wife, Helen. As he prayed for her, he wondered if he could spare
much more time away. He had planned to visit Sardis in addition
to spending some time in Ephesus on his way home. In Ephesus
he expected to meet the apostle John, the beloved disciple, who,
with Mary, Jesus' mother, Tyrannus and the church had invited to
make their home with them. His longing for Helen and the
uncertainty of the future, however, led him to pray again, as he
had so often before, the prayer of Jesus now called the Lord's
Prayer.

"Yes, dear Lord, your kingdom come. Your will be done in
earth, in Pergamum, in the life of my dear Helen, in all that takes
place tomorrow and this week. Give to Helen her bread for the
day, guide and strengthen her as you do me, and deliver us all
from evil.''

He went to sleep with that act of trust in the wisdom and
goodness of God.

Late afternoon the next day, Onesimus and Glaucon rode into
the city. That morning they had descended into the valley of the
River Caicus and followed it along the plain to a plateau that rose
one thousand feet above the plain where Pergamum was built
centuries before. With a population of over one hundred sixty
thousand, the city, with Ephesus and Smyrna, was one of the three
great cities of the province of Asia. As the riders left the plain,
they passed by the Beauty Springs, a small pool where bathers
were said to regain some of their youth and beauty.

Approaching the city from the west, they saw the remarkable
collection of imposing buildings forming the Asclepion, the several installations of which were a mile square. These buildings were
dedicated to the worship and ministry of Asclepius. In addition to
the great temple, they included the rooms for the sick.

Following the directions Tyrannus had given them, the two left
the main road from Smyrna and rode another two miles north to

the entrance of the Asclepion. As they approached the arched, red granite entry, they stopped to read the words inscribed in the stone over the arch: "In the Name of the Gods, Death Is Forbidden to Enter!"

As they rode into the giant square, they saw several structures erected for use of the physician-priests as votive offerings by wealthy persons who had been healed. Onesimus and Glaucon stopped to read some of the inscriptions over the doorway. One in particular impressed them:

> Mutes have had their tongues unfastened, the eyes of a beautiful girl were opened and people who spat blood, who had pleurisy, who had pains in their stomach . . . were healed here!

"No wonder Pergamum is so famous. Such great numbers of people have found health and comfort here!" Glaucon exclaimed.

The visitors looked at the stream of sick and injured before them, and turned their horses to the north to find the house of Antipas as Tyrannus had directed.

At the house, almost a mansion, they were directed to large stables in the rear for their horses. The grizzled keeper met and welcomed them as friends of Antipas the physician and his son, Theophrastus.

"You've had a long, hard trip, and you must be very tired," the stablekeeper said. "I'll care for your horses and donkeys, and the baggage will be brought to your rooms in the house."

Turning to a small boy, he said, "Timaeus, show these guests to the library where Bishop Antipas is waiting. He's expecting them."

A warm smile lighted his wrinkled face, and the old man extended his hands. "My name is Petronius, and I too am a Christian. I've heard of your experiences in Rome with two of the great apostles, and I'd like to hear your stories in person."

In lower tones he added, "You couldn't have come at a better time. Next week is the trial of our dear Bishop Antipas."

Onesimus and Glaucon openly displayed their shock. They had heard nothing of a trial.

"I'm glad you're here," the stableman continued. "We need all the help and encouragement our Lord can give."

Onesimus thanked him and followed Timaeus into the house, through the atrium, and to the door of the study. The boy knocked, and the door was opened by the young bishop himself.

"Onesimus and Glaucon!" he exclaimed. "I know you from Tyrannus's description."

All three embraced with the Christians' kiss of peace. The young bishop was of medium height with black hair, a well-trimmed beard, and smiling black eyes. His voice was rich and deep. Onesimus could see that he was a strong, confident, intelligent man, fit for the leadership of the Christians in this capital city at such a time as this. The bishop invited them to sit down in the comfortable study.

Onesimus and Glaucon gave a brief description of their recent victories in Smyrna, but they were more concerned in hearing about what lay ahead for the bishop and his trial. Bishop Antipas, however, exuberantly clapped his hands and celebrated their triumphant story.

"So, the miracles of Christ's love are continuing through his followers who have caught his spirit!" he exclaimed. "It was that same selfless love of Paul and the stories of Jesus' love and his healing of the lame, the blind, and the lepers that caused me to believe in Christ. I've seen so many instances of the healing, freeing power of forgiving love here in this city of healing that I praise God with all my heart day after day. I know from all I've seen that the resurrection comes not only at the time of physical death but also in the darkest hours of spiritual death and despair. How wonderful of you to come to refresh my spirit and to encourage my people as we face our own supreme test!"

As he spoke of the trials ahead, the bishop's voice remained calm, but concern for what was going to happen was written in his face.

"Let me bring you up to date on what's happening here. Our church has grown rapidly, and our members are vibrant and joyful. As a result, the leaders of several temples and members of the court of the Roman governor for Asia, L. Antestius Vetus, have become jealous of us. They're especially threatened by the number of young physicians in training under Ventulus and my father who, after hearing my witness of the healing love of Christ, are interested in the Christian way.

"When several of their young priests of Asclepius, much to the anger and dismay of their superiors, also began to attend our daily preaching and teaching, the chief priest consulted with Governor Vetus. Together, they called a meeting of the chief priests of the temples of the other gods, where the chief priest of Asclepius made an impassioned speech and made all kinds of false charges against us, such as sedition and disloyalty to Caesar and the Roman government, atheism and unbelief in the gods and the weakening of family life by discouraging marriage. He accused Christians of breaking up homes by refusing to join in the sacred family feasts in the temples and charged that we recommend poverty instead of wealth as a way of life. The most disgusting charge of all was when he accused us of cannibalism. He claimed that we take the blood of infants during baptism and drink it at the feast of the Eucharist! Not one person made any attempt to correct these lies!"

A look of horror erupted on Glaucon's face. Trying to calm him, Onesimus spoke with deep sadness in his voice.

"This is the same tragedy that took place after the burning of Rome when Nero began his persecution. Most of these charges were leveled at the Christians then, and there's no way for us to counteract such lies. We're different as Christians. We're a separate people in choosing love over hate, in our unwillingness to offer worship to idols or Caesar. Of course, that's the most dangerous charge because of the governor's power to punish and even kill those charged with disloyalty to Caesar."

"Onesimus, I'm so thankful for your coming. Between now and my trial next week, we'll hold several assemblies of our congregation. We'll worship and celebrate Jesus Christ as Lord. In these times together, you can be of great help to me and to all of us. You can help us to understand how such false charges could be made. Most important of all, through your preaching and witness, you'll help us receive the grace of our Lord to suffer whatever we must for our faith.''

''I thank God that my coming will be of help,'' Onesimus answered with deep emotion.

''The first danger we faced,'' Bishop Antipas continued, ''was an edict proclaimed by the proconsul immediately after the meeting of the leaders of the temples and the governor nearly four months ago. It was similar to the edict you were involved with in Smyrna calling for all citizens to perform an act of worship and loyalty to Caesar. Since that first edict, the charges against us have been amplified and spread among all the people of the city. The hatred of many citizens is beyond description. Our people feel it wherever they go. Some of them are not as grounded in their faith as others. We all need your witness to increase our trust in the living Christ, king and ruler of the universe!''

''We've heard all this from Tyrannus, and so far, it has nothing to do with your trial,'' Onesimus said.

''That's all happened since Tyrannus has heard from me. Two days ago, news came from Smyrna of the political compromise you've just told me about. Several leaders in the assembly recognized the sobering fact that if the original edict were to be carried through to the letter, some of the finest citizens of our city, including several of the best young physicians, would be liable to punishment and death. This action by our neighboring city leaders allowed a way out of that problem. Speeches were made by members of the assembly blaming me for bringing this 'strange superstition' to Pergamum and declaring that, as bishop, I should be the one to stand trial.

''For his own political safety, Governor Vetus brought the edict before the assembly for approval. It could have been done without the assembly's support, but enemies of previous proconsuls have caused Nero to depose and bring them to Rome for execution, so Vetus did everything by the book. When Vetus did present the new edict, only one voice in the assembly was raised in protest— the voice of my father, representing the physicians. But when he finished, shouts of protest came from over the house accusing him of trying to protect me.''

"You must be very thankful for such a father," Glaucon said.

"Yes. That was a courageous action, especially since, though he's attracted by Jesus' teaching and the way his miracles of healing include the whole person, he's unable to believe the truth of the crucifixion and resurrection. Anyway, after the one note of support, the assembly voted overwhelmingly for the edict."

"What exactly does this new edict call for?" Onesimus inquired.

The bishop took a deep breath and slowly began his answer. "On Wednesday morning at the tenth hour, only three days from now, I've been commanded to present myself before the governor, the assembly, and all the inhabitants of the city in the amphitheater. I am to declare my allegiance and to present a small quantity of incense on the altar fire before the image of Nero Caesar."

Glaucon sucked in his breath, amazed at the calm pervading his host.

"What's the penalty if you refuse?" Onesimus asked, expecting the worst.

"I'm to be put to death, in a method determined by the governor. The presence of the inflamed mob suggests to me that the governor would likely choose the death with the most suffering, being burned alive," Theophrastus said calmly.

Onesimus had seen this horrifying punishment in Rome too many times. In the silence that followed, he repeated the words he remembered the apostle Peter saying to prisoners awaiting the same fate. "Dear Theophrastus, through your faith you've been filled with a living hope through Christ's resurrection from the dead."

In his own words, Onesimus continued. "I will speak of this living hope and do all I can to comfort and strengthen the church in Pergamum. I'm thankful, as Peter put it, that your faith is like gold that passes through the fire so it will stand the test! Let's pray that the spirit of our Lord, in spite of human rebellion, may shine out through you and what you say and all that takes place on that day."

The three took each other's hands and prayed, "as only those who recognize the presence of the living Christ can pray," Theophrastus said as he thanked them when the prayer was ended.

That evening at dinner, the bishop introduced his guests to his father, Theodotus Antipas. It was obvious to Onesimus that the older man had undergone great suffering. He was of slight build with graying hair and beard. Beneath his tired eyes, sagging dark shadows revealed the cost he had paid even during this ordeal. He was cordial as he greeted the travelers.

"I've heard how much you've meant to Tyrannus and Joanna over the years," Onesimus said to the elder Antipas. "I honor you for your charity and your brave defense of your son before the assembly. I know these are some difficult and costly hours for you."

"Thank you, Onesimus, though I don't know if I deserve it. What more could an intelligent citizen do even if the one so falsely accused were not his son? I know the charges being brought against the Christians are untrue, every last one of them. I could hardly keep silence." With a smile, he added, "I suppose my stand was foolish, but I would have done it for anyone else accused so unjustly."

The dinner proceeded as the physician plied Onesimus and Glaucon with questions concerning their recent experiences in Smyrna. The elder Antipas found great satisfaction from the story of Onesimus's visit to the governor of Smyrna. Glaucon's story of his mother and Anacreon at times caused him to laugh softly.

"I think I know how my son is reacting to your experiences there!"

"Yes, Father, indeed you do. These are additional evidences of the power of love over hate, of the spirit of Christ over the evil spirits of selfishness and greed!"

They both laughed at the common joke between them. Glaucon thought that Theophrastus must put in his strong words for Christ on every possible occasion to the amusement of his father.

After dinner, Onesimus and Glaucon were shown their rooms.

"I look forward in the morning to a long talk with you, Onesimus; I need your counsel and support," the bishop said in retiring.

———————————————————————————— *5*

*O*nesimus was cheered greatly the next morning by the strength of his new friend, Bishop Antipas, as the two talked of the coming week's preparation for the trial. Onesimus proposed to read the descriptions of the death and resurrection of Jesus from parchment copies he had made of the Gospels Mark and his good friend Luke had written. Theophrastus welcomed the reading, fully expecting to be called on to identify himself with their Lord in his death on the cross.

"As you said last night," the young bishop told his friend, "only the divine love shining on the cross and the living hope of the risen Christ can enable me to go through with my fate. Please read again how Jesus met his death so that I may be prepared to share his cross."

Theophrastus sat silently with eyes closed as Onesimus repeated the description of Jesus' trial and crucifixion from both of the Gospels.

The bishop opened his eyes and said simply, "Yes, Onesimus, the Lord is preparing me for the darkness when the sun stops shining for me. By God's grace, I'll be prepared for the feeling of forsakenness and being utterly alone, just what Christ felt. Unworthy as I am, I'll experience the same death he died, the same feelings of abandonment."

The young man's calmness returned, and with a glad smile he looked at Onesimus and said, "The difference I have is that Christ's victory is there to encourage me and the presence of the living Christ will support me in that darkness. As Paul wrote in describing the difference Jesus' death and resurrection have made, 'God, who said, "Let light shine from darkness," has shined light into our hearts to give us his revelation in the shining face of Jesus Christ.'

"When I stand on the platform before the proconsul and the people of Pergamum and they light the fires around me, I pray only that I may see the light of God shining in the face of Jesus Christ!"

"You will, my dear friend, you will!" Onesimus exclaimed. "Just as Stephen saw Jesus sitting at God's right hand as the stones crunched into his body, and just as my friends, as they were mangled by wild animals in the arena, cried in exultation, 'Christ, you are with me!' They died with the joy of recognition on their faces."

"And by God's grace, so will I!" Theophrastus said with determination.

Onesimus recognized, deep within himself, that he was seeing a level of faith he didn't possess. He confessed his weakness to Theophrastus.

"All that I say, dear brother, is from the witness of others. I don't know how I'd face what you're facing. I admire the strength of your faith, but who am I to encourage you, when I'm so inadequate?"

Onesimus was surprised when Theophrastus rose from his chair to walk over and put his arm on his shoulder.

"I once felt like that. If and when the trial comes to you, dear Onesimus, you also will find the Lord near to you. It is not *my* strength or *my* courage I depend on, but the presence of the Lord himself who said to his disciples, 'I'll be with you to the end.' He's kept his promise. He's come to me in the darkness after the sun's ceased to shine, and he'll be with me in that hour on Wednesday."

Theophrastus joined Onesimus in prayer, and Onesimus felt strangely uplifted. He thanked God that the one he had come to encourage and comfort had encouraged and comforted him. The prayer ended. They went into the garden for lunch with Glaucon and Antipas.

* * *

Early on Tuesday morning, the members of the church in Pergamum gathered in the house of Antipas for a special time of worship. They were quiet with the sense of impending danger and suffering ahead for their beloved bishop. Onesimus brought the message in preparation for the Eucharist. He read the same passages of the trial and death of Jesus from the parchment Gospels he and Theophrastus had shared the day before.

"For you, my dear brothers and sisters of the church, at ten o'clock tomorrow it will seem as though the sun has stopped shining and darkness is over all the world! Mark tells us that he really *felt* forsaken by God and humanity as he cried, 'My God, why have you forsaken me?' He was not only the Son of God; he was also the Son of man. This was a human experience of Jesus as it will be for all of us.

"What will we do when we see only the darkness, when we feel utterly alone and forsaken, when the physical pain and the sharper pain of rejection as Jesus felt it takes hold of us . . . what do we do? In our darkest hour, we will be empowered to pray the sublime prayer of trust as Jesus did, 'Father, into your hands I commit my spirit'! Already your beloved bishop has made that commitment, and in the morning, whatever happens to him, by the grace of God he will make it again!

"Let us thank God, the Father of our Lord Jesus Christ, that one so loving and strong has been permitted to be Christ's representative in that hour. Let us pray for him and for ourselves the power to stand the test!"

As each worshiper took the bread and the cup from the hands of their bishop, Onesimus saw in their faces strong love for their young shepherd and for each other. They were accepting the love of Christ, who would give each of them strength for anything— even death!

The bishop gave the apostolic blessing with deep feeling, and the people came one by one to embrace him and then each other. Onesimus felt the power of the *koinonia* and knew that whatever happened on the morrow, they and their bishop would be Christ's victors!

* * *

Wednesday morning came bright and clear. The early sun shone through the window of Onesimus's room. Awaking and remembering the trials of the day, he immediately knelt by his bed and prayed earnestly with trusting submission to the mighty God in whose hands he committed his brother Theophrastus Antipas.

At breakfast Onesimus was greeted warmly by the young bishop and his father. Asked to offer a prayer of thanksgiving, Onesimus did, feeling his words were utterly inadequate.

"Thanks, Onesimus!" Theophrastus put his hand appreciatively on his friend's arm. "Your prayer was exactly what I needed to hear this morning."

Onesimus was glad. It wasn't the words but the love and trust that counted.

After breakfast Onesimus and Glaucon met Theophrastus and his father at the stables as the grizzled Petronius waited in the carriage. The four rode together in the carriage as Petronius drove down the street to the Smyrna road, crossed the river to the Acropolis, and entered one of the stables near the amphitheater.

Out in the warm sunshine, the elder Antipas embraced his son and said, "May the great God of love and justice whom you call the Father of us all bless and strengthen you, my son!"

Tears filled Onesimus's eyes as he and Theophrastus embraced each other. At the gates of the amphitheater, the centurion met them.

Before the soldier could speak, young Antipas said quietly, "I am ready!"

Turning to his father, Onesimus, and Glaucon, he said simply, "The grace of the Lord Jesus Christ be with you!"

The Roman centurion led his prisoner through the theater and to the rear of the platform where the officers of the proconsul's court were taking their places. As a member of the assembly, the elder Antipas was seated with his companions near the platform.

Whatever happens, Onesimus thought with a shudder, *we'll be near enough to see it all.*

The three engaged in no conversation—only nods of recognition from Antipas's friends were acknowledged.

The amphitheater was filling rapidly as citizens of the city streamed in through the several entrances. At the hour of ten, trumpets sounded and Proconsul L. Antestius Vetus, dressed in a crimson toga, strode in carrying the mitre and scepter as a representative of the emperor. As he entered, the people rose and shouted, "Long live Caesar!" The proconsul sat, a vice-consul on each side, on the richly carved dais before a huge image of Nero Caesar.

Onesimus was aware that every Christian in the city was present. For the time being, they were free of charges that could be brought against them.

The air was filled with tension. People talked in voices filled with hostility. A few shouted, "Let the Christians burn!"

At a signal from the proconsul, the centurion led Bishop Antipas onto the platform. The valiant young man was dressed in a simple white tunic with a toga over his right shoulder. He stood calmly before the proconsul, as the official struck the dais with his gavel and the trumpeters sounded the call to silence. The voices of the crowd quieted.

The pompous voice of Proconsul Vetus was heard clearly as he greeted the people. "Honored members of the assembly and citizens of Pergamum, we are here for the trial of Theophrastus Antipas. This man stands before you charged with the serious crime of sedition and disloyalty to the emperor."

Turning to young Antipas, he said solemnly, "You are familiar with these charges brought against you in this assembly?"

"I am, sir," Theophrastus answered in a clear, strong voice.

"Were you warned that unless you ceased teaching that this crucified Jewish rabbi, Jesus of Nazareth, is the Lord and King of all the world, you would be declared guilty of treason and suffer the consequences?"

Again, Antipas answered with fearless voice, "Yes, your honor, this was made perfectly clear!"

"And yet you have continued to preach and teach boldly this motley crowd of people called Christians. They call you their bishop."

"What you say is true. I am proud to be called their pastor and bishop. I have continued to proclaim my faith in Jesus Christ as the Lord and King of all and as my Lord! I worship God, the Father of our Lord Jesus Christ, as the only true God, for there is no other!''

At this, a rumble of anger rose from the crowd. The proconsul quieted them with his hand.

"And yet," he continued, "you claim to be loyal and obedient to Nero Caesar and to the laws of this great empire."

"Indeed, I do, sir, and so do all who truly follow Christ. We will obey Caesar as loyal citizens, but we will worship only Christ!"

"Emperor Nero is a god! If you obey Caesar in all matters of government, how is it you refuse to worship him?"

"Sir, I repeat, I worship only Christ!"

A roar went up from the crowd: "Kill the Christian! Burn the atheist!"

With a show of patience and an eye to possible enemy reports to the proud maker of "Roman justice," Nero, Vetus tried again.

"Here before the image of our great emperor is your last chance." The proconsul paused dramatically. "Centurion," he commanded, "bring the box of incense to the accused!"

With his head high, his black eyes flashing, Theophrastus Antipas rejected the incense. For the third time he said, "Sir, I say to you, to the assembly, and to all the citizens of Pergamum that I will not worship before the image of any man, even Nero!"

Howls of hate came from the throng, fast turning into an angry mob. "Let him die! Kill the traitor! Burn him!"

Onesimus froze in his seat. The hearts of the father and all the Christians sank. The case of Theophrastus Antipas was out of the hands of the proconsul. The suffering on the gray face of the elder Antipas was plain as the brave young bishop stood erect, his face turned upward.

Trumpets were blown as Vetus signaled for silence. Addressing the accused, he voiced his anger and irritation in a loud voice.

"Let all hear my verdict! I, L. Antestius Vetus, Roman Proconsul of the Province of Asia, in the name of the great Nero Caesar, do hereby declare Theophrastus Antipas guilty of sedition and disloyalty to the emperor. I sentence you to death by—"

"Burning!" the mob took over the sentence. *"Burn him! Let him be roasted alive in the bronze bull of Zeus!"*

The cries of the crowd, Onesimus realized, so unmistakably in unison, had obviously been planted by enemies of the small group of Christians. Onesimus shuddered and gripped the arm of Antipas, who had turned pale with horror.

Hatred and prejudice, fed by ignorance and jealousy, won the verdict. Knowing that the Roman guard was not strong enough to protect his prisoner from the unusual punishment called for by the mob, Vetus rose as the trumpets signaled for order.

"Citizens of Pergamum!" he announced. "I have pronounced the sentence. You the people have chosen the method. Roman law requires that treason and sedition be punished by beheading, but you call on me to go beyond that. Therefore, I order the priests from the altar of Zeus to bring the bronze bull of Zeus. Antipas will join the hundreds of years of sacrifices offered to this, the god of all gods. Bring also wood, and let the fire be lighted in which the condemned atheistic traitor receives the punishment he deserves!"

Howls of approval went up from the crowd, "Hail to Caesar Nero!"

Onesimus observed many among the crowd moving toward the exits. They would apparently be unable to stomach the grisly scene to come. He noticed a few Christians he had met the day before also leaving. Onesimus would not be one to run away. The elder Antipas, shaken as he was, showed no signs of leaving.

What a noble witness Theophrastus is giving! Onesimus thought as he prayed for his brother, soon to be the first Christian martyr of Asia.

Standing erect with remarkable courage, Theophrastus waited, face uplifted. It was obvious to Onesimus that he was praying. Onesimus joined the other Christians in supplication for their brother in a prayer too deep for words.

The mob watched the removal of the dais and the placing of bundles of wood in the center of the stage. Seven priests of Zeus wearing their ritual robes carried the bronze bull and placed it on the pile of wood. The carved animal was open, allowing the victim to stand upright. Theophrastus's head and shoulders would be seen by all. Everything was ready as the proconsul signaled for silence.

"Centurion, bind the hands of the traitor and place him in the center of the bull," Vetus commanded. "Let the chief priests of Zeus, Asclepius, and Roma join in putting the burning torches to the wood. But first, Roman justice requires the condemned be permitted to say his last words."

Addressing the condemned man, Vetus said, "I make my final appeal to you, Theophrastus Antipas. Do you recant of your atheism and offer your rightful worship to Nero Caesar?"

A strange hush quieted the entire amphitheater.

"Honored sir," Theophrastus began with a clear voice, "I say to you, to all the assembly, to all citizens of this city, and to all among you bearing the name of Christ."

His voice rose in eloquent passion; his words could be heard to the furthermost corner of the amphitheater.

"I witness with my life and now my death to the immeasurable, never-failing love of God revealed to us in Christ Jesus. Unworthy as I am of such love, I now offer up my life, even as he did, in order that you may know the mighty power of God's love for each of you and for all humankind. May Christ strengthen each of you with enough power to allow you to meet whatever comes with wisdom, patience, and joy. To him be the glory, the honor, the majesty, and the power forever and ever. Amen!"

His prayer was a blessing as he stretched out his hands over all the arena, beginning with the proconsul and the assembly. The concluding ascription of glory to God was a shout of exultation as his shining face looked upward.

The hush in the amphitheater continued after these final words as the chief priests of the three temples took the lighted torches in their hands and touched them to the pile of dry wood. As the wood began to burn, Onesimus and all in the theatre saw Theophrastus's face still lifted with radiant joy. The remarkable silence continued over the vast throng as the flames leaped higher until they surrounded the bronzed bull. At times they rose so high they concealed the crowd's view of the bishop. Theophrastus continued looking up, his face illumined by something more than the light of the flames.

Now all the wood was burning. The heat had ignited Theophrastus's clothes. Only once more could the uplifted face be seen through the flames.

Suddenly it was over. The strong, heroic form of Theophrastus Antipas had fallen into the hot oven of the bronzed receptacle, where it became part of the fire. Onesimus wondered at what point the martyr's spirit had ascended into heaven.

Onesimus was moved by the scene, but not into sadness. Instead, his heart was lifted in thanksgiving and praise to God. He could not imagine a more glorious and moving witness than this.

Theophrastus has proclaimed the most powerful message of his life, Onesimus said to himself, almost aloud. *The love of our Lord has been revealed to thousands who never would have believed in it. The seed is sown for a stronger and more powerful church in Pergamum, in all of Asia, and wherever this witness will be told.*

Antipas took Onesimus by the arm and began to lead him out. He said with husky voice, "It's over now. Let's go home."

The three slowly made their way with the still strangely quiet crowd leaving the amphitheater. Some were Christians rejoicing in their bishop's witness. Many were moved by such an unexplainable courage and love to think more deeply on their own faith. Some left with curses under their breath.

"Christ has won the victory again!" Onesimus murmured as they got into the carriage. Antipas nodded in assent, and they rode back to the house.

———————————————— 6

*U*pon entering the house of Antipas, the physician spoke his first words since the ordeal at the amphitheater.

"You'll want to go to your rooms to rest and pray for the worship service Theophrastus planned to follow his death. It will be a difficult time for you and for all of us who loved him. That love will undoubtedly grow now that he has joined the glorious company of the apostles and martyrs who preceded him."

Antipas then spoke simply with quiet assurance words that gave great joy to Onesimus and Glaucon.

"I'll be there, too. If my son could die in such a triumphant witness to the love of Christ, then I'm ready to live by that love! I've been waiting for tangible evidence of the truth of the Christ and the resurrection, and today I saw it. It wasn't the scientific proof my colleagues and I have demanded, but it was the evidence of my son through whom the nature of God was revealed. I'm ready to wager my faith that this is the spirit of the mighty God, creator, ruler, and redeemer of all who trust in him. From now on, I'll say by both my life and my death when it comes, Jesus is Lord!"

"Praise God, Antipas!" Onesimus exclaimed as he embraced the sorrowful but victorious father. "What more fitting evidence of the truth of your son's witness than for you to be the first fruit of his sacrificial death!"

"Share this with the congregation, Onesimus, and tell them that from now on they can count on my presence, prayers, and support in every possible way!"

That evening the members and catechumens of the church gathered in the atrium of the Antipas house. As Onesimus watched, he saw on their faces the paradox of sorrow and joy. *How could there be such great joy in the midst of such sadness and tragedy?* he asked himself as he had so often before.

When Onesimus rose to begin the worship, the words he used took on a new and deeper meaning. "The risen Lord is with you!"

The people responded with full voice. "And with you also."

"Lift up your hearts!"

"We lift them up to the Lord."

"Praise and honor, glory and power belong to God the Father

of our Lord Jesus Christ who today has manifested the mighty power of his love that surpasses all understanding.''

The people responded, ''Amen!''

''With our own eyes, we have seen the victory that Christ has given to our beloved bishop, Theophrastus Antipas.''

As Onesimus continued, the words poured from his mind and heart.

''Only the inspiration of the spirit of the living Christ could have given him the courage, the strength, and the power to make such a noble witness.''

The people as with one voice cried, ''Amen, alleluia!''

Onesimus told the congregation of his time with Paul and Peter as they gave their final witness before their deaths in Rome, Paul by beheading, Peter by fire and the cross. He compared them to the powerful testimony of Bishop Antipas to the love of God.

''We are here tonight to celebrate his full entrance into Christ's unseen but very real kingdom,'' Onesimus continued. ''Let us now join in singing the song of our Lord's victory.''

Some psalms of David had been set to music and taught to the church by one of the Christians in Pergamum. Onesimus asked him to lead the people in one of them:

> ''Sing to the Lord a new melody;
> He has done wonderful things!
> By his own power and holy strength,
>   He has won the victory!
>
> The Lord is Ruler, all will be glad!
> Rejoice all you islands of the seas!
> Clouds of mystery envelop him;
> . Justice and righteousness undergird his throne,
> For in the Lord is love unfailing
> And great is his power to set us free!''

When they finished singing, Onesimus spoke out from his heart. He shared his own doubts after the martyrdom of Paul when he had witnessed the overwhelming victory of evil incarnate in the performance of brutal acts of pain and death to hundreds of Christians. How could Jesus, the loving, compassionate man of Galilee, be Lord, if this kind of evil is the ruler?

The best answer Onesimus could give them had been declared in the psalm. "The Lord is Ruler," Onesimus said, "but clouds of mystery envelop him. Indeed, these clouds obscure the reasons why God, in creating us free, permits evil and hatred to exist, which is a mystery no one can fathom. Nevertheless, we have seen Jesus through the eyes of his disciples, and we have witnessed Antipas reflect Christ's radiant image. The spirit we saw in the face of Antipas and that could be seen in the face of Stephen as he was being stoned is the spirit of the Lord! The Holy Spirit teaches us to say by faith, 'Jesus is Lord indeed! And the Lord is King!'"

Onesimus saw in the faces of the people something much more than sorrow over a lost leader. He saw the light of understanding in listening minds and hearts. He knew his message was being accepted with joy and thankfulness.

"What a wonderful fragrance comes from the victorious life and death of our dear brother Antipas. We were among many in that amphitheater who caught from him the aroma of life to life that Paul described in a letter to Corinth. Surely, there are many not in our congregation who have been saved by the fragrance of his victory. Like him, they and all who accept the good news of Christ will live even though we die!

"Through the Holy Spirit's gift of faith, let us continually invite God to renew *our* inner beings. Day by day, let us look not at what is visible, temporary, and easily destroyed, but at what is invisible, eternal, incapable of destruction!"

The congregation was quiet, awed by the mighty truth offered to them. Following the preparatory prayers, Onesimus and the deacons distributed the bread and wine of the Sacrament to each of the Christians present. Onesimus saw in their tear-stained, illumined faces the first fruits of the precious seed sowed by the Holy Spirit in Antipas's victory. As Onesimus gave the words of institution, he knew that through the Living Presence these elements were the bread and wine of hope to those who formed the body of Christ in Pergamum.

Before closing the service, Onesimus promised his prayers for the church and the new bishop they would choose. Finally, with obvious emotion, Onesimus beckoned Antipas to stand with him at the lectern.

"I have an announcement to make," Onesimus began, "that beautifully climaxes this day of sorrow and joy, of tragedy and hope. As we returned here this afternoon, our beloved friend and physician Theodotus Antipas shared with me his decision to be a disciple of Jesus Christ."

The people broke into spontaneous applause, and tears of thankfulness coursed down many faces. Onesimus concluded the service with his blessing and benediction. All the people cried fervently, "*Amen alleluia! To God be the glory both now and forever. Amen!*"

In the next few minutes, Onesimus experienced *koinonia* as powerfully as he had ever known. Though weary, Onesimus was exhilarated as each member of the church embraced him and thanked him for his words of encouragement and hope. They promised to carry on. With God's help they would reap a rich harvest. Antipas's witness to his new life in Christ was only the first fruit.

Physically and emotionally exhausted, Onesimus and Glaucon went to their rooms to sleep, but sleep did not come quickly to Onesimus. This had been the hardest and best day of his new life and ministry. As he reviewed it, he knew that his times of doubt had not ended and realized that the strength of his faith was the will to believe in spite of doubts. As he looked through the window at the full moon and stars, he was honest enough to admit how shaken he'd been before the evils of ignorance, jealousy, and hatred that had taken the life of Theophrastus Antipas. He prayed that, whatever happened to him and his family, he'd be able to rise above his doubts and go from faith to faith.

His mind leaped the distance to the bedroom in Colossae where his beloved Helen lay sleeping, and he thought of her beauty of both spirit and body. How he loved her! He wondered how she and the baby she carried were doing. What would the future hold?

One thing he decided as he lay in bed was that he'd change his plans. He simply couldn't be away from Helen any longer than necessary. He and Glaucon would have to return to Ephesus where the apostle John and Mary, Jesus' mother, would soon arrive. He couldn't take the time he had planned to visit the church in Sardis. That could wait for another time, maybe when Helen could be with him.

For the time being, he'd spend a few more days in Pergamum with the deacons and Christian leaders who'd survived the fires of this first persecution. He'd need to teach and guide them as they chose another bishop, and he'd do all he could to help Antipas build his new faith firmly. Breathing a prayer of thankfulness, he fell asleep.

Early the next morning after a good breakfast, Antipas invited Onesimus into his study. It was a large, comfortable room with walls covered in parchment scrolls and memorabilia of his fruitful life as a physician.

"I need your guidance, Onesimus," the physician said. "I feel your mind is kindred to my own. Share with me your own struggle to believe and how you've continued to struggle with doubt."

Onesimus spent the morning sharing his intimate experiences in which his philosophical mind met the amazing facts of the freedom to love in Christ. He told his story of utter despair and black doubt after he had bidden Paul good-bye as Nero's Praetorian Guards placed him in the prisoners' cart to be taken to his decapitation. The last words of Paul had seemed utterly preposterous. "In everything, we win the fullest victory, because Christ loves us!"

"I walked blindly down the street, wondering what kind of victory it is to give your life in love for others and then lose your head to the executioner of a crazed boy emperor? And then I realized that here is the highest truth, the deepest reality in the victorious love of Christ! But sometimes it's hard to see.

"It's amazing how I found the answer not by philosophical reasoning, but as I witnessed to Marcia, the young woman ex-slave and prostitute who had betrayed me when I first came to Rome. Why, as I met her in the street, was I now willing to forgive her?

"As I look back, there have been many other times when doubt seemed victorious, but my faith was restored through the continuing presence of the Holy Spirit and the Christlike love that surrounded me. Last night before I went to sleep, I confessed to doubt that arose over me yesterday as I watched the cruel powers of this world take the physical life of your son. His faith and the love with which he died brought me out of the doubt. And you helped my faith by your decision to be a Christian. The worship, the Eucharist, and all the love of the people in the church made my faith stronger than ever!"

"I take it the war with doubt is never over," Antipas replied. "Every time we win a battle with the darkness, our faith grows brighter."

"What a beautiful way to say it. You're so right, Antipas. We never arrive. We're always on the road from faith to faith. But we're never alone—the Holy Spirit, our guide and counselor, is always with us."

The sharing continued all morning as the wise old physician found the healing medicine that Onesimus, himself young in the faith, was able to give.

At the midday meal, Antipas proposed a visit to his physician friends and to the Asclepion. Glaucon and Onesimus were delighted at the opportunity.

The group first visited the home of the aging Ventulus, the author of many valuable parchments on various diseases and their treatment.

"The dear man is now over eighty years of age!" Antipas explained. "His mind is alert, but he's become a cripple and is unable to walk. Nevertheless, he's still active in leading us in consultations with each other and visiting physicians. We come to his house and sit at his feet. More than any of us, he's inherited the knowledge and wisdom of Hippocrates. You know it is from Hippocrates that we get the Hippocratic oath that defines the ethics of a good physician. All of our young doctors take the oath before being allowed to practice medicine.''

Antipas was admitted into the presence of his aging friend, who was propped up by pillows on a couch near the center of the large room where he met physicians and patients. After the introductions, he reached out for the hand of Antipas.

''I've been told of the trial and cruel execution by fire of your son.'' The old man spoke with obvious sympathy in his voice. ''I want to tell you that my heart goes out to you and to all who loved him dearly. I heard that he died with remarkable tranquility. His final witness before the mob was said to be deeply moving!''

''Thank you for caring,'' Antipas responded. ''It was a terrible morning for us all.''

''This kind of persecution and cruelty is part of the deadliest disease of our humanity,'' the aged physician continued. ''As we have seen so many times, hatred is the enemy of healing, and love is the door to wholeness and health. Some of the young physicians who were present told me that a transforming love shone in Theophrastus's face as he met his death. They were very impressed by that, and they're interested to know the cause or source of that love. What happened yesterday may have done more to open minds to the Christian faith than anything that could have happened.''

''I'm sure I know what they're thinking,'' Onesimus spoke up. ''I was also brought up with the philosophers, and I attended the Gymnasium here for two years. The same quality and power of love were what I saw in the Christians in Rome that convinced me of the truth of Christ!''

Ventulus looked at Onesimus with interest and responded to the young man. ''Yes, philosophy alone, as good as it may be, can't provide that kind of love. I'm not a prophet, but I can see that you and others like you are going to help change the superstitious, self-centered ways of our empire. Antipas and I and others in this city have sought to bring the healing powers of love to bear upon the sick. I have to admit that I still have difficulty with the Christian teachings of Jesus' resurrection from the dead, but I can and do believe that the love that gives, serves, and heals is eternal.''

Antipas quickly spoke up. ''At some other time, Ventulus, I

have some things to tell you about what's happened to me, to my thinking, and to my faith during these last twenty-four hours. What you say is most encouraging to me right now, as I'm sure it is to my young friends.''

As the visitors left, the revered old physician bade them the blessings of the God of self-giving love.

During the remainder of the morning, Antipas led his guests through the various buildings making up the huge space called the Asclepion. They visited the library and its two hundred thousand scrolls to be used by the sick, by visitors, and by the students in the various schools. They saw the theater with seating for forty-five hundred spectators. Therapeutic plays were performed nightly for both patients and patrons of the arts.

The group next went to the round Temple of Telesphorus, where the patients slept and allowed their dreams to be influenced by suggestion. As Antipas explained, this was where sacred snakes were kept as well. If a snake crawled over a sleeping patient, it was taken as a sure sign of healing. These snakes, wrapped around a staff, were used as a symbol of medicine called a caduceus.

Patients were brought to the temple through a sacred cellar where, as they walked, suggestions are made to them through openings in the walls. These suggestions often brought healing, sometimes gradual, occasionally instantaneous. Antipas led his visitors around the square to three sacred ponds and a fountain in which hundreds of persons with various kinds of sicknesses were bathing.

As they returned home, Antipas told stories of the various superstitions that ruled the majority of people in the Graeco-Roman world. Though belief in the gods had lessened and almost disappeared among those better educated and philosophically trained, most people were terrified more than helped by their belief in the gods and goddesses when faced with illness or accidents causing pain and death.

"These are the people," Antipas explained, "that we are seeking to free of superstitious beliefs in vengeful and evil deities. They seek to pacify and win the favor of these gods through offerings like those presented to Zeus in the fires of the bronze bull or brought to the altars of Asclepius. As I begin my worship and give my love to the mighty God and Father of our Lord Jesus Christ, more than any one prayer I pray, Onesimus, is that as a physician I may help free many from the destructive cynicism that results when, regardless of their votive offerings and acts of sacrifice, their dear one is still crippled, blind, or dead!''

"Tyrannus told me of Theophrastus's rebellion after your young daughter died," Onesimus said. "The same thing happened to Tyrannus and Joanna when their two-year-old son died in spite of all that you and the other physicians and priests of Asclepius could do. Your new understanding acceptance of the love of God revealed in the cross will surely be your most blessed means of therapy.

"Indeed it will," Antipas exclaimed, "for, as Ventulus said, healing the hurt mind and heart comes through love. Only thus can the whole person be healed. There's no greater love than the love of Christ! I can see a whole new world of help opening up for my ministry of healing!"

Onesimus spent many of the following days in conversation with the leaders of the church of Pergamum. He was amazed to see little jealousy in the church, but a strong desire to discern the will of God in finding the best bishop possible. He was impressed by their humility and hunger to know more about Jesus of Galilee, the risen Christ, and the Holy Spirit of God. Onesimus shared with them the teachings of Jesus he had learned from Luke, John Mark, Simon Peter, and Paul.

A meeting of the entire congregation was called for Wednesday evening, a week from the "great day of Antipas," their name for the day on which their bishop had been offered up. Their new bishop would be chosen this night. When the final vote was taken, the eloquent, warm-hearted, young physician Severus was elected with enthusiastic unanimity. Severus had worked in the church as one of Bishop Antipas's closest friends. They had studied together as young physicians. Severus was held in high esteem and respect by all in the church.

*   *   *

Onesimus and Glaucon remained in Pergamum for several days to share in the ordination of the new bishop. When the consecration service concluded, Onesimus took Severus's hand, lifted him from his knees, and embraced him.

"My dear brother Severus, you are now the bishop of the church in Pergamum! May your life as bishop be one of joy, love, and quiet strength."

To the waiting people, Onesimus said, "Here, beloved, is your new bishop. Embrace him, love him, pray for him, obey him in the Lord, and the Lord bless you all!"

The people crowded forward. With tears of joy and prayers of blessing, they embraced each other and Bishop Severus.

7

n their return journey to Ephesus, Onesimus and Glaucon were delighted to spend a night in Smyrna. They were warmly welcomed by Bishop Tavius and his family and by Erica and Anacreon.

They arrived early in the afternoon, and word soon spread to all the members of the Smyrna church. The news of the costly but victorious martyrdom of Bishop Antipas had already reached the community, and everyone wanted to hear the full story. The Christians in Smyrna knew only too well that their narrow escape from similar persecution had come through the influence of Onesimus.

The once dreaded day on which Governor Tavius's first edict would have punished by death all who refused to worship the emperor had become instead a day of celebration. All the Christians gladly had brought coins with the image of Caesar to deposit in the urn before Caesar's statue in the Assembly Hall. There had been no open challenge by the priests of Asclepius or the Templum de Roma. Even the enemies of the Christians had gladly accepted the "Medal of Honorable Citizenship" presented by the governor to all who fulfilled the requirements by registering in the Templum de Roma and before the bust of Caesar in the Assembly Hall.

The atrium of the Tavius house was full of eager Christians waiting to hear the terrifying details of Antipas's death and the inspiring witness of his last words. After Onesimus described the scene in the amphitheater and the worship of the church in Pergamum before and after the trial, Bishop Tavius called his people to prayer. For an hour the people prayed for their brothers and sisters in Pergamum and expressed fervent exclamations of praise and thanksgiving to Christ for the victory! Onesimus had never seen such intense devotion and joyful worship.

In benediction, Bishop Tavius declared, "As Paul wrote, 'The cross is the wisdom and the power of God. To the Jews it is troublesome and to the Greeks ridiculous, but to those who hear the call of Jesus, even Jew or Greek, it is indeed the wisdom and power of God!' Christ was again on his cross suffering with Antipas, as he will be with us when our time comes. Through our suffering love, we give witness to the mighty wisdom and love of God—more powerful than all the armies of Nero!"

After the people left, Tavius and Onesimus talked long into the night, sharing their concern and strengthening each other.

As Onesimus was eager to return to Helen, the two travelers left Smyrna early the next morning. As they came upon the steep mountain pass where they had spent the night with the bandits, Onesimus told Glaucon some of what Tavius had told him the night before.

The bandits' chief, Carias, had paid a visit to the bishop, and spent an afternoon seeking more about the life and teachings of Jesus. He wanted to know everything about the crucifixion and resurrection that Tavius could tell him. Carias had been so interested that he had stayed for the night to attend a class of catechumens and the church's worship service the next day. As he left to return to the bandits, Carias had promised to return. Tavius had told Onesimus, "I believe he'll continue his quest and become a Christian disciple."

"Tavius said that Carias warned him not to let us seek out the bandits when we reach the pass. Some of them weren't too impressed by our witness, and they're blaming their captain for treating us so well. They regretted losing the silks and woolens we carried, not to mention our money and jewels."

As they reached the spot where they had stopped on their previous trip, however, the two young Christians did stop to offer prayers for Carias and his bandits.

Onesimus and Glaucon had no shortage of conversation on their first day's ride from Smyrna to Ephesus.

"These have been the richest three weeks of my life!" Glaucon said exuberantly. He shared his own experience the night before with his mother and new father. "The change is so remarkable, I wouldn't have believed it possible. Anacreon is indeed a new man in Christ. He and my mother have become an important part of the Christian *communitas* in Smyrna."

In the late afternoon of the second day out of Smyrna, the young travelers turned off the Via Augusta in Ephesus and entered the short street encircling the large six-story apartment house of Tyrannus and Joanna. The place was familiar to Onesimus, who had been the guest of these Christians as he returned from Rome with Paul's letter to Philemon that helped set him free.

"It's remarkable and providential," Onesimus said to Glaucon, "that Tyrannus was one of Paul's first converts. His provision of the lecture hall he owns and his strong backing of Paul in the dispute and riot led by the silversmith Demetrius, one of his competitors, saved Paul's life. It also gave Paul a base of operations during his two years in Ephesus."

At the stables to the rear of the building, the riders left their horses to be curried and fed. They hurried inside and climbed the stairway rapidly to the sixth floor.

Tyrannus and Joanna met them at the door.

"Wonderful to see you," Tyrannus said as he embraced his guests. "From Antipas's note, we were expecting you either today or tomorrow. We've heard about your remarkable experiences! Come into the atrium and sit for a few minutes while we have some fresh grape juice. We're still enjoying the grape harvest." He led the way.

"We can't wait to hear all about your experience, but we most want you to meet the apostle John and Mary, who arrived from Joppa last week."

"Great!" Onesimus exclaimed. "We'd heard they were coming, but we didn't know when."

As the three were seated on a comfortable couch, Joanna brought in a tray with glasses of purple grape juice.

"What a blessing to have Mary along with the apostle!" Joanna remarked.

"Yes," Tyrannus added, "we've had some remarkable times listening to these two dear people who were so close to Jesus. When we heard about the martyrdom of John's brother James by Herod Agrippa and John's danger of being caught in the same vicious persecution in Jerusalem, our church asked me urgently to invite John, Jesus' only living disciple, to come as our bishop. We also invited Mary, Jesus' mother. Jesus entrusted her to John's care when he hung on the cross that day. I sent a special messenger to Jerusalem and, fortunately, reached John. He was in Galilee when his brother was murdered. The two of them immediately traveled to Joppa and set sail for Ephesus."

Tyrannus showed them to their rooms before dinner to freshen up. At dinner they would meet John and Mary and hear stories of Jesus.

"John calls his stories signs that Jesus is truly the Christ," Tyrannus added. "His close relation to Jesus lets us be inspired by some of the very words that Jesus said to help us in our understanding of his good news. But John is still volatile and fiery. He speaks as if every word is significant and every sentence a jewel to be examined and revered. And, despite his temper, his love and kindness set him apart from anyone I have ever known!"

Tyrannus paused and wiped his eyes.

"You've been deeply touched by this man," Onesimus observed. "Jesus' beloved disciple has evidently caught some of Jesus' love and reflects it in all he says and does!"

"Indeed he has," Tyrannus exclaimed. "But come, let me show you your rooms, the same ones where you stayed before."

Once in his room, Onesimus stretched his weary limbs on the

bed and again offered thanks to the Lord for the three weeks in Smyrna and Pergamum. On top of all of that, he would soon meet this great man of love and power and Mary, Jesus' mother. What sort of influence might this man have on his life in the years to come? Onesimus was excited at the possibilities and was more than ready when the call to dinner came.

As Onesimus first entered the atrium where dinner would be served, he was struck again, as he was each time he visited, with its elegant appointments. The spacious room was furnished with Lydian and Persian rugs, colorful drapes, and tables and chairs of polished mahogany.

In the center of the room were Jesus' beloved disciple and Mary, Jesus' mother. Onesimus, his pulse racing, walked over to meet them.

"Onesimus," Tyrannus spoke, "it's my great joy to present to you our beloved apostle John, and Mary the mother of Jesus, our Lord."

"I'm thankful for this opportunity to meet you," John said. "I've heard so much about you from Tyrannus and Joanna and from others who knew you in Rome."

Mary, equally glad to meet the young Christian, smiled and put one arm around his waist. "Onesimus," she said, "I'm so glad to see you! I've also heard about you and your witness, for which I'm very thankful. I'm looking forward to your sharing with us more about Paul and Simon Peter. From the first, Peter was one of my favorites of the disciples. I'm also interested to hear about Lady Pompania and your friend Marcia. From what Joanna has told me, she, like our blessed Mary Magdalene, has come a long way through the love of Christians like you. And of course I'm eager to hear about your wife, Helen."

Onesimus was deeply touched. She was older, but not as tall as his own mother. Her voice was soft and musical. Her hair, gray with flecks of brown, framed a face marked with suffering. Her dark blue eyes had a quality of loving-kindness that drew others to her. Onesimus would always remember the moment when he was first embraced by the mother of his Lord! Afterward, he tried many times to imagine how it must have been to care for such an unusual son as a boy. How difficult it must have been to have held his broken body in her arms at Calvary.

After a moment, Onesimus was able to speak. "Meeting both of you is something I've looked forward to for many months. I've wanted to meet you ever since hearing Simon Peter tell so much about you and the times you shared together with our Lord!"

"Onesimus," John responded, "you have so much to tell us about your work as Paul's *amanuensis* and the time you spent with Peter during his last trying days. Your intimate acquaintance with Luke, John Mark, and the Elder Linus, who's now a bishop, as well as with other brave Christians, has given you a priceless understanding of the good news that makes us victors in life and death. In your latest travels, you witnessed much that we're waiting to hear about. I especially want to know about blessed young Bishop Antipas's witness as the first martyr of Asia."

"Thanks for all you've said," Onesimus replied. "I pray that I'll always be worthy of your trust and confidence."

"Dinner is served," Joanna interrupted. She showed her guests to their places at the table set with white linen and laden with much fruit, milk, and cheese and with a large loaf of fresh bread waiting to be broken.

After a brief blessing of thanksgiving and words of remembrance and intercession for the church in Pergamum, the meal began. Onesimus sat between John and Mary. A large platter of roast lamb was brought in by one of Joanna's servants.

As the food was passed and the others began to eat, Onesimus was so overwhelmed with the poignancy of the moment that he had difficulty in swallowing. Sensing his problem, Mary reached out her hand and touched his, whispering, "You've been through a lot recently. We understand how you must feel."

As she said this, Onesimus was calmed. He thanked her and began to eat.

Tyrannus had briefed John on the situations in Smyrna and Pergamum in which Onesimus had been so effective, but neither he nor John had heard of Onesimus and Glaucon's evening as guests of the bandits of Mount Mimas. Tyrannus asked Glaucon to relate the episode. When Glaucon, giving full credit to Onesimus for the way they responded to the robbers, described the remarkable event, John became more and more excited.

"Here's one more evidence that loving one's enemies is indeed Christ's way to meet evil and to win the hearts of those who use force to gain their ends!" John exclaimed. He paused and rested his chin on his hands, a faraway look in his eyes.

"How well I remember that terrible hour when Jesus stood before Pilate in the outer court of the palace. I was standing as near as I could to see what was going on. Pilate asked him if he was the King of the Jews. I could hear Jesus' clear reply.

My kingdom does not belong to this world.

And so it was and is!"

After another pause, John went on. "It was the authority of the love of the mighty God that was in Jesus. And it was the same kingly authority of the love of Christ in you that those desperate bandits recognized. They saw that you really cared for them—a love they'd never seen before—and they couldn't rob you!

"Unfortunately," he continued, "desperate and fearful humankind does not always respond to such love. Pilate didn't and let the mob have their way! Nevertheless, it was Christ's love on the cross that was the victory that dark day, just as it was when young Antipas went to a fiery death!"

After describing the various aspects of their successful time in Smyrna, Onesimus related in detail the difficult events in Pergamum. "You're so right in your thinking, Bishop John, not all people respond positively to the love of Christ."

The little company around the table were moved to tears at Onesimus's description as they visualized what took place. The silent hush was broken by John's exclamation.

"Surely Antipas's witness by his words, his life, and his death revealed the wisdom and power of God's love as nothing else could have done! Hundreds of those there, indifferent and hating, will never be the same. I predict remarkable growth at the church in Pergamum!"

"Yes," Onesimus declared, "that witness was enough to win the mind and heart of Antipas's father, the beloved physician of Tyrannus, Joanna, and, doubtless, many others in Pergamum!"

"Do you mean . . . did . . . did he come to faith in Christ after the ordeal of his son?" Tyrannus and Joanna asked almost in unison.

"Yes, he did. It was my privilege to present him before the congregation that met that evening in his house. As he stood before them, I shared his words of decision, 'If my son could die in such triumphant witness to the love of Christ, then I'm ready to live by that love!' He said that, though he didn't have the scientific proof of the resurrection that he and his colleagues had demanded, he'd seen the resurrection in the spirit of his son."

Onesimus concluded his account of the worship service that evening. "I'm sure you're a prophet, John. There will be many more Christians, not only in Pergamum, but throughout Asia as a result of Antipas's noble witness."

As Onesimus described the new Bishop Severus, he noticed Tyrannus and Joanna both were smiling and nodding their heads.

"We know Severus," Joanna said. "He was the young doctor who worked with Antipas when our son was dying. We were both impressed by his compassion and skill."

"He'll make an excellent bishop, a spiritual and temporal leader," Tyrannus added. "There could be none better."

"So the work of the Lord will be carried on with strength in Pergamum!" John exclaimed. "It is well to have a bishop who can proclaim the healing powers of Christ for the whole person. Onesimus, you've again done the church a good service."

That night, after prayers by Bishop John, Onesimus was awake for some time, his mind and heart too full for sleep. He would have so much to tell Helen!

If only she could have been with us tonight, he thought. In his sleep, he dreamed of Helen joining Mary in a prayer for him. The dream was incomplete, but it seemed he was in some dark forest and could not get out. He saw the two kneeling with clasped hands before a cross. Awakening abruptly, he thanked God that, even in his dreams, he had the love of two such wonderful women.

Part Two

The Confrontation

$\mathcal{8}$

$\mathcal{E}$arly on the morning after Onesimus and Glaucon's return to Ephesus, four other men calling themselves Christians entered the city by way of the harbor. They had sailed from Alexandria in Egypt on a large merchant ship that was now entering the largest and best natural harbor of the Mediterranean world. The harbor, crowded with ships from the world over, was formed at the confluence of the muddy Cayster and the little Meander rivers, which brought fresh water from the east and the southeast.

Cerinthus, a tall, handsome, young man, mature for his age of eighteen, stood on the captain's deck of the *Cybele* as it neared the dock. The huge ship belonged to his father, Charon, a prosperous merchant of Alexandria. Charon owned a fleet of ships that carried trade between Alexandria, Rome, Corinth, Joppa, and Ephesus.

In addition to being a shrewd merchant, Charon was a philosopher and former student of Philo, Alexandria's famous Jewish philosopher. The father encouraged his son to study philosophy and sent him to the finest school in Alexandria. Charon took him, even as a boy, to read together with him in the huge Alexandrian library, said to be the largest in the world. Cerinthus shared many conversations with other young men he met there over Philo and other Greek and Roman philosophers such as Aristotle, Heraclitus, and Plato.

Not long ago, John Mark, a brilliant young Christian Jew sent by Peter, brought new excitement to Alexandria with the good news of Jesus Christ, the Son of God. Cerinthus and his friends were fascinated and became disciples of Jesus of Nazareth. They were intrigued by his teaching, particularly the account of his resurrection. They believed they had found the end of their quest for truth.

In Alexandria, a movement of philosophers claimed special knowledge, or *gnosis*. This *gnosis* of the *Logos*, the Word of the supreme God, defined a God who was so far above the evil, suffering world that he was, in effect, completely separate from it. God's only contact with the world came through a series of aeons or angels—some evil and some good. Cerinthus and his friends saw the Christ of John Mark's teachings as one of these divine agents of the ineffable and unknowable God sent to bring salvation from the evils and frailties of human life.

The four young seekers were curious as to how John, the only remaining disciple with firsthand knowledge of Jesus, considered these teachings. They had arrived at their own belief that through the right *gnosis*, the select could escape pain, suffering, and death. After listening to John Mark describe the terrible suffering of the Christians in Rome, Cerinthus and the others wondered if such martyrdom, though a brave act, was simply foolishness. With true *gnosis*, they wondered if martyrdom was unnecessary. They did not suggest these ideas to Mark, for they knew how he revered the martyrs, especially Simon Peter.

Perhaps John, who was closest to Christ, could clear up this and other troublesome questions for them. So they had come to Ephesus. They were full of youthful vigor and enthusiasm as they joyfully anticipated their visit to the fabled city where they would meet John, the "beloved disciple" of Jesus.

The sight of the great city gleaming white in the early morning sun made them even more excited and enthusiastic as they pointed out the magnificent buildings, world-renowned for the beauty and grandeur of their size and architecture.

"There's the huge theater carved into Mount Pion!" Cerinthus exclaimed. "Twenty-five thousand seats and loges built out of limestone quarried from the mountain! What a sight that must be on a moonlit evening as fifty thousand hands applaud the artistry of the actors in a chorus from Euripides or a farce from Aristophanes!"

"I can't wait to join that crowd—maybe tonight!" Michael affirmed enthusiastically. A diminutive Greek, he made up for his height by the quickness of his thinking. Michael's love for classic Greek drama was the strongest of the group.

"Well, you can keep us informed about theatre schedules and get us the best seats," Cerinthus rejoined.

Cerinthus was obviously the leader of the quartet. Taller by half a head than the others, he had a strong, tanned face, dark brown hair, and piercing black eyes, and spoke with a voice of quiet authority. His penetrating mind and mystic visions made him the natural head of the questing spirits in Alexandria. He exuded confidence as he spoke of their coming experiences with the Christians in Ephesus and of what they would learn from the apostle John, known for his philosophical interests.

Cerinthus pointed out the other notable edifices that adorned the city. His father loved to travel with his famous ships and had drawn a map of Ephesus, his favorite city after Alexandria. Charon had described the city so vividly that his son had no difficulty in identifying the most important buildings.

As the *Cybele* drew nearer to the dock, Cerinthus pointed his friends to the grandest building of all.

"There's the Temple of Artemis, one of the Seven Wonders of the World!" he explained. "Artemis is the fertility or mother-goddess. Her Latin name is Diana, but it's not really the same deity. The original mother-goddess in this region was Cybele, the namesake of this ship. When the Greek influence came into the area, the people adopted the Greek Artemis as the closest manifestation to their Cybele. Look at the 127 graceful pillars surrounding her temple. They were gifts from the wealthy King Croesus. When we get closer, I'll show you the elaborately sculptured bases of each pillar. They depict erotic dancers, male and female copulation, and the birth of infants. The famed sculptor Praxiteles made them."

The three friends listened in silent wonder until Claudius burst out, "What do you think Artemis is saying now that our ship bearing her ancient namesake is entering her port so proudly?"

The question was disrespectful, but Claudius, his sandy hair blowing in the wind, asked it with a grin. Cerinthus bristled slightly. Claudius was the quietest of the four, but he had a sharp sense of humor and the depth of his thinking often went to the heart of a problem. He had had some strong disagreements with Cerinthus in the past. He spoke now in jest, but the question had a barb.

"Cerinthus, since you're the son of the man who used her name so irreverently," Claudius persisted, "she'll expect you to atone for his sin by participating in an erotic dance with her choicest priestess in the fertility rite celebrated on the temple's steps!"

His face wrinkled with subdued laughter as he said it, and the other two exploded in loud guffaws. Claudius's words were few, but when he spoke, he always drew the attention of the others.

"How about it, Cerinthus?" Michael broke in. "Are you equal to the occasion?"

Cerinthus, never at a loss for words, retorted with a chuckle, "Did you ever know me to fail such an important responsibility?"

Unsure whether his friend was serious or jesting, Heracles said gravely, "But what will the Christians here think and say about your fling with the flesh?"

Heracles was always the cautious and sober one, concerned with the practical outcome of their philosophizing.

"Well," Cerinthus responded, "that would be an interesting situation. From what I've seen of many Christians in Alexandria, there's a danger that many of them forget the wonderful freedom to enjoy the pleasures of the flesh given to all who possess the *gnosis* of Christ. Plato said sensual pleasures are only shadows of the real ones, which are a thousand times more enjoyable. We should eat and drink with the Pharisees' 'sinners' like Jesus did, so why not a little dancing in his name?"

The laughing stopped as the group considered this controversial question. What was the place of sensual pleasure in the morality of those who had the *gnosis* of Christ? Hours of discussion and sometimes angry disagreement were passed among the Gnostic Christian friends. Two extremes had emerged. One practiced either an extreme asceticism, with little or no room for sexual or other sensual enjoyment, or a radical demonstration of one's freedom from the evil angel who made the world and, with it, human sexuality and animal-like appetites. Heracles and Claudius had disagreed violently with Cerinthus's easy dualism, which separated the sensual from the spiritual. They both questioned this interpretation of Mark's understanding of Jesus.

"Oh, come on, let's not fight about that again," Cerinthus interposed. "This isn't time for debate over such small differences. Let's wait to see what John has to say about it. Mark said that John's favorite teaching about Christ is the simple idea that we should love one another because love is from God, and God is love. After all, don't forget that *eros* exists alongside *agape*. Both are gifts of Christ from the supreme God! I'm surely going to ask the apostle what he means by this."

A sailor knocked on the door of Tyrannus's house and was admitted to the atrium where Onesimus and his friends had just finished breakfast. They were still talking about Onesimus's journey to Smyrna and Pergamum. The sailor asked for the apostle John.

"I am John," the apostle replied, rising to meet the young man.

"Allow me to introduce myself," the sailor began. "I am the servant of Cerinthus and his father Charon of Alexandria. Cerinthus and three companions have just arrived from Alexandria to have conversations with you as the leader of the Christians. The four of them would like to meet you when it is convenient."

"Do you mean to tell us that these young men have made this long voyage just to talk to me?" John exclaimed in astonishment.

"Yes sir, that's it! They became Christians along with Charon's family—and that includes me. Can you meet with them?"

"That I can, young friend. And I'm sure my partners in the gospel of Christ here will be happy to meet them also. What's your name?"

"My Christian name, given to me by John Mark at my baptism, is Petronious. Cerinthus and the others call me Peter!"

"Well you couldn't bear a more honored name than that! Go tell your master that we'll be happy to see him and his friends. Ask them to come at ten this morning."

When the young sailor had left, Onesimus expressed his joy at the arrival of the four young men, which he said indicated the widespread growth of the Christian church.

"I'll be glad to see them," John said. "I've read some of Philo of Alexandria, a Jewish philosopher. During my last years in Jerusalem, Paul, James, and other apostles urged me to become more familiar with the leading Greek and Roman writers. They had already started doing that to enable them to interpret the gospel in ways better understood by the Gentile world. I've also read Plato and some of the other philosophers. I must say, I heartily disagree with Philo that God is so far away from our world that he's above virtue, above knowledge, and even above good. That's not the Father of our Lord Jesus Christ! I hope these young men aren't too fond of Philo's approach. But we'll soon see."

"I'd never thought of that, but thankful that you have," Onesimus thoughtfully said. "I'm sure that if we're to proclaim the good news so that the people of the Roman world will begin to grasp its mighty meaning and power, we'll need to begin where they are. These are days when the old religions have lost their appeal for many. People are tired of the inferior manlike gods and goddesses who possess all our human weaknesses and evils. Most people only think in terms of appeasing the gods for their needs or of joining the Eleusia or other mystery cults so they can demand health and assurance of life after death. Paul said that we won't win people by philosophy or words of human wisdom, but by proclaiming Christ and him crucified and risen in our own new life!"

"I can see already that these young men will be a challenge to us all," Tyrannus added. "I've heard Christian brothers traveling from Alexandria say that there's a small group of Christians calling themselves Gnostics and claiming to have a special kind of knowledge of Christ. They're causing division and confusion in the growing church. We may have to deal with this in these young men."

"We shall see! Anyway, it'll be an interesting morning," John

replied as they each went to their room for a few minutes before
their guests arrived.

———————————————————————————— *9*

At ten o'clock, the four young men appeared right on
time. They were welcomed by Tyrannus and introduced to John
and Onesimus. Mary and Glaucon waited in the atrium, where
fresh autumn flowers had been placed. Tyrannus took his visitors
to join them where Joanna served wine and cheese. At the
apostle's invitation, each of the young men introduced himself
and explained why they had made the long journey to Ephesus.
When it was Cerinthus's turn, he came right to the point.

"What a signal honor and blessing to be able to meet with you.
As you've no doubt heard, we've come out of our honor for you
as our father in the gospel of Christ, the Son of God.

"We've come to learn more of the sacred mystery, what we call
the sacred *gnosis*, from the supreme God revealed in the Son.
We've also heard that you're familiar with the writings of Plato
and Philo, who have been our guides in the study of divine
philosophy. We're eager to learn how you relate Jesus' life and the
coming of Christ to their teaching. We believe Christ has come to
help us go far beyond the Greek teachings. My father was a
student of Philo, but he is now an ardent Christian inspired, as we
were, by the teaching of John Mark. Father wants us to take as
much time as we need to learn from all of you."

"I'm glad that you've come, my friends," John said thoughtfully, "but you're mistaken about my being a student of Plato and
Philo. I've done nothing more than read and consider some of
their writings. Instead, I'm a disciple of Jesus, a learner in his
school, and it's only through him that I've come to the knowledge
of the love of God. This knowledge, or *gnosis* as you call it, is
very simple. It can be understood and accepted both by the

uneducated and by highly trained minds like yours. I'd be delighted to talk with you about Jesus. We can discuss what the great
signs of his life and actions say about the love of the mighty God,
whom Jesus called Father.''

John paused, and a faraway look passed in his eyes. Suddenly,
the apostle turned and looked squarely at Cerinthus.

''I'm sure of one thing, my dear young friends. All that Philo
and the Greek philosophers have been thinking, dreaming, and
writing about the *Logos* of the supreme God is fully and truly
known in Jesus. Jesus is the Word of the almighty God made
flesh, becoming man!''

John's words made the air in the room vibrate with excitement.
All four of the young men bristled with electricity.

''That's exactly what we want to talk to you about!'' Cerinthus
cried. ''How did the *Logos* of the God who transcends all the evil
and sufferings of our world become flesh and live among us as a
man?''

To Onesimus's ears, the young Alexandrian spoke as if he had
come to teach his own *gnosis* to the apostle instead of to be open
to the apostle's teaching.

''Plato believed that our life in this world is only a shadow of
true life,'' Cerinthus went on. ''Philo wrote that reality is so far
above the evils and imperfections of this world that there's no way
humanity can see or understand it. The four of us thought and
talked about this for long hours, but finally something happened
to help it all make sense.''

John's ears perked up and Cerinthus paused for dramatic
impact.

''I had a vision,'' Cerinthus grandly continued. ''It came to me
one night after John Mark had talked of Christ's gospel. I saw
clearly that the utterly unknowable supreme God in some mysterious way did send his Son, the Christ, to live in Jesus the man.
Jesus himself was a man, but the Christ who came to live in him
as God's Son did not suffer when Jesus suffered. Otherwise, the
Christ couldn't've been the son of the perfect and unchangeable
God.''

John's eyes flashed as he broke into Cerinthus's speech. His voice sounded like the "son of thunder" Jesus had described.

"What are you trying to do?! Are you telling me that when Jesus was tempted, suffered, and died, he wasn't really the Christ? Do you mean that God cannot and does not suffer? If that's true, then Jesus' life and death were a sham, and our hopes in him are in vain!"

He paused to collect himself, but calm did not come. His voice continued like thunder.

"What you say about Jesus is a lie! There's no truth in it! I was there when he prayed in the garden and when he hung with excruciating pain on the cross."

The apostle's energy was spent, but his anger was not. His voice lowered, and he continued in hushed tones.

"I know it was real nails they nailed in his hands, and it was real blood and water that spurted from his side when the soldiers pierced him. But I also know that, even in his suffering and pain from the worst evils men could do to him, he forgave those who crucified, cursed, and spat on him. He loved them with a love that could have come only from the eternal one he called Father. In him, the love of the supreme God who's above all the universe is made known, the same God who sent his only Son into the world so that we might live through him!"

Onesimus was deeply stirred by the heated exchange. He observed Mary and saw her concern and the painful recollection of her son's agony written plainly on her face.

At the conclusion of John's fiery oratory, Cerinthus's eyes flashed in anger. He tried to subdue his indignation over the apostle's condemnation of his mystic vision and the precious *gnosis* he had shared with his companions. He realized that if he wanted to be accepted by the church in Ephesus, he would have to come to some kind of peaceful terms with the apostle.

In as conciliatory tone as he was able, Cerinthus, trembling with visible emotion, answered, "Honored sir, I did not mean to upset you with my visionary dream. You must not understand all I was saying. Please be patient with me, for I really do want to know more about the marvelous acts of Jesus. We will think over what you've said. You were there, and you did see amazing love revealed in those difficult experiences. Will you let us talk with you again? Perhaps we can learn from you more about Christ and his good news."

John rose and walked over to Cerinthus with the loving pastoral concern for which he had become known. Taking the young man's hand and putting his arm around him, he said, "Cerinthus, I love you and your friends as Jesus loves you. I believe you're sincere in your thinking, but I hope you're open to hear and understand the grace and reality I've seen in Jesus, who I believe in all his humanity is the Christ. God loved the world so much that he sent his beloved only son to reveal that love. I'll be glad to talk with you again—say this afternoon at the fourteenth hour."

"Thanks for your confidence, John. We will return at that hour. We're thankful for this opportunity to know you, Mother Mary, and your associates."

As the four Alexandrians left the room, John blessed them with the apostolic benediction.

"What a remarkable witness to the Christ you gave," Onesimus said to John when they were gone. "We could tell you were shocked by their denial of Jesus' humanity, but you remained so forgiving in his love. You gave them kindness and consideration even though some of Cerinthus's ideas are repugnant to you. What do you expect from giving them the help they need in their understanding of Christ as the human Jesus?"

"Well, Onesimus, I know this," John replied. "Jesus himself said he had come to give sight to the blind, but he knew that some who thought they already see would become blind because of him. All of us are blind until he gives us sight, but some of us remain blind because our pride dulls our vision and we will never see. I'm not sure how much self-centered pride these young men have, but I am sure that Cerinthus has had a vision of some kind when he saw Christ coming from God to live in our human frame. I'll ask him to describe the vision and his interpretation. It's that interpretation that concerns me. If Christ only *appeared* to take the form of a human being, only *seemed* to be in the flesh of

Jesus, then we're faced with a costly and dangerous falsehood. We'll see how open these men are to the sharing of my experience with Jesus, whom I knew truly as a man. He was tempted and he suffered, just as any of us would suffer, and yet did not rebel or distrust the love of our Father in heaven.''

A reverent awe enveloped the listeners as they grasped the importance of the apostle's words. They remained in silence until Onesimus could restrain himself no longer.

''You've spoken to the very heart of my own need, dear John, and I'm sure to countless other Christians who are facing the vicious cruelty and brutal evil of those who hate and would destroy us. The breathtaking good news I heard from Paul that you're now saying as well is that, even while we were still sinners, Christ *died* for us! You and Peter and—''

The young man stopped with embarrassment as he saw the tears on Mary's cheeks. ''Forgive me, Mother Mary, for reminding you of those terrible hours.''

''Onesimus, you don't need to be forgiven—John and I saw him cursed, beaten, spit upon, and crucified. It was terrible . . . awesome . . . his sufferings. He did suffer and die; we saw him. It was no 'appearance' of suffering; it was real. And even in my hour of sorrow there was a powerful light shining on me from his sufferings and death, the very light of the mighty everlasting God in the life and death of his Son!''

''That's what the supreme truth is, Onesimus.'' John spoke with fire burning in his eyes. ''In Christ was life, and that life was the light of all humankind; he was the very Word, the very intention of the eternal Word of love made flesh. And the light shining in his life and victorious death shines in the darkness of our own human sin and folly and in the hurts and pain of our frailty and suffering. But that darkness, no matter how black and appalling, can never overcome his light.''

After the noon meal had been served and eaten, Tyrannus suggested that he and Onesimus join John in meeting with the Alexandrians. ''Perhaps your acquaintance with Paul and Peter will enable you to give us some real help to change their thinking.

We need strong minds and straight thinking as well as loving in Christ's family today.''

When the second hour of the afternoon arrived, the young men were warmly welcomed again by Tyrannus. Onesimus greeted them with a smile. Opening the conversation, John asked the four about their Christian training.

''It was a high moment in our intellectual lives,'' Cerinthus began, ''when John Mark arrived from Rome bearing the good news of Jesus Christ, the Son of God. After listening to Mark, we began to grasp the startling news that the supreme God had bypassed all the lesser gods he had already created by sending Christ, a higher power. Mark called him God's beloved Son. God sent the Christ to live in the human Jesus and to lead humankind to the saving *gnosis* that brings eternal life.''

''Did John Mark teach you all of this?'' Onesimus queried. ''I spent a lot of time with him in Rome before and after Simon Peter came, and I don't remember him saying anything similar to that interpretation of the gospel. He received his understanding of Jesus from Simon Peter, and I'm sure neither of them ever suggested that, although Jesus was the Son of God, he wasn't also a man in every way.''

''That's what John Mark told us,'' Cerinthus responded, ''and it does certainly appear to indicate that Jesus was a man. But we've been taught by Plato, Philo, and other great thinkers that the almighty supreme God is so far removed from the evils of our humanity, so good and so righteous, that he couldn't possibly be tainted with the evils of the world of nature and man. In fact, it's our belief that this world wasn't even created by God! The infinitely good God couldn't be responsible for such an evil world, a world with the cruelty and hate that crucified such a good man as Jesus.''

''I'm aware of Plato's teachings,'' Onesimus rejoined. He wanted these philosophers to know that he had faced the same logical questions. ''I'm familiar with the conversation between Socrates and Adeimantus quoted in Plato's *Dialogues*. Socrates presses Adeimantus on the point that nothing good is hurtful, so that something that does no evil can't be a cause of evil. Indeed, my teacher in Pergamum insisted I memorize the first part of that dialogue. Following his line of reasoning, Socrates argued that the good isn't the cause of everything but only the cause of the good. God, Socrates said, if he's really good, can't be the author of everything, but only of the good things, which leaves out most of the things that occur to men. There are many evils in this life, and only a few goods. It is only the few that can be attributed to God alone. The evils, according to Socrates, have their sources elsewhere.''

"My point exactly," Cerinthus brightened. "This is the reason that we interpret John Mark the way we do. Christ, the Son of the eternal Father, was first sent to live in the human Jesus at his baptism. Mark told us that as soon as Jesus rose out of the water he saw the sky tear open and the Holy Spirit, in the form of a dove, came down on him. Then he heard a voice from heaven that said, 'You are my beloved Son, and my favor rests on you.' From then on it was Christ, the Son of God, living in Jesus, the man. Therefore, Mark said, when Satan tempted Jesus in the wilderness, angels waited on him so that the Christ in him was never really tempted. How could he be when he knew who he was and that the eternal Father wouldn't let him suffer and die?''

A look of shock and indignation flooded the faces of John, Onesimus, Tyrannus, and Joanna.

Ignoring the obvious protest his hearers were ready to make, Cerinthus continued. "When Jesus hung on the cross with the cry of despair, asking God why he had been forsaken, he really had been forsaken. Christ was no longer with him! He had already ascended to the Father, and Jesus was alone.''

John had released his anger that morning. He now sat still, letting someone else speak.

Unable to restrain his own indignation, Onesimus was the first to break the silence. "That completely destroys the very basis of our faith as Christians!" His face flushed with anger. "My whole mind and heart rebel at your distortion of the gospel! This is the opposite of all we've been taught by Peter and Paul, and John Mark and Luke.''

"And the opposite of all that I experienced as Jesus' disciple," John added. He waited quietly as Onesimus continued.

"Each of these teachers declared that Jesus, the very human man born of Mary, is truly the Word, the Christ, the Son of God made flesh. This is our elemental statement of faith, which everyone I've ever known as a Christian professes: Jesus *is* the Christ. We call him Jesus Christ our Lord! *You can't separate Jesus the man from Christ the Son of God!*"

Onesimus finished with his voice raised and his whole being aflame with deep conviction. Before the room could regain its stillness, John spoke in strong affirmation, and Joanna and Tyrannus nodded their heads in complete agreement.

"Onesimus, you have summed up the gospel," John told him. "Jesus is the Word—the *Logos* made flesh—human, yet divine!"

"Are you saying, then, that God, the infinite, illimitable, almighty God suffers with us?" Cerinthus asked, baffled. "That's impossible! The supreme God is too far away, separated by aeons of space and time. Only gods he has created deal with our evil world. God could not suffer!"

"Oh, Cerinthus," Joanna exclaimed. She had been listening with all her being. Her voice, almost to the point of tears, trembled. "You haven't really heard the good news as we heard it from Paul, from what Onesimus has said of Peter, and from what we've learned this morning from the beloved disciple, John. My strength has come in times of my own despair and doubt. As we have heard of Onesimus's danger and imprisonment and of the fifty young Christians nailed to crosses with boiling oil poured over them and then set on fire to make light for Nero's garden party, my strength and hope have come through my faith that Jesus of Nazareth is truly Christ. I couldn't have borne these evils but for the faith that the mighty God is our heavenly Father who cares for us enough to suffer with us."

"Dear Joanna," Claudius interposed, hoping to prevent an open break, "we're not saying that God doesn't care for us. We believe God is love, but his love so transcends this world of sin and evil that he sends Christ, his own dear Son, to remove us from the evil world of human nature and material objects. We disagree only on the way the almighty God works. You'll understand our views better if Cerinthus tells you of his mystic vision of the kingdom of God to which we may enter by the special gift of *gnosis* if we accept that gift."

As Onesimus listened, he began to realize how far apart he and John were from these brilliant young philosophers. He could still see that they deserved the chance to tell their story and to make their positions clear.

"Yes, Joanna," Onesimus agreed, "Claudius is right. Let Cerinthus tell us about his vision and what he means by the *gnosis*. It seems an entirely different kind of gospel than we've been taught, but let's at least be open enough to hear him out!"

"Yes, Cerinthus," John interrupted, "we need to understand as much as possible about your experiences and why you're making such bold and hurtful statements about our Lord."

"Thanks," Cerinthus responded curtly. His pride had obviously been wounded by their negative response. He had remained standing during the entire argument. "There are other persons to whom God has revealed his secrets, you know. My vision also has some truth and reality that should be respected. I'm here to learn from you, John, and from Onesimus and anyone else who can teach me, but perhaps you can also learn from me."

Cerinthus sat down on the couch. His feelings had been cut deeply by the outburst of indignation and lack of appreciation of his vision of Christ. They were now willing to listen only grudgingly. Putting his hands over his eyes, Cerinthus waited in silence for a few minutes. He knew how important his sharing of his mystic vision with these leaders of the Asian church was, and he wanted to describe the vision as clearly as was possible to convey the ecstatic revelation experienced by him alone. He began speaking softly with deep conviction the others could feel.

"My brothers and sisters in Christ, I pray that you will indeed be open to what I now tell you, for it is no fantasy or mere dream. Indeed, it is a revelation given to me from the supreme God, the Father of the universe, through his Son, the Christ who made his dwelling in the human Jesus from the time of his baptism until his crucifixion.

"The mystic vision came to me on a clear night, the heavens full of stars. I walked home from the hall where John Mark had finished telling his story of the gospel, where I had been deeply moved by his account of Christ's miracles: the healing of the leper, of the blind, and of the deaf and dumb, the casting out of demons, the stilling of the storm on the lake. I was especially stirred by his story of Christ's appearances after the painful death of the human Jesus on the cross: how in differing guises he revealed himself to two of the disciples as they were walking, to the eleven disciples as they sat at the table, and to many others who believed. I found myself crying a prayer from the depths of my heart as I stood looking at the brightest stars: 'O Christ, if you will only appear to me!'

"I came into the garden outside my father's house. I prayed again and again and again for Christ to let me know him as he really is.

"Suddenly, a bright light lit up a shining figure, his arms outstretched, standing under a large acacia tree. My eyes, like Paul's in the desert, were blinded by that light. Then a voice full of power and music—I can't describe it properly—was calling my name:

" 'Cerinthus, Cerinthus! I have heard your prayer, and I have come to open the door of heavenly *gnosis* to you. Do not be afraid, for I am the Christ, the Son of the illimitable God, Father of all the gods and all that is. I have come from the almighty Father to bring you and all who will listen and accept it, salvation from the evils of this world. If you receive this *gnosis* of my revelation, you will have life of the highest order and will never die!'

"I stood in awe before the one who spoke, but before I could answer, he continued: 'I have come to establish my kingdom on earth. It will be ruled by divine love and filled only with those who receive the perfect *gnosis*. This will allow the divine spark of the spirit-seed that the almighty Father has put into them to burst into a living flame.'

"Again he called me by name. 'Cerinthus, you are to be my messenger. Tell the good news that all who have the perfect knowledge are set free to live in the flesh, no longer bound by the evil angel who made the world and laid down such harsh and burdensome laws!'

"And then the light within him grew even brighter. He said, 'My kingdom is a kingdom of the goodness of pleasure. You and all who by *gnosis* are set free from bondage to the flesh may enjoy the physical and sensual pleasures a thousand times more than those who remain bound by the law. And you, Cerinthus, are to encourage those whom knowledge of me has freed to express fully and completely their physical desires and passions, thus declaring their victory over the evil angel who made the earth. The almighty Father has sent me to demonstrate victory over the evil ruler and to show the corrupt and disastrous folly of creating humanity with strong physical desires and causing them to suffer by denying these desires their fullest expression.

" 'This is your good news, Cerinthus: By the will of the supreme God, you and all who are spiritual in their *gnosis* of me are free from the evil ruler of this world. For he is hostile to God and seeks to keep all creation hostile and alienated from the supreme God and from each other. When you live in my kingdom on earth, you will not be subject to pain or sorrow or suffering of any kind. As I healed the blind, the lame, the leper, and the demon possessed through Jesus, so I will heal you through my Spirit! And when you come to what the evil ruler of this world calls death, it shall not touch you. You will pass immediately into the blissful realms in the heavens that cannot be entered by those who are only fleshly and material.' "

Cerinthus spoke with an exalted fervor and eyes uplifted scarcely looking at his hearers. It was as if he were seeing another realm. He paused to catch the horror and disgust plainly written on the faces of the Asian Christians. The same look held the faces of Claudius and Heracles, with whom Cerinthus had often engaged in hot argument concerning this earthly kingdom of sensual enjoyment he described as the intention of Christ.

Understanding the reaction he was generating, Cerinthus made his strongest appeal to his audience.

"This vision, my fellow Christians, was the highest moment of reality and truth of my life. It has given me my vocation. I have been called to proclaim this good news of Christ, the Son of God, and his earthly and heavenly kingdom. Before my vision ended, I was humbled and awed by the Christ. He stepped out of the light, touched his hands to my forehead, and called my name."

Cerinthus paused. With deep feeling, he recounted what Christ had said to him. " 'Cerinthus, you are my apostle of this love of the mighty God who calls on all to whom he has given the divine spark. You are to proclaim this good news wherever you go.' And this is the reason I am here."

The drama of the moment was suspended in the air. Cerinthus continued, now his voice soft and beckoning. "Yes, I want to learn more from you, John, the beloved disciple, the last of the twelve who knew Christ best when he was living in the human Jesus. But his revelation to me has also made me an apostle. I have something I must share with all his people, as Christ uses me to free them from their slavery to the ruler of this evil world."

Turning unexpectedly to Tyrannus, Cerinthus made a statement that stunned the entire room. "Since this is my calling, Brother Tyrannus, I desire to share my understanding in your hall. If you and the elders of the church are willing, I will do so at the time for teaching the members of the church."

The looks on the faces of the church leaders suggested to the Egyptian that his argument was not yet won. "If you are still unconvinced of my revelation," he added, "I trust you will give me the privilege of teaching at another hour and inviting all who desire to come hear me."

He paused, looking from one to the other, hopefully. The four Christians remained shocked by the enormity of the gap between what Cerinthus had taught and what they believed.

Onesimus was the first to speak.

"Cerinthus, we've listened to you with open minds. You're obviously sincere. You believe your vision was of the true Christ, but you can see from our reactions how utterly astonished we are to hear such a clear perversion of the faith we've received at so great a price. There are several points that your vision of Christ raises that, in all honesty, I must reject. But I earnestly want to

share with you some of the teachings of Paul you might not have
heard yet and some other reasons for my present rejection of
what you've said. As to whether you should teach this strange
new 'gospel' before the church in Ephesus, this is for Tyrannus
and John to decide. John has been called to oversee and guide the
church in its thinking and living. Your proposal is primarily to
him.''

"Onesimus is right." Tyrannus at last found his voice. He had
listened with mingled astonishment and disgust at Cerinthus's
proud claim to be an apostle, daring to ask for the church as a
platform to teach his heresy. In Tyrannus's mind, it was pagan
morality too closely resembling the philosophy undergirding the
worship of the fertility goddess Artemis.

Tyrannus spoke calmly but firmly. "Since I am only an elder of
the church, Cerinthus, I don't have the authority to give you an
invitation to teach our congregation. You'll need to spend more
time with our bishop, John, our shepherd and overseer. As for
me, after hearing the very earnest account of your special revelation, I admire your sincerity, but there's no way I can encourage
you to spread this kind of teaching about Christ and his kingdom.
Doubtless, this will appeal to some Christians who haven't yet
overcome their old nature and who are looking for an excuse to
abandon themselves to the life of sensual pleasures that your
vision invites them to. Indeed, and I say it with love for you and
your companions, the one who you call Christ sounds to me more
like the devil himself, a messenger of Satan, than it does the one
sent from God to save us from the evil and hurt of our sins!''

"Wait, Tyrannus," Joanna broke in. She had been sitting
uneasily during the interchange between her husband and Cerinthus.
"Though I feel as you do about the kingdom Cerinthus's vision
describes Christ as establishing, the Lord would have us be kind
to this confused young man and do all we can to show him the
errors in his thinking. There would be untold suffering and hurt if
all people set out to gratify their sensual desires. I've seen it
among the temple prostitutes and the families broken up by the
jealousies and fighting of husbands and wives. Too many women
have told me of the heartbreak of their husbands who stopped

loving them as they became attached to one of the beautiful
temple priestesses. Tyrannus, you've told me of men whose wives
were alienated by the same unbridled passion encouraged by the
fertility rites of Artemis. I don't want to see our Christian families
destroyed by the church's being open to encouraging its members
to give themselves in wild abandonment to their desires and lusts.
I feel just as strongly as you, Tyrannus, that Cerinthus's vision
doesn't come from the loving Father who sent his Son Jesus to be
the Christ. But, we can't cast him out entirely.''

"Thank you, Joanna,'' John said softly. ''I was thinking
precisely along those same lines.''

John's anger had cooled. As Onesimus and Tyrannus had
spoken, he had been praying silently for Cerinthus.

"I'm glad Cerinthus speaks of the supreme God as the God of
love,'' John quietly and thoughtfully continued. ''The freedom
he sends Christ to give us is the freedom to love even as he loves
us. This was what Jesus taught us, even in his last hours with us
in the upper room before his trial and crucifixion. 'The commandment I leave you,' he said, 'is that you love each other.' However,
the freedom to love is not a license to give way to passions and
lusts. An earthly kingdom of unbridled physical self-gratification
would not be heavenly, but would be a satanic kingdom resembling the fires of hell. Yet, I agree with Joanna in saying that we
must be charitable in our dealings with Cerinthus.''

Bishop John turned to the Alexandrian. ''We think you're
wrong in some of your understandings, Cerinthus, but we want
you to know that you belong to our beloved *communitas*. We
want you to be a part of our *koinonia* and to worship with us.
I want you to know that I'm going to pray that your relationship
with us will help you to know the freedom of true love that never
hurts, destroys, or fails, but rather heals, builds us up, and makes
us strong!''

"How beautiful these words you say to me, John.'' Cerinthus
was deeply moved. ''I was beginning to think I was an outcast
from the church in Ephesus. I was afraid my vision, as dear to me
as it is, had alienated me from this community of Christians! I'm

sure there are still many things I can learn from all of you, and I pledge to you that I will not share my vision with others in the church in Ephesus until you, John, as our bishop are willing!''

"Thank you for that assurance," John spoke in reconciliation. "Joanna has led the way to the only appropriate manner of living together in the coming days. As we seek to know each other better, I want to understand you and your vision. We must forbear, forgive each other, and seek to learn from the Holy Spirit. We need to test your vision, my brother, by the life and teachings of Jesus. As Paul wrote to the Romans that God's kingdom isn't made up of consuming passions like eating and drinking, but rather it's built upon the Holy Spirit's justice, peacefulness, and happiness."

"We all have much to learn," Claudius concluded, speaking for all four visitors. "We're glad to be in such a loving company."

Joanna rose quickly and, with warm hospitality, offered everyone a cup of wine. They stood to clasp each others' hands and to express personally their desire to understand the true meaning of Christ's kingdom. As Cerinthus and his companions rose to leave, Tyrannus invited them to return the next morning to visit with Bishop John.

"Yes, I want to understand your vision, Cerinthus," John spoke with warmth. "I'd like to find some way that I may be of help to each of you as you prepare to be messengers of the good news. I'm sure that with the Holy Spirit of love uniting our spirits, there ought to be some way to reconcile your beliefs with my experiences of Jesus. I trust you'll be open to what the Spirit is saying to us all. We have to test these spirits to find out if they're from God or the evil one."

"Thank you for your reconciling love," Cerinthus answered as they departed. "I'll ask the Lord to keep me from being as cocky and self-assured as I was today. I'm sure my pride was showing, but I truly did have the vision of Christ. I realize now that I need to test it with you and your knowledge of Christ in Jesus."

As the four visitors walked down the stairs, John, Tyrannus, and Onesimus heard them bantering among themselves and with their wounded young leader who remained rather quiet. Evidently, he had much to think of before he returned to meet with John the next morning.

—————————————————————————— *10*

*J*ohn stroked his beard and spoke thoughtfully. "There's an element of truth in what the Egyptian says, Onesimus. When we truly receive Christ, the Word of the eternal God made flesh, he gives us the power to become God's children and to enjoy the pleasure of physical and material things here on earth. During those wonderful days we spent together, Jesus enjoyed good food and drink and fellowship around the table. The scribes and Pharisees criticized him as a glutton and a wine lover, but that was farfetched indeed. The first miracle I ever saw him perform was at a wedding feast for a relative in Cana of Galilee. When the wine supply was exhausted, he saved the host from embarrassment by supplying plenty of good new wine. He certainly wasn't a killjoy."

As John continued, his voice was raised and fire flashed again from his eyes. "Jesus' joy, however, was never one of abandonment to lusts and passions that consume and hurt. It was always a joy resulting from loving consideration for the health and well-being of everyone, including ourselves. He led a balanced life in which the pleasures of physical existence were good in time and place but were never supreme. At the last Passover meal before his crucifixion, he prayed his last great prayer of intercession for us as his disciples and for all who would come after us. He prayed that God not take us out of the world, but instead keep us safe from the evil one in the world. He taught us that we are to be *in* the world but not *of* the world, following the pagan practices that produce such hurt and suffering, like, as Joanna reminded us, always take place in the worship of the goddess Artemis."

"John, that clears the question up quite a bit for me. Thanks,"

Onesimus said for the family around the table. "That goes right to the heart of Cerinthus's problem. He spoke as if Christ's kingdom consists primarily in the gratification of our physical and sensual desires. Paul warned the Corinthians who said that once they believed in Christ they were free to do anything but not everything was for their good. Paul had no doubt that he was free, but he wasn't going to become a slave to his desires. And then he wrote words to the Romans that have helped me to discern when pleasures are good and when they are evil:

> Do you not know that your body is a shrine of the indwelling Holy Spirit, and the Spirit is God's gift to you? You do not belong to yourselves; you were bought at a price. Then honour God in your body."

"Onesimus, you help us all by sharing from your experiences with Paul," John declared. "As I listened to Cerinthus's vision, I realized that Paul, Peter, my brother James, and all of the other disciples would've been as horrified as we are to hear the teaching that separates Jesus, the very human man we knew so well, from the Christ. To dare say that Christ was never really tempted, hurt, or in pain. I remember that morning on the way to Caesarea Philippi when he called us to sit with him. In his quiet way, he asked us who other people thought he was and then who we, his closest disciples, thought he was. We had all talked about it in his absence many times, and we were in hearty agreement with Simon Peter when he said we thought he was the Christ. We knew him as Jesus, the Son of man. He was born of this dear woman, his mother Mary. The longer we lived with him, seeing his loving concern and amazing miracles and hearing his incomparable teachings, the more certain we were that he was indeed the Christ, the Son of God! I can almost hear Peter roar out in indignation over Cerinthus's saying that Christ, as the supreme God's Son, couldn't and didn't suffer. The strongest rebuke Jesus ever gave any of us was when Peter protested that Jesus, in foretelling his coming suffering and crucifixion, was talking about something that mustn't happen to him. Jesus accused Peter of representing

Satan. 'Get away from me, Satan!' he shouted. 'You're a hindrance to me. You're thinking like people, not like God!' ''

"That's the very heart of our faith!" Onesimus cried excitedly. "And Cerinthus is denying it! When you talk to Cerinthus again, John, that story should help convince him that he's on the wrong path."

"Yes," John replied, "I'll share it with him and give him several other illustrations from my time with Jesus that are clear signs pointing to Jesus as both Son of man and Son of God! Any time we separate these two understandings of who he was and what he did, we lose the precious heart of our Christian faith."

After this proclamation, John became quiet, thinking back on his own experiences with the Christ. "I'll always remember the morning before I became his disciple. I'd journeyed to the Jordan to hear that remarkable prophet, John the Baptizer. What a fascinating, powerful preacher John was! I was attracted to him and was there when Jesus came to the river for his own baptism. I was standing close enough to hear John, pointing to his cousin Jesus, say that he was the Lamb of God, who would take away the world's sin."

The apostle stopped speaking and looked up as if he were again seeing that remarkable scene. The little group around the table hushed in silence as they watched him.

He turned to look at them with a warm smile and said, "There are so many of these signs I long to share with you, my dear family. Many of them, Mary, you saw, also!"

She nodded her head in strong agreement. "That's right, and with all that's in me, I'm confident of two things. He was my own son, borne in my body as any other human child is borne, and in him, even from his birth and childhood, there was something so unusual, so lovingly magnificent, that as I looked at him hanging on the cross—''

Her voice broke, and she was overcome with emotion for a few moments. "—I knew that he wasn't the only one suffering. The whole of humankind's suffering was there, too. As I remember that awful hour, I know now *his* heavenly Father and *our* Father was there suffering with him!''

She was crying now, unrestrained tears coursing down her cheeks. "John," she began slowly, "tell Cerinthus what we saw, you and I and the others who stayed by his side! Tell him that the Father didn't abandon Jesus then or when he was in the tomb. God raised him up, and he's alive! I saw him and so did Mary Magdalene and our other friend, Mary. Many of us saw him . . . my son . . . my son! Yes, my son is God's own beloved Son!"

John put his arms around his adopted mother as she spoke with such deep feeling. He strongly answered her plea. "Yes, indeed I will, dear mother Mary. Let's pray that they'll listen and understand."

As Mary finished speaking, her face, though lined with wrinkles, seemed more beautiful to Onesimus than any human face he had ever seen. His own mother and Helen were, of course, beautiful, yet here was the mother of Jesus, their Lord, whose heart had been pierced as if by a knife, just as Anna the prophetess had said it would. But she was not thinking of her sorrow; rather, her thoughts turned to the brash young philosopher, Cerinthus, as she prayed for his eyes to be opened to the truth she knew so well!

"John and Mary, your witness to us cannot be forgotten," Onesimus exclaimed. "If anything can change the proud mind of Cerinthus, your witness will!"

11

The next morning, Cerinthus and his friends had again arrived early to meet with the apostle. John shared some of his most precious recollections of his years with Jesus. The four young Christians from Alexandria listened with reverence and awe as John told of memories and interpreted them. Cerinthus was particularly impressed by the story of John the Baptizer's announcement as he saw Jesus coming down the road to be baptized.

"Did John say that *before* Jesus was baptized?" Cerinthus questioned.

"Yes," the disciple answered. "He was known by the people of his hometown, Nazareth, as a carpenter, the son of Joseph, who had taught him to make the best oxen yokes, tables, and doors to be found anywhere in Galilee. My own father, Zebedee, was a commercial fisherman, and he lived with my mother, Salome, my brother James, and me in Capernaum, near the Sea of Galilee. As a boy of ten years, I went with James and my father on a short trip to Nazareth to buy two of Joseph's yokes. Father had ordered the yokes several weeks before for the oxen we used to carry our fresh fish to Jerusalem. The shop was small but clean, and smelled of fresh-cut wood. I well remember Joseph's son, Jesus, but it was only after we both grew to manhood and I had become his disciple that my father reminded me of the trip."

"What did he look like as a boy?" Michael asked eagerly.

"He was strong, even then, evidently working many hours alongside his father in cutting and chiseling the fine oak timbers into the yokes and tables. As Father and Joseph talked in completing the sale, Jesus invited James and me to go to a nearby hill where some of the most beautiful flowers grew. Ordinarily I wouldn't've been interested in flowers, but he was so eager and enthusiastic that I went with him. We marveled at the way he talked about the flowers and the birds like they were friends. I asked him if he liked games, and he said he had a good time with his friends. Just then, his father called, and we ran down the hill. He was quite fast and lithe. We said good-bye, and that was the last I thought of him until the day he came with excitement on his face to be baptized. I heard from others later that when his father died, he took over the work in the carpenter shop with his brothers and continued the same kind of fine craftsmanship."

"Are you saying," Cerinthus persisted, "that the Jesus who came down the road to be baptized was in all respects a man, just as we are?"

"That's exactly what I am saying. From what I've heard from those who knew him, and especially from his mother, who's been with me now nearly thirty years, he was unusually strong, both physically and spiritually. He cared for his mother with a thoughtful tenderness that left nothing to be desired. He led his brothers in the work of the carpenter shop. His mind was unusually keen and perceptive, and he always asked questions of the rabbis who taught in the synagogue school. He learned fast, and by the time he was twelve, he knew most of the psalms, the books of the prophets, and even the books containing Hebrew history and the Torah. When he was old enough, he was occasionally called on to read from the scrolls in the synagogue meetings.

"As he grew older, Mary has said, especially during the last ten years of his life in Nazareth, he'd go out to his favorite hill or even to the more distant Mount Tabor. Mary recalls that during the later years, he sometimes spent an entire night on the mountain."

Mary broke into John's story. "He always told me where he was going, and when he returned, his face was lit with a glow of happiness. He said little about what happened at those times, but he would say that he enjoyed the solitude and his communion with God, whom he continued to call 'our heavenly Father.'"

"Then you weren't too surprised," Michael asked excitedly, "when he told you he was going out to meet John the Baptizer?"

"Not at all," Mary replied. "John was the son of my cousin Elizabeth and Zechariah, one of the priests of the temple. Jesus and I talked about John's strange prophetic ministry, and Jesus was intensely interested in John's call for repentance and the announcement of the one sent from God, the Messiah, whose shoelace John felt unworthy to untie. One day, after he spent the night on Mount Tabor, Jesus announced that he had to leave our home and the carpentry shop in the care of his brothers so that he could begin his ministry. He said that he didn't know all that he had to do, but he had to identify himself with the poor, the hungry, the hurt, and those in bondage, the people who were coming to be baptized by his cousin, John. He only said that he'd let the Spirit lead him!"

"Did you know then that he was the Christ?" Claudius asked.

"I knew he was special, and I knew it before he was born. Elizabeth talked to me about it, and I had my own vision."

"What was your vision?" Claudius leaned forward to ask.

"I've told my husband, Joseph, John here, and Luke, but I really don't like to talk about it. It was very personal."

"Is all this the reason, friend John," Cerinthus rudely questioned, "that you say we can never separate Jesus from the Christ, that he is both the Son of man and the Son of God, borne in his mother's womb as every human being is born and born of the Spirit as a Son of the most high God?"

"Yes, Cerinthus, you couldn't have put it in better words," John replied.

"You've almost convinced me that Jesus, as the Christ sent from the most high God, is both human and divine," Cerinthus continued. "Your teaching has assured me that he's truly divine, but I'm having trouble with the human part. What you've said about his remarkable abilities as a youth combined with all I've been taught by Philo and others cause me to reaffirm my first conviction that he wasn't really human as we are human. But when I hear from you and John Mark the stories of his life that tell of his temptations, his sufferings, and finally his cruel death on the cross, it's inconceivable to me that the Son of God could really be tempted or suffer hunger and thirst and pain the way we do, much less die! My vision of Christ tells me that these are the very human experiences from which Christ was sent to deliver us!"

John sat quietly for a few moments as he sensed the distance between Cerinthus's vision and his own experience with Jesus. He prayed silently for the wisdom and skill to help this earnest young man overcome the evil influence of the *gnostic* teaching. Finally, he spoke with the fire returning to his voice.

"Cerinthus, I respect your sincerity, but the major question of faith you must settle is whether you are going to believe the word of men such as Philo and the Gnostics or whether you are going to accept the word of God spoken to us in the life of Jesus Christ. I recall Jesus' rebuke of the teachers in the temple, many of whom said he was leading the people astray. His words made them angry, but I believe you, too, need to hear them. He said:

> The teaching that I give is not my own; it is the teaching of him who
> sent me. Whoever has the will to do the will of God shall know

whether my teaching comes from him or is merely my own. Anyone whose teaching is merely his own, aims at honour for himself. But if a man aims at the honour of him who sent him he is sincere, and there is nothing false in him.''

John allowed the words to sink into his listeners. "So I ask you, Cerinthus," John challenged, "how do you know the teaching of Philo is the truth? On the other hand, how do you know that the teaching of Jesus when he proclaimed that the infinitely good and righteous Father created the earth and humankind and set us free to obey or disobey is false? How do you know that it's false when by implication he taught that the righteous Father shared in the suffering of his disobedient children, and, therefore, the Son of man had to suffer and be crucified and then, on the third day, rise again? If Jesus the Christ, the Son of God, did not suffer and die, then the good news I heard from his lips and life is false, and we're left in our sins without the forgiveness and grace of our Father, whose very name is love!''

John realized that his anger was beginning to get the best of him, so he slowly took in a deep breath and continued quietly. "I tell you, Cerinthus, if we lose that faith, we're indeed without hope and without God in the world. Remember the words of John the Baptizer as he saw Jesus coming on the road. As a Greek, you may not know our Hebrew history. The lamb that is slain at every Passover feast is to remind us of the lamb slain one night in Egypt as a sacrifice for the saving of God's people. John was saying that Jesus is the Lamb of God. Therefore, he too must suffer and die in order that we may live.''

"I'm sorry, John," Cerinthus spoke emphatically, "but I can't accept your thinking. You're mixing up the writings from the Hebrew scripture with the new revelation of Christ from the supreme God. He wouldn't and couldn't permit himself to be in the position of a lowly lamb led to the slaughter! That very idea is repugnant to those of us who believe in the infinite holiness of the mighty God! But, contrary to your argument, we're not without hope, as my vision of Christ shows. God has sent Christ to take all to whom he has given the saving *gnosis* out of the evils of this material world with its shadows and suffering. Possessing this *gnosis*, we won't have to suffer such a death as Jesus suffered!''

John sat again in silent frustration, hurt by the stubbornness of this brilliant young man who preferred the wisdom of the Gnostics to the rich Hebrew heritage that had been fulfilled in the life of the one who spoke of true greatness as the willingness to be the servant of all. John spoke, slowly and distinctly, but with strong conviction.

''Cerinthus, if what you say is true, then the great God of all doesn't really love us enough to suffer with us and for us. But this is the very heart of our gospel. The apostle Paul said it so well, writing to the church in Rome: 'If God is for us, who is against us? He who did not spare his own Son but gave him up for us all, will he not also give us all things with him? . . . Who shall separate us from the love of Christ? . . . I am sure that neither death, nor life, nor angels, nor principalities, nor things present, nor things to come, nor powers, nor height, nor depth, nor anything else in all creation, will be able to separate us from the love of God in Christ Jesus our Lord' (RSV).''

As he spoke, his face flushed with a radiance that touched Claudius and Heracles. Both were visibly moved. Sensing that he was finally reaching their minds and touching their hearts, John again assumed his pastoral role.

''The second major difference between your thinking and mine in regard to the nature of the kingdom Christ came to establish,'' he began again, directly addressing Cerinthus, ''is caused by this very lack of acceptance of God's love revealed in his Son Jesus Christ. You've asked me to tell you what Jesus said and did that led me to believe he is truly the Son of man and Son of God. Before we part, let me tell you one more thing that couldn't have happened but for the love of God revealed in Jesus.''

He went on with deep feeling to tell the account of a woman taken in adultery and brought by the Pharisees into the presence of Jesus and the crowd around him. ''They reminded Jesus that since this woman had been taken in the very act of committing adultery, the law of Moses ordered that she be stoned. Then they asked him what he had to say. Jesus stooped over and started writing in the dirt with his finger. They kept asking their question, and Jesus finally looked up to say that if anyone there had never sinned, he should throw the first stone at her. Then he bent down and started writing on the ground again. One by one the Pharisees went away. When they were gone, I remember our amazement as Jesus, alone with the woman, looked up and asked where they had all gone. 'Didn't anyone condemn you?' he asked. She said that none had, and Jesus replied, 'Then I won't condemn you, either. You can go, but don't sin again.' "

Onesimus had heard the story before, but he would continue to be moved by it each time he heard it anew.

"Cerinthus," John concluded, "don't you see how the character of caring love that you deny in your picture of the highest God was truly in Christ Jesus? Jesus didn't say that it was good for this woman to give her body to whomever chose to have her. He knew the loneliness and suffering she'd endured and the hurt she'd caused others. He called her adultery 'sin,' but he didn't condemn her. Instead, he forgave her and told her to go and sin no more. I take it, Cerinthus, that this story runs directly counter to your vision of the earthly kingdom of Christ as the rule of unrestricted pleasures. However, I call to your mind Jesus' clear statement that he had not come to destroy the law but to fulfill it! We believe freedom in Christ isn't freedom from all law. The law is the teacher that brings us to Christ. People in every culture and time have found laws necessary to prevent chaos and destruction. Christ came to set us free from bondage to rules that always kill life in the spirit of loving harmony with each other. Now, love fulfills the law! The kingdom of Christ on earth as in heaven is a kingdom and rule of Christlike love. If we love each other as Christ does, we'll do nothing to hurt or destroy the dignity and value of any of God's children. When we believe that Jesus is the Christ, we believe we're the children of God. It follows that when we love God and obey his commands, we love his children, too."

"What you're saying is beautiful, John," Cerinthus interrupted. "I agree with much of it. Indeed my vision shows us that in Christ's kingdom we're to love each other not only with *agape* but also with *eros*, the sensual love that gives us physical and emotional pleasure. Christ revealed to me that, living in his earthly kingdom, we're to celebrate his coming as the nuptial festivals of a new age where the pleasures of eating, drinking, and sexual relations are to be enjoyed freely. Christ told me to forget the old Mosaic-Hebrew laws and teachings that caused the Pharisees to bring that woman before Jesus to humiliate her and demand she be stoned. Those old laws and customs are to be superseded by the new freedom to gratify our human desires for all kinds of sensual pleasures.''

Cerinthus was enjoying the abandon with which he presented his argument. He continued with strong feeling, ''I have to disagree with your interpretation, John, and I say that humbly, knowing that I'm so much younger and should defer to you. But I must be honest and declare that your interpretation of what Jesus meant when he talked to the adulterous woman is wrong. Jesus was really saying to the woman, 'I don't condemn you for enjoying your sexual relations with men. Go, enjoy it, and don't worry about what the Pharisees call sin.' I'm confident that Christ was saying to her, as he said to me in my vision, that physical gratification of the senses, including and best of all sexual pleasure, is *good*, not evil!''

As Cerinthus said these last words, John became so disturbed that he leaped from his chair and, in a voice truly belonging to the son of thunder, exploded with indignation. ''Cerinthus, I don't care whether you're young or old, what you've just said is heresy at its worst! Like all false teachings, there's a half-truth in it: pleasure is good, yes. We all agree. But only when it's accompanied by *agape* is *eros* made holy and beautiful. Without *agape*, pleasure only for its own sake, with no consideration for the well-being of others, is destructive. You're right in thinking the pharisaical condemnation of the woman was wrong, but the other side of the truth is that adultery and fornication bring deep hurt to many and are degrading acts. The pleasures of eating, drinking, and sexual relations are good in the pathway of caring *agape* and in the right time and place.''

John's anger had taken everyone, including the apostle himself, by surprise. Regaining his calm, John put his hand on Cerinthus's arm, saying, ''I hope that you'll reconsider your understanding of your vision of Christ. Indeed, your Christ, if I heard you correctly, is my idea of evil incarnate—Satan or whatever name he be called. In all the ages of human experience recorded in Greek, Roman, and Hebrew history, *eros* on the level of lust has caused untold suffering. It could never be in the mind of Christ as the will of the mighty God!''

The room had been broken into factions. All four Egyptians were on their feet, and Tyrannus was shaken to the core. Claudius and Heracles nodded their heads in agreement with the apostle. Michael alone stood with Cerinthus. From his diminutive stature, he looked up with anger and open disgust at the aged apostle in hot rejection of his friend's position.

For a few moments, everyone stood in silence. Cerinthus, practical as well as visionary, saw that the disagreement among his friends could mean the end of that relationship, something he did not want to occur, now of all times. With careful words, he tried to smooth over the breach between them.

''John, you're indeed the apostle of love. You've accepted us this afternoon, even though you knew it was likely we would violently disagree. I ask you only one thing: Let us remain in your love, even though, as your words declare, you do not accept my vision of Christ's earthly kingdom. I desire, and I'm sure my companions desire, to be a part of the beloved *communitas* of the church in Ephesus, to worship with you, and to hear you share more recollections of our common Lord.''

Cerinthus appeared to John to be sincere in his desire. John was not so sure, however, what to make of the young man's next statement.

''What you said about the Christ who appeared to me was rather drastic! I know, though, that you were speaking in the hot anger of your indignation, and I can and do forgive you. I trust you will also forgive me.''

The apostle looked at him, incredulous. He sought desperately to find what the spirit of Christ would have him say to this wily young man in that moment. With a prayer for the help of the Holy Spirit, he answered.

''Cerinthus, since I follow Jesus the Christ, indeed I do forgive you as I saw him forgive those who nailed him to the cross. But I want you to know that this part of your vision, which I consider to be a revelation of the evil one, should not be taught in the church in Ephesus or anywhere else. My interpretation of the words and acts of Christ may not have been understood or accepted by you and some of your companions, though I notice that Claudius and Heracles are not in agreement with you on this. Yes, I'll grant your request and welcome you in our worship services. If you really want to hear more of my recollections of Jesus, I'll share them with you. Tomorrow morning is the first day of the week, so we will be having our regular worship services. You're invited to worship with us.''

As the four young men went down the stairs, John prayed for them and the church in what he knew would be some trying days ahead.

After the visitors had left, John led the remaining Christians in prayer. He was deeply concerned for what he saw as a blind and conceited young man and his friend who supported him. John prayed for Claudius and Heracles, who he thought were beginning to be disillusioned and disenchanted with their leader.

"May your spirit open their eyes and help them to use their great talents to the glory of the only wise God, our Father, under whose loving care all things are created and will be redeemed. In conclusion, I pray for this church that will be tested severely by such false and hurtful teachings. Give us, O heavenly Father, the grace and wisdom to help keep your church strong and undivided, in the name of Jesus Christ our Lord.''

The agitation and strain in the mind of John were obvious to all. This was a crisis of no small import. Other churches were faced with the same problems that threatened the fledgling religion.

Joanna had been busy with her household duties and had made a trip to the market for Sunday's food. As usual, she was anxious that lunch not be neglected.

"Bishop John,'' she implored, "I know you have much on your mind and a heavy burden on your heart, but please eat some of this delicious fruit, fresh from the market. You need it to keep your strength up after so much arguing.''

Mary joined Joanna in her request. John obeyed, and with an affectionate smile helped himself to several figs, pomegranates, and grapes.

They ate in silence for a few minutes before John spoke. ''I'm so disappointed in these young men, so brilliant, so gifted as thinkers and speakers! What great leaders they could be in the Alexandrian church and elsewhere! But I'm sure that Cerinthus is determined to hold on to his 'great wisdom' and his interpretation of what he believes was a powerful vision of Christ. I'm afraid he'll insist on calling all Christians to his 'celebration of the nuptial feast' in the years to come. All well and good, our Lord Jesus Christ often spoke of his kingdom as a wedding feast. But such lawless exaltation of physical desires and pleasures as Cerinthus proposes will lead to utter chaos. Cerinthus is a voluptuary in his thinking—I don't know whether he lives as he talks. If so, he's living outside the loving rule of Christ, whose love is the fulfillment of the law. I tried to explain our need for law as a guide and to show that the only true freedom is freedom to love each other within the law of mutual respect and concern for the well-being of others.''

In complete frustration, the apostle threw up his hands. ''I've done all I know to help them see, but Cerinthus and Michael are stubborn in their closed minds. Onesimus, what do you think? Did I do right, or should I have forbidden them to come?''

''John, you continue to be the apostle of love. Your forgiveness and acceptance of these young men in spite of your repugnance for their evil teaching are Christlike. We're all proud of you. I'm not sure I could've been as restrained as you were. I'm looking forward to hearing you preach in the morning. For the first time, I'll share with you and Mother Mary in the Eucharist of her son Jesus as the Christ. I think we should all spend time in prayer tonight that, through you and the holy Eucharist, Christ and his truth may be known to these young men. I'm glad that Claudius and Heracles are willing to learn. I'll pray for them, the other two, and for you, our dear father in the gospel!''

12

As the four Egyptians left the worship service in the lecture hall the next morning, they were still under the spell of the most memorable Eucharist they had ever experienced. The spirit of love evidenced by John, the strength of his charisma, his genuine appeal for their acceptance of his understanding of Christ's offer of the bread and water of life—all had impressed Cerinthus. The mystic part of him had been deeply touched as he received the bread and wine from the hands of the apostle.

"I felt anew the power of my vision of Christ!" he exclaimed to his friends as they walked together down the broad Via Augusta. "I may have to disagree with some of John's interpretations of the kingdom Christ came to bring, but I thankfully accept the reality of Christ present with us through the Eucharist. The Eucharist always increases the strength of our *gnosis*, but this morning was special in its gloriously strengthened assurance."

Each of the Alexandrians heartily agreed. They walked quietly toward the harbor, where they planned to lunch in a famous tavern Charon had recommended.

At the close of the morning worship, the quartet had been warmly welcomed by a great many of the Christians who mingled in the hall. No one had been in any hurry to leave, for it was several hours before noon. Those who did not need to go to work remained to greet one another and to share their happenings since they had all last been together. All wanted to greet Mary to receive her blessings. Of course, everyone also came to get the warm handshake and hearty commendation of their bishop.

Tyrannus and Joanna had been kind enough to stand with the four young men. Cerinthus said later that their forbearance and love were true tests of their faith in Christ. Tyrannus had introduced them to the members of the *communitas*, including all six of the other elders and deacons. The young Egyptian had worked hard to remember their names. One, Euplus, especially seemed attracted to the Alexandrians. He, too, was young and trained in the Gymnasium at Pergamum under Phineas, the philosopher who had taught Onesimus.

The four entered the tavern, which fronted on the Via Augusta near the harbor, found a table, and ordered the best dinner in the house. As they sipped their wine and waited for the roast lamb to be served, Michael could no longer withhold a comment he had wanted to make as they left the lecture hall.

"John was really aiming at you in his message this morning, Cerinthus!" he said with a twinkle. "His quoting Jesus' words to the people who followed him around the lake to see another miracle of the loaves and fishes was a broadside attack on your vision of the kingdom of heaven as a perpetual nuptial feast! And that reading from the letter to Colossae—the first time I've heard it read—is certainly contrary to your kingdom of freedom to enjoy food and drink and sex without limit! Has it had any effect on your thinking?"

"I'm sure the dear man hopes it has!" Cerinthus responded. "My problem with this approach, even though it comes from good sources like Paul and John, is that they've mixed up the old Hebrew scriptures with the teachings of Christ. The revelation given to me is a new truth that sets us free from the old law!"

Claudius and Heracles said nothing, but Cerinthus observed their discomfort. As the main course arrived, they enjoyed the succulent lamb and fresh vegetables. Conversation lagged until Michael spoke again.

"Last night as we watched the priestesses of the Temple of Artemis do their sensuous dances on the temple steps, I thought for sure you'd go forward to make amends to Cybele, whose name your father so irreverently used to name his ship!"

Between bites of lamb, Cerinthus smiled and answered flippantly, "I don't think I need to atone for any sin of my father, Michael. Indeed, I think the great Artemis will appreciate naming such a fine ship after her predecessor. From all that I saw last night, her lovely priestesses are doing about as well in attracting young men to their celebration as Cybele ever did!"

"All right, Mr. All-Wise," Michael said with a mischievous smile, "if you're on such good terms with her majesty Artemis, aren't you going to accept the invitation of one of her most beautiful young priestesses and do a little dancing yourself?"

"Why not?" Cerinthus laughed. "I'd better practice what I've been preaching, don't you think?"

"Cerinthus," Claudius interrupted, "surely you are not serious! What a scandal your participation in the fertility rites of Artemis would make among our new Christian friends. John, Tyrannus, Onesimus, Mary, and Joanna are not the only ones in the hall of Tyrannus this morning who take seriously the preaching of the apostle!"

"Aw, don't be such a prude," Michael protested. "I think we ought to enjoy all the pleasures of the nuptial feast Christ has provided! How about it, Cerinthus? I'll go with you, for I believe your vision is the truth!"

"Wait a minute," Heracles warned. "You've never done anything like this before back in Alexandria. You know what your father would think! Surely there's truth to what John and Onesimus said about pleasure being good in its place accompanied by *agape*. You two will be making a grave mistake to do such a thing ... that is if you're serious!"

"Serious?" Cerinthus laughed. "What do you think my vision of Christ means if not that we should be celebrating good pleasure. I'm very serious. Christ called me to help save his body, the church, from bondage to the Hebrew laws that deny a full life rather than open the way to it! So, Michael, tonight you and I are going to celebrate the nuptial feast of our Lord and thoroughly enjoy it!"

Heracles and Claudius stopped eating and looked at each other. Claudius said firmly, "If that's your decision, we can't stop you, but we won't be with you!"

That evening the four friends parted. Cerinthus and Michael made their way up the Via Augusta to the Temple of Artemis. Claudius and Heracles, shaking their heads in disappointment over what they considered their friends' perversity and foolishness, walked in the direction of Tyrannus's home. They stopped to sit on a bench under a large oak tree near the Odeum.

"Did you tell them we were going to visit Onesimus?" Heracles asked.

"No, I said we'd take a walk through the city," Claudius answered. "After what was said at dinner, I had no stomach for more argument."

"Neither did I. I knew we had a problem here, but not this much." Heracles sighed in his sadness.

"John Mark gave us a parchment containing Paul's letter to the Roman Christians," Claudius reflected. "I can't believe Cerinthus would think so highly of himself and his vision of Christ that he'd completely ignore Paul's clear words about the judgment of God on those who claim to be wise but become fools."

"We've had arguments before on the place of pleasure in the kingdom," Heracles pondered. "But Cerinthus's extreme permissiveness is a different matter from Paul's freedom of Christ that's set us free. The four of us have been such good friends, Claudius, that I hope this won't destroy that friendship. I'm really confused after all I've heard these past few days. Let's go see Onesimus. He knows Paul and Peter better than any of us other than John. He's also better versed in Plato and the other philosophers than we are."

With determination to settle the debate in their own minds, the two walked rapidly to Tyrannus's apartment, climbed to the sixth floor, and knocked on the door. Glaucon opened the door and greeted them.

"We're not expected," Claudius apologized, "but we were walking by and thought we'd enjoy a brief visit with Onesimus."

"I'll see if he's free," Glaucon said and left the visitors standing at the door.

In a few minutes, Onesimus appeared.

"Glad to see you, Claudius and Heracles. Come in. We've just finished dinner and were sharing our joy over today's events. Wasn't that a memorable hour this morning—the Eucharist and the message of Bishop John?"

Both agreed with enthusiasm. "It was a morning we'll never forget!" Heracles said.

Onesimus led them into the empty atrium to be seated on a comfortable divan.

"Onesimus, we don't want to infringe on your time, but we're disturbed and really confused by our conversation at noon with Cerinthus and Michael." Claudius proceeded to tell the whole story as frankly as he could.

"We left them tonight as they walked toward the temple. I'm sure that they're carrying out their expressed purpose and sharing with the priestesses in ways that, frankly, make us ashamed for them!"

Onesimus struggled to contain his anger. The folly of this brash philosopher from Alexandria was dangerous. With only a brief introduction to Jesus through John Mark, he now took it upon himself to act out his egoistic vision. Onesimus was silent for a few moments, praying for help to know what he should say to the disaffected friends. Finally he spoke slowly and thoughtfully.

"I understand how deeply you feel about this rift between you and your companions. You've come a long way together. As you say, you've had arguments over Cerinthus's kingdom of 'good pleasure' before."

"What we want from you, Onesimus, is some light on our own thinking. Are we right in believing his interpretation contrary to all that Paul and Peter and John have taught? You were with Paul and Peter, and you wrote several of Paul's letters. Can you help us?"

"I'll do all I can," Onesimus said simply. "The kingdom of unrestricted pleasure as Cerinthus describes it is not the kingdom of Christ as Jesus described God's rule on earth. Indeed, I can hear Paul and Peter as well as John cry their indignation at such perversion of the meaning of Christian freedom. As a student of the writings of Heraclitus, I remember many times when he made fun of the excessive licentiousness of the fertility rites offered to Artemis and spoke of the debauchery of uninhibited passion as unbalancing the soul and body. 'It's hard to fight your heart's desire,' he said. 'Whatever it wants, it buys at the cost of the soul.' Heraclitus would agree with Paul that true freedom is in the proper balance between soul and body. Paul said, and he had me write it to the Colossians, that love has to bind everything together and complete the whole. Where there's no loving concern for the well-being of others, especially for those who may seek to use others to gratify their passions, there is sin—the sin of self-love that becomes our idol. In the dialogue between Socrates and Protagoras, Plato indicates that pleasures are evil when their consequences are painful and destructive.''

Onesimus looked at his two companions and wondered if the conversation had become too philosophical for them. He decided to bring it back to a more everyday level.

''Last night Joanna, who's familiar with many of the priestesses through a Christian helper who was once a priestess in the temple, told us of the jealousy and strife in many broken homes as a result of the husbands' participation in the fertility rites. Joanna's friend told her also of the loneliness and suffering of many of the priestesses who long for *agape* love in society and children of their own.''

''Are you saying,'' Claudius asked, ''that there's no way that one who's committed to new life in Christ can participate in the perversion of erotic love in the temple rites?''

''That was the judgment of all of us as we talked of Cerinthus's kingdom of 'good pleasure,' '' Onesimus replied. ''There's no truly good pleasure that uses our sexual natures to exploit and injure the bodies and minds of any of God's children!''

''Then, Cerinthus and Michael are hurting not only themselves, but the whole church when they join in the incredible evils of the temple worship!'' Heracles concluded.

''Yes,'' Onesimus agreed. ''As our bishop, John has been given the authority to lead and protect the lives of the members of Christ's body in his charge, and he'll never permit this kind of heresy to be encouraged in the church!''

''Heracles and I agree with him. This confirms our thinking and clears our minds. But, what should we do in our relations with Cerinthus and Michael?'' Claudius threw up his hands in discouragement.

"Speak lovingly of the truth to them," Onesimus smiled sympathetically. "You might be rejected and ridiculed, but that's not important as long as you let them know they're still in Christ's circle of love. You can be friends even though strongly disagreeing. I understand the four of you have been invited to dinner at Euplus's home tomorrow night. Perhaps he can help you as you seek to show your two voluptuous friends how wrong and dangerous their teaching and actions are. Euplus knows Heraclitus well. Perhaps they will listen to him, even if they won't listen to Paul or John!"

"We'll do all we can," Heracles answered, "but I doubt Heraclitus will have any influence on Cerinthus. I've heard him make fun of the 'weeping philosopher,' as he's sometimes known. Cerinthus quoted one of his letters that the morals of Artemis's temple are worse than those of the beasts. He said that the pleasurable kingdom to which Christ calls will set even the pagans free from such dark philosophy."

"No doubt," Onesimus agreed, "there'll be many pagans in addition to weak Christians who'll be attracted to such false teaching. I can see that we're in for some difficult times."

Despite the frustration they all felt, Onesimus kept some sense of hope in his voice. "Nevertheless, the spirit of Christlike love never fails. I understand the church at Corinth was having similar problems, but Paul wrote to them offering victory."

As Claudius and Heracles arose to go, they thanked Onesimus for his helpfulness.

"This is a serious matter," Claudius said as they went to the door. "I know how hurt my family in Alexandria would be if they were infected by it. I love my beautiful Sarah too much to subject her to the pain of knowing that I'm a lecherous voluptuary!"

Onesimus impulsively put his arm around him as he spoke and then embraced them both.

"Let's pray for the spirit of *agape* to rule in our hearts!"

13

*O*nesimus spent only one more week in Ephesus with the apostle John and Mary. His heart was more and more with Helen in Colossae. Glaucon was busy buying materials for the silk and woolen business, so as soon as he had finished, they planned to leave.

The young Christians never tired of hearing John's moving stories and Mary's occasional witness of the life and teachings of Jesus, his response to the Jewish leaders, his trial and suffering, and his resurrection appearances. Onesimus had heard some of these accounts from Peter and Luke, but John had some recollections and interpretations of their meaning that were new to Onesimus, and he found his faith strengthened in the One who was both the Son of man and the Son of God.

"Sometime, Father John," Onesimus spoke emotionally at the close of their last morning together, "you must write down these stories and your interpretation of their meanings."

John answered with a deprecating smile. "I'm not much of a writer, Onesimus—you're the one with such skill! You were a great help to Paul and Peter . . . and to the whole church. I understand you've put some of the messages you heard Peter give to the imprisoned Christians in Rome on parchment. Perhaps sometime you can help me write my story."

"My friend," Onesimus replied, "I can't think of anything that would be more of a privilege. Hearing you and Mother Mary during these days has greatly increased my understanding and faith. I know how priceless such writing would be for others."

Several times in the last few days the conversation returned to Cerinthus and Michael. All were thankful for the strength of Claudius and Heracles to oppose their teachings and actions but were glad the love of the two young men was broad enough to hold them in the fellowship of the Gnostics.

John and the others had been shocked at the report of Cerinthus and Michael's visits to the Temple of Artemis. John exploded in furious anger when he first heard it.

"I don't want those two voluptuaries ever to be in the same place that I am!" he had cried.

After he had calmed his emotions, John had agreed with Onesimus, who had summed up what should be their attitude.

"If Jesus could accept and forgive the woman taken in adultery, surely we must be willing to accept these two young men."

"Yes," John agreed, "I can and will love them, by God's grace, but I don't need to be identified with them unless there's some chance of correcting their perverse thinking and licentious behavior."

Before breakfast on the morning after Euplus's dinner with the four Alexandrians, Claudius reported to Onesimus the results of their efforts to change the thinking of their friends.

"They're still adamant in their position concerning good pleasure celebrating Christ's nuptial feast in his kingdom, to which they're including such sensual experiences as they enjoyed with the priestesses in Artemis's temple. However, at Euplus's strong urging, they agreed to refrain from their visits to and sharing in the temple rites. Euplus quoted Heraclitus and Paul freely, but as we expected, Cerinthus had ready answers, claiming the gloomy philosopher didn't understand the *gnosis* by which the kingdom of Christ's good pleasures should belong to all Christians. And he held to his views of Paul's mixing the Hebrew scriptures with Christ's freedom from the law."

"What about Euplus's friends who were also present?" Onesimus asked with concern.

"Out of the five present, at least two of them seemed to agree with Cerinthus. After we came back to our rooms, Cerinthus and Michael were jubilant that at least two, Theatus and Sophorus I think their names were, invited them to a meeting tomorrow."

Onesimus shook his head sadly. "Thus heresy as a half-truth takes wings and spreads," he said.

He thanked Claudius for giving him the news. "At least they

won't be repeating the folly of their visit to the temple . . . for a while.''

That morning at breakfast, Onesimus shared the discouraging news with the apostle. He still urged John as bishop to do nothing that would prevent the two young heretics from attending worship services. John reluctantly agreed.

"But only until we've done everything the Spirit leads us to do to show them how wrong they are," he added with firmness.

Onesimus pushed hard for a delay in ostracizing the two Alexandrians from the Eucharist. "In the name of the love of God, we mustn't shut them out of our love. I want to have a chance to talk to them again before I leave for home."

John concluded the conversation, with words Onesimus would long remember. "We love even those whose words and acts we despise, because God loved us first. While we were still sinners, Christ died for the ungodly. We can't say, 'I love God,' while we hate our brother—to say that is to lie. If we don't love those people we've seen, we can't really love God whom we haven't. We're commanded to do this by Christ, who said that whoever loves God must also love those around him!''

The next week sped quickly by—though not quickly enough for Onesimus. The hours spent with John and Mary were precious times of growing in his understanding of Jesus the Christ and what his life, death, and resurrection meant. During one afternoon and several evenings, they read again the parchments that contained the letters the Ephesian church had collected—letters from Paul and a new one containing something called "The Gospel of Matthew," which had just arrived from Antioch. Onesimus asked Tyrannus for a copy to take with him to Colossae, where he would have the opportunity to read and study it in detail. The book was not complete, Tyrannus had been told, but it did contain more of the teachings of Jesus than any other parchment they possessed— several sheets contained teachings Jesus had given that Matthew had collected and put together as "Teachings from the Mount."

On the second Sunday of his visit, at the urging of John and Tyrannus, Onesimus told some of the inspiring stories during the worship service of his experiences in Smyrna and Pergamum, of Antipas's victorious witness, of the first worship services in the catacombs of Rome, of the hours he spent with Paul and Peter, and of the way, after Peter and his arrests, he had been saved from martyrdom.

Onesimus was able to spend another evening with the four Alexandrians, but it was an evening filled with disappointment and frustration, for it was a repetition of the same old arguments. The only difference was that now Heracles and Claudius were boldly on the side of *agape* as the final test. Onesimus's ire was kept in check, but as he said good-bye, he had to say what he felt.

"Cerinthus, you're a brilliant person. What an influence you can have as a leader in the church of our Lord! I must honestly say, however, that if you persist in your teaching of the *gnosis* that opens the door to lust without *agape*, you'll do untold harm to many in our *communitas*. Remember, I'll be praying for you as you remain in our love—and I hope to see you again."

Cerinthus was touched by Onesimus's kindness. "May Christ go with you back to your home in Colossae. Someday we will meet again," he said in response.

The morning came when Onesimus and Glaucon took their leave. Their horses were saddled, and the gifts they had purchased for their *familia* and the woolen and silk materials purchased for the business were packed on the backs of two donkeys. They said good-bye and began their three-day journey home to Colossae.

Part Three

Joy and Sorrow

14

*T*he setting sun reflected in many shades of red, orange, and saffron from the white limestone buildings of the little city of Colossae, which stood against the purple background of the Cadmus Mountains in the distance. Onesimus and Glaucon reined and slowed their horses on the travertine bridge over the Lycus River, which flowed from the northeast beside the plateau on which the city rested like a varicolored ruby in its setting.

The two young travelers sat on their horses and contemplated their home city for a few moments.

"Home!" Onesimus cried. "At last! A lovely sight. It's not as imposing or as noted for its architecture or history as Ephesus, but with Helen and our *familia*, it's a wonderful place to live!"

They urged their tired horses the final bit across the bridge and through the gates of the city into the courtyard of the house of Philemon and Apphia, now also the home of Onesimus and Helen.

The news of their arrival spread fast, and by the time they had dismounted, the entire *familia* surrounded them. Within moments, Helen was in Onesimus's arms with the kiss he had looked forward to for weeks! With warm embraces, he was welcomed by his mother, Alcestia, and his new family, Philemon, Apphia, and Archippus. Glaucon found himself surrounded by reunions of his own.

Philemon's *familia* now numbered fifty, many of whom had once been his slaves. Now in freedom, they voluntarily served their former master, who furnished them a home where they felt they really belonged—a place to live, work, and receive wages.

Everyone in the courtyard was delighted with the safe return of the young men. Onesimus had endeared himself not only to Helen's parents and brother, but to both the current and former slaves. With the exception of a few who still resented him, these newly freed persons and those still technically slaves had new hope and meaning for their lives because of Onesimus's courage and influence with Philemon and his son, Archippus.

Glaucon was one freedman who strongly felt his appreciation of his partner and friend on the long journey just completed. As they had ridden into the gate of the city in anticipation of their warm reunion, he had realized that he now considered this his home.

That evening, as the inner family reclined at the table for dinner, Onesimus told some of the significant parts of his experiences. The highlight of the evening was his description of the inspiring hours with John and Mary in the home of Tyrannus and Joanna. He was asked many questions about them. The women were interested in his description of Mary, but everyone found inspiration in the stories she and John told of the boyhood and early manhood of Jesus in the carpenter shop at Nazareth.

"We're thankful beyond words for your effective witness, Onesimus," Philemon said after Onesimus had related the extent of his adventures. "The story of these weeks away from home is a validation of your ministry as a messenger of Christ's love and peace. We're proud of you!"

After a brief but fervent prayer of thanksgiving by Archippus, they all embraced again. Onesimus, his arm around Helen's waist, walked to the new apartment prepared for them by Philemon and tastefully decorated by the two mothers, Apphia and Alcestia. Here they had spent the first night of their marriage.

"How wonderful to be home and loved in such a family!" Onesimus exclaimed to Helen as they closed the door. There was no need for words, but as he took her gently in his arms, he had a fleeting thought of Cerinthus and his twisted understanding of Christ's kingdom of love and good pleasure! But the thought lasted only for a moment as his complete attention was given to expressing his love for her with the enthusiasm and excitement of youth!

Much later, as the couple looked through the window at the full autumn moon, they talked of their coming child. The perennial question of whether the little one would be a boy or a girl was answered in complete agreement.

"The child can be either, but we pray he or she will be whole and strong!"

Helen confided in her husband that she had experienced several times of sickness and pain, but the physician had assured her that all would go well.

Locked in each other's arms, they prayed with thankfulness, trusting their little one and their own lives to the care of the all-wise and loving Father.

After breakfast the next morning, Onesimus joined Philemon, Archippus, and Theseus, their business clerk, in Philemon's office. As they sat around his polished oak desk, Philemon spoke words to Onesimus that again made the young man feel a warm contentment for the present and an enthusiasm for the future.

"As you are our partner in all parts of our business, Onesimus, I want you to know that the name I first gave you is even more appropriate now. You are truly 'useful,' not only in the deepest sense of having opened new doors to the meaning of our Christian faith through your costly experiences with Paul, Peter, the Christians in Rome, and now the apostle John, but also in the practical work of making and selling the best silk and wool in the whole Mediterranean world!"

"Be careful, Father, your pride is showing!" Archippus said laughingly.

"Maybe so, son, but it's a healthy pride! Paul told us to study so we could show ourselves to be workers who don't need to be ashamed. I'm proud of our work, and I'm thankful that Onesimus has so much to share with us!"

Thus resumed the business partnership of Philemon, his son, Archippus, and his adopted son, Onesimus. Onesimus was brought up to date by Archippus and Theseus on the happenings during the weeks of his absence.

"One thing I've discovered for sure," Theseus remarked, "the products of our looms and dye works are valued highly by traders all over the world. The purple dye from the Cadmus Mountains that we're using makes some of the most valued cloth to be found anywhere. Several of the merchants I've met in Ephesus told me that the care our workers put into the dying of the cloth improves its quality.''

"Yes," Archippus affirmed, "I've noticed that. Part of the reason for it is that our workers, most of whom are freedmen and women, put their hearts into their work. They're becoming more and more effective in the stewardship of their jobs, which they gladly do without force!''

Onesimus clapped his hands. "Where the Spirit of the Lord is, there's freedom! Paul was right! In that freedom the glory of God is seen, even in the making of beautiful colored cloth!''

15

*T*he quiet return to Colossae Onesimus had been experiencing was suddenly interrupted by the shouts of Glaucon, who came running through the gates of the house. Everyone who had been enjoying lunch around the table rushed out to the courtyard to be met with the entire *familia*. Glaucon was gasping for breath, having run until exhausted. Archippus met him and led him to a bench to rest.

At last he was able to speak, as all gathered near with anxious concern.

"The most terrible thing has happened. Horace, the son of Urbana, has . . . has . . . been beaten . . ." He still gasped for breath. "He may be dead. Angell, the slave Horace severely whipped to mar his face for having made love to his sister, has attacked him!''

Onesimus put his arms around Helen as they both remembered the day when she had been warned by her own father not to act foolishly with his slave, Onesimus.

As Glaucon's story was pieced together, the punishment had

left Angell with a burning hatred, and now he had taken his revenge.

"What happened to Angell?" Archippus asked.

"I walked up to the stables just as it was all over. Only one or two other slaves were around. They said that Angell struck his young master with a riding stick and knocked him down. Cursing strongly, Angell continued to beat and kick him until he was critically hurt and bleeding. The slaves who were there were either sympathetic or afraid to interfere. When Angell's anger was spent, he leaped on the fastest horse and rode out toward the mountains. I got there just in time to see him disappear in the trees along the river."

Once he had had a chance to catch his breath, Glaucon continued his story. "I knelt with one of the slaves to see if we could do anything for Horace, while the other ran for help. There was nothing we could do. Soon the stables were filled with Urbana's *familia*. Urbana himself, furious with rage and fear for his son, knelt beside him."

"Was Aurelia there?" Helen broke in, concerned for Horace's sister.

"No," Glaucon answered. "They said she was visiting a friend in Hierapolis."

"It's a good thing she wasn't there," Helen thought aloud. "It'll be hard enough when she returns!"

"As they waited for the physician to arrive," Glaucon continued, "some of the women brought fresh water to wash Horace's wounds. Seeing me and knowing that I'm one of Philemon's freed slaves, Urbana went into a tirade of curses on the 'foolish Christians' corrupting his slaves. He told me to tell Philemon that we'll have to deal with him and many of his neighbors who are distressed by what is happening in their *familias*. I started to express our sorrow and regret, but before I could say anything, he cursed me and told me to leave. I knew we'd all be hurt deeply by this, so I ran as fast as I could to tell you the story!"

Everyone continued to stand in the courtyard wondering uncertainly what this tragic event would mean to Philemon and their *familia*.

"Dear friends," Philemon took a few steps forward in addressing them, "let's lift our hearts in prayer for our neighbor who has been so critically hurt and for his family. Let's also remember the hurt borne by young Angell and the bitterness and hatred that led him to seek revenge in such a tragic way. This sad event proves that injustice and cruelty always breed more cruelty and injustice. I'll go to Urbana to convey our sympathy."

After a few moments of quiet, Onesimus spoke in a voice filled with compassion and concern.

"I'm sure most of you remember my own situation and the beating I received at the hands of my former master. Had I not discovered the forgiving love of Christ through the forgiveness of Philemon, Archippus, and the Christians so cruelly persecuted in Rome, I might have committed just such a desperate act—though Philemon's treatment of me was never as cruel as Horace's treatment of Angell. Nevertheless, only the love of Christ within us enables us to love and forgive when we've been hurt and wronged. I'm thankful for the divine love and compassion that have brought us back together as one family."

As he spoke, Onesimus watched Junius, one of Philemon's own rebellious slaves, standing with a grimace of disgust at one side of the group.

"I know there are still a few of you who question the genuineness of our forgiveness and love," Onesimus continued. "I beg of you to keep your minds open and to find in your own heart the love that will never fail. We may reject or ignore it, but the love of God in Christ is the only way to right human wrongs and to remain truly free!"

"Now, let's get back to work," Philemon suggested. "But please pray for me, for I'm going as soon as it seems wise to visit with Urbana. Let's all pray for Horace's recovery and the saving by the Spirit in the life of Angell. As we remember him and his brutal deed, let's remember that there, but for the grace of God, each of us would be!"

Three days passed before Philemon went alone to call on his neighbor Urbana. The neighbor received him coldly, unlike former times when they had enjoyed good times together. Horace remained unconscious and near death.

"I'm truly sorry about the injuries to your son," Philemon began.

Urbana responded with bitterness. "You and your Christian ways are to blame for this, Philemon."

"That's not possible," Philemon responded. "We hadn't even heard of Christianity when Horace first punished Angell. But that doesn't matter, now. We have to remember that slaves are human, too. No doubt Angell nursed his grievance until it finally burst out in this terrible crime."

"No, it's not as easy as all that." Urbana's voice was edged with venom. "You've set the wrong kind of tone by forgiving your runaway slave, Onesimus, and then by setting some of your slaves free. You and your son will have to account for this bad influence on our slaves. Several of our neighbors have told me of their unhappiness with you."

Seeing Philemon's shocked reaction, Urbana softened his voice a little. "I imagine you'd feel the same way if Archippus were lying at death's door. At least when Onesimus escaped, he did it without injuring anything but your feelings and finances! I was at his wedding to Helen, and I must admit he's likely to make a fine partner in your family's business. But I warn you that you'll have to pay dearly for your foolish Christian ways!"

"I'm ready to share the costs of unpopularity and worse, if necessary, if my neighbors don't believe in my integrity; but what I do, I do for a higher cause, a cause that—"

"I don't want to hear any of that nonsense! I've heard the rumors of the strange practice you have of drinking the blood of your Christ."

"That's not what we do at all!" Philemon insisted.

"Of course, you'd be a fool not to deny it. Get off my property, Philemon!"

When Philemon left his neighbor at the gate, Urbana was shaking his fist. "You'll pay for this!"

When Philemon returned home, his *familia* listened to the story with sorrow. Before they parted, Onesimus led them in a prayer for their new enemy, Urbana, and others who might join him. He prayed for the healing of Horace and for the courage and faith to continue loving and witnessing to the Christ in every way possible.

Onesimus thoroughly enjoyed his quiet new life with Helen and the *familia* of Philemon. He liked the measured rhythms of early morning worship, breakfast together, and sharing with his partners, Philemon and Archippus, and with their workers. Lunch came at midday and was followed by a brief rest and afternoons of occasional rides with Helen in the fertile, verdant plains to the north of Colossae.

Autumn was in the air. The farmers' crops of wheat, corn, and barley were ripe and being harvested. The fruit trees were filled with plump apples, grapes, figs, and pomegranates.

Once the couple took a picnic basket and rode farther up into the mountains. They found a perfect site to spread out their food and to look out over the city below. Some of the mountains were covered with chalky limestone deposits, making them appear white in the sunshine.

While the evenings were still warm, Onesimus and Helen spent an hour or two at twilight in the garden with the inner family or sometimes the entire *familia* joining them. On cooler nights, they chose the atrium. They would sing folk songs familiar to all, accompanied by Alcestia on the harp. Often she set one of the Hebrew psalms to music; other times they sang hymns she and two of the younger Christians had written.

At Onesimus and Helen's suggestion, at least two or three evenings each week, the entire *familia* joined with them to sing and hear Onesimus tell exciting stories of his experiences in Smyrna, Pergamum, and Rome, the terrible fire, the *koinonia* of the Roman church, and the heroic martyrdom of many who refused to deny their faith. Even the few disgruntled slaves listened with quiet attention as he told these and other stories he had heard of the life of Jesus from Simon Peter, Luke, and John Mark.

Always the best part of their time together was Onesimus's reading from the parchments he had brought back from Rome containing the parables and other teachings of Jesus. Onesimus had written them down while they were told by those who, like Peter, had been there to hear them, or like Luke and John Mark who had heard them firsthand from other disciples. The apostle Paul was a favorite of Onesimus! They had been so close as Paul dictated his letters to Onesimus. Onesimus had preserved several parchments on which he had copied the letters Paul had dictated in the house prison and later in the Mamertine Prison. Among these was the letter Paul had written to Philemon before Onesimus's return to ask forgiveness and receive his physical freedom. The *familia* was attentive to hear the letters Paul had dictated to the churches and Simon Peter's words of comfort and courage to the Christians in prison who were soon to be martyred.

Exclamations of wonder and amazement came from the group as Onesimus told the stories and read the words that stirred him so deeply. Many questions were asked that led to intense discussions of the meaning of what Jesus said and did, the reasons for the persecutions, and why Christians were willing to undergo such indescribable sufferings and death for their faith. During the weeks that followed Onesimus and Glaucon's return from Ephesus, a veritable school of Christ was held at Philemon's home with Onesimus as the teacher.

It was a good time not only for Onesimus and Helen, but also for the Colossian church that met in Philemon's home. Onesimus realized that its members knew so little about Jesus, the loving One who had begun as a traveling rabbi and whom they now confessed as their Lord and Master! He knew that these hours were priceless preparation for the costly and tragic experiences that would lay ahead for many of them.

16

One night early in the twelfth month of the year, Onesimus was shocked awake by Helen's cries of pain.

"Onesimus! This pain is much worse than what I had before! Please call Mother and Alcestia!"

With a comforting embrace and a word of encouragement, Onesimus put on his tunic and awakened his mother and Apphia and sent Glaucon to ride as fast as he could to the other side of the city for their physician, also a Christian.

Returning to the bedroom, he put his arms around Helen as she shook with pain. As the physician had calculated it, she had carried the baby for five months. What could be happening? Onesimus held her and prayed for her and for the child. He tried to speak words of comfort and assurance.

The two mothers came into the room and did all they knew to do. The physician soon arrived and gave Helen medication to stop her spasms. He said that it appeared to be a premature birth. In spite of all that was done, within the hour the baby was born. At five months, Helen and Onesimus's little son was unable to breathe and died. Onesimus paced up and down the hall until Alcestia came to tell him the sad news. He went into the room where the physician and Apphia were seeking to comfort Helen. Close to her breast, she was holding the form of her lifeless child.

"Oh my poor baby... my poor baby..." She saw Onesimus and cried, "Onesimus, our son ... couldn't breathe.... He's dead." She wept with uncontrollable sobs.

He knelt by her bed and held her close, his own tears mixed with hers. The physician patted him on the shoulder.

"I'm sorry, Onesimus. I did all I could do.... The baby's premature birth is one of those mysteries we can't explain.... I've given Helen some medicine to ease the physical pain. With your love and faith, you can help our Lord to ease her inner pain!"

To Helen he said, "I'll be back early in the morning. I'll pray for you and Onesimus in this terrible disappointment."

With tear-filled eyes, Apphia and Alcestia thanked the doctor. As he left, they stood by the bed for a few moments, not knowing what to say. Finally Alcestia spoke.

"We'll leave you alone for a few minutes, but we'll be in the library praying. God is love, and he cares for you in your sorrow.''

"We love you both so much, and our Lord loves you even more than we do," Apphia murmured. "We trust him to help you meet this terrible disappointment!"

Onesimus, through his tears, was able to say only, "Thanks to you, our mothers! Helen will need your prayers . . . and so will I!"

They kissed both Helen and Onesimus as they left the room, closing the door behind them.

For the next few minutes, Onesimus held Helen close to him as they wept together in wordless moments of poignant grief. The little one's body was still in the cradle where Apphia had placed it, covered with the white linen blanket she had woven for her first grandchild. Onesimus knew how many thousand times Helen had thought of the baby she carried and prayed for him. He realized how often he also had thought of and prayed for the coming one. He had all of his work and concerns; Helen must feel the loss infinitely more than he did.

He saw that she was feeling the effects of the medicine the physician had left. This was the first great trial of their faith, and he began to pray audibly the prayer he had been praying silently.

"O Lord Jesus, you know and carry our pains and sorrows. Comfort and strengthen my dearest Helen. Heal her body and spirit as she sleeps."

Helen's hand fell limp in his as the medicine took effect. He continued holding her hand, praying for the courage and strength he needed to help her come through these days of disappointment.

Alcestia opened the door. Seeing Helen asleep, she whispered to her son, "She'll likely sleep till morning, only a few more hours. Apphia and I will stay in the library with the little one's body. Philemon and Archippus are with us. As soon as it is light enough to travel, we'll send Glaucon to bring our good friend Bishop Papias from Hierapolis. It'll be good for you to get some rest as you stay by her side."

"Thank you, Mother, and thank Apphia for all you two have done! It's good to have our two mothers with us!"

Alcestia kissed him on the cheek, took the cradle, and left the room.

Onesimus closed the door and turned to see the lovely white face, now pallid, against the white pillow. He fell on his knees again by the bed and wept unashamedly as he poured out his grief for her and for himself. He had not realized just how much of his heart had been bound up in the expectancy of one small baby whose coming was so brief and whose going so quick. He became aware of the same rebellion he had felt when Paul was taken to execution and Antipas given to the flames. Now it was happening to him and Helen—the dark, mysterious side of life. He wondered what he would say when she awakened. What could he say to this rebel within himself? He knew the words of Paul, of Peter, and of John. He repeated them and the words of the Twenty-third Psalm. Just saying them helped. Even more important than these, he knew the Good Shepherd. John had told him that Jesus had called himself the Good Shepherd. "The Good Shepherd always lays down his own life for his sheep," he'd said. But why was this necessary? Why should the Good Shepherd let the thief come in to steal their little lamb? Their first. Their own flesh and blood! Why? My God, why?

Suddenly, Onesimus awakened to hear again the cry of his Lord from the cross: "My God, why? Why have you forsaken me?" He knew, deep down beneath the void of cold reason that always tried to take over within him, that the answer was not in logical words, but in the *word of life*. He had heard of that word supremely in Jesus and had seen it for himself in Simon Peter, in Paul, and in the young Christian mother whose little son was torn from her arms as she was pushed into the prisoners' cart with him and Simon Peter on her way to execution.

Peter had said to her, "It's not your Father's will that these little ones should perish."

She had said, "My little one won't perish. I'll trust the Father."

In the moment Onesimus remembered that, he knew that his answer was not in philosophical proof but in a presence, the Presence of the Lamb that was slain but is alive forevermore. In the awesomeness of that moment, he committed himself, Helen, and their little one to the living presence of One whose love passes all understanding. He arose quietly and lay down by the side of the sleeping Helen. He knew morning would come!

Morning did come.

It always does, Onesimus thought as he watched Helen regain consciousness after her drugged sleep.

She opened her eyes and looked at him. The remembrance of what had happened flooded over her. She threw her arms around him and wept silently. He waited for her sobbing to subside.

"Where's the cradle and . . . ?"

"Our mothers took it into the library. They've been there since you went to sleep. Your father sent Glaucon to bring Bishop Papias."

"Why did it happen to our little one? Why . . . ," her voice trailed off as she hid her face on his shoulder.

"I asked that after you went to sleep. As a myriad of mothers and fathers through the ages have asked it, I prayed and wept, pouring it all out, but suddenly I remembered that was the very same question our Lord asked as he hung on the cross. 'My God, why?' He didn't get an answer, but he did look to the Father he had known since he was a boy and who had never failed him, and by faith he prayed the prayers you and I must pray. Father, into your hands we commit our spirits and the life of our little son."

"But how could God our Father be a Father of wisdom and love and let our little one die?" she cried.

"Why this happened is a mystery, just as the physician said. God is the greatest mystery of all—the hidden God, as a psalmist wrote. But in the darkness of mystery that surrounds him and his purposes—why our baby should not be born normally and grow up to full stature and countless other mysteries—in the darkness there is a light shining in the face of Jesus Christ. You saw that light shining in your darkness while I was in Rome. I've seen it in the faces of Paul, Peter, and Antipas."

Onesimus told her the story of the young Christian mother's response to Peter's comforting remembrance of Jesus' words he had remembered the night before.

"She said, even as she went to her death and they took her little one away, 'My little one won't perish. I'll trust the Father.' So you and I will trust him, even in the painful mystery of our great loss."

Helen, wiping her eyes, said thoughtfully, "And so we will, dear Onesimus. How thankful I am for your love, your presence, your understanding. I'm sure Bishop Papias will say the right things to help us witness this kind of faith to all of our *familia*!"

"Your faith has always been simple and strong. Sometimes I have to fight the rebel within me in order to trust. But trust I will, by God's grace and your help!"

"Does this mean that we trust the Father to take the life of our baby and complete it?" she asked.

"Yes, that's the essence of our faith in Christ. God the Father is not a destroyer of any good thing. He knows even when a sparrow falls, as Jesus said. He's a perfecter and completer of all that is good. Surely your carrying our child for five months were good, in spite of the pain!"

"Oh, yes!" she cried. "I'm thankful for the privilege for even that long with his growing little body and mind and spirit within me."

"Yes, his small body and the spirit within him were good! So God didn't destroy him. In some wonderful way he took him from his imperfect state as a five-month-old baby unable to breathe like all babies are meant to breathe. His birth was painful for him, for you, and for me. But, Helen, I believe God is still creating our son, still perfecting this dear little one whom you held so close to you for five months. What that perfected life will be we can't know. It's too hidden in the mystery of God. But as John said when I was with him in Ephesus, 'What kind of love has the Father given us that we should be called the children of God? We really are God's children, though we don't know yet what we'll be, but this we'll learn when he shall appear—we'll be like him, for we'll see him as he is.' Someday we'll see our little son perfected in glorious liberty as God's son!"

The two knelt by the side of their bed and, in simple words, expressed their thanksgiving for the light shining in their darkness through Christ and for the confidence that into his love they could trust their son.

That morning at the hour of ten, the *familia* of Philemon and several of their closest friends gathered in the atrium for a service of love and praise to Christ before the burial of Onesimus and Helen's little son. Helen was carried by Onesimus and placed on a couch near the lectern. Bishop Papias read several psalms and, from the scroll of Isaiah, a passage that Helen heard now with new meaning:

> He will tend his flock like a shepherd
> and gather them together with his arms;
> he will carry the lambs in his bosom
> and gently lead the ewes to water.

The bishop spoke for a few minutes describing Jesus as the Good Shepherd who loved the little children.

"Christ, the Good Shepherd, has received this little lamb and will surely make provision in the Father's house for his care and feeding."

Alcestia, though fearful of her own emotions, sang a beautiful song she had written and sung for Onesimus's first return from Rome and then for the wedding of Onesimus and Helen. She had written a new stanza during the early morning hours of waiting by the cradle in the library:

> "Lord of all your great creation,
> You who made us to be free.
> Praise to you for love you give us,
> Breaking chains of fear and need,
> Bonds of love that can't be broken.
>
> "You who called us as your children,
> Take this one so small and sleeping.
> Hold him in your arms so strong.
> Make him grow in rare perfection.
> Shield him from all hurt and wrong.

> "Glory be, Eternal Father,
> Son of Love in Jesus living,
> Now, O Christ, your Spirit giving!
> Lord of all your great creation,
> Praise to you for loving freedom."

The closing prayers were offered by Papias. These were followed by an invitation for all to offer up their prayers of silent thanksgiving for the loving freedom Christ had given—freedom from fear, from hate, from selfish grief, and from the bonds of death.

After the benediction, all of the *familia* and friends came to express their love and sympathy to Helen and Onesimus. Helen had recovered her composure and responded with words of trust and hope as they spoke to her. Onesimus was proud of her spirit. He had never seen her look lovelier, though her face was whiter than usual. She had found the loving freedom of Christ even in her feelings of emptiness and loss.

The small body of the lifeless baby had been placed tenderly by the mothers within a little cedar box prepared during the early morning hours by Theseus and Glaucon, who had requested the privilege. Now led by Bishop Papias, they walked out to the garden where a small grave had been dug in a corner under a large acacia tree. After another brief prayer of thanksgiving, the Lord's Prayer was prayed by all the Christians, and Theseus and Glaucon put the box into the ground and covered it with earth and autumn flowers. Onesimus held Helen in his arms and carried her back to their room.

As they left the garden, tears did come. Helen whispered, "Onesimus, when I think of him, I'll remember that beautiful song your mother sang: 'Lord of all your great creation, Praise to you for loving freedom!' "

"Yes, my darling," Onesimus responded, "our little son has the loving freedom to live and grow in ways we can't imagine. We'll trust him there!"

Part Four

The Rebel

efore leaving the Philemon home on that sad but victorious day, Bishop Papias sat at lunch with the bereaved family. As he gave thanks for the food and for the victory of faith, he expressed their common appreciation that, through Christ, they need not sorrow like those who have no hope.

"I've been waiting for your return, Onesimus," Papias said, "from your journey to the churches in Ephesus, Smyrna, and Pergamum. I urge you to come to us in our neighboring church at Hierapolis. Our people have heard you speak of your experiences in Rome with Peter and Paul, but they're anxious as I am to hear of your fruitful weeks in your recent journey—especially of the martyrdom of Antipas. I don't want to take you away from Helen for long, but since she can't make even the short trip to Hierapolis, I wonder if you'll come on the next Lord's Day to share of your recent experiences."

"I think you should go," Helen exclaimed. "This is a good way for you to celebrate our faith in Christ. I know how inspired all of us were to hear of Antipas and Tavius, of John and Mary. I want you to go as much as I'd like you to be with me."

Onesimus agreed. "So long as I know you're all right, my dearest, I can do it."

All of the *familia* concurred. Since it was only about twelve miles—a three-and-a-half hour ride—he'd go on Saturday and return on Monday.

During the next several days, the two young lovers spent as much time as possible together. Helen regained her strength as they rode to their trysting place in the mountains. The leaves were gold, brown, and red mixed with the evergreens, making a breathtaking view from their favorite site. The air was cool on the sunny December day, and the crops had been harvested. Winter was slow in coming.

They talked of their future. Would they have another child? Yes, they both agreed, if this were possible. He told her of invitations from other churches in Antioch, Magnesia, and Tralles whose leaders had invited him to come for a week or so of proclaiming the good news. They wanted to hear it from him as he had heard it from three great apostles and Luke, John Mark, and Timothy, and as he had seen it lived out in the lives of Tyrannus and Joanna, Bishop Tavius and his family, and the brilliant young physician, Theophrastus Antipas, the story of whose courageous witness had spread throughout the church. Onesimus and Helen decided that he would accept as many of these invitations as he could and that Helen would go with him where it was feasible, unless another little one were on the way to keep her at home.

They were happy in the confidence of the future belonging to the kingdom of God with his will as their goal and his Spirit as their guide.

On the first day of the week following, Onesimus stood before the now familiar congregation of believers in the church at Hierapolis, one of the first Christian churches in that part of Ionia. Papias and his son, Protagoras, had been on a business trip to Antioch when they first heard Paul preach. The church in Antioch was vital and strong, and Papias was attracted by the apostle's preaching. He and Protagoras, then only twelve years old, were baptized. When they returned to Hierapolis, Papias began to preach and teach the good news, and a little church grew up around him meeting in his house. Later, when Paul came to Ephesus, Papias and his family had spent several days with him.

On this Lord's Day, the atrium of Papias's large house was filled with excited worshipers. Onesimus had preached for them several times since he returned from Rome. They were ready to hear him again.

Onesimus was just ending his testimony when he felt the building shake beneath his feet. The movement was so strong that a glass of water on the lectern overturned. The noise of some faraway explosion filled the room. Onesimus stopped speaking, realizing it was an earthquake. The house shook again.

Papias got to his feet and, as the tremors continued, admonished with a calm voice: "Peace, beloved. . . . Do not panic! Those of you nearest the doors go outside first. The remainder will follow. The Lord keep us all!"

Hurriedly but calmly, Papias led his sons, Gorgia and Protagoras, and Onesimus through a back door as people hurried through the front. There was no panic; Onesimus was thankful for that. Though the tremors continued, the people did not push each other in terror. Instead, they were amazingly quiet.

Outside the house, they saw that several of the mud-and-brick buildings had suffered some damage, but most of the stone buildings were still intact. People from all the buildings were milling around in the streets, many of them with terror on their faces. Earthquakes occurred in this region of Ionia at intervals over the centuries, and some had had devastating effects. Onesimus recalled stories he had heard during his first stay in Colossae of an earthquake that had destroyed whole villages—thousands had perished. A part of the Cadmus Mountains had been ripped and torn with a huge gash that had become a deep valley with sharp rocks on each side.

Onesimus was horrified as he looked to the southwest towards Colossae. A dark cloud of dust rose where the city stood.

Dear Lord, he prayed to himself, *that looks as if Colossae may be in the center of the quake.*

"I have to go home," he said to Papias. He started running to the stables with young Protagoras and his father behind him. One of Papias's servants had preceded them and had thrown the saddle on Onesimus's horse. Leaping into the saddle with the blessings of Papias and several of the Christians, he rode off at a gallop.

The twelve miles to Colossae usually took about three hours, but Onesimus made it in one. As he came nearer to the city, the smoke and dust became so dense that he had difficulty breathing. His faithful horse, Solon, was lathered with sweat and gasping for breath.

The scene was one of utter devastation. Just outside the city, he looked up in horror as he passed by a graveyard where the earth had vomited up the bones of the dead. Out of a huge chasm, waters gushed forth and ran into the swollen Lycus River. As he approached Colossae, he met crowds of refugees running from the city, some dazed with shock, others crazed with fear. He tried to stop several of them to ask the extent of the destruction. Only one waited to answer.

"The whole city is in ruins or else has disappeared," he cried. "You're a fool if you go into it!"

Onesimus spurred Solon faster in spite of the horse's exhaustion. Both horse and rider coughed and gasped for breath. Onesimus bound a turban cloth over his mouth and nose to keep out the worst of the dust and smoke.

The walls of the city were completely demolished. As he entered what once was the gate to the city, he dismounted and led Solon around the huge cracks in the streets into which many people and entire houses had fallen. Almost every house was leveled. Here and there a brick wall stood only a few feet high. All the houses made of mud and brick had been destroyed. Around him were a few survivors who appeared to be deranged, stumbling over the rubble, making guttural cries.

"My Lord and my God, how could you have permitted this?" he cried out to the blackened skies. "Where are you to let this happen?"

The domain of Philemon and his family was not too far from the entrance to the city near the River Lycus. As he drew near, Onesimus was relieved to see some of Philemon's houses, though in ruins, had not been swallowed up.

He knew the Christian members of the *familia* would have been at worship when the quake hit, so he made his way to the spot where the atrium had been. Onesimus was horrified to see that its walls and ceiling had collapsed on the worshipers. Arms and legs stuck out beneath the rubble. He could hear the groans of those still alive.

In a frenzy of fear, he climbed over the broken pillars and beams and found the spot where he guessed Helen, his mother, and Apphia would have been sitting. As he pulled a huge beam away, he saw his mother's white face, an ugly gash tearing through it. He felt for a pulse but, finding nothing, he knew she was dead. Powerful sobs overcame him as he pulled and tugged frantically at more rubble until he found Helen. She had been pinned beneath two columns that had fallen against each other miraculously to keep her from being crushed to death. When he knelt beside her, he realized that, though unconscious, she was still alive. Onesimus pushed against the column and prayed, but it would not move. He knelt beside her again and prayed more earnestly than he ever had in his life. Suddenly, he felt a hand on his shoulder.

"We're here to help you, Onesimus," a kind voice said.

Onesimus looked up and thankfully saw the faces of Papias, his two sons, and several other Christian men from Hierapolis.

"Thank God you've come." Onesimus's face was streaked with trails of tears through dirt and grime. "Please help me remove this column. Helen is still alive, but my mother and many others are dead."

The men struggled together, but the marble column was too heavy. Finally, Gorgia found a loose beam and inserted it under one end of the column. With great effort, the men slowly raised the column high enough for Onesimus to pull Helen from beneath it.

As he held his wife in his arms, Onesimus knew her body was seriously injured. Blood gushed from a gash on the side of her head, and both her legs appeared to be broken. She was breathing, though, for which Onesimus was thankful. He laid her carefully on the grass in the garden. One of the men had gone to the river and carried back water in a vessel he had gotten in what used to be the kitchen. As Onesimus looked on helplessly, Papias took his own turban, dipped it in the water, and washed and bandaged Helen's wound.

Onesimus suddenly remembered Philemon, Archippus, Apphia, and his mother! Leaving Helen in the care of Gorgia's wife, Sappho, who had arrived with several other women, Onesimus, dazed by the events, hurried to where men were removing debris to find the rest of the living members of Philemon's *familia*.

Beneath two beams that had once held up the ceiling of the atrium, they found the bodies of Philemon, Apphia, and Archippus, crushed and lifeless. Philemon still held the papyrus in his hand containing the cherished letter of Paul to the Colossians that he had been reading in the morning worship. With reverence, Onesimus withdrew it from the stiffened fingers and fastened it under his own tunic.

When the bodies were removed from the rubble and placed on stretchers hastily made from the wreckage, Onesimus felt orphaned, desolate, and wordless. Only a few people were still alive. Of these, only two were conscious: the clerk, Theseus, and the cook, Croto. Glaucon was unconscious but alive. Everyone suffered broken arms or legs and were in shock, moaning with pain.

As Onesimus walked from one to another of his dead loved ones and friends, the sight was too much for him. He sat down besides Helen's still form and wept.

"What would life be without you. . . . Everyone else is gone. . . . Lord, don't let her die." He put his arms over her lovely body and held her face cupped in his hands.

Onesimus's friends tenderly bore her and the other survivors to the carriages where their wounds would be tended. Onesimus sat on the grass, trying to pray. He found the words meaningless, and a deep emptiness and despair seized him. Suddenly, he decided he would at least be a man.

He rose and walked over to join Papias and his friends who now stood at one end of the garden trying to decide what to do next.

"Thank you, my brothers. Your coming has saved my life, Helen's, and the few survivors of our *familia*. Thank you, Bishop Papias."

Papias, his arms around his young friend, spoke for the group. "Onesimus, our dear brother, this catastrophe is too much for any human being to bear. Only our Lord, made perfect through his suffering, can enable us to bear it. At your deepest level of need, dear Onesimus, the Lord is near to help you. Trust him and you'll come through this hopelessness."

The words of affection and counsel comforted Onesimus and

raised his spirits. His mind was too dazed to think clearly, but he wanted to do all he could for Helen and the others. He welcomed Papias's next suggestion.

"Let's take Helen, Glaucon, and the rest of the survivors to Hierapolis as soon as possible."

The physician Hymanaeus nodded. He had done all he could under the circumstances. As a Christian physician, he was ministering not only to the Philemon family but to any others who needed his help.

"As soon as I've done all I am able for those who need me here, I'll be back at your house, Bishop, to do what I can for them."

"Thanks for your presence and help," Papias responded. "Onesimus, you should accompany Helen and the others while we join our fellow Christians and other helpers in searching the ruins for anyone still alive. Protagoras, you and two or three of our churchmen remain to guard the bodies of the dead. Gorgia, get some help to dig a long trench here in the garden. Tomorrow we'll return to bury their physical remains. In the morning during our worship, we'll celebrate the victory over death won by our Lord Jesus and now shared by these dear ones."

Turning to the victims, Papias demonstrated his sympathy. "Onesimus, ride in the carriage with Helen so you'll be near her as we take her to our home in Hierapolis. We'll see to it that your horse is back in the stable by evening. I'll stay here with the others to do what we can for the living and to prepare the dead for burial. Sappho will ride with you. Hymanaeus will join you before long. The Lord be with you!"

18

By early afternoon, Helen was safely in bed in one of the guest rooms of Papias's house where Onesimus had spent the previous night. Hymanaeus arrived as night came, after having cared for the living among the ruins of the devastated city. He dressed Helen's wounds, bound her broken legs with splints, and gave her medicine to enable her to rest.

"She'll regain consciousness within a few hours," he said hopefully. "Evidently, she's received a brain concussion. . . . Let's hope and pray it's not too serious. Since she's breathing normally, I think it's not critical, but some time will be required for her full recovery. In the meantime, Onesimus, I'll pray for her and you in addition to caring for her physical wounds."

"Thank you for your kindness and assurance. I need your prayers as much as she does—not physically, of course, but spiritually. It's been a blow to me—my faith is really being tried!"

"I understand how you feel! A wounded and injured faith is sometimes more difficult to heal than a wounded body! But from hearing and seeing your witness during the last several months, I'm confident your faith will recover and be stronger than ever!"

"Well, I hope so. . . . I wish I felt so confident. . . . You see, all the tests of my faith in the love of God have come through the terrible human evils I've witnessed. But this . . . this horrible convulsion of the earth . . . is . . . is . . . just too much for me."

"I understand, young friend." The kindly physician put his arms around Onesimus's shoulders. "As we trust the Great Physician to heal Helen's wounded body, let us trust him to heal our spirits!"

"Please pray for me," Onesimus whispered as the man gripped his hands and left.

For the next hour, Onesimus sat by the side of Helen grieving, hurting deep within. "My mother . . . Philemon . . . Archippus!"

As he called their names, he knelt by the bed and wept with uncontrollable sobs. Then he tried to pray. For a few moments the sobs ceased and he was quiet.

"Dear Lord, I thank you for Helen's escape. . . . She could have died, too!"

The storm was over, but the fog had not lifted.

Sappho entered with a lighted lamp.

"Papias has just arrived," she said encouragingly. "He'll be in to see you in a few minutes. We're so thankful Helen's going to recover!'' She smiled and Onesimus noted her genuine concern.

''Thank you, Sappho! All of you are so kind. Please tell the bishop I want to see him as soon as he's free. He has the burdens of so many. All of us need his love and faith right now.''

The door opened and Papias entered with his two sons. Sappho retired.

''How is she?'' Papias inquired anxiously.

''Hymanaeus thinks she's suffering from a mild brain concussion along with her broken limbs, but he says she'll recover consciousness soon.''

''Thank God,'' the bishop exclaimed. ''And how about you?''

''I'm stunned and hurt. So many questions and doubts fill my mind. I can't think clearly about it all. But tell me, did you find many more of our Christian community still alive?''

''Not many. One of the deacons and his wife escaped by some miracle. And Glaucon, Theseus, and Croto are still alive. Their bodies were shattered but, like Helen, the convergence of two beams sheltered them and they'll recover. I join with you, Onesimus, in thanking God for Helen's escape and theirs.''

Papias's tone suddenly became more solemn. ''I have one more piece of bad news,'' he began. ''The only part of Philemon's estate swallowed by one of the chasms was the shop and storehouse where all the materials and finished cloth were stored. The office and the safe containing the money, jewels, and records were buried. I regret to tell you, but there's nothing left of Philemon's houses and your rich business. The only material things you and Helen now possess are a bit of clothing and a few objects of little value we were able to salvage from the ruins.''

Stunned by this revelation, Onesimus was silent. ''Is there nothing left with which to begin our business again?'' he asked helplessly.

''Nothing as far as I could see. The huge crack in the ground is truly a chasm. It appears to be bottomless. We were concentrating on saving those still living and removing the dead bodies from the ruins of the atrium. There were other gaping holes in the ground all around, and none of us realized that all your prized looms and

dye works, your cloth and your capital are . . . gone!'' He spoke
sympathetically with his hand on Onesimus's arm.

"But . . . but . . . what can we do? Helen and I have no home . . . no
way to make a living. . . .''

"You still have each other—praise God for that! You have
youth and life and our Lord's continuing gift of his Spirit. And
you're always welcome to make our home your home!''

"Thank you, Papias.''

Dry-eyed and empty of mind and heart, Onesimus sat staring at
the symbol of a cross in the center of the wall. It was similar to
the cross in Papias's atrium where Onesimus had stood earlier that
day to give his witness to the assembled church. He had felt
warm and joyful even as he delineated the tragic happenings in
Rome and Pergamum and the faith that gave these first martyrs the
victory. Could he ever again speak so freely and hopefully?

Papias and his two sons sat in silence, conscious of the struggle
going on within their young friend.

"Well, at least we have each other!'' Onesimus spoke at last.
"As you say, we're young, I'm strong, and it appears Helen will
recover. We have you as our friends. Thanks for your help and
encouragement. . . . Somehow we'll come through!''

As he spoke, the words seemed hollow, as if someone else had
spoken them.

"Yes, you will make it by God's help. Remember Paul's words
as you read them to us. I may not quote them exactly, but this is
what I know he would be saying to you. 'Be happy in the Lord,
Onesimus; he's very near. Don't worry about anything. Let your
needs be made known to God with prayer and thanksgiving, and
the peace of God will keep your mind and heart!' ''

"Please, Papias, I can't stand to hear any more of Paul's
words. They were true for me yesterday, and with part of my mind
they're still true. But right now, I can't accept Christ's peace in
the depths of my heart. . . . Forgive me. It may be my pride of
intellect, but there should be some rhyme and reason even in the
worst horror that we've experienced today, and I can't see it. But
one thing I promise you: as stubborn and intractable as I am in
wanting a reason, I won't renounce the faith in God, the Father of

our Lord Jesus Christ, whom you ask me to trust and whom Jesus,
from the words of John, commands me to trust. Right now, I
can't. I'd give anything if I could. My feelings are so hurt and
torn. Please keep praying for me that before too long, even though
I can't see and understand this great mystery, I'll be able to trust
again. . . . Right now, it's just too much for me.''

Silently, the bishop took Onesimus's hand, embraced him, and
gently said, ''You're exhausted and too hurt to think. Don't
apologize for your honest feelings. The shock of this day, the
weariness, are too much for you. What you need is sleep. Sappho
and Arias will care for Helen. Perhaps when she awakens and
you've had a good night's rest, you'll think more clearly. Soon,
by the grace of our Lord, the gift of a strong faith will return.
We'll be praying for you.''

''Thank you, dear friends. I must get some rest, but now I want
to be alone with Helen for a little while longer.''

''When you're ready, I'll show you to your room,'' Protagoras
responded. They all embraced. Papias and his sons left the room.

Helen's medicine was beginning to take effect, and she slept
more easily. Sappho came in every few minutes to apply hot
towels to her bruises. Onesimus sat holding her hand, so limp and
lovely. He tried to think. He tried to pray, but a block was in his
mind. He knew he could not go to sleep yet.

Suddenly, it dawned on him why Cerinthus's *gnostic* teachings
were so attractive. In times like this, one did not have to blame
God the Father for the evils of natural disasters. According to
Cerinthus and other Gnostics, the Father of Christ had not created
the earth and our human bodies with such frailties and limitations.
Instead it was ''the Evil Ruler of this world.''

For the first time in that terrible day, Onesimus almost laughed.
*This is such an easy escape from facing the great mystery behind
the eternal Father's ways in the creation of the earth and humanity and in completing and perfecting that creation,* he thought. He
had seen the falsity of such an escape so clearly when he was with
John. Why hadn't he recognized it now? To accept this easy but
false answer to the tragedy of the day would be to denigrate God
the Father to a continuing struggle with an evil god or gods. This

would make the mighty faith of John an illusion, for John had said
several times that Christ the Word was with God in the beginning.

> Through him all things came to be; no single thing was created
> without him. All that came to be was alive with his life, and that
> life was the light of men. The light shines on in the dark, and the
> darkness has never mastered it.

The words of John were so clear and powerful that Onesimus
could not forget them.

"I'm in that darkness," he groaned to himself. "I can't understand
it, and so I rebel. Maybe the Lord will restore the light to me. Right
now, I'm in utter darkness. Somehow, dear Lord, show me the light!"

For the first time since before the earthquake, he'd prayed a
hopeful prayer!

Onesimus fell on his knees by Helen's bed. Still holding her
hand, he wept softly. He knew the battle within himself had just
begun, but he turned it loose for the moment, knowing it could
wait until the morrow. Kissing Helen on the cheek, he went out to
find Protagoras.

"We have an extra room. Arias prepared the bed for you."

Protagoras took Onesimus by the arm and led him to the room,
where they found towels and a basin of water. After he had bathed
and rested on the bed for a few minutes, he fell asleep with
exhaustion.

He awakened in the morning light as the sun was just rising.
Pulling his tunic around him, he hurried to Helen. As he entered
the room, he was met with a smile by both Sappho and Arias.

"She's so much better!" Arias announced. "She's moved her
hands several times. Soon she may regain consciousness."

"We're glad you are here," Sappho added. "I was on my way
to wake you."

Onesimus thanked them eagerly and went to Helen's side to
take her hand.

"My dearest, can you hear me?"

Slowly her eyes opened.

"Onesimus. . . . Where am I? . . . What happened?"

"You're all right now, my precious one! Just rest and go back to sleep!"

"But something's wrong with my legs! What's happened?"

"There was an earthquake. Your legs are hurt, but you'll be all right."

"I remember now," she said with fear in her eyes. "As Father was reading, a sudden noise filled and shook the room. The last I remember was the ceiling falling in on us. Something struck my head. . . . It was terrible!"

"You need to rest now," Onesimus urged as he bent over and kissed her. "We'll talk about it when you're stronger."

"But tell me. . . . Is anyone else—?"

"Yes, dear." He knelt beside her and took both her hands in his. "But close your eyes and rest."

Sappho came with the medicine that would help her sleep. Helen took it and closed her eyes. "I want to know. . ." Soon she was sleeping again.

"Thank the Lord!" Sappho said softly.

For the first time, Onesimus looked at the two young women who had cared for Helen. Both were lovely Ionian matrons with dark hair and eyes. Sappho was plump; Arias slim and petite. He thanked them profusely.

"You go and rest now," he told them. "I'll stay with her until she awakens."

During the hours he sat by her side that morning, he tried desperately to sort out his thoughts and pull his faith back together, but he was not successful.

When Helen woke up, she insisted on knowing it all. As tenderly and with as much assurance as possible, Onesimus told her the tragic story. She was braver than he expected.

Her eyes brimming with tears, she exclaimed, "Mother—mine and yours . . . Father, Archippus . . . all . . . all . . . dead! I can't believe it!"

"Neither could I. Yesterday was the most horrible day of my life. I'd heard of terrible earthquakes in many parts of Ionia and Asia, but I never thought that we'd be the victims."

He tried to reassure her with the strong faith he wanted but did not have. It was hard going. He quoted the same words Papias had used to comfort him the day before. *Wonderful words if they're true*, he thought as he said them.

Helen listened and smiled through her tears. Her faith was simpler and stronger than his.

He would have to tell her of his rebellion—this seething bitterness even worse than his sorrow. He couldn't tell her. She needed to regain her strength first.

"This afternoon, dear one, I must go with Papias and the other able-bodied Christians—the only family you and I now have— back to the ruins of Colossae. We must reverently bury the bodies of these our family and friends and trust God for the resurrections."

He said the words of his dimmed faith, for he knew she needed them. He could not let her down now.

"Some way, somehow, God will take care of them as he will us!"

The afternoon was like a nightmare for them all, but Onesimus's rebellion made the bad dream seem ever more loathsome. When they arrived on the scene of the disaster, they found some of the survivors still stumbling over the rubble, prying under beams and columns. Some of them cried and mumbled in madness. Others sat stupefied with grief watching the malignant scene. The stifling smell of death was in the air. It could only be kept out of the lungs by tying cloths around mouths and noses. Several of the Christians from Hierapolis had remained on the scene all night to help search for the bodies of relatives or friends and to guard the bodies of Philemon and his *familia*. These watchers were covered with the smoke and grime and were utterly exhausted. They had dug a trench in the garden and covered the bodies with sheets they had found in the ruins of the bedrooms. Papias thanked them and bade them return to Hierapolis, but most of them chose to remain.

Onesimus, his grief weighing heavily on his chest and holding his head as in a vise, was shown the body of his mother. He pulled back the sheet and looked at her once beautiful face, now swollen beyond recognition. Hurriedly he covered it and told Papias that he did not want to see any of the others.

The corpses were placed in the trenches and covered with earth. All stood around the spot as Papias spoke simply and hopefully of the tragedy. He called on Onesimus and all present to look beyond the things that are seen to those things unseen, for what is seen passes away, and what is unseen is eternal. Onesimus knew he was quoting from Paul's second beautiful letter to the church at Corinth, but he found the unseen victory difficult to achieve.

Papias continued to read from the letter:

> We know that if the earthly frame that houses us today should be demolished, we possess a building which God has provided—a house not made by human hands, eternal, and in heaven. . . . God himself has shaped us for this very end; and as a pledge of it he has given us the Spirit.
> Therefore we never cease to be confident.

Papias's strong, deep voice sounded over the cries of mourners still digging for their loved ones or a few of their cherished possessions. Onesimus listened and watched with an outer quiet the other Christians took to be a strong faith. If they only knew how bitter and disturbed he was. He could hardly think of himself as he had been yesterday—so calm, so sure of the love of God.

Now he heard Papias concluding with a sentence from Paul that had often challenged him but that now had a dull ring in his ears.

> The same God who said, "Out of darkness let light shine," has caused his light to shine within us, to give the light of revelation— the revelation of the glory of God in the face of Jesus Christ.

There had been a light shining in the face of Jesus. He had seen it in Paul and Peter and in the faces of the young martyrs in Rome. He had seen it in Tyrannus and Joanna, Tavius and Antipas. He wished he could see it now within himself. Yes, the light was in Papias's face as he spoke in the putrid air, having pulled off the cloth mask from his mouth and nose. Onesimus was glad. He wished he could regain it, but he had only darkness and moaning within.

That night he sat by Helen's bedside. She was much better. The color had returned to her cheeks beneath the bandages over her head.

"You're so beautiful," he spoke tenderly. "You're all I have now, my dearest."

"Thank the Lord we have each other; but even better we have his living presence, Onesimus. He'll be with us and those dear people. How gracious is the providence of our heavenly Father."

Onesimus described the service in the still green garden surrounded by the ruins of their once beautiful home. He quoted the words Papias had used. Onesimus wanted his wife's faith to be strong, and he would not hurt her any more than he could help. He told her about the loss of the business, the looms and dye works, the cloth, and the money. Much to his surprise, she responded with a smile.

"Our treasure is now in heaven, dearest one, where moths and rust can't get it or earthquakes break in," she paraphrased.

Of course, she always had plenty of material things, he thought. *She doesn't understand what this means. But that's just as well. I'll let her get stronger before she realizes the full weight of it.*

The next morning, a memorial service was held in the atrium of Papias's home. Helen was brought in on a cot and sat by Onesimus as the beautiful words of Paul and Peter were read. Hymns of faith and praise were sung, and Papias offered prayers of thanks for the lives of the fine Christians who had so unexpectedly experienced the victory of their Lord.

Papias read from Paul's first letter to the Corinthian Christians.

"Death is swallowed up; victory is won!" "O Death, where is your victory? O Death, where is your sting?" The sting of death is sin, and sin gains its power from the law; but, God be praised, he gives us the victory through our Lord Jesus Christ.

Therefore, my beloved brothers, stand firm and immovable, and work for the Lord always, work without limit, since you know that in the Lord your labour cannot be lost.

Could this really be true? He had once found such hope in it. Certainly, it had been true for Paul. His labor was not lost or wasted—or was it? Onesimus was ashamed of himself for his black thoughts.

That night as he sat by Helen as she expressed her joy over the victory their mothers, her father, and Archippus had won, Onesimus was compelled to share his thoughts. He could dissemble no longer. He told her of the darkness that had entered his mind as he rode into the horror of the earthquake's toll. Tears came to her eyes. She had wept that morning as Papias spoke of their dear ones, but had wiped her eyes and sung with the others the song of the resurrection. Now visibly distressed, she took his hand in hers.

"Oh my dearest Onesimus, this can't possibly be you, my strong arm of faith! You, who've won so many battles with doubt after the terrors you witnessed in Rome. How could you express these terrible thoughts? God's still with us. Trust in God, and also in Jesus."

"By all that's beautiful and holy, my dearest, I wish I could. But my mind still rebels. I simply can't let my mind trust a mighty God who could either permit or will that the earth should be so senseless and unconcerned with our frail human lives. I know there's love—victorious love. I've seen such love matching the inhumanity and lovelessness of human evil; but how can God love and let this happen? It's just too much!"

Helen gripped his hands. With a strength he did not know she possessed, she said, "There are some things, dear Onesimus, many things about our human life that are mysteries. We can't understand them now. But if you believe in the love that shone in the face of Jesus, in Paul and Peter, and in your mother and mine, can't you trust that love, even if you don't understand?"

"I do believe in that divine love. I've seen it in these great spirits. Pray for me, dear one, that the time will come when I can trust as I once did. For now, though, this contradiction of love is so abhorrent to everything in me that my mind seems shut. I can't change it. Since God is love, then some way, some time, he'll restore the joy and assurance I once had. Right now, I'll just have to live in the darkness and make the most of it.''

19

uring the days that followed, Papias tried several times to help Onesimus overcome the blackness of depression that engulfed him. Each time they conversed, Onesimus seemed to be farther away than ever. On the third morning after the earthquake, Papias invited him to join him in his study.

"As your bishop and friend, I want to be of any help I can as you pass through this time of soul darkness. In my own experience, there was a time when I was just as rebellious as you are. Remember, even our Lord as he hung on the cross shared your feeling of utter abandonment. In spite of the *gnostic* teachings you've described, though Jesus did feel forsaken, he wasn't left alone. The Father was there with him. We're told of the last cry from the cross: 'Father, I commit my spirit into your hands!' ''

"Yes," Onesimus affirmed, "Mary has been emphatic in her witness to his final hours. She declared that at the ninth hour Jesus cried those words of trust in his Father as with a loud voice he breathed his last. She and John were horrified when Cerinthus quoted John Mark as saying the only words at the end were 'My God, why have you forsaken me?' Cerinthus insisted that Christ had departed from the life of Jesus before the crucifixion because God is too great to suffer with us! John and Mary rejected this as wrong. They both insist that even though Jesus felt forsaken, the Father was with him. His last cry was a cry of faith!''

"So it was with me, Onesimus. A short time after I was found by Christ through the apostle Paul, I saw my dear wife dying with a malignancy, and I couldn't help her in her pain or stay the hour of her death. I prayed, but she didn't get well. I couldn't pray any more. I, too, felt abandoned by God. Then, as I waited in the darkness, after several days faith in the love of God did return.

What a precious gift! Some day, Onesimus, faith as a living trust
will be yours again. Now in your darkness, hold on to the light
that's still there even though you can't see it!''

Onesimus was deeply touched by Papias's honest confession of
his own time of rebellion.

"I'm glad for you, Papias. I love and respect you highly. I'll
hold on to the light of our good news. I'd won the battle with my
doubts after I witnessed the inhumanity and brutality of Nero's
persecutions and the martyrdom of Antipas. The difference is that
in those human events there were dignity and courage in Paul,
Peter, Antipas, and dozens of ordinary Christians who welcomed
the opportunity even in death to witness to their faith. They
suffered from the human abuse of freedom, and I can see meaning
in their suffering. I think—though who can be sure—that I could
have stood that kind of test. But in this . . . there's no shred of
dignity left. When God the creator makes a world that suddenly
swallows up or crushes such beautiful persons as my mother,
Philemon, Archippus, Apphia, and countless other noble spirits . . . to
love and trust that God is beyond me."

Onesimus paused for a few moments and put his head in his
hands. Soon, he continued speaking in firm voice.

"How can I ever square all this violence with the infinite love
and goodness of God the Father and creator? Jesus taught us to
pray that God's will be done, and he even committed his life to
him on the cross. God is to blame for this, because humanity
can't be responsible for an earthquake! But how could a God that
can do this be good and loving? But if he's not good and loving,
then how can he be God, the almighty Father, creator of heaven
and earth—the cosmic Christ Paul says is in, through, and above
everything? You can see my dilemma—my mind's too small and
weak to answer this. After seeing the horror of these three days,
the thousands dead, and the crazed grief of the survivors, I keep
asking how Jesus could say that we shouldn't let our hearts be
troubled! 'Trust in God,' he said, 'and trust in me, too.' I *can* trust
a good man such as Jesus, but he wouldn't permit this kind of
catastrophe if he had the power to stop it. His Father, the supreme
God who knows even when a sparrow falls, must have the power

to stop it. But then the supreme mystery is why God doesn't use this power. Paul's exclamation is my only answer, but it's still a question for me. 'How deep is the wealth of God's wisdom and knowledge, how unquestionable his judgments. His ways are past understanding.' ''

"Why don't you trust God even when you can't understand?" Papias interjected.

Onesimus smiled a wry smile. "I guess I'm right where Job was in the misery of his suffering. All he and I can do is to humble ourselves before the disturbing mystery and ask why."

"Yes, Job never understood why he suffered such calamities," Papias mused. "He also didn't believe it was brought on him because of his sins, as his counsellors claimed. But he did recover his love for the Almighty."

"So with me. All I can do is to say with Job that I know God can do anything, and God's purposes can never be stopped. Therefore, I speak of things I don't understand that must be too wonderful for me."

Onesimus stopped to think for a moment. "Yes, I'll continue to love God—the God Job knew even before Jesus Christ and continued to love. Nevertheless, I can't help rebelling at the dark mystery, the hiddenness of God. I don't renounce my faith in him even in the darkness, but right now I'm unable to live and act on it! Like Job, I abhor myself and repent in dust and ashes, but I can go no further."

"I understand. Such trust is given as a precious gift. It didn't come to me at first, but it *did* come, and it'll be yours again, of this I'm sure. The Loving One who has begun to live and speak through you won't let you go. Someday the joy of your faith will be restored and you'll continue your wonderful ministry!"

The two embraced, and Onesimus went back to Helen. He was now able to see a very small light in his darkness.

"Bishop Papias is a friend and brother, indeed," he said to Helen as he entered her room.

As Helen recuperated in the days that followed, Onesimus took long walks along the streets and into the countryside. The brown leaves falling from the trees and the cold winds of early winter matched his spirits. Several times he saddled Solon and rode along the River Lycus. He could not bring himself to go near the ruins of Colossae, so he generally rode to the west or through the fields to the foothills of the Cadmus Mountains to the favorite spot where he and Helen had often sat. He wrestled with the paradoxical rebellion that had suspended his faith in the justice and love of God.

One day he dismounted in that spot. He sat, lost in thought, on the windward side of a huge boulder that some previous eruption of the earth had deposited. He looked out over the familiar valley with the ruins of Colossae just beneath him and the cities of Hierapolis and Laodicea dimly visible in the distance. He recalled John's words as he sought to convince Cerinthus and his fellow Gnostics that almighty God loved the world so much that he was not content only to be its creator. In addition, he sent his beloved Son to save doubting, sinning humanity from its evils and hurts. Did these hurts include earthquakes and disease? he wondered.

He remembered John's description of that last evening in the upper room at the Passover meal with Jesus and the other disciples. Onesimus had written down much of what John said describing the remarkable scene of the teacher, the Son of man, whom they believed to be the Messiah, the very Son of God. He insisted on washing their feet, performing the menial tasks one of them should have done but was too proud to do!

"He did this," John had explained, "as an example that we're to be servants of others, even willing to wash each other's feet."

Cerinthus and the other Gnostics could not think of God in Christ stooping so low, but Onesimus marvelled as he thought of the greatness of Jesus revealing the majestic glory of God, whose gracious self-giving love was so amazingly revealed in his Son.

Yes indeed, the words and acts of Jesus have a note of reality in them, Onesimus thought. He pulled from his tunic the parchment on which he had written much of John's account of the words of Jesus to his disciples on that last dark night together. As he read, he recalled John's emphasis on the caring love of the Father. Jesus had said, "This is my commandment, that you love one another as I have loved you" (RSV).

The words brought him a strange comfort, yet filled his mind with torment as he considered the seeming contradiction of such love permitting the tragedy of the earthquake. Onesimus sat looking out over the scene of the horror. His eyes were misty as he thought of his mother, Philemon, Archippus, and Apphia. Are they in the other dwelling place conversing with their risen Lord? Onesimus felt the conviction that Jesus' words about the love of the Father were the deepest truth. But the same old question would not be hushed. *If God is love, we ought to love one another,* he thought, *and accept even this contradiction in the world created by love. But how can we be sure that God is love? How could God the creator be love in the demonic evils of an earthquake?*

The unanswered question was like an ulcer in his stomach. As he looked at the scene below, he remembered that some of the Christians in Hierapolis had chosen the *gnostic* way of escape from the responsibility of caring for the hungry and homeless victims of the earthquake. They had excused themselves from sharing the suffering of these victims and from giving their physical energies, time, and money to care for them. *After all,* Onesimus said to himself with growing indignation, *they claim to possess the precious* gnosis *of God's love in Christ who removes them from all suffering and trouble! The supreme God is too great to suffer! It wasn't the God of love but the evil ruler of this world who created the earth with its quakes and floods and plagues.* The more he thought of the folly of their position, the angrier he became.

"These Christian Gnostics rest serenely in their proud and selfish *gnosis* that God is not responsible for the evil, so that they're not! They don't have to worry. God will take care of them!"

Onesimus rose to his feet and shouted these last words furiously. The sound of his voice startled his horse, and a rabbit jumped from a nearby bush and ran down the mountain to a safer hiding place.

"A false and evil distortion of the love of Christ!" Onesimus continued his soliloquy aloud with less heat. "John and Mary, Peter and Luke said that Jesus *did* suffer and that God was suffering with him. But the Christians who follow Cerinthus instead of Jesus are only repeating the deadly error of the old pagan belief that the gods are unconcerned with the suffering of men!"

Onesimus seated himself more calmly on a rock as he recalled an old Homeric hymn that described the gods of Mount Olympus enjoying their unending gifts as gods and making sport of

> the sufferings of men,
> and all that they endure at the hands of the deathless gods,
> and how that they live witless and helpless,
> and cannot find healing for death
> or defence against old age.

The only difference, Onesimus mused, *between the Christian Gnostics and Homer's view of the gods is that the Gnostics teach that Christ saves from suffering and death all those who have the* gnosis! *This I reject as completely as John does and Paul and Simon Peter did. Indeed, I prefer the honesty of the pagans to the hypocrisy of these false Christians.*

Onesimus rose and mounted Solon. He rode down the mountain path with his mind far from settled and more confused than ever. He knew he could never accept the *gnostic* version of the spurious love of God who never suffers, but he still could not accept the contradictions of a loving creator God who would permit the demonic evils of the earthquake and other natural disasters for which man could not be held responsible!

Returning to Papias's home in Colossae, Onesimus shared with Helen the confusing experiences of his hours on the side of the mountain in their old trysting place.

"John's description of Jesus' words on that last night are comforting," he told her. "If only I could do as Jesus asks of his disciples—trust in God and also in him."

Helen listened helplessly. She had always admired the strong, brilliant mind of her lover, but now she was overwhelmed by the stubbornness and pride that prevented him from having the unfaltering trust in the highest truth without all the answers. All she could do was listen and pray for a miracle to remove the block that prevented him from becoming the man of faith she had known and admired him to be.

At breakfast the next morning, Onesimus said only the fewest words possible. After breakfast was over, he kissed Helen and walked out into the street.

He walked aimlessly until he passed a tavern from where the laughter of several inebriated men could be heard. On a sudden impulse, he entered and walked over to sit at an empty table. As the waiter brought him a glass of wine, he listened as three well-dressed, happy men about his age extolled the exploits of a band of daredevil bandits in the mountains. Onesimus had heard of this gang. He knew that most of them, including his old friend Angell, were runaway slaves. He had never heard their deeds praised like this, so he listened with interest. These men apparently knew the bandits personally. From their conversation, Onesimus learned that they specialized in robbing the camel trains laden with riches from the Far East. By necessity, all trade had to come through a narrow pass in the mountains not far from Colossae. The favorite targets of the bandits were the wealthy traders from Rome who represented Nero and who supplied his court with gold and silver cups, plates, and other vessels and ornaments in addition to silks, beautiful and costly paintings, rare birds, and most of the tigers, bears, and other animals used for the spectacles in the Coliseum.

The very animals who'll someday be killing our brave Christians in Rome, Onesimus thought. As he listened, the "crimes" of the bandits seemed less and less objectionable. *Why not?* he thought. *The men they rob are the predators of civilization, feeding the insatiable maw of Roman lust for blood, beauty, and excitement. What better could one do than rob them? At least with this group there's no pretense, no hypocrisy as with the Gnostics—and*

in myself. They're Epicureans living for the day and the hour.
Maybe Epicurus had something that I've missed. I've known
freedom from guilt and shame, but I'm certainly not free from the
vain opinions arising out of confusions that trouble my soul.

Suddenly his thoughts were interrupted as one of the three said
to him, "Friend with the lonely cup, come over and join us."

Relieved of his confused soliloquy, he got up and took a chair at
their table.

"I am Onesimus, lately arrived from the late, great city of
Colossae!"

The men caught the bitterness in his voice, and one responded
appropriately.

"What you need is to drink up that good wine. You don't have
to tell us how you feel, friend. It's written all over your face.
What a sorry trick the gods or fate or whoever made this beautiful
but dangerous world have played on you, your family, and people!
I'm Aristippus, this is Pyrrho, and this is Theodorous."

As Onesimus shook the hand of each, he felt relief at no longer
having to hide his bitterness.

"Thanks for your welcome. I gather from your names that you
men are Epicureans. I'm familiar with the original writings from
which you borrowed your copies. You couldn't have chosen more
interesting philosophers than these!"

"Well, Onesimus," Pyrrho responded, "perhaps some of our
medicine will do you good in your bitterness. Or do you prefer the
stoic way of grinning and bearing it?"

"No, at times I've preferred to think of myself as a Stoic, but
lately I like the realism of old Epicurus himself. I certainly agree
with him in the sensible question of how any truly divine creator
could've made so middling a universe, so confused a scene of
order and disorder, of beauty and suffering."

"Hear, hear!" Theodorous joined in. "My namesake, Theodorous
of Cyrene, would've applauded your honesty and good sense.
Surely religion is hurtful to most people. There are more confusions and questions in religion than an intelligent mind can bear.
But, throw off your gloomy face, and let's drink up!"

Onesimus knew he had gone too far. He realized the faith of

Christians he had known and loved was a faith that brings salvation from fear and evil. He had seen too much of Paul, Peter, John, and the dear Christians in Ephesus, Smyrna, and Pergamum to doubt that. But he was tired of dissembling and hiding his feelings with the Christians. The last few days he had found it difficult to say how he felt even around Helen or Papias, for he did not want to hurt them.

"There's a certain liberty here that I've missed," he admitted as he drank a toast to a life of pleasure with reason as guide! Deep within, he knew they had missed a great deal that he had found, but he had lost the way of it, so why not let reason take over, he wondered. The momentary escape, at least, was pleasant.

20

*T*ired of fighting his doubts and unwilling to trust like a little child as Jesus said he must, Onesimus went back again and again to the tavern. The only difficulty he had with his new life was when he returned to be with Helen and talk with Papias—he could not share with them his present state of mind. In order to escape one kind of hypocrisy, he was forced to accept another with those whom he loved and who loved him. But he would not let himself think of the consequences of his present state as he abandoned himself to his way of escape.

Helen recovered rapidly, though it would still be some time before she could walk again. She knew a change had taken place in Onesimus. He would not talk with her about his inner struggles, though time and time again she sought to draw him out. She shared her concern with Papias.

"You must commit him to our Lord," Papias counselled her. "We can't fathom the greatness of the gift of freedom God has given us. Onesimus has suffered deep wounds in his mind and heart. As you know, he's always possessed what might be called an 'Aristotelian mind.' He wants visible, sensible proof of the love of God that can overcome the horror from the earthquake experiences. You and I will have to understand and accept him as he is and pray that the Spirit will turn him around before too long."

"Oh, do you think he'll ever return to his strong faith and joy in our Lord?" Helen asked as she burst into tears. "I can't stand to see him draw farther and farther away from us as he goes deeper into the abyss of rebellion!"

"This is our test, little sister," Papias said kindly. "Our Lord is depending on us to trust, pray, and wait for his return. He will, I'm sure he will."

On the surface, it seemed to Helen the opposite was taking place. One night Onesimus did not come home when he was expected. She called Papias, and together they prayed for him.

"There's nothing we can do but wait and pray," he told her, "but that's perhaps the greatest work any believer can do!"

Onesimus did come later that evening around midnight. He knelt by Helen's bed as she put her arms around him, and her tears wet his cheeks as she held him close.

"Oh, my dearest one, can't you share with me what's happening? I know your struggles. I'll try my best to understand. . . . Please tell me."

Onesimus sat by her bed, holding her hand in his.

"My dearest, the last thing I want to do is to hurt you."

"But you're hurting me more by your silence than if you told me what you're feeling and thinking and doing. . . . Please."

"All right, dear one, but understand that I believe what I'm doing is for the best. I'm concerned about us, our future. I can't continue to depend on Papias for our living. I have no way of recouping the losses in our business or in my own mind. . . . The former is total, but someday I may recover my thinking. That's the reason I've been spending time with some friends I've met. I've decided to ride to the mountains and join for a while with Angell and the other runaway slaves who are now a band of bandits specializing in robbing Roman camel trains bringing the riches of the East to Emperor Nero and his court."

Helen looked aghast as he broke the news to her.

"Why—how could you?!" she cried in alarm. "What do you plan to do there? Surely you're not going to join them?"

"Yes, my dearest one, though it sounds strange and maybe even wrong to you, I've decided that it's the right thing for me now. They're robbing the predators of civilization who satisfy the Roman lust for blood, beauty, and excitement. I saw enough in one afternoon at the Coliseum with Marcia, Nicia, and their friends of the bloody gladiatorial combats and lions and tigers brought by these wealthy traders. Right now, they're continuing to supply the hungry animals tearing and devouring more and more Christian martyrs. I can't think of any better thing that I can do in my time of confusion than to join these desperate runaway slaves. They're stopping some of this nefarious trade that feeds the insatiable demands of Nero and his cruel followers."

"Oh, but Onesimus," Helen's shocked reply was said in desperation. "Surely you don't want to be classed as a criminal putting your life—and mine—in jeopardy again!"

"That's a real possibility for me, and I know it," Onesimus responded. "But you'll be safe. Somehow, I believe this is what I ought to do. I'm so disgusted with the *gnostic* Christians who appeal only to the safe and easy way of following Christ. I prefer the open honesty of those who, lacking the physical freedom I have, are striking a blow at the evils of Rome. Since I can't follow Christ with the same enthusiasm I did before the earthquake, at least I'll be doing something positive—more than staying around here nursing my rebellion. Getting out with these brave men will help me get my thinking straight. I'll at least visit with them for a while. If it seems right, I'll join them. Maybe I'll also share with them the experiences of Christ I've had—seeds of faith that might grow in them and again in me. Besides, I'm so filled with inner rebellion and my mind is so confused that I can't continue dissembling before this wonderful *communitas* of Christians. Nor can I go to other churches, though they desire to take offerings for our support. The people from the Laodicean church, from Magnesia, and from several other churches have sent words of condolence, sympathy, and offers of support to us, urging me to come and share with them the witness I've gloried in. Yesterday I received a deeply moving letter from John, saying some of the same beautiful words about the love of God that I've heard him say before. He suggested that I consider coming to Ephesus again. But right now I can't take these offers. I must be free!''

"Onesimus, what are you saying? You are free! You've found the only true freedom as you, yourself, have said so many times.''

"I know, I know. . . . It sounds contradictory. But since the earthquake and the sensible evidence of a universe in which there seems to be no loving God, or else . . . or else. . . . Oh, what's the use? We've been over and over this. Since I can no longer trust in the love of God, though in my deepest soul I really want to trust, I'm not free to live in this wonderful community of love as I once did. I must go and act with my hands and body, doing things in the wilderness that will at least strike a blow, however small, at the evils in Rome. And while I'm there, perhaps I'll rediscover for myself what true freedom is! I thought I knew. Paul had it and so did Peter—and even Nicia and Marcia. I had it—a blessed gift—but I've lost it. I must go now, dearest one. Believe in me. Pray for me. I'll send you word and money to care for your needs. When I return, by God's grace, I hope to have fought through my present barriers of doubt. But right now I must go.''

He kissed her as she wept. She clung to him, speaking her love, assuring him of her prayers, begging him not to go. Then, seeing that he really was leaving, she dried her tears and propped herself on her pillow.

With a light shining in her eyes that Onesimus would never forget, she said courageously, "I'll pray for you and love you as I trust you to our Lord. Remember the words Paul wrote to the Corinthians, 'If the Lord's Spirit is there, there's freedom.' I have confidence in you and in our Lord that you'll return filled again with his Spirit and that we'll both know more fully than we ever did what his freedom truly is.''

Once again he kissed her, and she returned it with the love and passion of her whole heart. And then he was gone.

* * *

By the next morning when she told Papias of Onesimus's decision, Helen had recovered her composure. During the night, she had wept and prayed before she slept.

After being carried to the early worship and singing the hymns of love and faith, she remained with Papias in the atrium.

"I'm not surprised," Papias said. "He has to get it out some way. I wonder what he's going to do."

"He said he was going to the mountains to act with his hands and body in a way that will strike a blow, however small, at the evil injustices of Rome."

She recounted as best she could Onesimus's justification for visiting the bandits and likely becoming a part of them.

"He's unable to accept the invitation of the churches or to accept their gifts in his present state of mind, so he hopes his experiences with these bandits will lead him to a new trust in the Lord. He remembers his good experience with the bandits on Mount Mimas, and he feels this is his mission right now. I tried to dissuade him, pointing out the risks of again becoming an outlaw, but he'd thought it all through and, in spite of my pleading, left promising to return with a new trust in the Lord."

As she finished, she broke into tears. Papias put his arm around her shoulder.

"Helen, I know how this hurts you, but I'm not too surprised," he said comfortingly. "He feels caught here, and he knows something has to help him break the chain of his depression. Though what he's doing is very risky, he knows that. Getting away will give him the perspective he needs to return stronger than ever to his sense of mission and the faith to continue it."

21

*C*he sky was full of stars. A half moon gave Onesimus enough light as he rode out of Hierapolis. No one but Helen saw him go—she embraced him with a tearful good-bye. A small bag of his warmest clothes was wrapped within a bedroll tied securely behind Solon's saddle.

The hour was late, but Onesimus preferred it that way. He wanted no embarrassing questions and farewells.

He slowly walked Solon to the street that led to the Galatian Highway eastward through the mountain pass to Antioch and beyond. This was the route over which the camel trains must pass to bring the treasures from the East to Ephesus and thence to Rome by ship.

Once on the main road, Onesimus loosed the reins and spoke to Solon as the horse began the slow, steady trot that would bring them to the foothills before morning. As he rode out of the city, Onesimus realized that he was making another attempt to escape to freedom, just as he had as a runaway slave when he boarded the ship in the harbor at Ephesus and set out for Rome. Yet, this night seemed different. Then he was a slave escaping from external bondage, but he remained a slave to his guilt, his hatred for his master, and his fear of being caught. Now he was a free man, no longer a slave to Philemon but a "slave of Christ." He no longer hated Philemon—he had forgiven his master even before his master had forgiven him and set him free from physical bondage. Now Philemon and his family were buried in the mass grave in the garden of his once palatial home.

Onesimus's memory returned to the vivid experiences on his road to internal and external freedom.

But now I've lost some of that precious freedom, he thought. *Why am I leaving Helen and these friends who have been so kind to us? Why am I reluctant to share with the churches who wait to hear the story that could bring them so much hope and encouragement—the good news of forgiveness and the freedom to love and be loved? I feel like a fool!*

He knew the answer that he had given to Helen and Papias that had been framed so often in the reasoned logic he could not seem to break. He recalled Paul's witness to the Romans of his own bondage to the old nature.

"I can will what is right, but I cannot do it. For I do not do the good I want, but the evil I do not want is what I do. Now if I do

what I do not want, it is no longer I that do it, but sin which
dwells within me.

"So I find it to be a law that when I want to do right, evil lies
close at hand. For I delight in the law of God, in my inmost self,
but I see in my members another law at work with the law of mind
and making me captive to the law of sin which dwells in my
members. Wretched man that I am! Who will deliver me from this
body of death?" (RSV).

*I didn't understand what Paul was saying when I first read
those words,* he mused as Solon continued the steady gait to the
east. *The sin of a proud mind unwilling to accept the mysteries I
can't understand! This is my enemy like a dead body hanging
around my neck. I can't deliver myself, but, thanks to God and
our Lord Jesus Christ, I'll win the victory. Someday!*

"That's it!" he said out loud. "That's the reason I'm going to
the mountains—to think and pray like a little child until this body
of death can be lifted from my mind. While I do that, I'll meet
Angell and his companions and see if by joining them in their
worthy cause, I'll help us all receive the freedom that Christ has
in store for us!"

As he rode along in the early morning hours, he began to pray
for the first time in the long weeks of rebellion. "Dear Lord, only
you can set me free from this proud mindset that holds me
captive. Through your providence, I'll be truly free to return to
Helen and a new life of loving ministry to others."

During the remainder of the journey that early morning, he
prayed for Helen and for the freedom of the spirit within to set
him free from the law of sin and death.

As dawn came, Onesimus turned Solon away from the road and
into a sheltered place behind a clump of trees in the Cadmus
foothills. Taking the bedroll from the back of Solon, he tied the
horse to a tree, spread the roll, and lay down to sleep. By the
time he awoke, the sun had risen. He found the bread and cheese
the cook had prepared for him the night before and found a small
stream of water where he sat on a rock to eat his breakfast. Then
he led Solon to the stream for a drink.

With both of them refreshed, Onesimus rode toward the nearby mountain pass where he expected to find Angell and the bandits. The road wound around the valley in which the Lycus River began. The forest of pine, birch, oak, and fir grew luxuriantly along the road. It was broken intermittently by huge crags of rocks—mostly granite and limestone.

As he neared the top of the pass, the lowest point in the eastern range of the Cadmus Mountains, Onesimus felt the excitement of meeting Angell and the other ex-slaves he hoped would be his friends in the days ahead. He knew they would be hard to find, for, like the bandits on Mount Mimas, they were outlaws who needed a hiding place safe from detection. Fortunately, just before arriving at the highest point of the pass, he heard voices. He dismounted and led Solon until he was within fifty yards of the curve in the road around which the voices came. Leaving the highway, he found a place hidden behind a rock where he could observe a robbery taking place.

He crawled on his hands and knees to the edge of the rock where the scene below him was in view and watched with fascination the holdup of a small caravan of seven camels by ten rough, unshaved brigands with spears and swords raised threateningly.

The tall, bronzed leader of the bandits shouted orders to a small, very angry Roman merchant, who cursed the bandits in Latin. The chief of the brigands commanded the merchant and his crew of dark-skinned Indian camel drivers to move to a place off the main road where they were to unload their cargo of gold and silver cups, plates, ornaments, Persian rugs, and bolts of silk. One of the camels, Onesimus discovered from overhearing, was loaded with tea and spice from southern India.

"May the gods curse you, you *diabolus*!" the angry merchant yelled. "These goods are the property of his majesty, Emperor Nero, and his court. If you take them or harm us, you'll be caught and punished by the legionnaires in Ephesus!"

"Ha! We've heard threats like this before," the chief retorted, laughing. "If the great Nero wants your goods so much, why didn't he send his famed Praetorian Guard to escort you through our domain?"

Onesimus knew the answer to the chief's question. Burrhus, head of the Praetorian Guard, a Christian beloved by Onesimus, had told him the reason that such brigands were able to get by with this kind of robbery. Nero was so afraid of losing his crown, knowing at least two strong generals who waited for an opportunity to kill him and take over, that he kept a large part of his legions in the main population centers. They had no time to chase occasional gangs of brigands such as the ones on Mount Mimas or here. He would share this knowledge with the brigands if and when he became a part of them. At the moment, the scene below him strengthened his sense of doing the right thing in helping to strike a blow at Nero and his malevolent power.

"Shall I let him have it, Diocletus?" one of the brigands asked as he held his sharp sword close to the neck of the little Roman.

"Not yet, Donatus!" the chief answered. "I think such an extreme measure won't be necessary."

The merchant, shaking with fear, was ready to obey. He climbed hastily onto the back of the kneeling dromedary and, with a hoarse voice, said to his men, "Come. We have no choice but to follow them."

Grunting, the dromedary rose from its knees, the merchant astride its hump. The merchant, cursing under his breath, followed Donatus, the other six camels falling in behind. Each of the other brigands rode beside one of the camel drivers with spears and swords raised lest they try to escape.

As the captured caravan moved off the main road, Onesimus waited a few minutes and then mounted Solon to follow them. To his delight, he recognized Angell riding the white horse on which he had escaped after attacking Horace in Colossae. Angell and another of the brigands were covering the rear of the caravan.

This is my chance to let him know I'm here, Onesimus said to himself. *After the empty caravan is sent on its way, he can introduce me to his companions.*

The noise of the camel train enabled him to ride up to the side of Angell and his companion without being noticed.

"Hello, Angell, this is your old friend, Onesimus!"

Angell, startled, recognized his former comrade in slavery and smiled.

"Well by the gods, it is you, Onesimus! But what are you doing here?"

"I've come to visit and join you and your comrades in this exciting and worthy way of striking a blow at the evils and injustice of Nero and his cruel associates."

"It's good to see you, Onesimus." Angell rode ahead and called to his companion, "Hermas, this is Onesimus, an old friend from the late, beautiful city of Colossae. He and I suffered similar humiliations at the hand of our masters for daring to show our love to their daughters. He says he wants to join us!"

Hermas, looking over the strong, handsome figure of their visitor and his beautiful white horse, almost a match for Angell's, nodded with a smile.

"Welcome to our band of brigands! I am sure our chief, Diocletus, will be glad to have a strong fellow like you working with us. Are you a runaway slave like the rest of us? From what are you escaping?"

Onesimus smiled. "I was once a runaway slave, and I know how it feels. But right now I'm escaping another kind of slavery. I'll tell you about it later."

After the merchant had been relieved of his burdens and sent on his way, Angell introduced Onesimus to Diocletus and the other brigands.

"We're glad to see you!" Diocletus welcomed him. "We're a rough, untidy band of men, but we enjoy our freedom. We're also making a positive protest against the evils of Nero while avoiding our capture as runaway slaves."

"I can understand your feelings, for I was once a fugitive slave myself. Though I'm now a free man externally, I'm looking in these beautiful mountains for an escape from another kind of slavery. When we have time, I want to tell you my story and share with you some interesting news from Rome, where I've spent several years."

By this time, more of their number had arrived leading several donkeys. Onesimus dismounted and helped them load the new treasures from the East on the backs of the donkeys. Then, led by Diocletus, they mounted and rode together for several minutes. Part of the time the horses and donkeys walked in the shallow stream of the river to hide their tracks if some inquisitive legionnaires came looking for them.

Onesimus rode beside Diocletus and told some of his experiences in Rome. He particularly talked of Burrhus and explained that Nero's legions were spread so thin that very seldom did any of them try to find and capture mountain bandits.

At last, having ridden through difficult paths on the side of the mountain, they came into a clearing in the thick forest of pine and oak trees. Here was a small, clear stream running from a grotto in the side of the cliff. Onesimus was amazed to see the similarity between their headquarters and the home of the Mount Mimas bandits.

"What a beautiful place to call home!" Onesimus exclaimed as they dismounted and unsaddled their horses.

"Yes, for some time to come, this is it!" Diocletus responded. "It's a good place to camp. You're welcome to join us."

That evening and on several successive evenings, Onesimus shared his story with this strange fellowship of new friends. He received the same kind of response as he had with the bandits of Mount Mimas. The men were fascinated by his account of the apostles Paul, Peter, and John and their good news of Jesus of Nazareth. Angell added his part to the story.

"I knew, as did all the other slaves in Urbana's *familia*," Angell said, "that some remarkable change had taken place in the life of Philemon and his son. We were amazed to hear of your return, Onesimus, with the letter from Paul to Philemon. Though we never knew all that was in it, we were overjoyed to hear of your being set free. We hoped that our master would also become a Christian and set some of us free. Instead, he turned the other way, and became a harsher master than ever. He warned us not to expect the kind of freedom Philemon was giving some of his slaves. Philemon's acts were becoming a scandal in Colossae.

This made my slavery even more galling and led to the beating I gave Horace.''

''I was in Colossae at the time, Angell,'' Onesimus spoke his concern. ''We all wondered what led to such a drastic action and your dramatic escape.''

''Horace was taunting me at the stables for some things he'd heard I'd said about the difference between Philemon and his father. He warned me that if I continued to talk and stir up trouble, he himself would see to it that I got what I deserved— another forty stripes at his own hands! That was too much! I grabbed a horsewhip, struck him across the face with all my strength, and hit him with my fists and kicked him. Then, realizing that I'd just endangered my own life, I jumped on the horse I'd saddled for him and took off for these mountains! These men are very kind to me and have become my family —but . . . I, I wish I could have known your Paul and Peter and had a chance to be freed.''

Then Diocletus asked the question all had been wondering. ''If this 'good news' has accomplished so much for you and these people you tell us about—such as Philemon and his family and many of his slaves who are now free—why is it you're here and not back home with your beautiful Helen?''

Onesimus opened his heart to his newfound friends. Sharing the story of the earthquake and the questions that had darkened his mind and clouded his thoughts, he talked of his dilemma. Only a few of the men really understood. Diocletus, once a student of the philosophers himself, was one who did.

''So you're here with us not only to strike a blow at Rome, but to get your thinking straight and reclaim your lost freedom to love as your Christ loves?'' Diocletus asked.

He quoted Socrates's well-known saying, '' 'We're all like an egg; we have to hatch.' But that's sometimes the hardest thing in the world. But who am I to tell you how to get this inner freedom you seem to have lost? Of one thing I'm sure: You'll have to break out of the shell of your proud mind and hatch out into a stronger faith. I'm entranced by your story of the Christians in Rome and especially by the 'good news' your Christ is spreading over the

world through such persons as Paul, Peter, and John. I'm glad
you'll be here awhile. I, for one, desire earnestly to know more
about this Jesus. I, too, want to be a follower of Christ if you can
answer some of my questions.''

Several of the other men joined in with similar statements of
interest.

"All right,'' Onesimus responded warmly, ''if you'll take my
witness as one who believes but can't trust—as one who's
experienced what Jesus calls 'living in the kingdom of heaven'
and then lost the way! I need to find it again. Perhaps my sharing
with you will enable me to be free of this rebel self that must hold
out! In the meantime, I'm glad to share this exciting life with
you!''

During the days that followed, Onesimus joined this rugged
group of new friends in the systematic business of stopping the
camel trains carrying riches for the corrupt Nero and his Roman
court. In the evenings, he spent several hours sharing the stories
and teachings from his experiences with Paul and Peter, Mark and
Luke, and recently John. He was amazed to see the way these
lonely and desperate men listened to the good news of the love of
God revealed in Jesus Christ for all humankind.

*Something's happening in Diocletus, in Angell, Hermas, Donatus,
and several of the others,* Onesimus thought one night as he lay in
his blanket looking up at the stars. *It's something that could lead
them to the precious freedom in the love of Christ—a freedom I've
known and hope to recover as I regain my trust in the surpassing
greatness of God's mercy even in the terror of an earthquake.*

Even as he thought it, he understood what was happening
within him. It had happened before on that dark day after he had
seen his beloved Paul carried away to his trial and execution by
Nero's men. His mind went back over the blackness of that hour
when he walked aimlessly along the streets and suddenly found
himself in the Subura, where he had met Marcia, his first friend
and first enemy in Rome. He recalled how his witness to her and
forgiveness of her and her brother had brought him back to his
trust in the goodness and loving kindness of God.

Now, he thought with thankfulness, *as I share the good news of*

*Christ with these men, my own trust in him is returning. I'm like
Socrates's chicken in the egg.* He smiled to himself. *I'm beginning
to hatch! But unlike the chicken that hatches only once, it seems I
must continue over and over to pip my shell of pride.*

That night he prayed more earnestly than ever before for the
return of his trust in God, for Helen and their future. He went to
sleep, feeling for the first time in months a quiet peace that he did
not need to explain!

One evening as the men sat around the fire after dinner,
Diocletus surprised Onesimus by asking him to take his place as
leader in their work of stopping the caravans.

"Onesimus, you're so much better with words than I. You can
speak to those whom we're robbing in such a way that they and
others who hear about us will understand what we're doing and
why we're doing it. Who knows? We may develop some friends
who'll help us find external freedom someday!"

All the others joined in with similar pleas.

Reluctantly, Onesimus agreed to their request.

"I'll do what I can, but even at best, our future away from the
safety of this mountain is not very bright. But there are some
things we can do, perhaps, to gain the respect and support of the
people in the cities of Ionia."

He explained some of the measures he would take as their
leader, and they were all enthusiastically behind him.

During the next few weeks, Onesimus saw to it that only
caravans going to Rome with wealth for Nero and the unprincipled
men who supported him were robbed. All other caravans were
sent on their way with cargo intact and with the encouragement
and best wishes of the bandits.

In addition to this tactic, Onesimus arranged through the group
of young Epicureans he had met to dispose of the wealth they had
garnered from the Roman caravans. The young allies sold the
jewels and other valuables and used the proceeds to help the poor
and needy, especially the victims of the Colossean earthquake who
still were desperately in need of help to get a new start in their
businesses or trades. As word of the bandits' magnanimity and

generosity spread throughout Hierapolis, Laodicea, and all of Ionia, they came to be called the "Benevolent Brigands." Their young philosopher allies were delighted to act as partners with Onesimus and his generous bandits.

-------------------------------------*22*

apias and Helen were encouraged by what was happening in the mountains. Most of the Christians in Hierapolis did not know that the chief of the Benevolent Brigands was Onesimus, but as they heard of the bandits' works of charity, they were thankful that the Lord was using even the bandits to minister to his people. Some of those receiving help were friends who had suffered the most from the recent earthquake.

"What Onesimus is doing," Papias gladly told Helen, "indicates that someday soon we may expect his return. I surely believe his trust will be restored, but he'll still be an outlaw!"

"Thank God, even this may be cared for!" Helen replied with hope. During the weeks since Onesimus left, she had regained her strength, and her broken limbs had healed. She looked forward to the weekly visit of the young Epicurean allies, who brought her word, sometimes a brief letter with words of affection, and some money for her physical needs from Onesimus. She wrote love notes to him, always telling him of her prayers and hopes that he would return. Each week, the notes from him became more cheerful. As time passed as she prayed for him, she knew he would return.

The apostle John soon came from Ephesus, as he had promised to do ever since the earthquake. He had been delayed by problems in the Ephesian church with Cerinthus and the Gnostics.

Papias welcomed the old man warmly and invited him to meet Helen. She was overjoyed to meet this dear man of whom Onesimus had told her so much.

After embracing her, John expressed his profound sorrow over the loss of her father, mother, and brother and the tragedy of the earthquake.

"I've come to love your Onesimus as my own dear son!" he exclaimed. "I understand something of the shock of sorrow and loss that you both feel. But where is he now?"

Papias looked tenderly at Helen. He realized how difficult the story of Onesimus's loss of trust must be for her as he told it now to John.

"Onesimus had been given the gift of a faith that enabled him to accept the vicious storms of human evil and suffering resulting from sinful rebellion and the proud misuse of our human freedom. But it is *natural* evil that Onesimus cannot accept. Helen and I have tried to help him accept such evils as the earthquake with the same trust in the love of God in Christ, but with his philosophical background and intellectual pride, Onesimus can see no meaning, no shred of human dignity in the victims of natural evil."

"I can understand Onesimus's struggle," John said after hearing the details of the situation. "I, too, felt the same way after our Lord was crucified and the earthquake tore the curtains of the temple in two. But where is Onesimus now?"

"He's the chief of the brigands in the Cadmus Mountains!" Papias said simply.

John sat for a moment stunned by the announcement.

Slowly, he spoke with a chuckle, "So that explains the name these bandits have been given . . . the 'Benevolent Brigands'! I can see the hand of Onesimus here. But what have you done to bring him back and restore his faith?" The apostle's eyes flashed as he asked the question.

"We've waited and prayed. Through a band of young Epicureans here in Hierapolis, we've continued to write to assure him of our love and urge him to return. What more could we do?" Papias asked apologetically.

"Well, I don't know about you. Maybe that's all you could do, but it's not all I can do! I am going to find him!"

John spoke these words with some of the courage and boldness, Papias realized, that had given him the appropriate name "son of thunder."

"Equip me with two or three camels and let two of your young Christians attend me. I'm going to find Onesimus and, by the grace of our Lord, bring him back!"

Helen was thankful and excited beyond words. During the weeks and months that had passed, as the notes and letters from Onesimus had become more helpful, her own hopes had been lifted.

"The miracle is going to take place!" she had said to Papias many times.

The little caravan made its way slowly through the pass at the top of the mountains. John rode the horse Tyrannus had loaned him. When the caravan arrived on the other side of the pass, it turned around and started back towards the Lycus Valley. John looked impatiently on every side hoping to see the robbers. When they did not appear, he called a halt. They stopped in the narrowest part of the mountain pass and waited. In a few minutes, the robbers came, riding swiftly out of the rocks and trees on each side. With their spears and swords raised, they surrounded John and his little caravan.

"Why are you stopped here in the pass, old man?" he was asked demandingly. The questioning bandit had a black beard and long hair and was dressed in a soiled tunic with a leather belt and sandals. "Where are you going and what cargo do you carry?"

"Young man, I am John, servant of Jesus Christ and a friend of your captain. Take me to him at once!"

Something in the apostle's imperious voice and quiet authority impressed the young brigand.

"Well, old man, if that's what you want, come with me. You must be the aged leader of the Christians. Our captain has spoken of you often. I'm sure he will want to see you."

Turning to his companions, the bandit ordered, "Examine their packs. See what they're carrying and keep the other two travelers and their horses and camels hidden behind the rocks until we return!"

John followed the brigand through the rocks and trees on a winding path that led to a large opening on the side of the mountain. Tents had been set up, and over a burning fire a meal was being cooked. John saw Onesimus seated in a circle with other brigands.

"What have you there, Diocletus?" one of the brigands shouted.

"An old man who says he's a friend of the captain and wants to see him."

Onesimus jumped up in embarrassment and watched as the white-haired apostle was led into the circle by his captor. As they drew near, Onesimus recognized John and stood transfixed. He loved John, but with his heavy sense of guilt and shame, he was not ready yet to meet this courageous apostle of God's love. The blood drained from his face, tanned and brown from the sun. As John came closer, Onesimus could stand it no longer. He turned and, to the surprise of his companions, ran toward the woods. His heart was bursting with sorrow and self-loathing. He simply could not face the beloved disciple of the Lord. He did not expect what happened next.

The aged apostle broke loose from his captor and, his white hair flying in the wind, ran after the brigands' chief.

"Why do you fly from me, child . . . from your own father . . . from this old . . . unarmed man? . . . Have pity on me, child . . . do not fear. . . . You have still hopes of life . . . I myself will give account to Christ . . . for you!"

Onesimus reached the edge of the forest before he stopped to listen to the old man approaching him. . . . At least he would listen to what this man who was risking his life for him said. . . . His own heart was pumping wildly. . . . All the pent-up anguish of the weeks seemed ready to burst from his chest.

The apostle was catching up to him. "If need be . . . I will willingly undergo your penalty of death . . . as the Lord did for us. . . . I will give my own life in payment for yours. . . . Stand; . . . believe; . . . Christ has . . . sent me!"

Onesimus waited as the aged apostle approached him, out of breath, but with fire burning in his eyes. Seeing the tears of loving concern on the apostle's cheek, Onesimus ran to him. With arms outstretched, John embraced him. Then the dam broke. All the loneliness and shame, self-disgust and bitterness of the past months poured out of him. He wept on the shoulders of the beloved apostle.

Onesimus's fellow brigands watched the scene in utter astonishment. They had known that something unusual had brought this brilliant young man to join them. He had shared with them his story and his struggle with doubt since the earthquake, but they were unprepared to see their iron-nerved leader thus broken and weeping. After they had chosen him as their captain, Onesimus had proved ardent and effectual in robbing the merchants of Rome. He had led them in daring and successful exploits. More and more caravans were robbed, their leaders turned loose with their horses and camels to enter the valley empty-handed. The brigands had enjoyed the good publicity given them by their charitable distribution of the results of their work. Now they watched with avid interest as Onesimus took the old man's arm and led him into the forest where they could neither see nor hear what was taking place.

The aged apostle and the young rebel walked into the thick woods where they sat down on a fallen tree. After a time of silence broken only by the twitter of birds, Onesimus poured out his story. He described the appalling and bewildering experiences after the earthquake that had led him to leave the loving *communitas* of Christians and find a place with the brigands. He described the terrible scene as he rode into Colossae on that fateful day.

"The only thing that prevented me from going stark mad was finding Helen crumpled, hurt, and unconscious but still alive, and the deep-felt hope that even in this, Christ could somehow still be trusted! But my hope was dim. As I tried to pray, a black cloud of doubt and rebellion engulfed me. Nothing that I ever thought, imagined, or experienced prepared me for the darkness of that awful hour."

He burst into tears as he felt the arms of the beloved apostle around him. Onesimus spoke the question he had longed to ask for several weeks.

"Father John, how can I ever be forgiven by our Lord Jesus who suffered so much for me? How could you, Helen, Papias, and our fellow Christians ever forgive me for my failure to trust our loving Christ and for such a cowardly act as running away?''

''We forgive you, Onesimus, in the same way our Lord Jesus forgives us and you. That's why the Father sent his Son—to forgive and to set free. For the mighty God, our creator, father, and mother, loved the world so much that he gave his only Son that whoever believes in him wouldn't perish in doubt and fear and self-despising, but would find life that's abundant and eternal. This is our good news, Onesimus. You've heard it from the lips of Paul, Luke, and Simon Peter—and if anyone ought to understand forgiveness, it's Peter. Every one of us is like him. Peter denied Christ, and we forsook him and fled. So have you, and so has everyone at times. Isaiah confessed:

> 'All we like sheep have gone astray;
>   we have turned everyone to his own way;
>   and the Lord has laid on him
>   the iniquity of us all' (RSV).''

Onesimus was quiet. The early afternoon sun shone through the branches. For a time neither spoke. Only the song of birds could be heard. Tears continued to flow for the first time in months down the tanned cheeks of the brokenhearted young man.

''I understand, Onesimus, just how you've felt,'' John declared, as his own eyes filled with the tears of remembrance. ''For three wonderful years, I was unaccountably blessed by my nearness to our Master. I shared his teaching and witnessed his acts of love and mercy. I believed, as we all did, that he was the Messiah— the One sent from God to deliver us from the evils that mar our lives. But after seeing him treated so brutally and unmercifully, I too rebelled. Just as you asked after the earthquake, I asked, 'How could the Father to whom Jesus taught us to pray permit his Son to be subject to such tragic evil?' I too kept asking, 'Who's responsible?' For three days I was in the depths of doubts and despair.

''Then on the morning of that third day, I saw him as the risen Lord of all the universe! First, I heard Mary Magdalene tell how she'd gone to the tomb early in the morning and found the stone rolled away from the front of the tomb and the tomb empty. She ran to Simon Peter and me and tearfully told us that someone had stolen the Lord's body from the tomb. Peter and I ran to the tomb. I ran faster than Peter, but I didn't go in. I bent over and saw the linen cloths lying there and the cloth that had been around Jesus' head. When Peter came up, he saw the same thing and went in. Then I also went in, and at that moment I believed!

"It was by an act of faith that I saw the empty tomb, and later that night I saw him enter the locked door of the room in which we were hiding in fear. I heard him say to us what he's now saying to you. 'Peace be with you.'

"Now, Onesimus, he's saying to you, 'Trust in God even as you've trusted in me. The present ruler of this world has no power over you, for it's God my Father who rules, even in the earthquake and the storms!' So now you're called to believe where you can't see and to trust where you can't understand!''

Onesimus was deeply moved as he listened to John's impassioned words. Jumping to his feet, he placed his hands on the shoulders of this grand old man and sighed a long sigh of relief.

"Ah,'' he began, "at last I see, thanks to you, Father John! The witness of your own victory of trust over the terrible evils you saw thrust upon the best man who ever lived has opened the shut door of my lack of trust. I see now that living faith is much more than intellectual belief. I never stopped believing that God, the mighty creator, was supremely revealed in Jesus, but during these months, I've closed the door to his loving presence. My proud mind has demanded to understand the mystery of how the God of love could possibly have been in the earthquake with its evil and destruction. What folly! No wonder Jesus' summary of the commandments, that we should love God with everything in our hearts, souls, and minds, puts our *minds* last. I've put my logical, reasoning mind first. I wanted to *understand* before I *trusted*. I desired to see with my intellectual understanding before I believed with my whole heart and soul! I wanted to know what only God can know! How utterly foolish I've been!''

"Indeed, my son,'' John replied, "often the foolishness of this world is the wisdom of God, which, in our proud minds, we deny. You're so right, Onesimus; indeed God desires us to use our minds. But when we've gone as far as the mind will go, we must take the leap of faith and trust in the eternal love of God!''

"Yes, my reason refused to go with Cerinthus and the other Gnostics," Onesimus responded. "It would've been easier if I'd done so. But such an easy answer is only a delusion. I recall your saying that there's only one God, not an evil god and a good god. My mind told me that God isn't only the eternal *creator* but also the completer and perfecter of all things. I said this to Helen as we mourned over the still form of our first son. But as I faced the horror of the earthquake and the loss of most of what I held dear, I demanded to know how the Christlike God of love could be completing and perfecting anything in such indescribable agony."

Onesimus stood at his fullest height with his head uplifted as he declared, "Now, as of this moment, I trust that God the mighty creator is also the God of wise love who's still creating."

Onesimus paused for a moment. Reaching into his tunic, he pulled out a parchment containing the encouraging words of Paul in his letter to the Romans. "I understand what Paul was saying much better in this moment of new trust."

Onesimus continued with exultation. "Of this I'm confident; God is still creating, completing, and perfecting not only our little son, but also the earth with all its costly convulsions of quakes and storms. How? This is a mystery I can't understand, but where I can't understand, I now trust! Of this one thing I'm sure from the teachings of our Lord, of Paul, and of yourself: that God our eternal Father-Mother is not unacquainted with the grief of evil and suffering! Our God has come very near to us in our pain and anguish and bears it with us. This is what you've said so often, that the real love isn't our love for God, but God's love for us that's so deep he gave himself to us in his Son. God not only suffered with his Son but even brought him through death. As Peter said on the day of Pentecost, 'God took him through death because it was impossible for the pains of death to hold him.' ''

John rose to his feet and put his arms around Onesimus's shoulders. With quiet fervor, he said, "This, my son, is indeed the victory that overcomes the world. Our dear Lord has kept his promise not to leave us alone and desolate. Because he lives, we live as well. Therefore, Onesimus, let's trust that the mighty God, Father of our Lord Jesus Christ, is indeed overcoming the world. He's using for his righteous purposes the evils of the death and destruction of the earthquake. The kingdoms of this world have passed to our Lord and his Christ, and he shall reign forever and ever, alleluia!''

His voice had risen in a crescendo of joy and exaltation. His face was suffused with light that shone even in the shadows of the forest. Then he sat down again on the tree trunk. It was an awesome moment for Onesimus. Both were still for a few moments.

John broke the silence and said quietly, ''Onesimus, you've come a long way today. I'm thankful for the privilege of being here to share your new birth of trust. You and I know that this truly is the victory that overcomes the world, the victory of our faith!''

''How can I ever thank you for coming to share with me in this hour? I see clearly now that the way to faith is not resignation to terrible evils we can't understand, the way of the Stoics, nor is the rebellion and forgetfulness the Cynics and others practice. It's the way of trust in the caring Christ, whose love is eternal and never-failing. His gift of courage and hope is a thousand times better than any intellectual answer claiming to be total. Life is a gift. The gifts of family, health, friends, and wealth are not ours to keep—why should we be angry when they are taken away? My finite mind can't prevent the darkness from swallowing up the light, but in your realistic words, 'In Christ is life, and the life is the light of the world. The light shines in the darkness, and the darkness can never put it out!'

''Dear Father John, I'm blessed to have known Paul and Simon Peter and now you! How simple it all is once I surrender my proud demands for my own kind of proof. The biggest and most intelligent proof anyone could have, whether Aristotle or Plato or Epicurus or anyone else, is the love that shines in the life of Christ through you and these great friends of mine. And the love that shines in Helen! How is she?''

''She's a brave young woman, Onesimus, one you can't deserve any more than I can deserve to be loved by my dearest ones. She trusts you and is looking for your return. She said as I left, 'It'll take a miracle, but a miracle will take place.' ''

''And so it has! And so it has!'' Onesimus exulted. ''Praise to our Lord who, in his mercy, has again set me free. This time it's a freedom that neither life nor death, earthquakes nor principalities nor powers, height nor depth nor any other creature can destroy! But let's go, Father John, and let me tell my companions what's happened. They'll be surprised, and some may not understand, but I owe it to them to do my best. This is my first and most important witness!''

Taking the arm of his aged friend, Onesimus led him back into the circle of brigands. Then, simply and with deep conviction, he reminded them of his slavery and first freedom and his bondage to the false pride of a closed mind. He ended with a glowing witness to his new deliverance to the freedom of truth. They listened with awe. As he spoke, Onesimus knew that some of them would find the same Lord and his gift of freedom that he had found.

23

Riding his white horse, Solon, many times the only creature to whom he had been able to talk in the preceding months, Onesimus entered Hierapolis at John's side. When they arrived in Papias's courtyard, they were greeted by a rush of friends. Papias embraced Onesimus as did Protagoras, Gorgia, and the others.

''Please let me go to Helen,'' Onesimus said. They all understood as he left them to open the door to her room, then closing it behind him.

Their meeting was tender and full of joy. He sat by her chair—she was now strong enough to walk several steps—and told her of his experiences with the old joy and a new, added power and conviction.

"You've found a better freedom than ever, dearest one," Helen cried. "It's the freedom from a proud mind, now open and humble and filled with the spirit!"

"Yes, you were right. Paul said that wherever the spirit of the Lord is, there's liberty. I've found this freedom through the indescribable love of our Lord, whose spirit reached me through Papias's and your love and prayers and through John's willingness to give his life for me. I don't deserve it, but I accept it with humble thanks."

The next morning Onesimus sat with Helen, John, and Papias talking of the future. Onesimus was concerned about his status in the eyes of the law.

"I'm a robber and thief who should be punished according to the law."

"You're a robber and thief no longer," Papias declared.

"There's a law higher than the law of punishment," responded John, "and that's the law of love and forgiveness. We've forgiven you just as God has."

"And here's another pardon," Papias said with a smile. "It's one that you deserve no more than any of the others, a full pardon by Governor Lintullus of Hierapolis, who's also a Christian. I went to him yesterday after John left in search of you and told him the whole story. He was deeply moved by it all. Without my asking for it, he took out this parchment and wrote a full and unconditional pardon. He added a note giving his blessings and a request to spend an hour or two with you. He wants to learn more about the meaning of faith through your witness."

Once more, tears of gratitude welled in the eyes of Onesimus as he took the note from Lintullus. As he read the words, he gave another cry of amazement.

"This is another manumission like the one Philemon gave me!

Now I'm set free from my sin of pride, and by God's grace, I'll not submit again to the yoke of bondage!''

"Onesimus," John said, "I'd like to invite you and Helen to return to Ephesus with me, where we want to ordain you as an elder and you can act as my assistant. The church there has urged me to issue this invitation. Tyrannus wants me to give you his special welcome and urge you to come and let Ephesus be your headquarters. You can go into the churches of Asia and share your witness as you were doing when the earthquake stopped you. Much of your time, however, can be spent in Ephesus. There is much work of teaching and witnessing to be done. Right now, an openness and willingness exists on the part of many people to hear. My invitation includes the offer of a stipend to care for your house and living expenses. We can't pay you for being yourself, but with you and Helen together, and now free in the spirit, there'll be some wonderful years ahead! What do you say?''

Onesimus was astonished by the offer. "What else can I say?" he responded with exuberance. "There's hope, indeed, and the future's open. Helen and I will go with you in the freedom with which Christ has set us free!''

Part Five

The Interpreter

24

$\mathcal{O}$nesimus and Helen's return to Ephesus with John was celebrated on the first evening in Tyrannus's hall with great joy and enthusiasm by the Christian *communitas*. Many remembered Onesimus's earlier visits and his stories of deliverance from both inner and outer slavery. They recalled especially his interpretation of the last hours with the apostles Paul and Peter and the victorious spirit of the brave, young, Christian martyrs in Rome.

The church was fascinated by the story that had been rumored of his recent battles for faith after the tragedy of the earthquake at Colossae and his restoration by Bishop John. Young and old were intrigued to learn that Onesimus had been the chief of the Benevolent Brigands.

That evening the hall was crowded not only by members of the growing church in Ephesus but also by their family and friends not yet Christians who had come to join in the celebration. Adding to their enthusiasm was the knowledge that Helen was with Onesimus. The couple's love for each other and their marriage had been a favorite topic of conversation. The people anticipated seeing her now for the first time.

A hush of awe and expectancy stilled the excited company as Bishop John entered with Onesimus and Helen. The congregation stood with applause to welcome these persons who meant so much to them.

John raised his hand for silence.

As the people became quiet, he said with fervor, "Children of God's family in Ephesus, the one who was lost is found! Onesimus has returned home!"

A great shout rose from the people.

John again lifted his hand. "And with him is his beautiful wife,

Helen. With God's healing help, she is almost recovered from her severe injuries in the earthquake that took the rest of their family. They are here tonight with us to declare their renewed faith in the light that shines in the darkness that the darkness can never put out. In a few minutes, you'll hear Onesimus tell the inspiring story of his return to a vital faith after months of doubt and struggles. But before he speaks, let's sing the great hymn of the resurrection that Onesimus taught us. It was used in the first worship service in Rome after the martyrdom of Paul.''

The people with joyful voices sang together:

> ''Christ the Lord is risen.
> Every mind and heart rejoice!
> Alleluia! Alleluia!
> Death is conquered.
> Life is given!
> Alleluia! Alleluia!
> God is love and rules all things.
> We shall love as he loved us!
> Alleluia! Alleluia!''

When the song ended, John declared, ''Now I present my son and your brother, Onesimus.''

Onesimus addressed the group, his voice filled with emotion.

''Dear sisters and brothers in Christ, you overwhelm me by this outpouring of love. I can't deserve any of it. I, like Peter and the other disciples, have followed along away from our Master. In my despair and hurt over our great losses, I've failed him. For months, I was unable to give the witness to his victory of love and truth so needed by you and the people in other churches of Asia. No, I didn't lose my faith. With part of my mind I believed in Christ, but with my heart—the deeper self—I lost my trust!

''Our beloved Bishop John has followed our Lord in risking his life to bring me back to a deeper faith and fuller commitment than I've ever known before. I felt guilt and shame for giving over to my doubts and losing the ability to trust, because I've witnessed such victorious love in Paul and Peter, in Tavius, in Antipas and others I've known. Now all my guilt and shame have been wiped away by the forgiving grace of Christ ministered to me through our beloved John, and through Papias, Helen, and many others. I'm thankful for the privilege of sharing with you this journey from being lost to being found, for I know there are times in all of our lives when we find it easier to doubt and despair than to believe and overcome. As our spiritual father, Bishop John, has said so often, 'This is the victory that overcomes the world—even our faith!' Now let me tell you about it!''

Onesimus presented an hour of clear, straightforward description of his journey from shock and despair to a trust that used all the evidences of God's wise and loving providence, even though his mind could not grasp its meaning.

Everyone in the hall listened hungrily to each word. As Onesimus spoke, many of his listeners recognized their own times when blows were too great to be borne and rebellion and unbelief had robbed them of their trust. Others who had not yet come to an act of faith in accepting the forgiving love of Christ were able to see and accept themselves as forgiven and accepted by the Lord of the universe! It was an hour of new insight and new discoveries, new commitments and renewed faith, even for many who had come only out of curiosity.

"I'm now one of you," Onesimus concluded. "By the grace of God and the magnanimity and love of Bishop John, I'm among you as your pastor and servant, your friend and God's minister. I invite any of you who have battled your own doubts and despair and received insight from my story to share with me that I may be your spiritual friend! To Christ be the glory, for he is able to do immeasurably more than all we can ask or think. Amen!''

After a memorable prayer by John and another hymn, Onesimus was embraced by John, Mary, and Helen. Almost everyone in the hall came by to clasp hands and hug him with deep feeling. It was a heart-melting time. Helen, of course, was greeted with warm affection. With tears of joy, John shared in the blessed *koinonia* that he knew was another sign of the living presence of Christ, his Master and Lord.

Later that evening, Onesimus and Helen received refreshments with the inner family in the atrium of Tyrannus and Joanna's home. John spoke of his great hope for the future of Christ's ministry in Ephesus and Asia.

"Onesimus, your witness this evening and the response of the people are more evidence of the way our eternal Father's providence turns the worst into the best. Your painful struggles, which seemed so meaningless and vain, have been transformed by the Holy Spirit into one of the finest opportunities for good that I've known. Your life and ministry as my assistant, with Helen by your side, will be blessed and fruitful indeed. Your time will be more than filled with opportunities to share your understanding of the faith with many who were present tonight and with others who will come."

All added their encouragement.

"You and Helen are welcome to make your home with us until you find a suitable house or apartment," Joanna said. "There's plenty of room for you in addition to John and Mary."

"Thanks, dear friends," Helen exclaimed. "This day has been one of the happiest of my life. Onesimus has told me so much about you."

Helen turned to Mary and continued. "And you, dear Mary, have added an extra dimension to our coming and our future. I anticipate sharing many good times with you. Onesimus and I could have no greater blessing than to be here in such wondrous company!"

The next morning, Onesimus met with Bishop John, Tyrannus, and several of the deacons and elders of the church at Ephesus. The group included Euplus, the deacon in whose home Cerinthus and his companions had been invited to share their story and who had rejected their *gnostic* interpretation of Christ. Also present were the elders Crocus, Fronto, and Burrhus the deacon, upon whose integrity and faithfulness Bishop John had depended for counsel and encouragement as he sought to counteract the hurts being done by the young Alexandrian Gnostic Christians.

As they assembled in their bishop's study, they greeted Onesimus warmly and expressed their joy over the response of the people the evening before. John opened the meeting with a fervent prayer for the leadership of the Spirit and the gifts of understanding in dealing with the crisis now threatening to tear the church apart. After the prayer, John asked for a report on what had taken place during his absence. Euplus, the one closest to Cerinthus, spoke first.

"Bishop John, I regret to tell you that Cerinthus and Michael are now openly in league with the chief priests of Artemis's temple and the silversmiths and merchants in opposing you. They abhor your interpretation of the morality of Christians based on love that declares any pleasure, however good in itself, wrong and forbidden if it's hurtful and destructive to others. Cerinthus and Michael have been teaching their vision of Christ's kingdom of good pleasure as one in which we celebrate the nuptial festivals of a new age in which eating, drinking, and sexual relations of all kinds are to be enjoyed freely as a witness to Christ's conquest of the evil ruler of the world. Cerinthus is teaching openly every day in the speaker's rostrum in the agora to an increasingly large crowd of listeners."

"And that includes, I'm sorry to say, several of our younger Christians," Burrhus broke in. "Obviously, his argument that self-denial and abstinence for any reason is folly has a strong appeal to anybody who'd like nothing better than to retain the hope of salvation from death to eternal life, while being able to share in the enticing fertility rites in the Temple of Artemis. Some of our young Christians have gone with Cerinthus and Michael to the temple to participate in the exotic dances and sexual intercourse with the priestesses there."

John shook his head in disbelief and sorrow as he heard this disturbing news.

"What do you mean, Euplus, when you say they're in league with the temple priests?" he asked.

"I can answer that," Burrhus replied. "It means that the

silversmiths and merchants who've been profiting from the sale of Artemis's images and amulets are spreading the word about the new Christian teaching that reverses our usual abhorrence of their trade. Now that the number of Christians in Ephesus is growing, their business is again threatened like it was in the days of the riot that nearly killed Paul. Therefore, they and the temple priests are glad to encourage people to attend the daily teachings of Cerinthus in the agora.''

"That is to say," Onesimus stated the clearly obvious danger, "that they're endorsing the Gnostic Christians who are advancing their business. If being a Christian means accepting the corrupt culture of the temple worshipers, then the very basis of our Christian discipleship is threatened!''

"Yes, Onesimus,'' John spoke with a sigh. "You remember when Cerinthus and his companions first came how we spent hours trying to help them understand and reject the folly of their heresy that Christ didn't suffer and that, instead of a holy life in which *agape* is the ruler, his followers may indulge in any kind of erotic pleasure they choose. With your counsel, I went the second mile—even the tenth mile—in permitting them to share in our fellowship and receive the Eucharist! We prayed that their minds might be opened! Instead, their proud minds remained closed. Now we face a destructive division that can produce costly injury to the body of Christ.''

After allowing the implications of that statement to sink in, John asked the question all were asking. "What shall we do, now? Onesimus, what do you think? You know how I went out of my way, over and over, to be compassionate with them.''

"Yes, Bishop John, I recall your love for them and your many prayers. I think you've done all you can do to change them. The time has come to make our position clear through you as our bishop, the acknowledged leader and spokesman for the Christians in all of Asia. When you say that God is love, you're talking about a love that's strong and wise, that leads us to take the difficult way of the cross, to declare the truth even though it makes us unpopular with the priests and merchants who profit by the debauchery of the temple worship. We can no more worship the goddess Artemis than we can the emperor as god, even if we pay a costly price for our stand!''

The others present agreed. "Onesimus is right! The sooner we make this clear the better!'' Euplus affirmed.

"I'll do it by the grace of God and your support,'' John declared. "We'll let all of Ephesus and Asia know that, as followers of the Christ, we vehemently reject the false heresy of Cerinthus and his followers! I'll make my statement very soon. When does Cerinthus speak? I'll declare our position before him and all who've come to hear him!''

"But dear bishop, that could be dangerous!'' Euplus said with alarm. "Cerinthus's fanatical followers and the temple leaders could mob you!''

"We'll trust that to the Lord. If I'm attacked, so be it. Since my first failure to be faithful, I've never yet forsaken my Lord or refused to bear his cross, and I don't intend to begin now. I don't seek persecution, but I'll not turn from it!''

"We'll be right there with you,'' Onesimus and Tyrannus said, almost in one breath. The others agreed.

"Thank you for your encouragement and support, my brothers. I'll need it. Onesimus, will you close our time together with prayer?''

Onesimus's prayer was short and to the point. With deep feeling, he thanked the Lord for the courage and love of his apostle John and asked for the power and wisdom to say and do what would be needed.

"The Lord be with us all!'' John cried. He embraced each of them as they went on their way.

Shortly before the eleventh hour the next morning, John, accompanied by Onesimus and the deacons and elders of his church council, walked into the agora. His assistants took their places near him. Word had gone out to the Christian *communitas* of his intentions, and many of them were also present, along with the considerable number of Artemis worshipers who had come to hear Cerinthus speak.

Cerinthus arrived, followed by several of his most ardent

followers. At his first glimpse of the bishop, he felt embarrassed and sensed what was likely to happen. He still held the beloved apostle somewhat in awe, even though he had condemned and denied John's position so many times during the months since their first confrontation.

His discomfiture, however, lasted only a moment. His fanatical devotion to his own vision of Christ and his conscious attempt during recent weeks to align himself and his followers with the priests and priestesses of Artemis did not require of him a public battle with the man who had sought to help him. With his head erect, Cerinthus walked up to the bishop and greeted him with a smile.

"Good morning, Bishop John. I'm honored that you've come to hear me at my regular time and place for proclaiming the Lord! I see you've brought my friend, Onesimus, with you!"

"Cerinthus, I'm afraid you've completely mistaken my reason for being here."

John spoke firmly so that all around could hear.

"I haven't come to honor you and your false teachings. As the bishop appointed and ordained by Christ as shepherd and overseer of his church and supported by these leaders of the church, I am here to disavow any relationship with you and your heresies. I shall never cease to love you and pray for you, but because of the great harm you and your followers are doing to the people who bear the name of Christ, I must make clear, contrary to your teachings, that Jesus of Nazareth is not only the Son of God, but also the human Word of God made flesh as the Son of man. In him is the truth of the mighty Father who created this world. Through him, all things came into being, and without him, no single thing was created. In Christ, the Word of the mighty Father became flesh—he came to dwell among us in Jesus Christ, our Lord and Savior. We who knew Jesus in the flesh saw such glory as belongs to the Father's only Son, full of grace and the truth of reality. Therefore, those who know the Son know also the Father.

"This, Cerinthus, is the basis of our faith as followers of Jesus Christ. If we are true to his spirit, we cannot accept your voluptuous and hurtful teachings that Christ's kingdom is the rule of sensual and sexual pleasures of all kinds, unlimited by moral requirements, regardless of the hurts to people and families. Your teachings contradict the basic spirit of Jesus Christ our Lord who summed up the commandments in the simple words that we are to love God and our neighbors as we do ourselves."

John turned to the motley crowd, which was amazingly quiet, and addressed it directly. "The love of Christ is the love of God. It will never encourage anything that injures the dignity and worth of any person. Cerinthus's personal participation and his encouragement of young Christians to join in the fertility rites in the Temple of Artemis in the name of Christian freedom is a contradiction to all that the love of Christ stands for. This must cease!"

As John spoke, his voice rose in eloquence and power, and his face was illumined with a radiance that for the moment quieted and shamed the young Christians who had followed Cerinthus and Michael and the throng of Artemis worshipers. But when John began to denounce the fertility rites of their beloved goddess Artemis, many of the listeners became angry. Led by the priests and several of the silversmiths present, they began to shout their contempt for these enemies of their favorite goddess and her exotic worship. Soon, most of the crowd was in a turmoil of scorn and vilification. John's voice could no longer be heard.

"Stop that foolish old man's talk!" one man with a strong voice cried, and others took up the shout.

"Get him out of here!"

"Great is Artemis of Ephesus!"

"She's our hope for sons and daughters!"

"Her priestesses bring us good pleasure!"

"Great is Artemis of Ephesus!"

Onesimus and Tyrannus stood near the aging bishop, who was now trembling with exhaustion and covered with sweat.

"This," Tyrannus whispered to Onesimus, "is similar to the riot that forced Paul to leave Ephesus for a while. We have to get John out of here, or he'll be beaten and hurt badly."

Before they could move, the crowd was suddenly quieted by another voice from the rostrum. It was Cerinthus, whose golden tongue had charmed them with encouraging words confirming their belief in the goodness of the temple worship.

"My friends, listen to me!" Cerinthus cried. "You who've heard me know that the charges of this old man are false!"

"Hear, hear!" the crowd now under the spell of the handsome young man's words shouted in agreement.

Cerinthus continued, "Though his interpretation of Jesus Christ, whom I also worship and serve, is twisted and mistaken, he's the last of the disciples who knew Jesus. He's a man who's always been kind to me, so I ask you to let him go without harm. He's indeed a great and loving man. Let him go, and I'll continue with my teachings!"

"You may continue your teachings, my son," John spoke in the moment of quiet following Cerinthus's words so all could hear. "But you know and all people should know that not one of us who knew Jesus as he was and is can accept what you teach as resembling the gospel of Christ! I'll go now; but remember, son, though I continue to pray for you, I can't associate with you and your false and hurtful teachings and example."

The crowd watched the interchange with fascination, and they saw a strange thing happen. John's concluding words were said in a voice of caring concern as he took the hand of the man who, though claiming to be a follower of Christ, had denounced the aged apostle's teaching as false. They had heard Bishop John called "the apostle of love." Strange love indeed for one so clearly his enemy! They watched in amazement as Onesimus, Tyrannus, and the other leaders of the church also took Cerinthus's hand. Then the little group of deacons and elders led their bishop away from the rostrum. The crowd parted in silence to let them through.

John leaned heavily on the arms of Onesimus and Tyrannus as the group made their way out of the agora and up the wide street.

"We're proud of you, John," Onesimus said as they reached the street where the sound of Cerinthus's voice could no longer be heard. "You said what needed to be said, and you did it with love. The Holy Spirit of our Lord was in you!"

"Indeed," Tyrannus affirmed, "turn and look back to the place where Cerinthus is standing and you'll see the most hopeful sign of all. Several of the young Christians who've been deluded by Cerinthus's enticing words have left the agora and are going their separate ways to their work."

"This hour was a greater victory for the spirit of Christ than I'd ever expected," Euplus cried exultantly. "I was looking for violence and hurt from the fanatical followers of Artemis! I am thankful for Cerinthus's love for you and his influence on that crowd. A few of our Christians will stay with him, but from the looks of the ones who are leaving, your witness and spirit have won the victory. The Christian church in Ephesus will not become a church of bland, pleasure-loving Gnostics!"

"God be praised!" John responded with a weak voice but a glad heart. "It was a task I had to perform. I trust our Lord was pleased. There's one thing of which I'm sure, my dear partners and brothers in the gospel. God is love, and those of us living in love are living in God and God is living in us."

25

*T*he days that followed were busy and happy for Onesimus and Helen as they began their new life together in Ephesus. Helen accompanied Joanna to several of the women's groups that met together for prayer and study of the parchments containing the Gospels of Matthew, Mark, and Luke and several of Paul's letters. Onesimus and Helen both shared in small group meetings of the *koinonia* in the evenings or early morning hours each day.

Helen immediately found a place in the admiration and love of the people. Her joyful spirit and ready wit made her most welcome. Her training under Onesimus in the philosophers and under Papias in the teachings of Paul gave her helpful insight. She began to lead in the interpretations of what the groups were reading and to share her remembrance of her experiences with

Paul, Epaphrus, and other Christian leaders who had come to her
father's house in Colossae. Sometimes Mary accompanied her.
Mary was quiet and spoke few words, but when she did, she was
heard with reverence and affirmation.

Onesimus began his ministry the day after the scene with
Cerinthus in the agora as several of the younger Christians,
confused by the conflict between Bishop John's and Cerinthus's
teachings, came to him for counsel and help. Every day, he spent
hours in conversation and prayer with those attracted to the gospel
as taught by John but enticed by Cerinthus's kingdom of good
pleasure.

Some of the younger church members were confused by the
group of Jewish Christians who insisted that the Hebrew levitical
law was binding on all Christians. These Judaizers, as John called
them, sought to encourage and enforce the practice of circumcision on male babies born to Christian parents in the church. They
also made much of the difference between clean meat and the
unclean meats from animals sacrificed on the altars of the pagan
gods that were then sold at much lower prices in the market. In
their prayer and study groups, the young Christians heard Paul's
words written in strong opposition to these practices. They were
utterly confused and needed the wise and understanding counsel
of Onesimus to help them understand to what the freedom with
which Christ has set us free really referred.

One evening at mealtime, John spoke of his warm and affectionate appreciation for Onesimus and Helen.

"Both of you in your small group sharing and in person to
person conversation are giving priceless aid to our people. Surely
your coming to Ephesus is the work of the Lord! And I ask you,
Onesimus, as my first assistant, to take several mornings with our
entire congregation to teach them your interpretation of Paul's
writings to the Galatians and Corinthians concerning the pressures
the Judaizers are placing on our people. There's as much confusion here as with the Gnostics and their teachings—one just the
opposite of the other. These questions are too important to be

dealt with singly, and no one is better suited than you to deal with them, since you spent so much time with Paul.''

Tyrannus agreed heartily. ''Your teaching, Bishop John, of the love commandment of Jesus must continually be interpreted, and Onesimus is fit to do this from his own experience and understanding.''

''Indeed,'' John responded, ''Onesimus can be a powerful interpreter of true freedom in Christ's love.''

At the meeting of the elders and deacons the next morning, everyone heartily agreed to set aside an early morning each week for the special teaching. Burrhus reminded them that the influence of the Judaizers was greatly increased now that the war between the Jews and Romans in Palestine was so bitter and destructive. Many Jews, especially Jewish Christians, were fleeing their homeland and making their homes in cities around the empire such as Ephesus.

Tyrannus nodded affirmatively and added, ''I know of at least twenty Jewish-Christian families who've come to Ephesus and are worshiping regularly with our congregation.''

''Some of these are the ones causing the division among our people,'' Burrhus said. ''I'm sure there'll be many more arriving in the months ahead. They're sincere followers of Christ, good and honest people, whom we need to teach and lead rather than to isolate and drive away from our *koinonia*.''

''Onesimus, you're one of the best interpreters and reconcilers among us,'' John concluded. ''So it's agreed that for the next several weeks, you'll preach and teach each Wednesday morning as the entire congregation meets. You can help heal the wounds and bridge the gap between these two groups dividing and hurting our *koinonia*.''

Spring arrived, and with it some warm days. On one of these, Onesimus counseled with a young Christian in the shade of the peach tree in the garden at the rear of Tyrannus's apartment. The young man confessed his seduction by Cerinthus who encouraged him to join in the fertility rites in Artemis's temple. His wife, who was pregnant, had become very angry when she heard about it through a neighbor.

"When I realized how much my yielding to the enticement of Cerinthus's gospel of good pleasure had hurt my dearest one with whom I'm bound in the covenant of faithfulness in marriage, I asked her to forgive me!"

"What happened then?" Onesimus inquired.

"She said she hoped she could but that our relationship could never be the same again. She said for the sake of my child she's bearing, she'd pray that my relations with the priestess and my lack of love for her would injure neither her nor the child. When I told her I was only following Cerinthus's teaching and couldn't see why she objected, she started to cry. She said over and over that what I'd done wasn't the way of Christlike love. In the days since, I've been so miserable and my thoughts so confused that I decided to come to you for help. Teach me. . . . Help me—Oh, please! What I did seemed right at the time, but now it seems wrong. . . . But I don't know. What shall I do?"

In response, Onesimus began sharing his understanding of the freedom to love as Christ loves us.

Suddenly he saw John running into the garden from the street wearing a towel and carrying his tunic. Onesimus knew something unusual must have occurred. He rose and ran to meet him, stopping him at the gate.

"What on earth has happened?"

John was out of breath. Onesimus put his arm around the shaken old man.

"Not here," John gasped. "Let's go into the house. . . . I'll tell you there."

Seeing the young Christian under the peach tree, John pulled the towel tighter around him and said apologetically, "I have had a sad experience. Please wait for Onesimus."

With that, he and Onesimus entered the doorway and climbed the stairs to the atrium. John sank into the couch and put his head in his hands. He caught his breath and rested for a minute or two before telling his story.

"On this very warm afternoon," John said, "I walked to the

bath house, looking forward to a refreshing wash in the pool. I undressed and carried my towel to the pool. When I came to it, I saw that Cerinthus was already in the pool on the other side. That filled me with indignation—I couldn't remain under the same roof with him or bathe in the same water! I picked up my clothes and only put on my sandals, and I exhorted everyone standing near, 'Let us escape, lest the bath should fall while Cerinthus the enemy of truth is in it.' ''

Onesimus listened with compassionate amusement to the old man's account.

"Did Cerinthus know of your hasty departure from the bath house and why you left?"

"I am sure he did!" John replied. "I've already told him that I'd continue to pray for him, and I have, but . . ." John, now somewhat relaxed, smiled. "I never told him that I'd associate with him in the bath."

The two laughed together as John realized the humor in his hasty departure wearing only the towel!

"One thing is sure, John. Your actions in the bath house unmistakably proclaim your disavowal of Cerinthus's teachings!"

"Yes," John replied apologetically, "but I trust this doesn't say to those who hear about it that I've ceased to love and pray for Cerinthus. I'll write him a note affirming my continuing prayers for him even as I must continue to oppose his heresies."

"Father John, you indeed continue to be what you've always been, the apostle of God's love and still very human! Thank God!" Onesimus affirmed as he rose to go back to the young Christian waiting for him in the garden.

He found the young man sitting under the peach tree, perplexed and uncomfortable. When Onesimus explained what had happened and why Bishop John felt so strongly about the evils of Cerinthus's teachings, a smile broke out on the young man's troubled face.

"I begin to see," he said, "that if this great apostle who was so close to Jesus Christ our Lord sees so large an evil in the *gnostic* teachings, then they must be wrong. Onesimus, will you pray for me that my sin will be forgiven and that I'll never repeat it?"

Onesimus put his hand on the young man's arm and prayed

fervently for his acceptance of the forgiveness that was his and for
the courage to withstand the enticements of the lusts that would
continue to tempt him.

"Help him see, O Christ, that the enjoyment of sex is beautiful
when accompanied by love, and grant him and his wife a new and
deeper love that binds their lives in perfect harmony and prepares
them for the gift of their child!"

Time passed rapidly as Onesimus continued his fruitful assistance to Bishop John, and Helen became more and more valuable
as teacher and friend to the members of the church. Onesimus's
weekly interpretations of Paul's writings to the Corinthian and
Galatian churches were increasingly effective in preventing a split
in the church over either the Judaizers or the *gnostic* heresies. As
he read and expounded the meanings of Paul's central theme that
love of God and each other as revealed in Christ is indeed the
highest law, he found it necessary to use as well portions of the
letters Paul had dictated to him while awaiting his execution in the
stinking Mamertine Prison. These were letters Paul was sending to
churches such as Lystra, Iconium, Derbe, Athens, and Antioch,
as well as a brief letter to the Ephesian church that Onesimus had
read when he first returned from Rome to Ephesus. Onesimus was
glad he'd made copies of each of them for himself.

One morning as he prepared to teach his early morning classes,
the thought occurred to him that he should combine these several,
mostly unknown, letters of Paul into what he thought Paul would
now say to the church at Ephesus. Onesimus had also received
some precious insights from listening to John. He decided he
would combine these insights with the brief letters of Paul into
what he would call "The Letter of Paul to the Ephesians."

Surely, he thought, *Paul would want me to use all that he's said
and written. I'm confident that he'd have me incorporate the
insights of John concerning the cosmic greatness of God's eternal
purposes in the creation of humankind even before the world with
the sun, moon, and stars of heaven was made.* With this thought
in mind, he prayed for the inspiration of the Holy Spirit and put
together "The Letter of Paul to the Ephesians."

In the latter part of the letter, Onesimus included an interpretation of the way husbands must love their wives as well as wives their husbands.

> Husbands, love your wives, as Christ also loved the church and gave himself up for it. . . . In the same way men also are bound to love their wives, as they love their own bodies. . . . That is how Christ treats the church, because it is his body, of which we are living parts. . . . Each of you must love his wife as his very self; and the woman must see to it that she pays her husband all respect.

Onesimus sat back after he had penned these lines thinking how very much the young Christian men with whom he had counseled needed these clear words from Paul, for these young Christians had come to him in despair after having followed the *gnostic* teachings of Cerinthus. They had hurt their young wives by giving themselves to the sexual enticements of the priestesses of the Temple of Artemis. Helen had shared with him the brokenness and bitterness of several of the wives who had come to her. They, too, needed to forgive and to love their husbands more fully, not only sexually, but with tender respect and companionship. He knew these words would be very helpful to those whose homes were breaking up because of the selfish misuse of their sexual desires and needs. All of those who were seeking earnestly to follow Christ would find Paul's words a priceless help in their quest.

"The Letter of Paul to the Ephesians" was concluded with the parable of the "whole armor of God" from Paul's letter to the church at Lystra, which had been dictated to Onesimus as one of the last letters written from the Mamertine Prison.

The composition of the letter was received with great appreciation. It combined so many of the priceless teachings of the great apostle Paul as collected by Onesimus over the months he had been Paul's *amanuensis*. It was written also with the insights and understandings Onesimus had gained from John. No wonder it proved to be one of the most popular and helpful of all Onesimus's contributions. When it was first read to the early morning congregation in Tyrannus's hall, the people listened with unusual intensity. When he finished reading it, they rose as one to applaud and thank Onesimus for what he had given them.

Bishop John rose to say, "Onesimus, you've brought our beloved apostle Paul close to us. His spirit and teachings are alive as never before. We'll always be in your debt. I propose that we ask our young Christians who are good at penmanship to make several copies of the letter. We'll send them to the churches in Asia, Rome, Alexandria, and wherever we know of other Christian churches. I predict that this new letter containing so much of Paul's unknown writings will be one of the most valuable helps to the churches and those who seek to be fully Christian all over the world!"

Part Six

The Revealer

26

*T*ime passed swiftly for Onesimus and Helen as they shared the struggles and joys of the growing Christian movement in Ephesus and Ionia. Their love for each other increased, but it was also marked with tragedy. Helen continued to experience miscarriage with every new pregnancy. In order to avoid the continual danger and disappointment, the couple decided to devote their time and loving service to the Christian family struggling to be born in the frustrated and hurting world all around them.

Thirty years had passed since their coming to Ephesus, a time in which Onesimus gave his undivided loyalty and service as Bishop John's assistant. Their lives had been difficult as they were faced with constant threats of persecution and problems of division in church. The couple had grown in their loving appreciation of the aging apostle.

In spite of the feebleness of his ninety years, John continued his growth in strength of mind and spirit and expanded his reputation as the apostle of love. He was the beloved bishop and father in the gospel, the only living disciple who had personally known the man Jesus. Invariably as he spoke to the people of the church, his message began with the same warm greeting.

"Little children," he would begin, "let us love one another, for love is from God and God is love!"

Christians from all over Ionia looked to him as their spiritual leader and teacher. They came from house-churches in Smyrna, Pergamum, Hierapolis, Laodicea, Magnesia, Philadelphia, Sardis, Tralles, and even from distant Antioch, Derbe, and Lystra. Some brought problems and reported sharp divisions within their churches. All came to sit with the beloved disciple to listen to his description of Jesus' acts and teachings and the meaning of his life, death, and resurrection.

John's authority as bishop came from an inner spiritual authority as one whose life was completely mastered by the love of Christ. Even those Christians who disagreed with him revered his memories of the life and victory of their Lord as the connecting link with the source of their own faith and life. Bishops and elders from churches in distant cities such as Rome, Alexandria, Corinth, Athens, and Philippi came by ship to spend a few days listening to John's stories and interpretations of his years as the disciple closest to their Lord.

Though John was loved and respected by all who professed Jesus as the Christ, strong disagreements were reported from leaders of house-churches that had sprung up in Ephesus and other Ionian cities.

One of these house-churches was the group of Gnostic Christians Cerinthus had begun. Although Cerinthus and Michael returned to Alexandria three years after they had come to Ephesus, the Gnostics had continued to meet in the house of Theatus for twenty-eight years. Claudius and Heracles remained in Ephesus and became two of the most devoted supporters of John's church, which continued meeting in Tyrannus's hall.

Most of the Gnostic Christians were led by Theatus and Sophorus, the two deacons who had defected from John's following. Participation in the exotic cult of Artemis had dropped, however, because most of the Gnostic Christians considered the practice repugnant. Cerinthus had twisted many of John's teachings concerning the *Logos* or Word revealed in Christ and the signs of his divinity. The Gnostics continued, however, in Cerinthus's antinomian approach to morality, and the number of Gnostic adherents remained steady.

"They still come occasionally to hear me preach," John complained to Onesimus one morning as they talked of their frustrations over this continuing division in the church. "They listen and then return to teach the opposite to all I've said!"

The aged apostle was exasperated and angry. He threw up his hands. "There's not a thing we can do about it!"

"You're right," Onesimus replied. "Their heresy is serious, but I believe there's something you can do about it. If you'll help us write down a clear account of your teachings about Jesus' life, death, and victory, we can prevent much of the twisting of the gospel by the Gnostics. And what could be even more important, you can present your interpretation of the meaning of all Jesus said and did in order to influence and change the attitudes of some of the Jewish Christians meeting here with Rabbi Ben Jacob and similar Jewish-Christian churches in other cities."

Onesimus had touched a sore spot in John's thinking, and John exploded! "What a shame to hear Jewish Christians speak as though Jesus were only another wise rabbi, a teacher, and a prophet, and miss the glorious truth of Jesus the Son of man and the Son of God without whom we can't know the Father or the eternal life that faith in him brings!"

"Yes," Onesimus responded, "and in addition to them, there are the honest, perplexed Jewish Christians continuing in the synagogue as good Jews who think that circumcision and keeping the laws are as important as their faith in Jesus as the Christ! How desperately these and many others need to have your complete account of the meaning of Jesus' life and teachings and death and resurrection. Please, let's get together with our bishops and elders who know the greatness of Christ through you so we can prepare the Gospel according to John for all to hear."

That time came sooner than Onesimus expected. One evening before he and Helen finished their supper, a young Christian appeared at their door. He was breathless from running, but he burst into the room with a cry.

"Hurry, Onesimus, come! Something terrible's happened. The bishop needs your help!"

"What is it?" Onesimus asked with concern as he donned his tunic and followed the young man out into the street.

Between breaths, the youth answered, "Rabbi Ben Joseph has been stoned and is nearly dead!"

"Where is he now?"

"Some of our Jewish Christians brought him, hurt and bleeding, to Bishop John. He's in the atrium of Tyrannus's house."

"Is he still conscious?"

They climbed the stairs to Tyrannus's apartment and entered the atrium. The disheveled rabbi lay on the couch, his head and robe covered with blood, his face and shoulders cut by the stones. Joanna and her helpers washed the wounds. John and Tyrannus stood nearby watching anxiously.

As Onesimus entered, John said, "I'm glad you've come. Menelaus, our physician, should be here soon."

John paced around the room and sorrowfully sighed.

"We have a sad witness to the conflict in the synagogue both here and, from what I hear, in many other places in the Roman world. Ben Joseph is the victim of a group of radical Jews, mostly Pharisees, who are rightly disturbed by the destruction of the temple in Jerusalem, the slaughter of so many people, and the new dispersion of thousands of the survivors over the world. With the temple leveled and Jerusalem gone, many of the Pharisees have become fanatical in their zeal to preserve the unity of the scattered Jewish people."

John sighed again and motioned for the visitors to be seated. "We might as well sit here and wait. Ben Joseph is badly hurt and unconscious by the stoning."

"How did it happen?" Onesimus inquired.

"All we know is that he was stoned by the Jewish temple police, the *Chazzan*," Tyrannus said. "They were aided by a dozen or more Jewish merchants angry over the loss of profits from the sale of amulets from the Temple of Artemis. They stoned him just outside the city. Two Christians were entering the city on the road from Smyrna and saw what was happening. They hid behind some bushes until it was over and the rabbi was alone. Then they picked up the bruised and unconscious man and brought him here as quickly as they could."

Onesimus thought for a minute and then began to speak. "I'm shocked but not surprised. The rabbi and I had a long conversation a few days ago. He told me that as a Jewish rabbi who believes in Jesus as the Christ he expected the worst from some radical Pharisees who came recently from the Academy at Jamnia.

After the fall of Jerusalem, several Jewish teachers, mostly Pharisees who escaped the terrible slaughter, assembled there and formed an academy to strengthen the unity of the dispersed Jewish people. The academy is regarded by many as the successor to the Sanhedrin. Ben Joseph said that one of their decisions was to stamp out heresies like the Jewish Christians, especially rabbis who believed and taught Jesus as Christ but wanted, as he did, to remain in the synagogue. He said he was expecting persecution, possibly expulsion from the synagogue and even, he told me, stoning if he continued to believe and teach that Jesus was the Messiah.''

Menelaus the physician arrived to examine the injured rabbi. After a careful examination, he explained thankfully, ''Ben Joseph has a concussion and severe bruises. He'll recover, but it may be several hours before he regains consciousness.''

''Andrew, help me carry him into our extra bedroom,'' Tyrannus asked the messenger who had brought Onesimus. ''Then go and bring the rabbi's wife.''

As the move was made, John spoke sorrowfully. ''The situation with Jewish Christians is serious indeed. It reminds me of the very same accusations made of Jesus when he taught that no one truly knows the Father except through the Son. The Pharisees called this blasphemy. After he healed the lame man on the Sabbath, the leaders determined to kill him. Now a similar fate is awaiting his disciples who want to remain faithful to their Jewish heritage in the synagogue and also believe in Jesus as the Messiah!''

Onesimus listened to John's comparison of what had happened to Ben Joseph and the death of Jesus. He placed his hand on John's arm and spoke with deep feeling.

''This is one of the great reasons why we've been appealing to you to tell us the whole story of Jesus' life, death, and resurrection and what it means so that we can write it down and make it available to Christians all over the world. How desperately they need to know the amazing love of Jesus, who laid down his life to reveal the love of the Father. There are likely others who will suffer as Ben Joseph has for the gospel. Shouldn't they have your full account of Jesus' life?''

John listened with a warm smile of affirmation. "You're right, Onesimus. You, Tyrannus, and many others have urged me to tell the stories of Jesus that haven't been told in the Gospels of Matthew, Mark, and Luke. There are a lot of precious words and parables that aren't available to those who haven't heard me share them. Let's invite the bishops and elders from nearby cities to come and set aside some time for me to tell as best I can all that I remember of our dear Lord's earthly life and the eternal significance of everything he did."

Onesimus and Tyrannus stood up and clapped their hands in approval as they heard John's promise.

"We've been praying for this decision for a long time," Onesimus exclaimed with joy. "Your interpretation of the meaning of Jesus will be of infinite help not only to Jewish Christians undergoing persecution, but to all who are suffering or will suffer for their faith at the hands of the Roman authorities. Just as important, The Gospel according to John will be of great use in refuting the twisted and dangerous teachings of the Gnostics."

"Thank the Lord for your decision," Tyrannus exclaimed. "I'll be happy to help in any way I can!"

"Thank you both!" John smiled with the old light burning in his eyes. "You've been most helpful. We'll begin writing just as soon as we're able to assemble the bishops and elders from the Ionian churches. Many of them have also asked me to tell my story. Onesimus, send out messengers to invite them to come on the second day of next week. Tyrannus, you and Joanna can arrange places in the homes of our Christian families where these visitors may stay!"

Four days passed before Ben Joseph recovered consciousness. John, Onesimus, and Tyrannus came into his room and greeted him and his wife, Deborah, who remained with him.

"Thank the Lord you're much better!" John said solicitously. "All in the church have been praying for you."

"Thank you, dear friends," Ben Joseph responded slowly in a weak voice. "Your care brings the love of Christ very real and near. Bishop John, I can never tell you how much your teachings of the last hours of Jesus in the upper room meant to me in those last hours of my trial and stoning. Through your witness of Jesus' last teachings, I was able to hear him say to me as he says to all of us, 'Peace I leave with you; my peace I give to you; not as the world gives do I give to you. Let not your hearts be troubled, neither let them be afraid' (RSV). Then I heard him say to me, 'In me you have peace. In the world you have tribulation; but be of good cheer, I have overcome the world' (RSV). I can't tell you how precious these words were to me as I stood before the whole synagogue.''

The rabbi was winded from talking. After a few moments of rest, he continued. ''The new head of the *Gerousia*, the ruling council of the synagogue, Rabbi Ben Thomas, tested me by asking me to give the eighteen benedictions prepared by the Academy of Jamnia. Of course, I could give all of the prayers except the twelfth, in which I'd have had to say, 'Let the Nazarenes and the Minim be destroyed in a moment and let them be blotted out in the Book of Life!' These are references to Christians and heretics. After I'd said the first eleven, I declared I couldn't and wouldn't say the twelfth. A loud cry went up from many persons in the synagogue. They shouted that I was a Nazarene and demanded that I be excommunicated and stoned.''

''We can imagine how you felt at that moment,'' Onesimus exclaimed.

''Yes, I knew what was coming. I prayed for and received Christ's peace, even as Rabbi Ben Thomas called for the vote that put me out of the synagogue and sentenced me to the stoning. The blessed presence of our Lord and his peace were mine as they dragged me blindfolded into a cart and took me outside the city. I could hear their jeers and curses as the stones began to hit me. The last thing I remember was the inner voice of the Holy Spirit, my counselor and advocate, saying 'Don't be afraid. I'm with you!' ''

''What a beautiful witness,'' Onesimus affirmed. ''We're thankful that you weren't killed. Now, let me tell you some good news. Next week these words of Jesus and many others that our beloved John remembers will be shared with Christian leaders from the

churches of Ionia. We'll write the whole account down and send it
out to all of the churches. What our Lord has done for you in the
words you remembered from John's lips will now be available to
countless others!''

That hour with the wounded Ben Joseph was one Onesimus
long cherished. Together the group by the bedside participated in
a service of the Eucharist administered by John. They each offered
their intercessions for Ben Joseph's recovery and for thousands
who, like him, would be blessed by the new Gospel according to
John.

27

"What an inspiring gathering of bishops and elders
from so many of the Christian churches in Ionia,'' Onesimus
whispered his excitement to John.

John, seated in the large, comfortable chair Tyrannus had built
for him, answered thankfully. ''Yes, I'm happy to see these dear
brothers here together. What a joy to have loved and shared with
them in their burdens and victories! This is a wonderful day!''

The colorful Christian leaders obviously were enjoying seeing
and sharing with each other. John lifted his hand for silence and
spoke words of welcome.

''Little children of God's family, grace and peace to you
through our Lord Jesus Christ. I've invited you to share my
recollections of how it was in Galilee and Judea when I became a
disciple of Jesus and lived and walked close to him for nearly
three years, hearing his words and seeing his marvelous works,
experiencing the sorrow of his death, the joy of his resurrection,
and the coming of the Holy Spirit as our counselor and helper.''

The excitement of anticipation showed on the faces of the
Christians around the room.

''Most of you have heard by word of mouth and have read
many of Jesus' teachings and stories of his life as recorded by the

Gospels of Matthew, Mark, and Luke, but there are other memorable events and precious sayings of our Lord that only I've lived to tell. I'll relate these to you in fuller detail, though all of you have heard them during these years we've known each other. I'll also explain as I'm able what these words and events mean. For sixty years, I've thought about all I've seen with my own eyes and heard with my own ears and experienced in my deepest soul. I now declare them to you. I'll point to a number of signs I see in Jesus' deeds that reveal clearly who he was as the Father's beloved Son.''

Onesimus proudly looked at each of the bishops and elders as John was talking. They would all soon be taking part in a historic process. He listened as John continued.

''I pray that what you write down and pass on to God's people will correct some of the false and foolish misunderstandings of Jesus that have arisen. I also hope that it will increase the strength of faith and the love of Christ in all who are dedicated to be true disciples. I think especially of the Gnostics who have been bewitched by the fanciful visions and artful words of Cerinthus and other Gnostic leaders.''

A murmur of approval could be heard as many in the room nodded their heads.

''I also think of the Jewish Christians who desire to remain in the synagogues but who are being expelled, hurt, and even stoned. Many of them think of Jesus only as a great teacher or prophet and thus rob him of his identity as God's Son and revealer. These mistakes need to be corrected and all God's people strengthened in their faith!''

As John finished, the room was filled with a thunderous ovation.

''Now I'm ready to begin!'' he announced with elation as he stretched his hands towards them. ''Tyrannus has provided each of you with parchment on which to record what I say that seems important to you. Onesimus has agreed to be our chief *amanuensis* to write the record in its final form that will be sent out to the churches. His experience with Paul and Peter will be valuable to us all.''

"Thanks for your confidence, Bishop John," Onesimus spoke up, "and for the trust you all have in me. I'll do my best, but understand that all of us together will be writing our new Gospel according to John."

Another chorus of affirmation rose from the group. Bishop Antonius Tavius of Smyrna put the feeling of the group into words.

"Bishop John, our hearts are full as we begin these days of intimate listening and sharing the wondrous good news you declare. We're thankful that, while your memory is bright and your strength sufficient, you give us this privilege. Your interpretations of who Jesus was and what he said and did will be a priceless spiritual Gospel for us and all who come after us."

Agreement was apparent in the room.

Tavius turned to Onesimus and added, "We're thankful for you, and we'll be happy to work with you in this, our most significant task!"

"Yes, yes!" the others cried and clapped their hands in approval.

In the silence that followed, John lifted his hands in prayer. His wrinkled face was illumined with a strange light causing all to believe the Holy Spirit inspired his story of all that Jesus said and did.

John's recollections of his experience with Jesus Christ and his disciples provided an opportunity for each of the participating Christians to broaden and deepen personal faith. Because of the excitement surrounding the project, each morning the work would begin well before breakfast and continue late into the night. Even then, work would end because of the sheer exhaustion of the writers. At the end of each day, no one ever wanted to stop until the next morning.

The last evening of the second week of their time together, the final night of the work, was a precious time of *koinonia* for them all. Bishop John thanked and blessed them for their faithfulness. He commended the new Gospel that was to bear his name and be used by and through them to the church in the world.

"Remember," John warned his co-workers, "this isn't *my*

Gospel. It bears my name only because I related it as an eyewitness to these things that tell the good news of our Lord, the very Word of God in human form! This is *God's* Gospel!''

The next morning before they departed, John blessed the Christian leaders with a benediction they would always remember.

''Peace be with you. Even as God sent Jesus into the world, so Christ sends you. Receive and live in Christ, with the Holy Spirit ever near to guide, strengthen, and protect you through all the temptations and trials that are to come! In the name of Jesus. Amen!''

—Part Seven—

The Bishop of Ephesus

28

*O*nesimus and Helen watched with concern as John grew more and more feeble during the intensive exertion of telling his story every day for two weeks. Though exhilarated as he remembered his precious years with Jesus, he paid a price in spent energy that hastened his illness and death.

In addition to these difficulties, John was weary with long hours of emotional strain as he encouraged and supported Christians who came to him from nearby cities where they were subjected to new persecutions under Emperor Domitian—the first widespread persecution of Christians since the reign of Nero. Under Vespasian, Nero's successor, there occurred only sporadic persecutions. Because Bishop John and Onesimus were held in such high regard even among many non-Christians, no serious attempts had been made by Roman officers to stamp out Christianity in Ephesus and nearby cities.

Indeed, Governor Marius of Ephesus became an ardent admirer of both John and Onesimus. Though not an open believer in the Christ, Marius and many members of his court and the business community appreciated the moral character of honesty and integrity displayed among the Christians. Over the years, Marius had spent several hours in conversation with John and Onesimus.

Under Emperor Domitian, however, the fiercest persecutions of the Christians began. An imperial decree was sent out to all the provinces that proclaimed Domitian lord and god and demanded public worship be given to him as *dominus et deus*.

The cult of emperor worship became popular. Governor Marius of Ephesus, now an old man, invited John and Onesimus to his palace to warn them of the coming fierce opposition they should expect and prepare their people to meet.

"I'm likely to be replaced soon," Marius informed them. "In

the brief time I have left, I'll do what I can with this new proclamation so as to do as little harm as possible to you and your people. I expect some of your leaders in other cities to suffer beatings, imprisonment, or exile. The governor of Laodicea is already at odds with John the Elder, as you know. He informed me yesterday of his intention to send John the Elder into exile on a remote and desolate island, and he's angry at me for seeking to intervene. I'm responsible for what happens to you, Bishop John, but he told me that he'd had enough of Elder John's defiance and he's going to make him pay for his folly!''

Bishop John was visibly upset by the news. As he and Onesimus returned home, he spoke sadly of the suffering ahead for their colleague in Laodicea and many others of the faithful.

That evening, he continued to share his sorrow at dinner with Onesimus and Helen in the home of Tyrannus and Joanna.

''My heart is heavy,'' he spoke softly, almost in tears. ''My burden is great, because I can't do anything to prevent this new suffering. My time is short, and you dear ones are my hope and my joy. I may not be with you long, for in the providence of the Lord, I too may join my brother John in exile. Or I may end my pilgrimage here and go to the work our Lord has prepared for me in those many rooms of his Father's house. Whatever comes to me, I rejoice, though I don't want to leave you to suffer. But you won't be alone. Whatever comes to you, the *Paraclete*, the One called to walk by our side, will never fail you!''

With a smile of confidence, John's voice became stronger. ''I'm ready for whatever it is! My body is weary and frail. These old bones are weak and hurting and will soon be at rest!''

The table was quiet as John's meaning began to sink in. Then, with the old light burning in his eyes, the aged apostle gave what was to be his last witness of faith.

''For sixty years, the love of God has been my song, the strength and joy of my life! I look forward again to seeing our Lord face to face, and I'm not afraid. I'll be glad to meet our Christ in all his risen glory! But let us pray for John the Elder and for those who must pay a greater price than we have paid for our faith. And may the Lamb's continuing presence in the Holy Spirit lead, comfort, and empower you, my beloved family!''

With awe and tears, everyone at the table embraced John and expressed love for him. Sustaining him with one arm, Onesimus walked with him to his room. Before entering, John paused and put his hands on Onesimus's shoulders.

Looking into the younger man's eyes, John said, "My son, you've been faithful to our Lord all these years. Upon your shoulders I leave the responsibilities as bishop. Be a good shepherd to Christ's flock, the people of God who know you, love you, and already look up to you as their spiritual leader. Teach them to love one another, for love is of God and never ends. Amen.''

Returning to their own house, Onesimus and Helen expected that this was the end of John's earthly life. They offered up tearful thanks for the inexpressible privilege of having known the beloved disciple for these thirty years. Before they retired for the night, a messenger came from Tyrannus to tell them that John had breathed his last shortly after going to sleep.

The news spread rapidly over the Christian community. By daybreak, Tyrannus's hall overflowed with sorrowful Christians gathering for worship. Governor Marius and other non-Christian citizens of Ephesus sent word to Onesimus of their sense of loss.

Onesimus conducted the Eucharistic memorial service to celebrate the life and victorious death of the last of the apostles who had known Jesus as a man. It was a sad but strangely joyful service as the congregation responded in the words of great thanksgiving they knew so well.

"Lift up your hearts!''

"We lift them up to the Lord!''

"Let us give thanks to the Lord our God!''

"It is right to give him thanks and praise!''

Onesimus spoke the words describing the wonders of God's gift in creation and redemption through his Son, Jesus Christ.

"The Lamb that was slain before the foundation of the world— the Word of God from the beginning!''

The people responded with fervent voice:

"Victory to our God who sits on the throne and to the Lamb! Amen!

Praise and glory, wisdom, thanksgiving and honor, power and might be to our God for ever and ever! Amen!"

After invoking the presence of the Holy Spirit, the people shared the consecrated elements with awe and reverence and sang a hymn of joyful praise.

As the service ended, Onesimus, followed by the elders, deacons, and many who had been close to the beloved bishop, walked behind the carriage that carried his physical remains. The procession passed through the city and climbed the steep road to the summit of the precipitous cliff outside the city. There, in a tomb hewn out of rock, the earthly body of John the beloved disciple was buried near the tomb of Mary, Jesus' mother, who had preceded him in death by fifteen years. Their lives and love had intertwined for nearly forty-five years; it was appropriate for them to be buried in such proximity.

On the first day of the next week, four days after John's memorial service, the congregation of Christians in Ephesus met in Tyrannus's hall to welcome Onesimus as their new bishop. Representatives of churches in several nearby cities were also present. Tyrannus shared the news of John's last hours with the leaders of the Asian churches assembled for the occasion.

Every one of the bishops, elders, and deacons of these churches was in common agreement that Onesimus should be the one to succeed John as bishop of Ephesus. They were glad that John had indicated so clearly his expectation that Onesimus would follow him as spiritual leader of the church. During the last few years of John's advanced age, Onesimus had served as preacher, pastor, priest, mediator, and teacher and was held in high respect and affection not only by the church in Ephesus but by the Christians in all of Ionia.

Bishop Tavius of Smyrna, the senior bishop among them, presided over the consecration of Onesimus as the new bishop of Ephesus. It was an awesome and inspiring moment for Onesimus as each of the bishops present laid hands on his head as he knelt before the table on which the sacred elements of bread and wine for the Eucharist were placed. Bishop Tavius called for silence and invited all to pray for the Holy Spirit to be poured out upon the life and ministry of Onesimus and his wife Helen, who had so beautifully joined in his labors. As the new bishop, Onesimus gave a brief, heartfelt message of acceptance, thanksgiving, and hope for these people of God, some of whom were to meet the trials of fierce persecution.

In a spirit of humility and joy, the memorable hour closed as Onesimus administered the bread and wine using the words so often heard from the lips of their beloved John.

"Take this in remembrance of the love of God offered to us in his Son, Jesus Christ our Lord. Little children, let us love one another, for love is of God, and God is love!"

—Part Eight—
The Martyr-Witness

29

"It's here, Helen. It's here," Onesimus sighed with sorrowful voice. He was deeply moved by what he had just heard from a traveling Christian merchant who brought a message from his longtime friend and colleague, Bishop Ignatius of Antioch.

"The dreaded persecution has begun!" He hung up his toga, walked over to Helen, and embraced her.

Both Helen and Onesimus had aged; his seventy-seven years had taken their toll on him physically. But with all his grey hairs and wrinkles, his appearance was even more impressive. He stood tall and straight, with kindly eyes and determined face.

Helen is even more beautiful than I've ever seen her, Onesimus thought as they shared their forty-eighth anniversary only the day before. Her snow-white hair was kept tied in a shapely knot; her face was thinner with a few wrinkles, but still ripe in its strong kindness.

She looked anxiously and lovingly at the troubled face of her partner. Since the deaths of Tyrannus and Joanna ten years earlier, the two had lived in the familiar apartment where they had spent so many interesting and inspiring hours.

"Yes, dear Helen, it's come—the persecutions by Emperor Trajan that our friend, Governor Junius, unreasonably thinks are both reasonable and necessary! Petronius brought the news. I remember him so well as one of our group of Benevolent Brigands. He now owns his own caravan, having received his pardon from the same governor of Hierapolis who pardoned me. It was good to see him again, but sad to hear the story of Ignatius's arrest and trial before the governor of Antioch. Several *delators*, those miserable paid informers, had accused him of not only being a confessor, but being a leader of the Christians. Petronius was present in the government hall when Ignatius was asked by the governor if he was a Christian. Ignatius answered with the fiery vehemence and impatience mixed with true Christian humility that we'd expected, knowing him so well. He said that if his confession meant his own death, he was ready. He said he would rejoice and be thankful to share the sufferings of Christ, who rules all things!''

Onesimus stopped speaking and wiped his tear-blinded eyes.

''Listening to Petronious recount the scene, I was deeply stirred, and I remembered the final message of young Bishop Antipas in front of the Roman proconsul and the angry crowd before he was roasted alive. Petronious said that the words of Ignatius burned like fire in his memory, and I know just what he means. He told me that the governor in Antioch turned red with anger and announced the verdict immediately after Ignatius's confession. He called Ignatius an atheist and traitor. His sentence is to be taken to Rome to fight to the death with wild beasts for the pleasure of the emperor and the defense of the empire! His logic for such a severe punishment was that Christians threaten the worship of the gods of Rome and of the emperor, upon whom the unity of Rome depends.''

Onesimus shook his head in sorrow. Helen asked him to finish the story.

''Bishop Ignatius was seized by the guard. He's now on his way to Rome with ten soldiers to guard him. The centurion's orders are to let him stop in any of the cities on his way to death to demonstrate to Christian leaders the punishment we can expect when accused of being confessing Christians.''

Onesimus embraced Helen. He was able to force a smile as he said, ''One good thing comes out of this tragic story, Helen. Several of the bishops from Ionia plan to meet Ignatius in Smyrna on his way to Troas and Rome. I've decided to take Burrhus, Crocus, Fronto, and Euplus with me. It will be a blessed privilege indeed to share with our first bishop martyr since the days of Antipas. This way, we'll be mutually prepared for whatever persecution may come to us. And providentially, we'll together reflect on the best of the writings from Paul, John, and Peter to help us in dealing with the heresies of the Gnostics and Judaizers.

These precious writings of the apostles will enable us to minister to our people called to accept martyrdom as Jesus and the early disciples did.''

"Oh, dear Onesimus, you may be the next to go!" Helen cried tearfully. "You no longer have a friend and protector in Governor Junius as you did with Marius!"

"Yes, I've faced that fact already, and by the grace of God, I'm prepared to meet it if and when it comes.''

30

Early the next morning, the Eucharist was observed in the new hall of Tyrannus that replaced the former hall in which the Ephesian church had met for so many years. The new building, made possible by the generous gifts of the enlarged congregation, added to the legacy of Tyrannus and Joanna. It was now primarily a church building, though, as they would have wished, it continued to be used as a meeting place for the city forum.

As news spread of Ignatius's arrest and the approaching meeting in Smyrna, the new church building was filled to capacity. Strong, deep-felt prayers of intercession were offered for Ignatius and others like him who would pay the supreme price for confessing Jesus as Lord.

After the service's benediction, Onesimus and his four companions slipped out the rear door and mounted horses loaded with provisions for their journey to Smyrna. With all of his years, Onesimus was still able to ride his horse with comparative ease.

As they traveled the familiar road to the mountain pass, Onesimus recounted the remarkable story of his and Glaucon's adventure with the robbers years before.

"One of the great miracles of the Spirit is that the robber chieftain and several of his men made visits to Smyrna and were baptized as Christians. Tavius's father, the governor, pardoned them, and they made a new beginning with a new life of freedom within and without!''

The travelers camped for the night in front of the cave where the bandits had once made their home. Around the campfire, Onesimus shared once more the stories of his own loss and restoration of trust.

"Of one thing I'm confident," he declared. "Any suffering we endure with trust in the amazing love of God revealed in Christ tries us as gold is tried in the fire. The cross is removed, and our lives are purified. This has happened in my own life and surely will happen in the life of our worthy colleague whose body is soon to be fodder for wild beasts in Rome.''

It was a clear, warm August night, fragrant with the smell of pine and balsam. The travelers watched the stars from their bedrolls and went to sleep with the comforting words of Paul as spoken by Onesimus. He prayed parts of the prayer in Paul's letter to the Colossians.

"Dear Lord, may we, together with our brother Ignatius, gain strength from your glorious might. Provide us with enough power for us to meet whatever might come with fortitude, patience, and joy. We give thanks to God for having made us ready to have our share of what he has reserved for his people in the kingdom of light. To you, O Lord, be the glory and honor, victory and power, forever and ever. Amen.''

When the five rode up to the gates of the house of Tavius the next morning, they were greeted warmly by the youthful Bishop Polycarp and several of his deacons and elders. Bishop Tavius and his father had died several years before. Governor Tavius had become a secret believer in the Christ his son worshiped and proclaimed. The governor had left the Tavius house to the church in his will for their continued use. The church had met there ever since it had been founded in Smyrna. Part of the house had been enlarged into a meeting place more adequate for the growing church. It had become the bishop's house as well as a place of worship.

"Little Peter," as Onesimus had known Bishop Tavius's son, had grown to be a distinguished physician. He had studied medicine in Pergamum and made the most of the great library and the teaching of the good physician Severus, who had followed Antipas as bishop. With his wife and three children, Peter Tavius lived in his own home in Smyrna as a loved and trusted Christian. His mother was now the aged head of the household of Tavius and was regarded with great devotion as the mother of that church.

The weary travelers were welcomed and invited to sit down to a meal with Bishop Polycarp as host and his lovely wife, Mary, as hostess. Just before the meal began, the arrival of the youthful Bishop Damas of Magnesia and Bishop Polybius of Tralles was announced. Lunch was postponed as all went out to greet them with warm embraces.

As the newcomers joined around the enlarged table, Polycarp announced joyfully, "Let me share some good news before we say our prayer of thanks. Sometime this afternoon, we're expecting the arrival of our brother and colleague, Bishop Ignatius. Word has come that Ignatius's inspiring witness to the churches where he's been allowed to visit has had the opposite effect from what the emperor expected. Ignatius's visits were supposed to threaten Christian leaders into backing down from their beliefs when they saw what the consequences could be. Instead they are encouraging the Christians to be even more faithful!"

"And so it will be here!" the visiting bishops exclaimed, almost in one voice.

Polycarp turned to Onesimus. "As you are our senior bishop, Onesimus, we want you to lead us in a prayer of thanksgiving and intercession for Ignatius and for all of God's people in these times of trial."

Onesimus responded with a gracious expression of appreciation to their host and offered a deeply moving prayer.

As the hungry travelers joined heartily in the tasty meal, Onesimus assessed the qualities of each of his companions, particularly the young elder Crocus who served so effectively as his chief assistant. *Crocus's wise and inspiring preaching and*

*warm pastoral care make him the elder most suited to succeed me
as bishop when the time comes,* Onesimus mused thankfully. *And
the church will be needing him soon!*

Onesimus's thoughts turned to Polycarp, the brilliant, warm-
hearted leader of the Christians in Smyrna. *His charisma and
love, joined with his ability to articulate the gospel and its moral
implications, make him the God-sent leader needed by the church
in all the world. How priceless a gift from our Lord that this
youthful bishop should be our host at this crucial hour—a worthy
successor indeed to Antonious Tavius.*

When the meal was finished, Polycarp invited Onesimus to talk
with him in the library. The walls of the room were covered with
scrolls of parchment that Bishop Tavius had collected and passed
on to his young successor. Polycarp pointed to the numerous
additions he had purchased for his own studies in the school for
young Christians taught by the aging Bishop Severus.

"We will miss Severus's presence," Onesimus said as they sat
at the reading table. "He's too feeble to make such a long trip."

Pointing to the new scrolls, made up not only of all the writings
of the Christian apostles but also of classic Greek and Roman
philosophers and historians and the disputed writings of those
dividing the church by their heresies, Onesimus continued his line
of thought. "I know what a valuable contribution Severus made to
you and many other young Christian leaders. We need him now
more than ever!"

"You're so right!" Polycarp exclaimed enthusiastically. "I owe
more to him, to you, and to Bishop Tavius, my fathers in the
gospel, than I can ever repay! From early childhood, I was
privileged to feast upon the meat of Tavius's preaching and learn
from his caring, effective administration as bishop. And from you,
my dear friend and father, we've gained inspired and helpful
interpretations of the lives and writings of Paul, John, and
Peter—all of this has helped me receive a faith in Christ I believe
will not fail! And I can never be thankful enough for the months
of teaching under Severus. I'm singularly blessed in sharing his
knowledge of medicine for the body and medicine for immortality,

as he calls the Gospels of John, Matthew, Mark, and Luke and the Epistles of Paul and Peter!''

"Thank the dear Lord, Polycarp, that you've had such strong teachers and that my life and teachings have been of help to you,'' Onesimus responded. "In this critical time in the life of the church threatened by heresies and divisions, there's immeasurable need for both the medicine of physical wholeness and the medicine of eternal life for the health of body, mind, and spirit. With all the fears and uncertainties through which the people of God must go, this salvation from fear and hatred into trust and Christlike love is indeed the medicine of life now in addition to the life to come.''

The conversation ended as James, Polycarp's ten-year-old son, burst into the room.

"They're coming up the street, Father!'' James exclaimed breathlessly. "We can see the horses. They've turned the corner off the highway!''

Polycarp and Onesimus followed the excited boy and stood with the others near the arched entrance to the grounds as they waited for the cavalcade to arrive.

"What a colorful procession,'' Polycarp exclaimed. The nine soldiers led by the centurion came first, their helmets shining in the afternoon sun. They were riding four abreast; the last two were leading a horse on which Ignatius was sitting, his hands tied behind him. In contrast to the colorful garb of the soldiers, the bishop wore a simple white tunic now grey from dusty travel. His face was burned from hours in the hot sun. His shoulders were erect; his dark eyes flashed as the soldiers leading his horse passed the other soldiers and came to a stop near the centurion inside the gates of the house of Tavius.

The centurion reined his horse in front of the caravan. For a few silent moments, he looked into the faces of Polycarp, Onesimus, and their companions. Then he turned his horse and spoke in a loud voice that could be heard by the growing assembly of citizens that had gathered around the procession.

"Greetings from his majesty, Emperor Trajan of Rome, to

you who dwell in the beautiful city of Smyrna. The emperor has heard of your devotion as Roman citizens and your worship of his divinity. He congratulates you on having built one of the first temples of Rome in the empire. He sends also his greetings and a message to your noble Governor Decius that includes full instructions concerning the appropriate way to deal with the people called Christians who confess their only allegiance to Christ as Lord rather than to the emperor and other gods of Rome.''

Turning to Ignatius, the centurion raised his voice in scorn. ''See this shameful prisoner on his way to feed the wild beasts in the arena at Rome! He is Ignatius, atheist and traitor from Antioch! Among the other atheists in this city who call themselves Christians, he bears the title 'bishop,' which means overseer. As overseer of these rebellious Christians, he has been declared as one deserving the most degrading of all deaths. He is to be made an example to other confessors and their leaders of a similar fate unless they renounce their atheism, confess their loyalty to our *deus imperator*, and curse their Christ.''

Addressing the people of Smyrna surrounding the Christian leaders, the centurion continued. ''Your noble Governor Decius has sent word that there are some Christians among the citizens of Smyrna who are decent, law-abiding citizens. As such, the emperor has no desire to harm them, but . . .''

In saying these words, he glared threateningly at all who stood in front of him. ''Though the emperor has decreed that no magistrate shall seek out and punish Christians, he made it plain that if any are accused by *delators* among you, and if the magistrate has been properly notified in writing concerning the accusations of atheism and disloyalty of the accused, they shall be tried. If they remain confessors, they shall be put to death.''

As the centurion said the last words slowly and gravely, a deathly hush fell over the assembled crowd.

After a long period of silence, the centurion dismounted along with the other nine soldiers and their prisoner.

Bishop Polycarp stepped forward and introduced himself as their host. Without apology, he surprised the centurion with a warm welcome, presenting his fellow bishops.

"You have honored us, sir, by permitting our brother and colleague to share with us for a short time, even though you are leading him to his execution by wild beasts in the arena. While your task is odious to us, we know you do this in the service of our emperor, whom we honor and obey in all matters of government and temporal order. We receive you as men who must do your duty. We offer places for you to set up your tents, since you will be staying near to guard your prisoner."

The centurion listened in astonishment. He replied, "Your fearlessness and warm welcome are surprising, since you may someday be accused and tried for the same crimes as your colleague. But I accept your offer. Dracus, one of my men, will by my order be chained to our prisoner at all times. The others will be camping nearby. After all, I am not your judge."

With this unusual understanding, the centurion ordered his legionnaires to their responsibilities. Dracus was chained to the arm of Ignatius and grudgingly followed Polycarp and his companions into the atrium of the bishop's house.

31

That night at the evening meal, Polycarp and his colleagues reclined at the spacious table and listened eagerly to the account of their brother Ignatius on his way to martyrdom. He spoke with intensity of feeling in fluent words that revealed his brusque and impetuous nature.

"Yes, my brothers, I'm on my way to Rome to be fodder for the wild beasts! But as Paul wrote to the Romans, I'm not ashamed of the gospel of Christ or of these chains as I'm led by this soldier, Dracus, and nine other leopards, as I call them. They've been rough on me, and they only get worse the better I treat them."

Turning to Dracus, a big muscular man who sat uncomfortably by Ignatius's side with a scowl on his face, Ignatius addressed him.

"Dracus, you've been kinder than the others, but all of you have accused me of being a fool in my refusal to act with a 'decent respect' for the gods of Rome and for your emperor, who was once only a soldier like you."

"You surely are a fool," Dracus growled. "And you've made our task harder by your constant talk about the man who was crucified by our legions over seventy years ago."

Dracus was plainly exasperated by the impetuous and passionate ways of his prisoner. He continued his criticisms. "You're a silly babbler of nonsense when you speak of Jesus as Lord of the universe. And your stupid passion to get to Rome where you say you look forward to the battle with the wild beasts! What nonsense! But I must see that you get there."

The big legionnaire heaved a sigh of disgust and resignation. "I'll not interfere with your conversation with your hosts, who seem ready to hear your imbecilities. So get on with it!"

His outburst ended, Dracus sat passively to endure the evening as best he could.

Ignatius now found his voice. He had sat with deep embarrassment as his captor vented his anger. "My dear brothers in Christ, you can see something of what I've had to bear. But all of this and what's to come is small compared to the sufferings our Lord bore for us. I'm planning to write letters to each of your churches that tell something of what I've gone through."

A note of exaltation entered his voice, and his face was suffused with joy. "Let me tell you what I'm writing to the Romans. 'Now is the moment I am beginning to be a disciple. May nothing seen or unseen begrudge me making my way to Jesus Christ. Come fire, cross, battling with wild beasts, wrenching of bones, mangling of limbs, crushing of my whole body, cruel tortures of the devil—only let me get to Jesus Christ. . . . "I would rather die" and get to Jesus Christ than reign over the ends of the earth. That is whom I am looking for—the One who died for us. I am going through the pangs of being born.' "

The church leaders remained in awed silence as they listened to this remarkable witness. They had not begun to eat as the drama of one preparing himself for painful martyrdom unfolded before them. Each listener thought of the time, almost sure to come, when he, too, would face such suffering.

Again Ignatius spoke, this time with subdued voice. " 'It is not that I want merely to be called a Christian, but actually to *be* one.' Since I've been selected by Trajan as an example not only in Antioch, but also in Asia and Rome, I trust nothing will prevent me from completing this privilege. 'Let me be fodder for wild beasts—that is how I can get to God. I am God's wheat and I am being ground by the teeth of wild beasts to make a pure loaf for Christ. . . . Pray Christ for me that by these means I may become God's sacrifice. I do not give you orders like Peter and Paul. They were apostles: I am a convict. They were at liberty: I am still a slave. But if I suffer, I shall be emancipated by Jesus Christ; and united to him, I shall rise to freedom.' "

As he said these last words, Ignatius lifted his hands in prayer, his face raised and tears streaming down his cheeks. His companions sat in reverent awe, not daring to interrupt their brother's impassioned declaration.

At last Polycarp spoke. "Ignatius, your preparation for the coming trial and suffering is inspiring to us. A priceless act of faith, indeed! We're indebted to you beyond words for spending this time with us, for we, too, may very well need the same preparation some day. But you've had a long, tiring journey. Onesimus, please offer a prayer of thanksgiving for this food and for the bread of Christ that Ignatius will become. We'll eat this physical food in order to be prepared for what tomorrow brings."

Onesimus lifted his voice in a brief, animated word of praise and adoration to Christ. He closed with a prayer of trusting intercession for their brother Ignatius and the courage and strength he would need for his trip.

They ate together without further conversation for a few minutes. Onesimus examined more closely the strong face of his colleague sitting across the table from him. His black beard was ragged and unkempt and his hair disheveled. His reddened face was lined with creases. Under his eyes, his skin was black with exhaustion.

What a price he's paying for his loyalty to Christ, Onesimus

thought. His mind went back to Antipas standing in the bronzed
bull of Zeus as the flames caught his clothes and devoured him.
He remembered Paul's emaciated body as he was carted off to
meet Nero. In them all, he had seen the fire of a victorious faith.
He wondered whether he, himself, could stand such a test. He had
failed it after the earthquake. He silently prayed that his faith
would be as strong as Ignatius's when his time came. *It won't be
long,* he thought, recalling the warning he had been given by
Junius.

When the dinner was finished, Polycarp suggested that Ignatius
and his guard go immediately to rest.

When morning came and breakfast was over, Polycarp invited
his guests into his library, where he asked the young Bishop
Damas to lead them in a brief worship. Damas read part of Paul's
second letter to the church at Corinth, describing the trials and
sufferings through which he had gone and which concluded with
the words of the Lord to Paul in his time of trial—words that had
encouraged Onesimus so often.

> "My grace is all you need; power comes to its full strength in
> weakness." I shall therefore prefer to find my joy and pride in the
> very things that are my weakness; and then the power of Christ will
> come and rest upon me. Hence I am well content, for Christ's sake,
> with weakness, contempt, persecution, hardship and frustration; for
> when I am weak, then I am strong.

As the fair-skinned bishop read these remarkable words, his
voice was strong and resonant. Onesimus watched the face of
Ignatius light up. When the reading was over, Damas prayed for
the same strength out of weakness for their guest, for himself, and
for all other Christians who were sure to be tried in the fires of
persecution.

When Damas finished, Ignatius burst out with a hearty exclamation. "Praise the Lord for such strong young believers and
messengers as you, Damas. I knew your father, and I was fond of
his sense of humor. Now to see and hear you following in your
father's steps gives me great encouragement that the cause of our
Lord's kingdom will be in good hands. I hope and pray that you'll

be allowed to live to a ripe old age and continue in your vital work."

"Thank you, Bishop Ignatius," Damas responded with modesty. "It's good to be here with you to learn from you and these other dedicated men the ways by which we may meet and overcome the problems that challenge those of us who seek to lead the church in these perilous times."

"Yes," Onesimus spoke with quiet strength, "you've brought hope to us all. We need not only your encouragement in the face of persecution, but also your wisdom in dealing with the Gnostics and others who would twist the gospel taught us by the apostles."

"Thanks for the kind words about my poor life and ministry," Ignatius responded. "I'm just beginning to be a disciple, and I'm a long way from perfection. But if my witness enables the bishops of Asia to be good shepherds during these perilous times, then my being offered up as a sacrifice in Rome, a cheap sacrifice of scum and criminals, will be to the glory of God. I'm taking this opportunity to write letters to each of your congregations for you to take back with you. I've already written to the churches in Tralles and Magnesia. I trust these letters and our conversations will enable you to deal firmly and wisely with the false teachers who are like bad yeast in the church that's gone sour and stale."

"Bad yeast!" Onesimus responded with a smile. "That's a description of what Cerinthus and other Gnostic heretics have been in our churches! But, Ignatius, we want you to know there's nothing cheap in your devotion—giving yourself in the same spirit Jesus gave himself as the Good Shepherd. He laid down his life for his sheep under his own free will. No one took his life from him, just as they don't from you."

Onesimus turned to his companions and said earnestly, "This is the reason we must do all in our power to see that everyone in the church everywhere will be able to read or hear the Gospel according to Matthew, Mark, Luke, and especially the Gospel of John. The four Gospels are the only true records of the life our Lord lived."

"Right!" Bishop Polybius declared. He had been quiet until now, but he spoke with strong conviction. Though not as old as

Onesimus, his hair and beard were almost white, and his body was stooped.

"For the very same reason," Polybius added, "we must encourage the spread of the collection of Paul's letters, which Onesimus has made possible. No one could've been in a better position to know which of Paul's epistles are genuine and which aren't. So many people have written falsely using Paul's name or Peter's or John's or the other apostles, but their writings aren't genuine. Paul's epistles are precious interpretations of the meaning of Jesus Christ our Lord for our daily living in the spirit of Christ, which Paul says is the real test of being a Christian—having the mind and understanding of Christ and living by the faith that works through love! Paul wrote again and again about the realistic teaching that no one finds God and eternal life by some kind of mysterious knowledge, but by continually dying to the old self and rising again in newness of life. How desperately our people need that!"

"You've summed up the meaning of the writings of Paul as he taught them to me and as found in his letters," Onesimus responded with thankfulness. "We're at a crisis in the life of the church. So many Christians are being tempted by Cerinthus and other Gnostics to think that a soft and easy *gnosis* of Christ might exempt us from suffering with Christ and that paying the supreme price as Ignatius will be paying is unnecessary folly!"

A chorus of agreement came from all who sat around the table. Ignatius rose to speak; as he did, he also jerked Dracus, cursing under his breath, to his feet. Ignatius paid no attention to his guard but spoke with great emotion.

"We're dealing here, my brothers, with a crucial test of our faith. There are many in Antioch and in each of your churches who say that Christ didn't really suffer and therefore the Father doesn't suffer with us. Polybius, I wrote about this to your church in Tralles last night. 'If, as some atheists (I mean unbelievers) say, his suffering was a sham (it's really they who are a sham!), why, then, am I a prisoner? Why do I want to fight with wild beasts? In that case, I shall die to no purpose. Yes, and I am maligning the Lord too!' I warned your people to 'flee, then, these wicked offshoots which produce deadly fruit. . . . It is through the cross, by his suffering, that he summons you who are his members.' Paul put it plainly. The Lord's spirit joins in witness with our spirits that we're all God's children. If that's right and we really are God's children, then we're also his heirs along with Christ. But part of that legacy is that we suffer along with Christ so we can also be glorified with him.''

As the animated discussion rose in intensity, Polycarp stood to address Ignatius. ''We all want to be true disciples like you. What you're doing and saying goes to the very heart of Christian good news and the hopes for the future of Christ's church. We want you to know that we stand with you against the Gnostic heretics who make fun of your suffering and the suffering of God in the life of his Son, our Lord Jesus Christ!''

A chorus of *amen*s came from the others.

Ignatius looked at the group in appreciation. He turned to Bishop Damas and continued. ''As I wrote to your church at Magnesia in a brief letter last night, we can compare ourselves to money. 'One might say similarly, there are two coinages, one God's, the other the world's. Each bears its own stamp—unbelievers that of this world; believers, who are spurred by love, the stamp of God the Father through Jesus Christ. And if we do not willingly die in union with his Passion, we do not have his life in us. . . .

'' 'You must have one prayer, one petition, one mind, one hope, dominated by love and unsullied joy—that means you must have Jesus Christ. You cannot have anything better than that.' ''

''You're right! There's nothing better than the unity of love that our common faith in Christ brings,'' Polycarp declared. ''As your host, I want you all to enjoy these hours together. They'll be short, because the centurion has declared that they'll be leaving early in the morning. Since it's nearly time for the noon meal, I suggest each of you take a few minutes to visit personally with each other.''

''We've had a rich time together this morning with Ignatius,'' Onesimus exclaimed. ''After our meal together, let's give him an opportunity to rest and write letters to our churches. Ignatius, from what you've said to us personally, I cherish the same kind of counsel for our people in the church at Ephesus.''

''Thanks, Onesimus. Since I can't visit your churches in person, these letters are my last will and testament for those who confess themselves to be Christians. I'm writing to them, indeed, that they may be true disciples of Christ. I'll next write to your church in Ephesus, but it will include encouragement for Christians everywhere 'to harmonize your actions with God's mind. For Jesus Christ—that life from which we can't be torn—is the Father's mind, as the bishops too, appointed the world over, reflect the mind of Jesus Christ.' I'll urge Christians to 'act in accord with the bishop's mind as you surely do. Your presbytery, indeed, which deserves its name and is a credit to God, is as closely tied to the bishop as the strings to a harp. Wherefore your accord and harmonious love is a hymn to Jesus Christ. Yes, one and all, you should form yourselves into a choir, so that, in perfect harmony and taking your pitch from God, you may sing in unison and with one voice to the Father through Jesus Christ.' ''

''This truly is indeed a beautiful message to our churches, Ignatius!'' Onesimus exclaimed. Everyone joined in his enthusiasm. ''Your ministry as a martyr-witness to the Lord will be of immeasurable value! As you know so well, our churches are torn with divisions by those who question our authority in keeping the message and moral teachings of the apostles. These are the real tests of the mind of Christ, for he's our guide in life and our hope in death!''

During the next two hours, the precious unity of fellowship was obvious. All of the church leaders embraced Ignatius and assured him of their love and prayers. The presence of the surly Roman guard only served to increase awareness of the value of their time together.

After the meal, Ignatius and Dracus returned to the library, where the bishop sat at the table to write letters to the Ephesians, Romans, and Philadelphians.

After Ignatius finished writing, he asked Onesimus to read them and tell him if he had written what would help bring courage and

unity to the people in Asia and Rome. Ignatius went to his room
to rest while Onesimus read with interest and thankfulness what
his colleague had written.

The bishop of Ephesus was deeply moved by Ignatius's generous description and affirmation of him. Ignatius had thanked the
Ephesian church for its prayers and for sending itself "in the
person of Onesimus, your bishop in this world, a man whose love
is beyond words. My prayer is that you should love him in the
spirit of Jesus Christ and all be like him. Blessed is He who let
you have such a bishop."

Onesimus paused for a few moments as, with tears in his eyes,
he recalled the times he had almost given up his faith when the
love of such persons as Paul, John, Tavius, and Severus had
brought him back to trust. *Yes,* he thought, *I've prayed to be a
man of love, able to reveal a love that's beyond words. I want to
be worthy of Ignatius's trust and the admiration and love of those
who seek to be like me.*

When Onesimus finished reading the letters, he thanked God
for this precious but costly meeting with Ignatius and for the
epistles that so humanly described his own struggles in addition to
those of Ignatius over his coming sufferings and death. *I, too, want
to share in the passion of my God,* he prayed. *I long to be a real
disciple, a genuine Christian, in the hours and days ahead.*

Even as he prayed, a young Christian arrived from Ephesus. He
had ridden his horse to exhaustion. Now he was brought to
Onesimus in the library.

"Stephanus, I'm glad to see you," Onesimus greeted the young
man. The other bishops gathered to hear the reason for his
coming.

"You look exhausted," Onesimus told him. "Why have you
driven yourself and your horse so hard?"

"B-b-beloved bishop," Stephanus stammered his reply, "I . . . I
bring you bad news! Yesterday Governor Junius publicly announced you are to be tried as an atheist and traitor as soon as you
return to Ephesus. In his proclamation, he spoke of the arrest and
death sentence passed on Ignatius of Antioch for the same crimes.
Evidently, he knows that you and these other bishops are here with

Ignatius. The governor said this close relationship with one already convicted of treason added to your well-known leadership of the confessing Christians in Ephesus and left him no choice!''

Young Stephanus fell on his knees and broke down in tears. "Bishop . . . Onesimus . . . ," he sobbed. "From my earliest memories, you've been the one I've loved and trusted most. . . . It hurts to think of you going . . . through . . . this shame . . . suffering . . . and likely death.''

Onesimus walked over, put his arms around his young friend, and lifted him up. He was one of the most articulate leaders of the younger element in Ephesus.

"My son, Stephanus," the bishop began, "I'm thankful for your devotion, not only to me but to our Lord. Remember that Jesus was only a young man when he was beaten, cursed, and then crucified at the hands of sinful men, but he didn't try to escape, though he could've done so, even as I can if I choose. He died that we might live. If this is the Father's will, I join with Ignatius, with Paul and Peter, and with thousands of others who must share the passion of God. For God is love, and if we love as he loves us, we must be willing to live and, if required of us, die in order that that love may be made manifest in us to all who see our witness. Pray for me that I may not fail in love, for perfect love casts out fear.''

"Yes, Bishop Onesimus, you've taught me ever since I can remember that God loves us so much that he sent his beloved Son to die so we can have eternal life. But why should you, our bishop, who's harmed no one, have to die such a painful death?''

"Stephanus, I don't know all the reasons, but I'm sure of one great fact. Paul wrote that if we die with Christ, then we'll also live with him. It's through Jesus' cross that God's love is most clearly known. I must follow him, even to death, if his love is to be revealed to those who curse and hurt me. Never forget, my son, that Christlike, forgiving love is the greatest thing on earth. Pray that I may share in the loving joy of our Lord as I meet whatever comes.''

Ignatius entered the study just in time to hear the announcement of Onesimus's coming trial and likely martyrdom in Ephesus. He

walked over and placed his free arm around Onesimus and spoke
words that were most appropriate and deeply meaningful for all
who stood around the table.

"Congratulations to you, my friend Onesimus, and to you,
Stephanus, for you're now going to be real disciples of our Lord.
As Onesimus has said, the sharing of Christ's cross is the only
way to share his love. For some, that means martyrdom——that
may be your privilege, Onesimus, as well as mine. For others it
means living lives of love, as Onesimus has for these many years.
Let many others, as I just finished writing your church, 'learn
from you at least by your actions. Return their bad temper with
gentleness; their boasts with humility; their abuse with prayer. . . .
Return their violence with mildness and do not be intent on
getting your own back. By our patience let us show we are their
brothers, intent on imitating the Lord, seeing which of us can be
the more wronged, robbed, and despised. Thus no devil's weed
will be found among you; but thoroughly pure and self-controlled,
you will remain body and soul united to Jesus Christ.' "

"Thank you, Bishop Ignatius." Stephanus spoke now with
strong voice and flashing eyes. "This hour is one I'll never forget.
I wish all of our people in Ephesus could be here in this time of
light in darkness. My greatest desire is to be like you, Bishop
Ignatius, and you, Bishop Onesimus!"

"My dear son, Stephanus," Onesimus replied, "Ignatius has
written these words and many others in a beautiful letter to our
church in Ephesus. It will be your privilege to take his letter and
share it with all of our people. My time will soon come, and I'll
likely not be there to read it. Your new bishop, Bishop Crocus,
Euplus, Fronto, and I will return to Ephesus with you. Burrhus
will accompany Ignatius as far as Troas."

Onesimus stopped for a moment, overcome by emotion. After
regaining his composure, he continued. "I'm grateful for all of
you! I'll need your love and prayers more than ever in the days to
come!"

That evening's dinner with the group of church leaders together
was a blessed time of caring—a true *koinonia*. Their final act was
to receive the Eucharist as Ignatius's last request. Even though the

guard could not participate, the bread and wine of Christ's body and blood were shared by everyone else. It was likely to be the last Eucharist for both Ignatius and Onesimus. Knowing that his trial for "atheism" by Governor Junius was almost sure to result in his death by torture, Onesimus realized, as he received the bread and the cup from young Polycarp, as he had never understood before, the quiet assurance that he belonged to Christ as Christ belonged to God and that he would soon know even as he was known.

— Part Nine —

"It Is Enough..."

arly the next morning after tearful farewells, the centurion and his nine soldiers led Ignatius, his hands in manacles, away to continue their journey to Rome. The bishop was accompanied by the strong, kindhearted Burrhus as the group set out on the highway north toward Troas. A few minutes later, Onesimus, riding with his faithful deacons and elders and the youthful Stephanus, traveled toward the mountains to the south on their way home to Ephesus. Damas and Polybius and their companions began the journey home to Tralles and Magnesia.

Polycarp and many of the Christians in Smyrna gathered in the early morning light to bid them good-bye and to enter the chapel to pray for these whose faith would be put to the test.

As Onesimus rode beside Euplus and Stephanus, he shared with them his thankfulness for the many years he and Helen had been privileged to live and work with John and their many friends in Ephesus.

"It's healthy for me to go back over the many ways God's providence has turned all things for good," Onesimus said. "I need to keep my trust strong so my witness can be real and vital!"

Because they had left early, they were able to reach Ephesus in one day, although they did not arrive until late in the night. The last hours of the journey were spent in silence. Their way was lighted by a full moon, and the only sound heard was the *clip-clop* of the horses' hooves.

Arriving at the familiar apartment house, Onesimus was embraced by his companions and by a few Christians who were still there at the late hour. No one had known the exact time they would arrive.

Helen waited at the top of the stairs.

"My dear one!" she exclaimed as they embraced. "How blessed to have you home and in my arms once more!"

Kissing her tenderly, Onesimus said, "I've heard the bad news. Stephanus brought it yesterday. Do you know when we are to expect my arrest and trial?"

"As soon as the governor hears of your return," Helen spoke calmly, "you'll be taken and given a public trial. You've heard the charge, I'm sure. It's atheism in denying the gods of Rome and disloyalty to the emperor. Junius calls you a traitor. He says you'll be punished for treason unless you recant and curse Christ, which he knows you'll never do!"

She shuddered and turned away for a moment. "Oh, Onesimus, how I and the whole church in Ephesus have prayed that this wouldn't happen. Now that it has, I pray that you'll be granted courage and peace within and the power of a loving witness to our Lord. Beyond this, my only desire is to be with you!"

"I know how you feel. . . . I understand, dear Helen," he said after kissing her again and again. "But you're needed here as long as possible. Your loving strength will help hold our people together. As we've said so many times, one doesn't seek martyrdom. If this is my lot, your presence and courage will sustain me to the end and afterward. The Lord has a priceless ministry here for you to perform!"

"I know you're right. I've prayed and overcome my greatest temptation. When you go, whether tomorrow or the next day, I'll be there to help and sustain and not hinder and complicate your sufferings."

The couple knelt with their arms around each other to pray their thankfulness for the joys and victories of forty-eight years as partners in marriage and ministry. They closed with the Lord's Prayer, every word speaking their adoration and trust in the Father whom Jesus revealed and their commitment that God's will be done on earth as in heaven. They ended with the doxology: for God's is the kingdom and the power and the glory forever. After the prayer, they went to sleep in each other's arms.

* * *

The next morning before Onesimus and Helen had finished breakfast, heavy footsteps on the stairs and a knock on the door alerted them to the arrival of the squad of legionnaires who had come to arrest Onesimus. Before answering, Onesimus embraced Helen. He whispered his love and devotion to her.

"Evidently," he said quietly, "Governor Junius had a good source for my arrival. Before our people are aroused, he's sent his soldiers to arrest me. Remember, dear Helen, the words of Peter that we should cast all our cares upon Christ, because he cares for us."

The second knock came as Onesimus went to the door and opened it.

"Come in, my friend. I know your mission, and I'm ready."

The centurion was surprised. He had known of Onesimus for some time. He admired him as did so many others in the emperor's legion.

"You've come to take me to the governor for trial as an atheist and traitor. I'm neither, but I'm in your hands, so do your duty. I'll not resist you."

"Then you don't need for me to read the order for your arrest!" The centurion spoke for the first time. "I am Marcus. I've heard you speak in the agora, and I've seen you in several visits with our former Governor Marius."

Turning to Helen, the centurion sympathetically said, "I regret that I must take your husband away. I only do my duty as a soldier of the emperor."

"Thank you for your concern," she said bravely. "We were expecting this, and by the grace of God, we're both ready."

She again gave Onesimus an embrace and a tearful kiss as she whispered, "The love of God our Father and the grace of our Lord Jesus Christ and the presence of the Holy Spirit are with you, my dear Onesimus."

The centurion bowed, took Onesimus by the arm, and led him down the stairs to the carriage used for transporting the emperor's prisoners. Helen followed them to the entrance and watched as they put him in the carriage and drove away surrounded by the governor's guard.

As the carriage passed down the street to the governor's palace, Onesimus was surprised to hear Marcus, who sat beside him, begin to speak to him in a low voice so that the driver could not hear.

"Onesimus, though I'm not a confessing Christian, I think that the faith for which you're willing to give your life is indeed true, and that Jesus Christ is good news to us if we can accept him as the truth, the way, and the life, as I once heard you preach. I'm not yet ready to confess him publicly, because I'm still not sure, but I want you to know that after the sentence is passed, I'll do all I can to help you, though that may be very small."

"Surely God is good to let you be my captor," Onesimus answered abruptly. "Some day you'll come to the glorious assurance of which Paul wrote in his letter to the Romans: 'For all who are led by the Spirit of God are sons of God. . . . We suffer with him in order that we may also be glorified with him' (RSV). I pray that you'll soon find that assurance. It's this confidence that I'm loved without limits by Christ that enables me to be unafraid as I face the pain and suffering that's coming. So, my brother, pray for me that I may keep the faith to the end!"

The secret conversation ended as the procession arrived in the courtyard of the palace. Marcus led Onesimus up the marble steps into the governor's judgment hall. This early in the morning the hall was already filled with the governor's friends and members of the assembly who hastily had been called. The hall was familiar to Onesimus. He and John had often visited here with Governor Marius. The room was not large, but it provided a convenient place for the governor to meet delegations and pass judgment in cases where large numbers of citizens were neither needed nor desired.

This new governor, Onesimus thought, *isn't too sure of the popularity of what he's about to do. He's afraid to try me in the amphitheater as Antipas was tried, because he knows that the numerous Christians and citizens of Ephesus friendly to the Christian churches could easily cause him trouble.*

Governor Junius was seated in the huge chair in the center of the platform. He was dressed in a toga, symbolic of his royal relationship with the emperor, and he held in his hand the mace representing his power of life and death over those who came before him. He was short of stature and had a thin face covered with a dark beard. He had a scar on the left of his forehead.

Marcus stopped with Onesimus on the lower step of the platform and was presented to the governor by the prosecutor, Flaccus. Onesimus recalled that several years before Flaccus had represented the merchants who sought redress before Governor Marius for the loss in sales of the gold and silver amulets of Artemis. Marius had made short the trial and rebuked Flaccus and the merchants who brought the complaint. Ever since, he had been an enemy of the Christians and their bishops.

Flaccus stepped up and began his prosecution in a stentorian voice. "Your honor, Governor Junius, this man standing before you is Onesimus, called Bishop of Ephesus by many, a confessing Christian and leader of the Christians who have made so much trouble for the government and the people of this city for many years. Members of the assembly and other citizens of Ephesus in this room join me in accusing this man with the crimes of atheism and treasonous disloyalty to our divine emperor, Trajan. According to Trajan's edict regarding the accusation of being a confessing Christian, if the person accused does not deny his allegiance to the one called Christ, is unwilling to show his loyalty to the emperor as his supreme lord by proper signs such as the offering of incense on the altar before the image of *emperor deus,* and refuses to curse Christ, he shall be sentenced to death in the manner the governor or other judge may elect as proper."

Turning to the people in the governor's hall, Flaccus asked with bold voice, "How many in this room join me in making this grave accusation?"

With one voice, the assembly and most citizens present shouted, "We do!"

"Do you believe," Flaccus continued, "that this man, posing as shepherd or bishop of the Christians in Ephesus, is dangerous to the state and family customs of our people? Do you accuse him of being an atheist who refuses to believe in the gods and goddesses of Rome?"

"He's guilty!"

"Dangerous!"

"A traitor!"

When the shouts of accusation ceased, Flaccus turned to the governor.

"Honored Junius, I present these accusations by members of the assembly and other citizens of Ephesus against this man Onesimus. I ask you to judge him according to the emperor's edict and sentence him to the penalty of death in the manner you choose!"

When Flaccus finished his accusation, he took his seat on one side of the governor's chair. Onesimus stood alone in front of the governor, but he was not alone in the hall. Several Christians, including Crocus, Euplus, and Fronto, had heard of his arrest from a Christian legionnaire. They sat in vacant seats in the back of the hall.

The governor addressed the accused with unveiled ridicule in his voice. "Onesimus, you've heard these accusations by your fellow citizens. You've lived in this city for many years, much of that time under the protection of my predecessor, Marius, who has been exiled by our divine emperor. You've openly taught that Jesus, your Christ, is Lord and King of the universe. Before you're sentenced as the law of Rome requires, you have the right to admit or to deny these accusations. I command you now to offer due signs of your repentance of this traitorous teaching and to show by acts of obeisance that you now recognize as lord only Trajan, the *emperor deus*. If you renounce your Christ, you'll be set free. What is your answer?"

As the governor asked the question, his eyes flashed hatred for this man who was loved by so many Ephesians.

Onesimus's first response was silence as he lifted his eyes in prayer. In the breathless stillness that followed he spoke in a firm, clear voice heard by everyone in the judgment hall.

"Yes, I *am* a Christian! I am a follower of the man of love and peace, Jesus Christ our Lord! He was crucified, dead, and buried, but the mighty God whom he called Father raised him up and exalted him as King of kings and Lord of lords forever. He has made known to us that the eternal Creator and Sustainer of all is love, and his love never ends. During my life, Christ has never failed me. I will not by God's grace fail him now! I cannot curse one who is my friend and Savior and who I believe is the hope of the world. He gave his life for me, and I am ready to give mine for him. Here I am!"

The silence that followed the bishop's impassioned words was broken at last by the governor. His rage was visible in his flushed face as he exploded in anger.

"Traitor, your own words condemn you! Loyalty to one you call Jesus Christ declares your disloyalty to the emperor. Your refusal to worship Trajan, *emperor deus*, and the other gods and goddesses of Rome seeks to destroy the great Pax Romana the whole world enjoys. You and your Christians are betrayers of Rome!"

Rising from his chair and standing at full height, the governor pronounced his verdict.

"Onesimus, since you refuse to recant and curse this false god you call Christ, I now pronounce the sentence of death upon you."

He spoke each word slowly and distinctly.

"I order my chief centurion to tie you to the back of my own royal chariot with a rope as an example for others who hold your atheistic belief and are not yet accused. The rope will extend around your neck and under your arms so you will be dragged behind. The chariot will be driven at full speed through the streets of Ephesus until you are dead! Whatever is left of you will be thrown from the cliff on the banks of the River Cayster. This is my will and the will of the *emperor deus*! So be it!"

As the sentencing was finished, shouts went up from most of the crowd.

"Death to the atheists!"

"Kill the traitor!"

"Show who's lord!"

"Take him away!" the governor shouted with disgust. "Marcus, I depend on you, as chief centurion, to carry out the sentence of death upon this traitor and unbeliever!"

Marcus took Onesimus by the arm and turned him around. The two walked through the hall with the boos and jeers of the Christian-haters sounding in their ears.

It's over! Onesimus thought. *Now I'm on my way to meet Christ and all who've gone before me face to face.*

The faces of Paul, Peter, Antipas, Philemon, Archippus, Apphia, and his own mother flashed before him. A smile came to his lips as he realized he would be joining them all soon.

Suddenly, as if awaking to reality, his arm was jerked by Marcus. For the first time, he saw his brothers in the faith, Crocus, Euplus, Fronto, Stephanus, and others, standing in the rear of the hall. They extended their arms toward him in assurance of their love.

Marcus and Onesimus walked out to the street where the governor's chariot was waiting with two strong white horses champing at their bits. One of the soldiers handed Marcus a rope, one end of which was already tied to the rear of the chariot.

"It'll all be over in a few minutes," Marcus whispered. "I'm truly sorry I must drag you to your death. I suffer with you and care for you even as I drive the chariot."

Breathing his blessings on this unexpected friend, Onesimus permitted the rope to be tied under his arms and around his neck. By the time the preparation was complete, a large crowd had assembled. Word was spread to all the Christians by messengers who rode up and down the streets announcing that the governor's sentence was about to be carried out.

The crowd very quickly became a mob. It was almost evenly divided into two opposing camps. There were those who hated the Christians and hurled epithets at Onesimus, urging the centurion on with his deadly business. The other part of the crowd was made up of Christians or Christian sympathizers who watched with mingled awe and fear as one whom they loved and admired bravely allowed himself to be made ready for a cruel and disgraceful death. In the Roman Empire, only the lowest criminals and enemies of the state were put to death in this degrading manner. Those who thought well of Onesimus were greatly angered, and only the forbearance and forgiveness of Christians near them prevented a riot with the Christian-haters.

With a whisper of encouragement, Marcus left Onesimus and mounted the chariot. "Let them go!" he shouted at the soldiers who held the horses by their bits.

As the chariot lurched forward, Onesimus was abruptly wrenched from his feet and thrown to the road below. He felt the continued pull of the rope around his neck and shoulders as the stones bruised his head and his body. In all his pain, he breathed a prayer of thanksgiving that he was found worthy to die as witness to the love of God in Christ. He committed himself to the Father and to the Son and to the Holy Spirit. By the time the chariot turned onto the marbled Via Augusta that led from the harbor to the Temple of Artemis, Onesimus had lost consciousness.

Crowds lined the wide street to jeer and cheer as the famed bishop of the Christian church was dragged to his death by the governor's golden chariot. The Christians scattered throughout the crowd prayed and wept as they watched their beloved friend and shepherd raked and battered over the rocks of the street.

As the chariot passed the place where Crocus stood with a group of Christians, all could see the blood flowing from open wounds on their bishop's head and torso. The words of scripture from the prophet Isaiah were silently formed on Crocus's lips:

> "he was wounded for our transgressions,
> he was bruised for our iniquities;
> upon him was the chastisement that made us whole,
> and with his stripes we are healed" (RSV).

Other groups sang songs of praise to the Lord of eternal love who gave them hope even in the pangs of death. Onesimus could no longer hear their songs, but Helen did. She insisted on standing with the wives of Euplus, Fronto, Burrhus, and Crocus.

With deep horror, Helen watched the chariot dragging her beloved's body, bouncing and torn, in the street. When the chariot came close enough for her to see the wounds that covered his lacerated and bleeding form, she knelt and prayed that she might be able to hear once more the words of Jesus that she and Onesimus loved. Even with the noise and clamor about her, she stretched out her hands toward him and said with a strong voice parts of Jesus' last message before his crucifixion.

> Peace is my parting gift to you, my own peace, such as the world cannot give. . . . I have told you all this so that in me you may find peace. In the world you will have trouble. But courage! The victory is mine; I have conquered the world.

As her companions listened, they were strangely comforted by her heroic declaration of faith. They, too, knelt to pray for Onesimus, for Helen, and for themselves.

Marcus observed Helen and her friends as the chariot passed. He turned to see Onesimus's body severely broken and bleeding. His toga and tunic had been completely ripped off his mutilated form. His remains were clearly ready to be thrown over the cliff. He had already arranged with a Christian legionnaire, Thucydus, to inform the Christian leaders where the body would be left. This task was indeed the most painful that Marcus had ever been ordered to perform.

The centurion had driven the chariot from one end of Via Augusta to the other and now took to a side street that led to the cliff. *Surely,* he said grimly to himself, *no person could survive so much torture*.

The chariot arrived at the appointed spot. Two legionnaires who followed on horseback drew up by the side of the chariot. Marcus had made sure that one of them would be Thucydus. The Christian legionnaire helped Marcus untie Onesimus's body from the chariot. The two lifted the bleeding, shattered body as gently as possible and turned it loose over the side of the escarpment. They watched it roll to a stop several feet below. Marcus had gained the consent of the governor to leave the body where it fell, so Onesimus's wife and friends could take it for burial.

As Thucydus and Marcus stood over the mutilated form of the martyred bishop, Marcus whispered his concern. "I'd halfway hoped that some life would still be left in the old bishop's body when the Christians came to get him, but I'm sure he's dead.''

Thucydus knelt to see if any signs of life remained but shook his head. ''Yes, our beloved Onesimus is dead. But, Marcus, you did the best you could under your orders.''

Marcus offered his first prayer to Christ as he mounted the chariot and drove the horses back to the stables. He decided one thing for sure. If Onesimus could live and die with such fearless love because of his faith in Jesus Christ as Lord, the centurion could and would do the same. In his stumbling way, he prayed for faith as he thanked Christ for giving him the blessing of experiencing the noble and brave witness of Onesimus in this last terrible hour.

33

That night a small group of Christians—deacons, elders, and close friends of Onesimus—stood with Helen around the bed that had been prepared in the atrium for his bruised and broken body. His wounds had been washed and bound by their old friend and physician, Menelaus, who had surprised them all in his own health and life span.

''There are no signs of physical life,'' the physician shook his head in sorrow. He had accompanied the two strong young men assigned by Euplus to recover Onesimus's physical remains and had walked with them as they carried the stretcher up the steep bank of the river and placed it in the church's carriage. Now his lifeless form was resting on his own bed.

''Thank you, dear Menelaus,'' Helen spoke as she held the cold, bandaged hand of her loved one. ''You've been such a good physician to us all through these years.''

Her face bore the evidence of her suffering and also of the sublime faith that had strengthened her all through this terrible day.

Turning to Euplus, she said, "You were one of the closest to
Onesimus in these later years. We've all been praying through the
day, but please lead us now in a prayer of thanks and intercession
for Onesimus as he's entering those glorious other rooms our Lord
has prepared for him. And pray for us who still live, that we may
have the grace and strength to carry on the good news of Christ's
kingdom to the poor and hungry people of Ephesus and the rest of
the world. Pray that we may successfully interpret the message of
God's love near us through the living Christ whose victory
overcomes the evil and suffering of the world! This was Onesimus's
last request of me as he told me farewell this morning."

"I'll be glad for the privilege, Helen. Your courage has inspired
us. Let's now join hands and lift up our hearts to the Lord!"

All in the room joined in a circle as Euplus led them in prayer.

"We lift up our hearts to you, Abba Father. We hallow and
revere your name of love, your nature of compassion. In your will
is our perfect freedom, even in the pain and hurt of death. You
hold the life of our beloved Onesimus in your caring hands.
Nothing can separate him or us from your love—not the hatred of
our enemies, the treachery of those heretics who profess your
name, or the breaking and bruising of our bodies—nothing can
defeat your purposes.

"In this moment, as your family gathered around the mutilated
body of your son and servant, we praise you for his life and
ministry, for the victory of his faith that time and again overcame
the temptations of doubt and despair over the evils that threaten
us. The mysteries of life and death are beyond our understanding,
but of one thing we are sure: when we are weakest, then we are
strong in your strength! We have seen this in Onesimus as he, like
our Lord, gave his physical life for us. Because you love us so
much that you gave your beloved Son to die for us, we know that
you are holding him in your love and giving him the place
prepared for him in your other rooms beyond our physical sight!

"We praise and thank you, and for the sake of your church, we
ask for the strength to take up Onesimus's mantle and do the work
he no longer can do. We are not worthy, but through your love,
you made us and called us to follow in his steps as he followed in

the steps of our Lord. The grace of our Lord Jesus Christ be with our spirits. Amen.''

As Euplus concluded the prayer, a sense of joy and victory broke through the tears and pervaded the minds and hearts of these who were now the servant-leaders of the church in Ephesus. They embraced Helen and each other with the kiss of peace.

Helen fell to her knees by the side of her husband's still form and bent over to kiss his forehead. With a cry of thankfulness she said, "Dear, dear Onesimus, even now as you share the blessedness of our Lord, you hear and understand our love and give us your blessing!"

She looked upward in silent adoration for a few moments, then turned to her friends around the bed.

"This is what I'm sure Onesimus is saying to me and to us all: *'Nothing is greater. . . nothing better. . . nothing more lasting than to love as Christ loves. . . . Love one another, for God is love!'* "

Helen caressed his bruised face, but Onesimus's spirit was no longer there. "He's with Christ . . . and Christ is with us," she whispered. *"It is enough. . . ."*

Appendices

Cast of Characters

Historical Characters are indicated by bold type

ANGELL: Slave in Colossae and brigand in the Cadmus Mountains.

ANTIPAS: One of the first Christian martyrs in Asia (Rev. 2:13); fictionalized as the first bishop of Pergamum.

ANTIPAS THE PHYSICIAN: Father of Bishop Antipas.

APPHIA: Leader of the church in Colossae (Philem. 2); fictionalized as wife of Philemon.

ARCHIPPUS: Leader of the church in Colossae (Philem. 2); fictionalized as son of Philemon.

BURRHUS: Deacon in the church in Ephesus, mentioned in Ignatius's Letter to the Ephesians.

CARIUS: Chief of the bandits on the road to Smyrna.

CERINTHUS: Young Gnostic leader whose teachings were denounced by John of Ephesus and Irenaeus as dangerous heresies.

CLAUDIUS: Young friend of Cerinthus from Alexandria.

CROCUS: Leader in the church in Ephesus, mentioned in Ignatius's Letter to the Ephesians.

DAMAS: Bishop of Magnesia, mentioned in Ignatius's Letter to the Magnesians.

DIOCLETUS: Chief of the brigands in the Cadmus Mountains.

DRACUS: Roman guard for Ignatius during the journey from Antioch to Rome.

EUPLUS: Leader in the church in Ephesus, mentioned in Ignatius's Letter to the Ephesians.

FRONTO: Leader in the church in Ephesus, mentioned in Ignatius's Letter to the Ephesians.

GLAUCON: Freed slave of Philemon and Onesimus's travel companion.

HELEN: Daughter of Philemon and wife of Onesimus.

HERACLES: Young friend of Cerinthus from Alexandria.

IGNATIUS, BISHOP OF ANTIOCH: Christian martyr and author of letters to the Ephesians, Magnesians, Trallians, Romans, Philadelphians, Smyrneans, and Bishop Polycarp.

JOANNA: Wife of Tyrannus.

JOHN THE APOSTLE: Original disciple of Jesus, later bishop of Ephesus and author of the Gospel of John.

RABBI BEN JOSEPH: Jewish-Christian rabbi in Ephesus.

JUNIUS: Governor of Ephesus.

MARY: Mother of Jesus, traditionally believed to have lived in Ephesus under John's care.

MENELAUS: Physician ministering to Helen and Onesimus.

MICHAEL: Young friend of Cerinthus from Alexandria.

ONESIMUS: Slave of Philemon returned to his master by the apostle Paul in his New Testament letter to Philemon; believed by several early church historians to be the bishop of Ephesus described in Ignatius's Letter to the Ephesians.

PAPIUS: Pastor-bishop of Helen and Onesimus; father of historical Bishop Papius of Hierapolis described by Eusebius and Irenaeus.

PHILEMON: Leader among the Christians at Colossae and recipient of Paul's letter requesting the release of Philemon's slave, Onesimus.

POLYBIUS: Bishop of Tralles, mentioned in Ignatius's Letter to the Trallians.

POLYCARP: Bishop of Smyrna; his Letter to the Philippians still survives.

SEVERUS: Second bishop of Pergamum.

ANTONIUS TAVIUS: First bishop of Smyrna.

TAVIUS THE ELDER: Governor of Smyrna, Antonius's father.

TYRANNUS: Christian leader in Ephesus; the hall of Tyrannus was the first meeting place for the church in Ephesus (Acts 19:9).

L. ANTESTIUS VETUS: Roman proconsul of Asia under whose judgment Antipas was martyred.

Chronology of the Life of Onesimus

With Approximate Dates

	Roman Emperor	Onesimus's Age
Birth of Onesimus	33 A.D.	
Sold as slave to Philemon	50	Claudius (41–54) 17
First trip to Ephesus	56	Nero (54–68) 23
Escape to Rome	60	Nero 27
With the apostle Paul	60	Nero 27
Return to Colossae with the Letter to Philemon	61	Nero 28
Freed, he returns to Rome	61	Nero 28
Execution of Paul	62	Nero 29
Burning of Rome and execution of Simon Peter	62	Nero 29
Return to Colossae and marriage to Helen	62	Nero 29
The Reconciler—Visit to Smyrna, Pergamum, and Ephesus	63	Nero 30
The Confrontation—The apostle John and Cerinthus	63	Nero 30
Joy and Sorrow—At home in Colossae with Helen	63	Nero 30
The Rebel—Earthquake destroys Colossae	64	Nero 31
The Interpreter—Return to Ephesus as assistant to John	66	Nero 33

With Approximate Dates

		Roman Emperor	Onesimus's Age
The Revealer—Sharing in writing of the Gospel of John	90	Domitian (81–96)	57
Death of John	92	Domitian	59
Onesimus as bishop of Ephesus	92–110	Nerva (96–98)	59
The Martyr-Witness—Meeting with Ignatius and other bishops of Asia in Smyrna on Ignatius's way to martyrdom in Rome	110	Trajan (98–117)	77
Death of Onesimus	110	Trajan	77

The chronology of this novel begins in 63 A.D. when Onesimus was thirty and ends with his death as a martyr in 110 at the age of seventy-seven. The dates obviously are fictional except within the framework of the historical facts known.

Acknowledgments

My first historical novel, *Onesimus*, was published in October 1980, and is currently in its sixth printing. During the years since then, I have been pushed inwardly and encouraged by others to undertake a sequel. I have been asked what happened when Onesimus returned to marry Helen after his harrowing but inspiring days with the apostles Paul and Peter and the early church in Rome during the Neronian persecutions? How were Onesimus and Helen affected by the earthquake that destroyed Colossae? How did Onesimus become Bishop of Ephesus as the letter from Ignatius to the Ephesians describes him? John Knox, Edgar Goodspeed, William Farmer, and other reputable scholars indicate that this "Bishop of Ephesus" could very well be the runaway slave mentioned in Paul's Letter to Philemon. What would Onesimus's relationship with the apostle John, who tradition declares lived in Ephesus until his death, have been like?

These and other questions plus the exciting prospect of recreating the time and events of the early Christian churches of Asia during the last part of the first and first part of the second centuries moved me to undertake the writing of this book. For seven years, I continued research, begun nineteen years before, to create a novel that would be as historically and biblically accurate as I am able to make it.

Obviously, this book is not purely a historical account but rather a plausible, imaginative recreation of the lives of Onesimus and other historical characters based on various legends and factual sources.

Let me here acknowledge the invaluable help of several consultants in church history. Professors Albert Outler, William Farmer, and Victor Paul Furnish of Perkins School of Theology and Professor Robert Jewett of Garrett-Evangelical and Professor William Beardsley of Candler Schools of Theology have given generously of their time and counsel concerning books and other sources of information relating to this era.

Professor Farmer, in *Jesus and the Gospel* (Fortress Press), strongly supports the principal assumptions I am making about Onesimus and his relations with the Ephesian church and other churches in Asia and especially the importance of the meeting of Ignatius and bishops from Asia in Smyrna as Ignatius was led to his martyrdom in Rome. Professors Outler and Farmer have been especially helpful in reading major portions of the manuscript and making suggestions that keep the story as historically accurate as possible within the limits of available information.

Understandably, church historians disagree on the interpretation of the scarce historical evidence for this period of church history. I have chosen between several interpretations concerning the identity and work of John of Ephesus. There is some question as to whether this was Jesus' beloved disciple, the author of the Gospel of John as well as the exiled author of the Revelation to John. Allusions by early church historians to John the Elder, also of Ephesus, further confuse the question. I have chosen the viewpoint, as represented by William Barclay in his *Daily Study Bible Series* (Westminster Press, 1955) and the traditional view supported by many scholars, that Bishop John of Ephesus was indeed one of the twelve original disciples and wrote the Gospel of John. John the Elder, therefore, was exiled to Patmos, where he wrote the Revelation to John.

In answer to many readers' questions, the following is a brief bibliographical list of the major sources I have used:

Descriptions of Ephesus, Smyrna, Pergamum, Colossae, Hierapolis, Laodicea, and the surrounding topography are derived from C. J. Cadoux, *Ancient Smyrna* (Blackwell Pub. Oxford); *The Westminster Historical Atlas to the Bible*, edited by George Ernest Wright and Floyd V. Filson (Westminster Press, 1956); several booklets from the Ministry of Press and Tourism of Turkey; and my own travels in the region.

Sources on Cerinthus and other Gnostic Christians are Irenaeus, Bishop of Lyons, *Early Christian Fathers*, *The Library of Chris-*

tian Classics, vol. I, translated and edited by Cyril C. Richardson (Westminster Press, 1953); *Oxford Dictionary of the Christian Church*, edited by F. L. Cross (Oxford Press); Eusebius, *Ecclesiastical History* (Baker Book House); Robert M. Grant, "Rival Theologies," *Crucible of Christianity*, edited by Arnold Toynbee (World Publishing Co., 1969); Walter Bauer, *Orthodoxy and Heresy in Earliest Christianity* (Fortress Press, 1971); and Elaine Pagels, *The Gnostic Gospels* (Random House, 1979). The story in chapter 25 of John and Cerinthus in the bath can be found in Irenaeus, whose original dialogue I have used.

Sources for Greek and Roman philosophers referred to can be found in *Great Books of the Western World* and *The Harvard Classics*. The Homeric hymn quoted in chapter 19 is translated by H. G. Evelyn-White.

Sources for the cults and beliefs of the masses of people in competition with the Christian faith are Frederick C. Grant, editor, *Hellenistic Religions: The Age of Syncretism* (Bobbs-Merrill, 1953); Rudolph Bultman, *Primitive Christianity in Its Contemporary Setting* (Meridian Books, 1956); A. D. Knock, *Conversion: The Old and the New in Religion* (Oxford, Clarendon Press).

My treatment of John as an apostle and how the Gospel of John came to be written is derived from several sources mentioned above: Irenaeus, Eusebius, Papias, and recent commentaries such as that of William Barclay. Clement of Alexandria relates the story of John and an apostate robber, who, in chapter 22, I have chosen to dramatize as Onesimus. This story can be found in Clement's "The Rich Man's Salvation," in *Clement of Alexandria*, translated by G. W. Butterworth (Harvard University Press, 1939). I have used Clement's original dialogue.

Information concerning the persecution of Christians including Ignatius's and Onesimus's martyrdoms during the reign of Trajan is found in "Letters of Gaius Plinius Caeclius Secundus," *Harvard Classics*, vol. 9 (P. F. Collier & Son, 1909); and Herbert Brook Workman, *Persecution in the Early Church* (Oxford University Press, 1980). In chapter 31, I have quoted from Ignatius's letters to the Ephesians, the Magnesians, the Trallians, and the Romans as translated by Richardson in volume 1 of *Early Christian Fathers*.

The Discussion Guide was prepared by my daughter, Mary Edlund. A similar guide for *Onesimus* was so well received by adult and youth classes that it has been added to later printings of that novel, where it has been widely used in many churches— United Methodist, Episcopal, Roman Catholic, and others. Mary's preparation of the guide for this sequel adds greatly to its value for personal or group study. I am thankful for her helpful insight and questions concerning this story and its parallels in our lives today.

Professors Jerry Campbell and Roger Loyd, librarians for Bridwell Library at Perkins School of Theology, have provided generous aid with books and documents for my research. J. Edwin and Mary Fleming have given valuable suggestions on wording and arrangement of material. Mr. Anthony J. Tolbert III gave me encouragement and aid as my agent in seeking the best publisher. I am grateful to Janice Grana, World Editor of the Upper Room, Charla Honea, Book Editor, and Douglas Tonks, Assistant Book Editor, and all on the staff of the Upper Room who saw the vision of what this sequel to *Onesimus* can mean.

I am also grateful for those who have given secretarial help in typing the manuscript: Mrs. Clara Jessee, Mrs. Nell Thompson, Mrs. Marianne Blackwell, Mrs. Kay Hendricks, and Mrs. Sharon Sumner. Mrs. Doris Coombs, my former secretary in Columbus, Ohio, and the Reverend David Bort of Arlington, Vermont, read and suggested improvements to the manuscript. I am also grateful to Mrs. Peggy Learner, my present secretary, for her invaluable assistance.

Lastly, Elizabeth, my dear wife and companion in all my work, has listened eagerly and patiently as I read the pages I wrote each day. My story would have lacked much if she had not said after my reading, "No, Mary would not have said that," or, "You need to make this part clearer." She has been my best critic and encourager in making this an exciting and realistic story! I trust this book will be just that as the lives of these noble Christians in the church of the first and early second centuries become real in our imagination and understandings of the One who taught by telling stories and whose own story is the best good news for all humanity in every age!

Thankfully,

Lance Webb

Discussion Guide

These questions can be used as starting points for small-group discussion or as stimuli for thought and reflection by the individual reader. Some questions are divided into *A* and *B*. These divisions separate the questions about the story and its themes from questions concerning how these themes reflect upon our contemporary personal journeys. Participants are encouraged to use all questions they deem appropriate to their group or to their own understandings.

Session 1

Part I: The Reconciler, Chapters 1 and 2

1. A. Discuss why Onesimus and Glaucon were able to give up their possessions so willingly to the robbers who held them up—"agreeable victims"!

   B. What makes it easier to love someone who hurts you? Have you ever seen a change take place because you have shown that kind of love?

2. A. The robbers would not have been interested in Onesimus as a person if they had not seen the physical evidence of his persecution. Describe some of the effects Onesimus had on Carius and the other robbers as the robbers began to identify with Onesimus's history as a slave.

   B. Think of a person in your life who influenced you in some way because of a triumph over difficulties similar to your own.

3. A. Chapter 1 gives evidence that God brought Glaucon to these robbers for Glaucon's encouragement as well. How does the bandit Clarus minister to Glaucon without realizing it?

   B. How are we used by God to minister to others? Does God use only committed Christians in the ministry of love?

4. What is the new freedom that Onesimus describes to the robbers? Why is it more attractive than their release from physical slavery?

5. What can Onesimus do as an outsider to help reconcile the alienation between Bishop Antonius Tavius of Smyrna from his own father because of his family's commitment to Christ? What part does little Peter play in the reconciliation?

6. A. Pyrrhus Tavius, the Roman proconsul, held Onesimus in high regard, despite differences in faith and belief. Why did the non-Christian governor consent to listen to Onesimus tell about the Christians in Rome? How did Onesimus answer the proconsul's question, "How could the Christians pray for Nero?"

    B. How do you relate to those who hold different beliefs from you? How can you work with them so that they will respect your beliefs, even if they do not share them?

7. A. Why were Christians so determined to die rather than put a pinch of incense on Caesar's image? How did Paul's teaching help Onesimus come up with a way to demonstrate Christians' loyalty to the emperor?

    B. What are ways we are tempted to compromise our belief in Jesus as Lord in our work? Our family? Our church?

8. Why did Governor Tavius intervene for Glaucon to help free Glaucon's mother?

9. A. Anacreon had been a very unjust man with Glaucon's family. What caused him to change? How was Glaucon able to forgive him?

    B. Is there someone you need to forgive? What would be your first step?

Session 2

Part I: The Reconciler, Chapters 4 and 5

1. A. What conditions or series of events took place in the life of Bishop Antipas as a young man to lead him to Christianity?

    B. Share a time when you felt you became a "new creation in Christ."

2. What frightened the Roman leaders in Pergamum about the Christians and made them persecute their local church? Why did they choose to execute only Antipas?

3. A. How was Antipas spiritually prepared to accept his execution and death?

   B. Have you ever known any Christian who was willing to or had to die for his or her faith? Tell about that person.

4. How did Antipas, as he prepared for his own suffering, encourage Onesimus?

5. How was the martyrdom of Antipas a powerful witness to the love of God?

6. What was the evidence of the truth of Christ and his resurrection that convinced the elder Antipas and led to his decision to become a Christian?

7. A. Discuss this Christian mystery: Jesus is Lord, even though the evil of the Roman persecution still ruled the land.

   B. How do you know that Jesus is Lord today?

8. A. Why does either superstition or philosophy fail to satisfy the lives of unbelievers, leading them to cynicism?

   B. What is a key to Christian faith that has helped you and others you know to cope with tragedy in your lives?

9. A. How were Tyrannus and Joanna instrumental in building the Christian community in Ephesus?

   B. What is God's purpose for you in building your Christian community?

Session 3

Part II: The Confrontation

1. A. What was the basic difference between the *gnostic* approach to Christianity through Cerinthus's vision and that of the Christians who had known Christ? Why did the four young Gnostics consider themselves Christians?

   B. What are some modern practices and beliefs of professing Christians that parallel Cerinthus's vision of the "Kingdom of Good Pleasure"?

2. A. Why was it so important to John and Onesimus that Jesus was completely human *and* divine— both the Son of man and the Son of God?

   B. What difference does this make in your faith journey?

3. What do you think of Cerinthus's vision? Was it genuine or mistaken?
4. What was the essential difference in John's and Cerinthus's understanding of the story of the woman taken in adultery?
5. How was John able to disagree completely with Cerinthus and still love him? What difference did this make in settling the issue?
6. Have you ever felt that offering unconditional love to those who do what you despise is a waste? Why or why not?
7. A. How do John, Onesimus, and Tyrannus test Cerinthus's vision of the kingdom? What are they testing for?
   B. Are there issues today that need to be tested? What are they?
8. What are the signs of Jesus' divinity before his baptism?
9. What are the signs of Jesus' humanity?
10. What blocked Cerinthus and the Gnostics from accepting Jesus as a fully human person, despite the apostles' firsthand witness?
11. What was Jesus' attitude toward pleasure-seeking? Why were the Christians of Ephesus so opposed to it as practiced by some of the Gnostics?
12. What was the issue that led Claudius and Heracles to leave Cerinthus and Michael and go to the Christian community?

Session 4

Part III: Joy and Sorrow; Part IV: The Rebel

1. A. How does Onesimus interpret Colossians 3:22 because of his conversations with Paul? How does Philemon deal with the tension in the community caused by his action of freeing some of his slaves?
   B. What explosive issues divide your Christian community? How would you follow the example of Philemon?
2. A. The pain of losing a child or a loved one is difficult to bear, and questions such as *why*, "How could a loving God allow this to happen?" and "If God is all-powerful, couldn't God have prevented it?" torment the family. Discuss these questions and the comfort Onesimus and Helen find in their faith.

B. How do Christ's death on the cross and his resurrection comfort you in times of sorrow and loss? What does Onesimus mean by saying God is a perfecter and completer of all that is good?

3. What does Onesimus mean by the mystery of the "hidden God"?

4. A. What was the inner rebellion Onesimus felt after the destruction of Colossae and his business, and the deaths of so many he loved? Why was this more difficult for him to deal with than the death of his child? Helen accepted the losses much more easily. What made the difference?

B. Who are you more like when you face a painful or difficult situation— Onesimus or Helen?

5. Why, as Onesimus discovered, would the *gnostic* teachings make these losses easier to bear? Why, then, would Onesimus refuse them?

6. What is the difference in Onesimus's intellectual belief in Christ revealing the love of God and his ability to trust that love?

7. A. Why couldn't Onesimus continue to discuss his doubts with his Christian friends or, for a while, even Helen? Did they do anything to discourage his honesty with them? What was the only thing they could do for him?

B. How can we help our friends work through their doubts and pain without making them feel guilty for having them?

8. A. What did Onesimus discover the role of "mystery" in our Christian faith to be?

B. Is it ever all right to question God's actions? Do we always have to accept whatever injustice comes to us?

9. Why is it more difficult to accept natural evils such as cancer and earthquakes than to accept human evil? Or is it?

10. How is the Aristotelian mind of Onesimus similar to the mind of many in our scientific age?

11. A. What attracted Onesimus to the band of robbers in the Cadmus Mountains? How did he justify his activities? Was he punishing himself for lack of faith? Why did he feel the need of separation from the Christian community?

B. What are some ways you tend to take out your own discouragement and loss of faith?

12. A. Read Romans 7:18–25. What is the promise that is found in this inner struggle?

   B. If this passage is not meant to excuse our sinfulness, what hope does it offer? Read Romans 8:1–3, 14–17.

13. A. What experiences in the band of brigands help Onesimus start to "hatch out of his shell" and reclaim his loss of freedom?

   B. The renewal process takes many forms. Describe the process that helped bring you to renewal of faith after a burnout or period of loss of faith.

14. When Onesimus became the leader of the bandits, what did he do to make them become known as the Benevolent Brigands?

15. A. How did John's visit make the difference in Onesimus's faith struggle?

   B. Why is it that one person can accomplish what others have not been able to do? Should you feel you have failed if you are not that one person? Does Christ ever send us to fail?

16. What new trust did Onesimus learn through his rebellion? What did he have to surrender to God?

17. A. How did God provide for Onesimus and Helen's basic needs for living after they lost everything in the earthquake?

   B. Recount a time when God surprised you with provision for your daily needs.

Session 5

Part V: The Interpreter

1. A. In Onesimus's first sermon to the Ephesians, what did he cite as the sources of guilt and shame that paralyzed his mind and soul and blocked his acceptance of God's unconditional love?

   B. What can God do with the guilt and shame in your life? How?

2. A. What good came out of Onesimus's struggles and doubts?
   B. Does struggle always bring some good? How?

3. A. How has Cerinthus's *gnostic* teaching been hurtful to others in Part V?

   B. What is the difference between Christian love and being a prude?

4. What similarities, if any, are found in the "sexual freedom" of today and Cerinthus's teaching?

   A. How was the spirit of the Lord present in the public rebuttal of Cerinthus's *gnostic* teachings that John made?

   B. When has the spirit of the Lord helped you to speak out on your Christian convictions in an unfriendly atmosphere?

5. A. What was a "Judaizer"? Why were they a destructive force in the early church?

   B. What legalistic forces exist in our churches today that would destroy our Christian unity?

6. A. Was the apostle John's refusal to bathe in the same bath house as Cerinthus humanly or divinely motivated? Why did John laugh at himself?

   B. Loving others with whom you have deep moral differences is difficult. How far does God expect us to go?

7. A. According to the author's dramatization of the origin of the letter of Paul to the Ephesians, Onesimus brought together many of Paul's letter fragments with insights from John and his own prayers for the inspiration of the Holy Spirit. When Onesimus read the letter in the service, the congregation applauded to thank him. Was such recognition appropriate in that community? Why? Why not?

   B. Why and when do people need to be recognized for their work, even when it is the Holy Spirit working in them?

Session 6

Part VI: The Revealer; Part VII: The Bishop of Ephesus; Part VIII: The Martyr-Witness; Part IX: "It Is Enough . . ."

1. What law did Rabbi Ben Joseph break to be punished by stoning? How is this similar to the Roman persecution of the Christians? How does it compare with the death of Jesus— were the causes similar?

2. Say the words of Jesus that Rabbi Ben Joseph remembered

from the teachings of John that gave him comfort and peace during his stoning: John 14:27. If you have not already committed them to memory, copy them down on a note card and carry them with you as you go about your work this week, referring to them often.

3. What was the purpose of John's telling the story of his memory of the teachings of Jesus? What groups did his letter address? Why is it called the "spiritual gospel"?

4. Discuss the many reasons why the various Roman leaders continued to persecute Christians in the years following the death of John.

5. What was the Roman rule of thumb under Emperor Trajan for choosing which Christians to persecute and execute? What did this do to the Christian community?

6. A. The Christians accepted martyrdom with resignation and faith. Even the Roman emperor's plot to scare the Christian community into submission using Bishop Ignatius's arrest as an example backfired. What was in those Christians' faith that brought out such a sacrificial commitment?

   B. Do we find this quality in our Christian community today?

7. According to Onesimus and Ignatius, what is the role of suffering in a Christian's life?

8. A. Onesimus prayed to become a real disciple and genuine Christian and to share in the passion of God. Was it necessary for him to be executed by the Romans to accomplish this?

   B. How do modern Christians show that we are real disciples and genuine Christians sharing in the passion of our God?

9. What does Onesimus mean when he tells Helen that one does not seek martyrdom?

10. How does Onesimus's death as a martyr convince Marcus of faith in Christ's love and power?

11. Read Daniel 3–6. Why did God not save the Christian martyrs as he did the young Jews in the passage? What is the real issue here?

12. Discuss the meaning of Helen's last words spoken at the side of her martyred husband's body, quoting Onesimus and revealing her own firm faith: "Nothing is greater . . . nothing better . . .

nothing more lasting than to love as Christ loves. . . . Love one another, for God is love! . . . He's with Christ . . . and Christ is with us. It is enough!''

Lance Webb, a bishop in the United Methodist church, is retired from administrative responsibilities. His first novel, *Onesimus*, was published in 1980. Bishop Webb has spent the time since then researching and writing this, his second novel.

Before his election to the office of bishop, Lance Webb pastored two large university churches in Texas and Ohio for a total of twenty-four years. During his career, Bishop Webb has blessed many through counseling and through teaching about prayer. He is currently a consultant on spiritual formation with The Upper Room. In addition, Bishop Webb is active in leading seminars, workshops, and retreats for both laity and clergy.

Bishop Webb is the author of numerous books of non-fiction. His books include *The Art of Personal Prayer, Making Love Grow, Disciplines for Life,* all published by The Upper Room, and his first book, *Conquering the Seven Deadly Sins*, recently reprinted as *Sin and the Human Predicament*.

With his wife, Elizabeth, Lance Webb currently resides in Dallas, Texas.